Quest For The Sword Of Anthrowst
By *Katrina Mandrake-Johnston*
World of Zaylyn

Order this book online at www.trafford.com
or email orders@trafford.com

Most Trafford titles are also available at major online book retailers.

Print information available on the last page.

ISBN: 978-1-4120-5422-5 (sc)

Trafford rev. 05/20/2019

Trafford PUBLISHING® www.trafford.com

North America & international
toll-free: 1 888 232 4444 (USA & Canada)
fax: 812 355 4082

Quest For The Sword Of Anthrowst
By *Katrina Mandrake-Johnston*
World of Zaylyn

Enter the World of Zaylyn. This is a world filled with strange creatures, magic, and mystery. In this book, you will be introduced to several characters, many of which you will learn more about in later books. This story revolves around a particular group, who through peculiar circumstances, find themselves partaking in a quest for the Sword of Anthrowst.

This is a world filled with many different races: humans, elves, dwarves, fairy folk, centaurs, dragons, dragon-like humanoids, goblins, trolls, shape-shifters, and many others yet to be discovered. With warriors, thieves, wizards, treasure, magic, strange creatures, danger, and adventure, this world is never dull.

Evil, malicious creatures have entered this world to do the bidding of an insane wizard. Can this horrible man control these beasts as he believes, and for what purpose?

Vordin, a teenaged boy, narrowly escaped the fate of his village as the creatures slaughtered everyone there, including his parents. Vordin is told by a tiny fairy queen, whose race had always been thought of as myth, that the evil wizard had to be slain by the Sword of Anthrowst in order to send the creatures back to where they came from.

Two thieves, an elf named Candra and Dendrox her human companion, join Vordin in the quest as does an amateur wizard named Weena. The mysterious being they encounter, half human and half spider, is she friend or foe?

When a dwarf, Nodwel, pleads for their help, they find themselves on a rescue mission to a small village under attack by these same creatures. Nodwel's group had been at the village when it had been attacked and he greatly fears for their safety and that of the villagers.

Will any of Nodwel's companions be alive? Were they able to hold the beasts back long enough for Nodwel to return with help? Is it even possible to defeat these beasts? Will there be anyone left to save by the time they arrive? Will they fall prey to the horrid evil monsters as well, trapped in a malicious web of spells and ripped to pieces by huge dagger-like teeth and claws?

Is this quest simply impossible? How are they to even find this sword, wherever it may be, and the wizard for whom they only know a name?

This group find themselves in many different and exciting situations, wondering if they will even live long enough to find the sword or even discover where it is.

Among their encounters are a mischievous fairy queen and her followers, many vicious monsters, giant spiders within ancient underground passages, bounty hunters after the two thieves, plus so much more. Could there be bandits within the forest, and perhaps even a werewolf lurking about as a few believe?

Meanwhile, a romance begins to stir, as well as a vicious jealousy.

But, worst of all for this little group of adventurers, is the presence of a mysterious and evil vampiric being with immense power, called simply The Black Shadow.

Could he have something to do with this group coming together? If so, what purpose does he intend for them? He wants them to complete their quest and save Zaylyn from the evil wizard and his army of creatures, but why, especially when he could easily take care of the problem himself?

* *

The World of Zaylyn is an elaborate mystical place, and I hope you enjoy exploring it through this and many more books. Enter the World of Zaylyn website at: www.webspawner.com/users/worldofzaylyn

Welcome to the World of Zaylyn by Katrina Mandrake-Johnston.
****
THE WORLD OF ZAYLYN SERIES
****
BOOK #1 = = > Quest For The Sword Of Anthrowst

See website for order information and special features.
****

(World of Zaylyn website = http:// www.webspawner.com/users/worldofzaylyn)

****

<Zaylyn ><Quest For The Sword Of Anthrowst ><By Katrina Mandrake-Johnston >   <Ch 1>< 1 >

CHAPTER 1 = VORDIN

Vordin was fifteen and an only child. He had a mother and father who loved him dearly and they lived a happy and peaceful life together in the village of Nilnont. One day that happiness violently ended.

On this day, Vordin had spent most of the morning in his room trying to solve his latest puzzle box which he received the month before. He was wearing a grey tunic with his brown pants and a well-worn pair of brown leather shoes. His hair was a light brown and he wore it long at shoulder length. As usual, his hair was tied back at the base of his neck with a strip of leather.

As Vordin went about his usual activities, he was unaware such horrors existed and that such an ordinary day could bring such terror and so abruptly.

Vordin had been at the edge of the forest on the hilltop, when it had happened. Just below him, at the bottom of this small hill lay his village, Nilnont. He had been passing the time away as he waited for his mother to finish preparing dinner. He had made a nuisance of himself by snatching samples of the whipped potatoes with his finger and had been sent out of the house until the dinner was ready.

It had been a warm and pleasant day, still being the beginning of autumn. Sunset was approaching and Vordin had been watching the horizon. He could see the road which made its way over the grassy hills and then up to Nilnont. He knew that this road also continued up through the forest, eventually winding up and over the mountains into the valley beyond. Dee'ellkka Valley was its name.

The vibrant colors of the sunset were incredibly beautiful. There were wonderful shades of red, orange, pink, and yellow. He had said to himself that he ought to come up to the hill more often to watch the sunset, but he knew that he would probably be too preoccupied with other things to actually do so. Then, as he watched, he had noticed a black mass which appeared to flow over the hills out from the horizon.

He hadn't known what to think of it, his mind puzzling over what he was seeing. As the mass got closer, he had realized that he was not seeing one large mass, but many black shapes.

***

Something was heading toward Nilnont. Confused, he stood up, his eyes staring.

He watched the shapes approach and then he heard the awful shrieking howls. Whatever these creatures were, Vordin was sure that they had a malicious intent. Shouts came from the village. People started to run about grabbing what weapons they had. Panic welled up inside him. He was in danger. Everyone was in danger.

The howls grew louder and louder as the creatures got closer. They were moving fast. Vordin's mind was racing. A story he had been told came out of memory.

"Like demons they are, created with evil intent. They are filled with hate and malice. They revel in pain and suffering. They will bring death. A hollow tree can be a savior. The tree was once alive. You will be a being within a being. They will not see you. As a child within the womb of its mother cannot be seen directly, so shall you be hidden from sight."

He could remember asking many questions about this and why the mysterious man in black from the story had said these things. The storyteller, Rasindell, had replied that he too had been puzzled when these words had been spoken to him long ago, as this had been a true story. He told him that

<Zaylyn ><Quest For The Sword Of Anthrowst ><By Katrina Mandrake-Johnston >   <Ch 1> < 2 >
when he had heard the shrieking howl and saw the black shape, he knew to follow the advice no matter how strange it had been.

Vordin was afraid. There just happened to be a hollow tree on the edge of the forest where he stood. He looked at his village, then the approaching creatures as they neared the edge of the crop fields just outside the village, and finally to the hollow tree. The fear was too great. He wanted his parents. He wanted to run. He wanted to live. There didn't seem like there was any time to act. The creatures seemed so close. There was safety in the tree. It had to be true. He went over to it and frantically searched for a way inside. He found an opening and crawled in.

As he wriggled around trying to situate himself better, he couldn't help but wonder what the creatures looked like. It sent waves of fear and panic throughout his body as he imagined visual images to fit the malicious noises the beasts made.

He could hear people screaming. His face was wet with tears.

"*They'll be okay,*" he told himself, "*My parents… They'll escape. I know they will. Somehow they'll be safe.*" He was too frightened to move a single muscle. "*What if they don't try to escape? What if they stay, hoping that I will come back?*" he asked himself, "*They must be so worried. They'll wait for me and they'll be killed, and it will be my fault. There wasn't enough time… It would be impossible to escape the village… No, they'll hide. They'll be safe… But the story spoke as if it didn't matter if people hid… as if the creatures could somehow see exactly where all living things were and that the only hope was to hide within something that had been living, or once was or something like that. I'm just assuming that these are the same creatures too. My imagination runs wild sometimes. I don't really know what these beasts are or what they look like, so how can I tell? There are some pretty tough people in my village, my father included. They'll fight them off, and all will be well.*"

He knew that his feeble thoughts of comfort weren't going to fool himself away from all the things he was dreading. He knew things had to be much worse, and if it were these 'demon' creatures like he thought, he knew that no one in his village would be able to survive, including his parents. He also knew that he could perish very easily along with them if this hollow tree trick didn't work.

Vordin thought about all the times he had been unkind to his parents, every time that he had lied to them, and all the times he hadn't really appreciated all that they had done for him. He cried and cried, knowing that he would never be able to tell them that he was sorry and how much he really loved them. He thought about all the happy times that he had spent with them and how he would never get to see them again. "*They'll be okay,*" he lied to himself, "*Everything will be fine.*"

He cried until it felt hard to breathe and his stomach ached. His eyes stung from rubbing his tears away with his dirty hands. Now all that was left for him to do was wait in the darkness of the tree and listen helplessly to all the horrible sounds coming from his village.

***

These horrid beasts had come to prey on the village of Nilnont. The crop fields were reduced to ash, as the creatures invoked spells of fire breath upon themselves enabling them to expel magical flames from their throats. The villagers' homes were burned and smashed. The animals of the village had been helpless, having no choice but to face the evil onslaught as their bodies were torn to shreds. The frantic screams of the villagers and the evil howls and shrieks of the creatures filled the night air. The creatures killed without mercy.

These innocent people could hold no hope of salvation from these foul beasts. Some villagers, the lucky ones, were killed before being feasted on, while the unlucky ones were eaten alive as they watched chunks of their own flesh being devoured before them by huge gnashing teeth. The ground was heavily stained with blood. Everyone was slaughtered.

***

Vordin listened from his hiding place to the horrors that were happening. As the screams quickly ceased, he feared that he had become the sole survivor of his entire village. He desperately hoped that these terrible evil creatures would creep back to wherever they came from when morning arrived. Dawn was far away, as the night was still young. Still, it gave him something to focus on. He would wait for the sun to rise. He told himself that things would be better then, all he had to do was wait. He

<Zaylyn ><Quest For The Sword Of Anthrowst ><By Katrina Mandrake-Johnston >   <Ch 1> < 3 >
could do that.

Why these 'demon' creatures would overlook him if he were hidden inside a tree, he didn't really understand. He desperately tried to remember the story he had been told, wondering if it were in fact these same creatures as he had thought.

Slowly, bit-by-bit, the story began to come back to him...

It had been around the time when Rasindell had first begun to learn magic. He had met a woman whom also was studying magic. They would spend hours together practicing their new spells and became quite good friends.

Unknown to Rasindell, she had an admirer. She was not interested in this other man at all, as he was known to practice dark and evil magic.

Unfortunately, this evil wizard had laid claim to her in his own twisted mind. When he discovered the friendship she and Rasindell had, he was furious. He could see that Rasindell and the woman were clearly interested in each other and perhaps even falling in love. The wizard left to hunt the two of them down and exact his revenge, for in his mind she had betrayed him.

This evil wizard discovered them in a rocky yet forested area where they had been practicing their spells. The wizard had come across them during their first kiss and had caught them unaware.

"How dare you!" he had screamed at her.

She tried to explain, yet again, to the delusional man that she was not interested in him and that there was no relationship between them as he imagined. She explained that she was in love with Rasindell and not him.

This just infuriated the evil man further. In his rage, he summoned a Killnarin, using very strong magic to do so. The beast easily slipped into this world using the incredible hate this man possessed as a conduit from its world into Zaylyn.

As the foul beast emerged from what looked like a tear in the very air around them, it growled maliciously. Its body was a deep black and it looked wet and slippery. This beast looked similar to a salamander, but with six clawed legs and a huge mouth of sharp jagged teeth. Its eyes were completely black and it never took its gaze off the woman.

"What have you done?!" she asked the wizard in terror, "It will kill us all!"

"As long as you die, I do not care," was his cold and heartless answer.

Vordin remembered that Rasindell had a very difficult time speaking of this and had never told him the name of the woman or the evil wizard.

The Killnarin pounced onto the woman as a cat would a mouse, killing her instantly with its dagger-like claws. There was nothing he could have done. If he could have given his life to save hers, he would have, but everything had happened so fast. Even in his grief, Rasindell knew that remaining where he was meant his death as well.

Next the Killnarin turned on the wizard that had summoned it. His death was slow and painful. Rasindell had taken this opportunity to run as fast as he could into the forest, trying to escape the terrible beast, as it would surely come after him.

Within the forest, he was stopped by a mysterious man dressed all in black and wearing a hooded cloak. Rasindell could not see his face, as it was cast in shadow beneath his hood. There was something about this figure that had made Rasindell very nervous, although he didn't know exactly why.

"Like demons they are, created with evil intent," said the man in a calm soothing voice, speaking of the Killnarin, "They are filled with hate and malice. They revel in pain and suffering. They bring death. A hollow tree can be a savior. The tree was once alive. You will be a being within a being. They will not see you. As a child within the womb of its mother cannot be seen directly, so shall you be hidden from sight."

Rasindell immediately questioned this mysterious man about what he had told him, fearing that the beast was close behind.

"Their vision is different from ours," he explained, "They can see the life force of others.

<Zaylyn ><Quest For The Sword Of Anthrowst ><By Katrina Mandrake-Johnston >   <Ch 1> < 4 >

Therefore, it matters not where you hide, as they can see within and beyond what we see. Your only hope is to mask your life force with that of another. It does not matter whether the tree is alive or dead and hollow. The fact that it once was alive and had a life force of its own is what is important."

"Where am I to find a hollow tree?" Rasindell asked, frantic to try anything at all to save his life, "The chances of finding one are so slim and then of finding one large enough to conceal me within are even less!"

The man directed him over to a large tree. Rasindell was about to protest that this tree was in good health and not at all hollow, when the mysterious figure pushed him gently forward into the tree as if it had been made of air.

When the Killnarin came into the area a few moments later, its large head moved back and forth searching for any sign of Rasindell. Rasindell tried to understand how he could be standing within a solid tree as he was, but couldn't come up with an explanation. The Killnarin couldn't see him; he was sure of it.

The mysterious man in black stepped forward toward the Killnarin. The creature actually seemed to fear him. The Killnarin reared up until it was standing on its back four legs reminding Rasindell of a centaur he had once met. The creature swiped at the air in front of it and snapped its massive jaws toward the man in black, but dared not approach him. The mysterious figure just stood there making his presence known.

The Killnarin finally dropped its upper body back down to the forest floor again, the ground shaking with the impact. It let loose a terrible shrieking howl in defiance. It stomped around as if it were trying to decide what to do, and then a tear in the air appeared as before. The tear looked similar to the distortion heat from a fire makes in the air, if you look at it a certain way. Rasindell had expected yet another Killnarin or some other terrible beast to enter their world through the portal. To Rasindell's surprise, the Killnarin instead left the world of Zaylyn, returning to wherever it had come from.

Once the Killnarin was gone, the mysterious man helped Rasindell out of the tree, and then he leapt up into the sky and disappeared from sight. Rasindell decided to build a home for himself and devote the rest of his life to magic. Having lost his one and only love, he had nothing else.

"*Could the mysterious man in the black hooded cloak be The Black Shadow?*" Vordin asked himself, "*The Black Shadow is supposed to be an incredibly powerful and evil being. I have heard awful things. Things that one could only imagine in the worst of nightmares. Surely it cannot be the same person. Perhaps I am remembering the story wrong.*"

Inside the hollow tree, it was damp and cold. For once, he was thankful for his short height and thin frame as these qualities allowed him to maneuver into his chosen hiding spot and therefore were responsible for saving his life.

He could feel bugs starting to crawl through his hair. It got to the point where he couldn't tell if it were some of his own hair that had made its way down inside the collar of his shirt or if it were some creepy insect squirming about. The wood was damp and had an earthy smell to it. Many times his hands found themselves sliding over slimy bits of fungus. Vordin wanted to get out of his cramped position and stretch, but he knew that he couldn't take the risk.

He continued to wait. He could smell the burning remains of the village from where he was. Luckily, he was far enough away to not have to worry about his tree catching fire. Vordin waited and waited, and finally the crackling fires became nothing more than smoldering embers.

After dawn, he emerged with great caution. The morning sun's rays were warm and bright. From where he stood at the crest of the hill at the edge of the forest, he could see the grassy hills rolling into the horizon. The road made its way up and over these hills until it reached Nilnont. There was no sign that the creatures had remained or where they might have traveled to afterwards.

He did not want to look at his village. He did not want to see the destruction. He knew it had happened, but if he didn't look at it, he could pretend that everything was fine.

Before this day, Nilnont was a happy and lively place. The small buildings had thatched roofs and the walls were made from stone. Nilnont's buildings had been constructed in this fashion for centuries.

<Zaylyn ><Quest For The Sword Of Anthrowst ><By Katrina Mandrake-Johnston >   <Ch 1> < 5 >

When a new building or home was to be built, it became a village project and everyone contributed in some way or another.

Almost every house had a garden of flowers, and it was a beautiful and peaceful place to live. Nilnont was known for its pottery. Some would be handcrafted for every day use and some would be made with artistic designs and paintings for decoration. On the rare occasion that travelers came to stop at Nilnont, they would always marvel at the quality and beauty of the pottery that the village produced.

It had been his village and his home. Finally, he made himself look down to Nilnont. He could see now that it had been reduced to smoldering piles of rubble and debris.

"*My parents are somewhere down there. Everything is destroyed. Everything and everyone is gone. Everyone's dead. No one could have survived. My parents are dead,*" he tried to explain to himself.

He turned his eyes away from it. He stared at the road, following with his eyes as it continued past Nilnont and up into the forested hills to eventually lead into the mountains.

Vordin had never been to Dee'ellkka Valley, as the trek over the mountains was a long and strenuous one. It was rumored that trolls and dragons inhabited the mountain range, although few had ever seen them.

Vordin reluctantly returned his gaze toward Nilnont again, and then he forced himself to travel down to it. One of the persuasions he told himself was that perhaps he would find some survivors. He would rescue them and be a hero. Deep down, he knew that he would not, but he bravely continued.

He now stood at the edge of his village. There was nothing left of what he had called home. There was an eerie silence which emphasized the fact that he was alone. Everyone was gone. Nothing in the village had survived except for him.

Even though he expected the worst, he wanted to run desperately toward his house, to look for his parents and to see if they were all right. The fear and shock of what had happened and the sight of the devastation in front of him held him back.

At the edge of the village, from where he was standing, he saw the blackened and crumbling walls of many homes and buildings. He saw charcoaled remains of various pieces of wood furniture scattered about in the rubble. The street appeared empty from where he stood, but he knew there would be bodies. It was so very quiet. Usually, he would be able to hear the livestock in their pens at the far side of the village, but there was nothing. The crops were now blackened earth.

The winds changed and the foul stench of burnt flesh reached his nose. He felt numb and emotionless. It was almost as if his body wouldn't accept the devastation in front of him as being real.

After many unsuccessful attempts, he finally was able to force himself to slowly walk down the street. As he walked, he was conscious of every reluctant step and of every tiny detail that he beheld.

He tried desperately to hold his sanity together as he passed the body of a middle-aged man lying face down in the gravel, a large pool of blood beneath him. The crackling embers seemed to taunt him, as if they knew all that had been taken from him and they had remained to gloat.

He felt empty. He thought he should feel at least something, but he just felt hollow and empty. It was as if it were impossible for him to be seeing all of this. It somehow couldn't possibly be real.

He walked past the remnant of a house. Its garden of roses had been trampled along with the white miniature fence that surrounded it. The thatched roof was in ashes. Several of the stone walls had been bashed in, obviously by the incredible strength of these creatures. Vordin could see the destruction inside. Then he noticed the lifeless hand still reaching desperately for the sky beneath the rubble.

He moved quickly past with a lump in his throat as he imagined that it could have been him caught under the rubble like that. Guilty thoughts entered his mind as he passed more and more bodies and severed limbs among the debris and what was left of the houses and buildings.

"*Why should I be the one to survive,*" he thought, "*I hid like a coward while everyone else died.*"

He couldn't help noticing that many of the dead strewn about were young children. "*I should have stayed. Maybe I could have saved some of the children,*" and then disgusted with himself he thought, "*I'm a selfish coward. I was frightened. I panicked. I ran and hid. I should have tried to help. I could have brought someone with me. I could have saved at least one child. There was enough room in the*

<Zaylyn ><Quest For The Sword Of Anthrowst ><By Katrina Mandrake-Johnston >   <Ch 1> < 6 >
tree for that."

Vordin now approached the side street where his home should be. He hoped that by some miracle it still stood there intact, with his loving parents alive and well inside. He knew that this could never be true.

He could now see the smoldering remains of his home. The walls and roof had been torn down. Everything that had not been burned, had been smashed or ripped to pieces.

"Mother... Father..." he whispered, and such a combination of fear, anguish, and panic welled up inside him so strong that he would have never believed someone could feel that way.

Without thinking, he blindly made his way toward what was left of his home through the debris and mangled corpses. When he reached his goal, he rummaged around frantically in the rubble without purpose. Vordin suddenly recoiled at the sight of a charred severed arm. At the same time, a wave of reality and clarity was shocked into him. He recognized his father's ring on the burnt and blistered flesh.

"No..." he choked out, "Father... No..."

He looked away with freshly shed tears streaming down his face. That was when he saw the leg of his mother beneath a pile of debris.

"Mother..." his voice said, "I'll help you. Don't worry. I'm here now. I'll help you. I'm here."

He began uncovering her in a desperate hope that she might still be alive. Upon discovering that her head was missing, he just sat there staring blankly into the ashes. His mind was fighting against itself, not wanting to accept the fact that this was real and had actually happened.

As he sobbed heavily, images of his mother and father kept flashing through his mind along with images and memories of his entire family, his home, the village, and the people that lived there. He sat there alone and distraught for most of the day.

As he mindlessly gazed about him, he happened upon a broken piece of mirror. He held it up and looked at the face which was reflected back to him. He knew it was him. It was his square jaw; the same as his father's. He could see his dark brown almond-shaped eyes and his full lips; the same that his mother had. The face was his, but it seemed unfamiliar to him now. It was a jumble of features from people he would never see again.

His mourning turned into a helpless frustration. That frustration turned into anger. In his rage, he made a hasty vow that his family's death would not go unavenged. Then he admitted to himself that for him to pursue vengeance would be impossible and deadly.

He staggered away from the village in the late afternoon. He would have to find shelter and if Rasindell's old home still stood, it would be the best place for him. Also, he hoped that it would give him some emotional comfort. Being around his village and dead parents only brought him incredible distress. He needed to be somewhere familiar and to be somewhere untouched by this massacre.

Vordin walked along an overgrown path which would eventually lead him deep into the forest and to the old hut. As he walked, his thoughts wandered back to his childhood. He had always been mature for his age and therefore didn't really fit in with the other children and their games. He usually played alone with toys, crafts, and other small projects. He was more interested in puzzles and games that challenged his mind, rather than the physical games and activities that most of the other children enjoyed.

Vordin had often ventured deep into the forest against his parents' wishes. He had known by heart the way to the old storyteller's hut. Vordin had often crept out to the hut after dark just to hear the wondrous stories he had to tell. Rasindell had become his only friend.

To see the warm welcoming glow coming from Rasindell's wooden hut had always been well worth the journey through the dark and gloomy forest. Rasindell, expecting him as usual, would often step out awkwardly to greet him wearing his light grey tattered robes and leaning on a gnarled and twisted cane. The wizard would wait patiently as Vordin made his way down the forest path and into the clearing where his home was situated.

Vordin remembered how the old man's grey eyes seemed to sparkle with excitement at yet another

<Zaylyn ><Quest For The Sword Of Anthrowst ><By Katrina Mandrake-Johnston >   <Ch 1> < 7 >

chance to have someone to share his wondrous tales with. Vordin could remember wishing that he too had eyes of a mystical color instead of his plain brown eyes.

Rasindell's round wrinkled face always wore an inviting smile. The wizard would greet Vordin at the door often and beckon the boy inside with a callused hand. He could remember how the hut would smell of potions, spices, and mystical powders.

Rasindell had been a heroic adventurer in his younger days and then had become an expert wizard as he grew into old age. He had become a lonely old man after his full and exciting life, and Vordin was glad that he had been able to spend the time he did with him.

Rasindell was an old man, and when his time had come to die, Vordin had been there for him. He sat there as the old man spoke his last words. Rasindell had pulled him close and spoke of how he had been cursed long ago. He had said that this curse was one of the reasons that he had started to learn magic, in hope that one day he might stumble on a way to break it. He was cursed to recite the legends of their world, Zaylyn, for all eternity after his death. Rasindell had told him that becoming a storyteller to him and seeing the joy and excitement that he could bring with a few words, that his curse had actually become a blessing to him.

Then Rasindell had died and Vordin returned home. After that, he never returned to the hut. He had never spoken of Rasindell, not even after he had passed away. The wizard had been his secret. Vordin now knew that he should have told someone. He had been a small child. He hadn't known how to react to his friend's death.

The old man had always said to remember the stories for the knowledge hidden in them might one day save his life. This was how Vordin had survived. He hid inside a hollow tree as in Rasindell's stories, and he had lived.

The path he had been following soon became non-existent to the point where he found himself stumbling over fallen logs and had brambles and bushes constantly scratch at his legs and arms. His skin itched and several large scrapes and scratches had begun to bleed.

The light began to fade and it became even more difficult for him to travel. He was lost, but he struggled on in the direction he thought Rasindell's old home lay. He was sure that it had not taken so long to reach the hut as a child. He wondered if the creatures would return.

After detangling his hair from a tree branch, Vordin stopped to rest. The sunlight had been replaced by the pale glow of the moon. He smoothed his hair as best as he could with his hands and re-tied the leather strip holding it.

The air was damp and cold. He was scraped and bruised from trying to maneuver through the thick brush in the dark. He had no idea of where he might be now, and he felt and knew that he was extremely vulnerable. The woodland creatures made eerie sounds, which only put him more on edge. He also expected at any moment to come across one of the horrid beasts that had attacked his village.

He figured that it was best to keep moving. As he continued to scramble through the vegetation once more, he heard the loud crack of a branch breaking. Vordin froze, afraid even to breathe. He heard nothing but the gentle night breeze through the trees for a few moments, and then from behind him came a deep bellowing laugh. Vordin spun around to face his unknown adversary, but there was no one to be seen. He heard footsteps and could not tell from which direction they came. His eyes darted around frantically in the dark, as his heart pounded hard in his chest. Then another deep laugh filled the air around him.

Vordin panicked, knowing the damage these beasts could inflict, and he frantically stumbled his way through the brush and brambles in the dark as quickly as he could. His leg had become caught between two logs, and as he fell, he felt the bone in his leg snap. The pain rushed through his entire body and in his agony he cried out.

He struggled in his helpless state, but to no avail. He heard the malicious laughter again as the footsteps quickened and started to move toward his location.

<World of Zaylyn ><Quest For The Sword Of Anthrowst ><By Katrina Mandrake-Johnston ><Ch 2>

CHAPTER 2 = THE FAIRY QUEEN

<Zaylyn ><Quest For The Sword Of Anthrowst ><By Katrina Mandrake-Johnston >   <Ch 2> < 8 >

Suddenly a beast appeared out of nowhere to stand in front of him.   The incredible pain in his leg began to numb slightly as his body reacted to the shock of the broken limb. All Vordin could do was stare, his dark brown eyes wide in amazement and fear at this foul creature.

It stood upright on short legs ending in clawed feet. Its body was covered in a golden brown fur except for its feet, hands, and face. Its overly long arms hung almost to the ground and the claws could easily tear a person apart. On top of its massive head were long pointed ears. The creature was just standing there looking with bulbous blood red eyes at the crippled adolescent. A long and tubular green tongue lay in a gaping mouth of jagged teeth. Large quantities of drool dribbled from its mouth down into its fur. The wrinkled skin of its short snout wiggled as it sniffed the air with its four nostrils.

Vordin was terrified and suffering horrible pain from his leg. It opened its jaws and a low growl resounded from its throat. The revolting stench of its breath and body made him gag. It snapped its jaws in the air in front of his face and he could feel the hot steamy breath on his face and neck.

Just when he thought the beast would rip its teeth viciously into his flesh, it started laughing hysterically. The laughter rumbled and gurgled deep in its throat and then gradually became a high-pitched giggle. The creature started to emit brilliant colored sparks of light from its body until the beast was transformed entirely into many glowing lights.

Each spark of light trailed a hue of color as it darted about wildly in the air. Vordin now realized that each spark ridiculed him with its laughter. It was obvious that they thought their cruel prank to be absolutely hilarious.

A larger spark grew to about the size of a small apple and hovered in front of his face. This delicate creature now before him had the wings of a beautiful butterfly and the body of a young girl. This small being wore a tiny dress made of pink flower petals and a tiny crown of silver rested on her head. Her light blue hair floated about her on the gentle breeze that her wings created, and she glowed with a beautiful lavender light. Her eyes were a deep purple, and her pale white skin glittered and sparkled. The fairy gazed upon him in curiosity for a moment and her manner seemed to show power, wisdom, and a hint of childish humor. She put a finger to her rosy lips and the laughter ceased.

She then asked in a high-pitched voice, "Did we frighten you?" She giggled slightly and then continued, "You don't seem as if you are very dangerous. Shall I fix your leg?"

The fairy queen closed her eyes and cupped her hands upward above her head.   In her concentration, she slowed the beating of her wings to an extremely slow rate, somehow managing to still stay afloat. As Vordin watched, a lavender mist began to drift slowly upward from her hands and then encircled around Vordin's body. The pain from his injury slowly began to fade. He floated free of the logs which had entrapped his broken limb and then he drifted back down to the ground. The mist then concentrated around his leg and he felt the bone right itself in one violent jerk. Soon Vordin was completely healed, including even his tiny cuts and bruises.

He stood and the fairy queen rose up to meet his eye level once more.

"You are one of great luck to have escaped the fate of your village," the fairy queen said to him, "The one responsible for this evil deed is Dranngore. He is the one who rules over the creatures that killed your village. Beware the night, as that is when they enjoy their hunt; under the cover of darkness. Do not be fooled, as this does not mean the daylight will provide you with safety from them. These creatures are not natural beings. They are Killnarin. They have six limbs, as do centaurs. They are hairless with black, oily skin. They have razor sharp claws and teeth. They are strong. They can cast magic on both mind and body. They are 'demon' creatures, summoned with evil intent. They will revel in the pain, suffering, and torment that they will cause, even delaying a kill to prolong it. Their magical source of life extends from Dranngore. Destroy the wizard Dranngore with the Sword of Anthrowst and all shall be well. Farewell human."

Then without hesitation, she darted quickly away with all her fairy subjects following.

So Vordin was left standing in the dark with many unanswered questions. He continued to scramble through the forest and he figured that by now he must have traveled very deep into it. Vordin crawled over and under fallen logs and fought his way through the thick brush until he stumbled into a clearing.

<Zaylyn ><Quest For The Sword Of Anthrowst ><By Katrina Mandrake-Johnston >   <Ch 2> < 9 >

He tripped and landed on dark green grass illuminated by the light of a full pale moon. The grass was cool and lush. As he picked himself up, his gaze fell on a small decrepit log hut.

With great relief, he realized from his childhood memories that this was Rasindell's old home. When Vordin reached the damp rotted door of the hut, he opened it wondering if the roof would collapse or not. Vordin took the risk and stepped into the blackness.

He slowly moved across the floor, sliding his feet across the ground trying to detect anything that might be in his way. Cobwebs clung to his face and as he tore them away, he began to think he had made a very foolish choice. His eyes strained into the darkness as he told himself, *"There could be other creatures who have also taken shelter in this hut. What am I doing? I could be walking into a pair of hungry jaws right this minute!"*

The clouds shifted and moonlight began to filter through several large holes in the roof, illuminating the room enough for Vordin to see that there was no apparent danger.

Then there came a sound above him. As he looked up, an immense spider, about the size of a dinner plate, dropped down to land on his face. Vordin immediately froze. He fought desperately with the instinct to jump around madly in panic trying to fling the thing as far away from him as possible.

He stared in horror at the hairy legs and fangs positioned just above his eyes. He could see the roof, and through the holes, patches of the night sky overhead. He tried to focus on the roof instead of the spider, as the fear was almost completely consuming him.

"Don't move," he pleaded with himself, *"Don't move! The thing will sink its fangs into you if you move!"*

The thought sent a shiver throughout his body and the panic intensified. He felt it slowly moving its legs gently against his vulnerable skin. His heart was pounding wildly.

"Don't move," his mind shouted at him, *"Please, please, don't move! What can I possibly do?! Even my breathing, as shallow as it is right now, might make it attack!"*

Then he thought he ought to do something now, before it got a chance to bite him, but the fear was too great. *"Get off me! Get off me!"* he screamed inside his mind.

Vordin then heard the flap of wings and the cry of an owl. The spider remained balanced on the boy's face, continuing to caress his skin with its many legs as it kept repositioning itself. The owl, now through an opening in the roof, soared through the air with its sharp talons outstretched to snatch the spider from his face.

"Please no! No! No! This thing's surely going to bite me, and if that doesn't happen, the owl's talons will rip my face to shreds!"

The owl was closing in on him fast, and he had to make a decision.

His arm seemed like a separate entity as it slowly and calmly picked up the spider by its mid-section and removed it. The owl continued its dive toward Vordin's face. He winced, helpless against the attack. The bird came extremely close to him with its talons, but then pulled up at the last moment seeing that its meal had vanished. Vordin felt the rush of air against him and he watched the brown and white owl fly up into the rafters where it perched. Its large yellow eyes began searching hungrily for the spider.

He felt something wriggle between his fingertips. For a moment, he had forgotten that he still held the large spider. He recoiled in terror and disgust, dropping the spider to the ground. It scurried toward a small crevice in the wooden floor to find refuge.

Vordin shuddered and felt a cold chill all over his body. He was amazed that the spider's fangs hadn't been imbedded in his skin. He shuddered again and wiped frantically at his face where the spider had been. It felt like it was still there; his face having an itchy, tickled feeling. He couldn't believe that the ordeal was over now and that he had gotten through it unharmed.

The spider was almost to the crack in the floor now. The owl dove down for another attack. As the spider crawled into the hole, the owl landed beside it and managed to sever a piece off one of the spider's legs. Then finding that its attempts to pry its meal out of the hole were futile, the owl flew off through the roof and into the surrounding forest.

Vordin slowly made his way over to what he thought would be the fireplace. There had been a

<Zaylyn ><Quest For The Sword Of Anthrowst ><By Katrina Mandrake-Johnston >   <Ch 2> < 10 >

small table on which Rasindell had kept a lantern. He hoped that the lantern was still there and intact. Reaching the now dilapidated table, he rummaged through the dust-covered debris and eventually he touched cool metal. He turned the object over and over in his hands until he felt a small clasp on one side.

As he opened the front of the metal box, the room was immediately illuminated by a strong glow coming from inside. How he had overlooked the makeup of this arcane and incredible device as a child, bewildered him. Upon further examination, he discovered that although it had been used as a lantern, it was in fact a flask containing a mysterious glowing potion in an elaborate metal case. There was no heat produced by the flask, and there was a metal handle in the top of the case so it could be handled easily. The purpose of the case was obviously to hide the glow of the potion when light was no longer needed.

Vordin looked around the now dimly lit room finding it cluttered with debris and covered in a film of dust. The windowless, one-roomed cabin had only one door leading to the outside and he knew that he should barricade it for the night. Beside the fireplace was a small but sturdy trunk. After dragging the heavy object to the entrance, he realized that the decayed wood of the door wouldn't be that difficult to break through but figured that it would have to suffice.

In one corner of the room was a straw mattress, and in the center of the room was a small table with a chair neatly tucked beneath. Beside the fireplace, on the left side, was a large cauldron, and on the right side, close to where he had found the lantern, was a pile of logs meant for the fire.

Vordin closed his eyes and tried to remember how inviting this old hovel had once been when the fire was roaring, making the shadows dance playfully on the walls. Rasindell would tell his tales of adventure and mystery with a smiling wrinkled face. The cauldron would bubble with a spicy stew or with a mysterious concoction. He remembered Rasindell's home as being warm and cozy with almost a friendly life of its own. Now as he examined his surroundings, he found himself in a cold and undesirable place.

He set the mysterious lantern on the table in the center of the room, and he proceeded to examine the trunk. The lid of the trunk opened easily and Vordin lifted out two thick grey blankets which he placed on the floor beside him. Under these blankets was an empty brown leather backpack and beside this was a wooden bowl, a small wooden spoon, a small dagger, a large wooden spoon for the cauldron, and also a small cracked mirror.

He picked up the mirror and took a look at himself. His hair was filthy and hung loosely at his shoulders, his hair tie lost. His eyes showed every bit of the hollowness he felt. He looked sickly, his skin paler than it should have been, and completely exhausted.

He replaced the mirror, and then he looked down at his clothing. His clothing and shoes were covered in patches of dirt and debris from the forest, but he found he no longer cared about his appearance. He removed the backpack and the dagger and then he closed the lid of the trunk.

He carried the blankets over to the straw mattress and laid them over it. Exhausted, he climbed under the top blanket and was soon fast asleep with the tiny dagger beside him and the backpack on the floor.

A dream came to him…

Vordin stood on the edge of his village. The warm afternoon sun felt good on his skin. The air smelled sweet with the fragrance of roses. A crow cried out from somewhere above, and as he looked up to the clear blue sky, he caught a glimpse of the bird as it beat its black wings against the wind. He walked down one of the busy dirt roads in the village. An old woman wearing a cheerful smile on her face was sitting on her porch with a clay pot in front of her. Her white hair, ruffled by the breeze, was tied back in a loose knot. Vordin watched as she took a small brush, dipped it into a small jar of dark red paint, and began to paint an intricate design onto the surface of the pot. She had a beautiful bed of bright red roses growing in the front garden with a white miniature fence surrounding it. He had seen her before, but he couldn't remember her name.

"Hello there! Vordin is it? Enjoying the day are you?" said a middle-aged man as he walked past.

<Zaylyn ><Quest For The Sword Of Anthrowst ><By Katrina Mandrake-Johnston >   <Ch 2> < 11 >

He had short black hair which had started to grey. His round happy face smiled at him. He had seen this man before too, but he couldn't remember when or who he was.

A small child laughed cheerfully and then several others. A black cat chased a butterfly. Vordin walked past several houses and shops. All of them were busy with life.

Then, he came to his own home. He couldn't remember a time when it had looked more inviting. The light blue flowers in the flowerbed were blooming and brought to him the smell of home. He stepped up to the front door. Something was cooking and the smells coming from the house were wonderful. His mother would be home and his father would be too in a short while for dinner. He opened the door and stepped into the warm cozy kitchen.

"Vordin, there you are!" his mother exclaimed when he entered the house, "I've been calling you for some time now. Dinner's almost ready. We're having stew. Would you mind setting the table dear?"

Vordin went to the cupboard and took the dishes from their place and began setting the table. His mother was wearing her light blue dress. It was the one with the pink flowers. She only wore this dress on special occasions. Her white apron was tied around her waist. She gave him a look that was warm and loving. Her reddish-brown hair shone in the firelight.

"Okay, look out now. This is very hot," she warned him as she set the stew pot on the table. She then gave him a concerned look. "Are you okay honey?" asked his mother, "You look a little pale." She felt his forehead. Her touch was warm and soft.

The door opened and Vordin's father entered the house. "How's my boy? Oh, that smells absolutely wonderful, Hun. I'm just going to wash up a bit and change my clothes," he said leaving the kitchen and went into the bedroom.

"Come sit down, dear," she said as she sat at the table and poured glasses of water for all three of them.

Vordin sat in his chair and took a sip of the water. It was deliciously fresh and icy cold. The smell of the stew made his mouth tingle with anticipation of the hot and juicy meat and the hearty vegetables. A large bowl of whipped potatoes was on the table... and he could see where he had swiped a taste earlier. He noticed that there was also a large loaf of warm crusty bread on the table and a plate of butter. A small knife was laid beside the plate and the flames from the fire danced in their reflection along the length of the metal.

Vordin's father returned, and they began their meal. The food was delicious, better than he could ever remember. He let the flavor of each mouthful linger a few moments before he swallowed. It was as if the creatures had never...

Suddenly, his parents vanished. Their plates were still on the table; their meals half eaten. He swallowed the bit of bread he had been chewing, but it felt like it had lumped in his throat.

The fire in the hearth slowly died out and now the only light in the room was the sunlight coming through the window. He wanted the smiling faces of his mother and father to return. There was a place deep down inside him that knew they wouldn't and in that spot it felt empty, cold, and hurt.

Vordin got up from the table. There was complete silence in the room. It was an eerie silence. Vordin left the house and stepped outside.

Silence. Nothing stirred. The streets were empty. The wind whistled through the trees and shrubs. The wind was cold and bitter.

He heard the cry of an eagle. Darkness fell over the village as if someone had pulled a black blanket up over it. He heard a scream. He heard a blood-curdling howl. Then there were more screams, panicked cries, and frightened words spoken to loved ones. It was everything he didn't want to hear.

He couldn't see anyone around him, but he could feel the presence of many. He could almost feel the hot breath of the beasts upon his skin. Tortured screams and fierce bellowing howls echoed in his ears...

He awoke from a restless sleep. He could see through the roof that the day was already half over.

<Zaylyn ><Quest For The Sword Of Anthrowst ><By Katrina Mandrake-Johnston >   <Ch 2> < 12 >
He had slept clear through most of the day, which disturbed him greatly, for with the night came the possibility that the creatures might return.

<World of Zaylyn ><Quest For The Sword Of Anthrowst ><By Katrina Mandrake-Johnston ><Ch 3>

CHAPTER 3 = LORENTA

His stomach grumbled at him. Vordin got up from the mattress and left the cabin. The air was fresh outside and he breathed in deeply. His body ached and felt stiff. Birds sang happy songs and insects buzzed from bush to bush. This place had a peaceful atmosphere and he was glad for it.

Lying down, he stretched himself out on the cool grass with his hands behind his head and looked up to the blue sky. The last time he had been here, he had been only seven years old. Now, it was eight years later and things here hadn't really changed all that much.

He thought about Rasindell and realized how much he missed his old friend. Now was a time when he wished most that the old man was still here and alive. The night that Rasindell died, Vordin had been so very frightened.

"*What's a kid supposed to do?*" Vordin thought to himself as he remembered that night, "*I had thought about burying him, but that would have been impossible. I couldn't have dug a grave very well and then there was the task of dragging the body to it. I didn't want to have to do that to my friend. I just left him there and went home. That's all I could have done. That's probably how he would have wanted it. If he hadn't been so secretive, things would have been different. I don't think a single person except for me even knew about him and his cabin here in the woods. Why aren't there any bones? Surely after all these years, there would be something. Maybe some animals had carried bits of him off into the woods until there was nothing left. What a horrible thing to imagine, what's wrong with you? Maybe being a wizard, he just magically disappeared. There, now that's a better explanation. Oh stop it, what a stupid thing to be thinking about.*"

Noticing a bush with clusters of ripe red berries growing on it, he got up and walked over to it.

"*What a great idea,*" he said to himself with sarcasm, "*Eat some poisonous berries and die. Then maybe some animals will drag pieces of you away over the years until there's nothing left.*"

He left the berries on the bush and roamed around the surrounding forest in hope of finding food, as it had been over a day, almost two now, since he had eaten anything.

The daylight had begun to fade. His efforts at finding food were useless. He felt incredibly weak, cold, and extremely exhausted. His stomach ached with hunger and his mouth was dry with thirst. He entered the cabin once more.

The lantern was still glowing brightly from where he had left it on the table. He crawled under the blanket and tried to figure out a course of action. He was still puzzling over what the fairy queen had said to him.

Through the roof, he could see that the sun had set and he became annoyed at how quickly the day had passed him by. Then out of the corner of his eye, he thought he saw something stir on the floor.

Vordin noticed that the huge spider was slowly crawling out of the crevice in the wooden floorboards. He had completely forgotten about it when he had laid down to rest the night before and was amazed that he had remained safe during his slumber. The thought of the thing crawling over his skin again sent shivers down his back.

He found the small dagger and held it tightly in his hand wondering how he would catch or kill the thing. Vordin watched the spider very closely as it crawled to the middle of the room. Vordin noticed that the lower half of one of its front legs on its right side had been severed by the owl. It was a wolf spider, greyish in color, and Vordin had seen many of them before. They were normally small, but once he had seen one that was so large that it was near half the size of his fist. This one before him was monstrous. The spider's large round eyes seemed to be watching him as well. He did not want it to scurry off into some unknown location where it could jump out at him unexpectedly.

He thought about maybe crushing the huge spider with the cauldron, but he realized that by the time he reached it, the spider would be long gone and the cauldron would be too heavy and clumsy to

<Zaylyn ><Quest For The Sword Of Anthrowst ><By Katrina Mandrake-Johnston >   <Ch 3> < 13 >

accomplish the deed. To attack it with the tiny dagger was absolutely ridiculous. So he decided to throw the blanket over the spider, thus trapping it underneath, and then crushing it under his shoe. He sat up and held the blanket ready.

Just before he was about to execute his plan, mysteriously, the body of the spider was instantly engulfed in magical green flames. The spider's body seemed to melt into a thick black puddle under the flames, and then, while Vordin sat on the mattress in utter amazement, the puddle slowly increased in size. The black mass traveled upward from the puddle and eventually formed into a humanoid shape.

As the emerald flames subsided, Vordin now saw the figure of a beautiful young woman before him. She was a few inches taller than Vordin, and black web-like robes clothed her slender form. Her long dark brown hair fell gently below her shoulders, and she had smooth pale skin. As the woman took a step closer to him with a dainty bare foot, he could see that she moved with great agility and grace. With her beautiful light brown eyes, she gazed at Vordin slightly puzzled. Then after a moment's hesitation, her pale lips broke into a smile.

She had large curious eyes and they studied his every move and feature.

"Hello," she said in a sweet voice, "Thank-you for saving my life." Vordin did not know what to say to this strange being. The woman continued, "I know you didn't intend to do so, but I thank you anyway. I know that Rasindell probably never spoke of me to you. I think he was a bit ashamed of me, although he would never have admitted this. He probably would have used the potion on a creature more beautiful than I, if he had known the power that it held. He enjoyed your visits so much. I think that he was afraid of what your reaction might be if you knew of me and of my true form. I did not want to stress the friendship between you and him, so I agreed to spend time away from the hut during your visits. He left years ago, and I've remained here ever since in hope that he would some day return. Also, I have nowhere else to go and so far no reason to leave."

"But who are you?" Vordin asked intrigued by this creature's strange story.

"I am Rasindell's daughter," she said as if that would be a sufficient explanation. She curiously felt at her face, tracing her fingertips over her deep-set eyes and high cheekbones, and then over her small round nose, her plump lips, and rounded chin. "Sorry, I have not been in this form for such a long time," she explained.

"What potion? What exactly are you?" he asked.

She sat herself upon the floor with her legs crossed beneath her and smoothed out her wispy black robes. Then she replied, "Years ago, Rasindell gave me my human form through an incredible magic potion that he had acquired in his journeys as an adventurer. He had not known at the time what the potion would do and he had been wary of using it for many years. I guess one day he decided to not let the potion go to waste and poured the contents of the flask onto a large spider which had found its way into his home. I was this spider. Perhaps at the time, he thought the potion would kill or mutilate me in some terrible way, but instead I gained the ability to transform into the form of a human. Rasindell told me that I had transformed immediately into a small child. I discovered that I am able to change my form at will, although only at night, and that I had gained the life span of a human as well. Rasindell from that day on had raised me as if I were his very own daughter. Oh, and as you probably noticed, my size in spider form increased by about ten times."

"That truly is an incredible and elaborate story," he exclaimed with suspicion.

"By the expression on your face, I can tell that you don't believe a word I'm saying," the woman said with extreme disappointment. The excitement in her eyes had vanished and it had been replaced by great despair. "I don't know the real reason why he would not tell you about me, but I suspect it was out of fear," she said to him, "If you had told one of the villagers, they might have come here to destroy me. I am different. Humans don't usually like things that are different."

"If this is all true, then why did you attack me?" he questioned.

She replied despondently, "I would have transformed to escape that horrid owl, but there wasn't time. I dropped down onto you in hope that I could save myself by doing so. Besides, I thought that you might have been Rasindell. You're the first person to come here since he left so many years ago. I am glad to see that you have returned here, Vordin. It's nice to see a familiar face after all this time.

<Zaylyn ><Quest For The Sword Of Anthrowst ><By Katrina Mandrake-Johnston >   <Ch 3> < 14 >
I'm very sorry if I have frightened you."

"Don't you know that Rasindell is dead? He died many years ago," Vordin said with further doubt about her true identity. Why she would not know about the death of her so-called father was even more disturbing.

She was sitting on the floor between him and the door which was still barricaded by the old trunk. He was sitting on the straw mattress with his feet positioned on the wooden floorboards. He still held the small dagger hidden within the folds of the blankets. It was obvious that she could sense his fear. He knew his only defense was to keep her talking, as he was extremely vulnerable against her and had nowhere to run.

"At first, I thought he did die," she said, "but then a strange event occurred that has puzzled me for years. When you left for the village that night, I came back to the hut and found that the old man had finally died. I sat by the fire, not knowing what to do. You had left without discovering that I even existed, and I found myself truly abandoned. After several hours, Rasindell just got up from his resting place and walked out the door as if nothing had happened. If he wasn't dead, then why did he just leave me like that? Was I that much of a disappointment to him? He always said he loved me as if I were his very own child. I don't understand. It doesn't make any sense."

"Did he really just get up and walk out the door?" he asked in amazement, because she had spoken with such sincerity.

"Yes," she replied, her eyes seeming to beg for any explanation that he could give her.

Vordin put aside his suspicions for a moment as he said, "He did speak to me about a curse."

"A curse?" she interrupted.

"He said he was cursed to recite the legends of Zaylyn for all eternity, or rather blessed to do so as he had said. He probably just got up to fulfill his destiny."

She took a moment to ponder Vordin's explanation and then said, "He always told me that one day he would have to leave me, but I always thought he meant in death and not in such a bizarre way."

"I don't understand it either," he admitted.

"I had always hoped you would return. Even though I had never met you then face to face, I had always thought of you as a little brother and part of our strange family." As she spoke, she broke eye contact with him. She knew he did not see it this way and his presence here did not mean her loneliness had come to an end.

Vordin realized that if her strange story was indeed true, he was the only other person besides Rasindell that she had ever known. When Rasindell died, and his visits to the hut had ceased, she had been left in bitter solitude. Vordin found himself truly feeling for her, for he too was now alone. Still, he decided that she couldn't be trusted no matter how convincing she became.

"How old are you now?" she asked.

"Fifteen," he replied.

"It's really been that long?" she paused a few moments, as if this loss of time had saddened her, and then she continued, "I guess that would make me seventeen, or maybe eighteen then. I'm not quite sure. Your village, its name is Nilnont, right?"

"It doesn't matter anymore. It's been destroyed. Everyone is dead," he said in a sullen voice.

Her light brown eyes showed a hint of remorse, as if she understood what he felt and what it was like to loose one's whole world and everything familiar to it.

"Would you like me to light the fire?" she offered.

"Sure," he said.

"I can bring you some food if you like as well. Are you hungry?" she asked.

"Sure," he answered again. He knew that she would have to leave the cabin to do so.

She gracefully moved across the floor and picked up a log by the fireplace. The woman then placed the log in the ashes and stood there waiting. Vordin almost laughed at these ignorant actions. Then to his amazement, the log burst into flames.

"There," she said obviously pleased with herself and the astonished look on Vordin's face, "It still works fine. Rasindell hated to light his own fires. I'm not sure how he did it, but all you have to do is

<Zaylyn ><Quest For The Sword Of Anthrowst ><By Katrina Mandrake-Johnston >   <Ch 3> < 15 >
toss a log in and it will light."

Vordin walked cautiously over to the fireplace and warmed himself by it. "You said something about being able to find something to eat?" he reminded her.

"Oh, of course. I'll be back in awhile then," she said with a cheerful smile.

She displayed exceptional strength as she easily pushed the heavy trunk aside and left through the door. Vordin watched the fire and the shadows dance on the walls as they had so long ago. He listened to the flames crackle and let the heat warm him. He realized that if he were in danger, he wouldn't be able to protect himself. Vordin decided that the only thing he was able to do was to wait for dawn, when she would have to revert back to spider form, and for the chance to escape unseen.

A heavy rain began to fall just as the woman was entering through the cabin door. She approached him with her hands outstretched and cradling a large leaf which held a plentiful amount of wild orange berries. He noticed that she only had a thumb and forefinger on her right hand and realized her missing fingers were the result of the wound caused by the owl's attack.

"Here you are," she said as she handed him the berries.

Vordin accepted her gift and they sat in silence in front of the fire for some time.

"*I wonder if these are poisonous? Maybe if I taste one, I'll be able to tell. If they are really bitter, I think that it means they are poison. I don't know. I have no clue of how to tell something like that. But what will she do if I refuse to eat them?*" he thought to himself.

"Aren't you going to eat?" she asked him.

Vordin popped one of the berries into his mouth. It was slightly bitter, but it tasted all right. The berries weren't poisonous, because he had eaten these same berries before. Rasindell sometimes had a bowl of them for him to snack on during the stories.

He ate the rest of the berries hungrily and wished that there had been more. He noticed how she kept looking sadly at her hand and tried to keep it hidden from sight within the folds of her clothing. Vordin tossed the empty leaf into the fire, and they watched as it sizzled and smoked.

"What's your name?" he asked, realizing he did not yet know it.

"Lorenta," she answered, pleased he had asked.

"It's pretty," he commented and then asked, "Did Rasindell name you?"

"Yes, and thank-you," she said with a smile.

Again there was a long period of silence. The rain beat a soothing rhythm on the roof overhead, and the fire spread its warmth throughout the cabin despite the few large holes in the roof where the rain came in. Soon Vordin had fallen asleep where he sat.

Another dream came to him this night…

Vordin found himself in a dark and damp cavern. Water dripped from stalactites above. A tunnel could be seen to his left and he made his way into it. The tunnel sloped gradually downward and he had difficulty maintaining his footing. As he descended farther, a soft glow steadily increased making it easier for him to see his way.

Eventually the tunnel opened up into another cavern. A pool of lava bubbled up through a fissure in the cavern floor. The heat was intense.

As Vordin approached the pool, a hideous creature arose from the molten rock. It leapt up into the stale air of the cavern and its leathery wings beat the air as lava rolled down its body to sizzle on the rocks below. Its man-sized body was covered in coarse hair and its massive jaws were filled with foul jagged teeth. Its bat-like face turned toward him and it let out a blood-curdling howl. Its beady blood red eyes were fixated maliciously on him and it clenched its sharp talons.

Vordin backed slowly away from the creature, and then he couldn't move. He was trapped in a giant spider web. No matter how hard he struggled, he could not break loose from its sticky embrace. The creature let out a growl that rumbled throughout the cave.

Lorenta came toward Vordin from out of the shadows. She had an evil smirk across her lips. The creature bellowed a wicked laugh and Lorenta joined it in its mirth.

From Lorenta's black cobweb-like robes came forth a horde of tiny spiders. Vordin's struggles

<Zaylyn ><Quest For The Sword Of Anthrowst ><By Katrina Mandrake-Johnston >   <Ch 3> < 16 >
were futile against the web, as they swarmed his vulnerable form. Thousands of tiny fangs pierced his flesh, as they crawled up his legs, inside his clothing, and up to his arms and face. Lorenta watched him writhe in pain, with a sneer and a look of satisfaction on her face. He opened his mouth to scream, but no sound came forth as the tiny spiders made their way into his mouth and down his throat…

He awoke early the next morning gasping for air. His mouth tingled with the memory of his nightmare. Lorenta was nowhere to be seen. She had wrapped a blanket around him while he had slept.

He unwrapped the blanket, got up from the floor, and went to the table. Vordin closed the door of the lantern and tossed it inside the backpack. After tucking the small dagger into a little side pocket on the backpack, he slung it onto his back where it rested comfortably. His dream had confirmed his decision to leave before Lorenta returned. He didn't want anything to do with her, no matter what crazy story she had for him.

Vordin then opened the door and stepped out into the cool, crisp, morning air. He heard birds singing their songs in the trees as the sun's rays filtered down through the treetops. He walked through the dew-covered grass as he headed in the direction of the mountains. On the other side of the mountain range was Dee'ellkka Valley and this was the path he had decided on. He did not know what he hoped to find there, but at least now he had some sort of destination to travel toward.

He traveled long and hard through the dense forest. By nightfall, he had emerged into the open and walked until he met the trail-like road that would lead him up into the mountains.

Reluctantly, he decided to stop for the night as it would be difficult to travel in the dark, even with his mysterious lantern. Vordin curled up by the side of the road for there was no place to hide himself from view. He shivered in the cool air and wished that he had remembered to take one of the blankets from the cabin with him. He hoped that his grey tunic and brown pants would offer him some kind of camouflage, but he highly doubted that.

Vordin tried to rest his weary body, for the hike along the mountainous trail would take a lot of endurance. Vordin found himself drifting off to sleep after several hours.

He awoke suddenly to the sound of heavy steps along the road. Vordin stayed low to the ground, as he couldn't detect who or what was coming toward him. A fierce howl resounded through the air that struck great fear in him, as he had heard this same noise at the massacre of his village. He was helpless against this vile beast and he knew it. In a few moments the 'demon' creature would be upon him. He couldn't see the beast from his position where the ground dipped slightly and because he was so low to the ground. Wondering how close his death was, he took the tiny dagger from the pocket of the backpack. Vordin held it tightly and noticed how badly his hand trembled.

"So, this is it. Fifteen years of life and now it's to be cut short. Looks as if they won't allow anyone to escape. What possible chance do I have? All that's left, is to accept my fate and try to be brave," he told himself, trying to force some courage into his last moments, although tears had begun to stream down his face and his whole body was weak with fear.

Before the creature could attack him, a black mass fell from the sky and landed a few feet in front of Vordin. This strange person, who had his back turned to Vordin, wore a black cloak with its hood covering his head. The cloak flapped in the breeze as Vordin stared in amazement. He could see that the mysterious man wore a pair of black pants and had a pair of well-worn black leather boots which came to mid calf.

The man turned his head to look down at the boy who was staring in astonishment at him, but did not utter a single word. His face remained unseen, as it was cast in dark shadow beneath his hood. With a gust of wind, the dark black cloak moved slightly to reveal a sword sheathed in a black scabbard at this man's waist.

The Killnarin shrieked and howled at the sight of this new stranger who had suddenly made his appearance along its path. As this man continued to look at Vordin, in the blackness under his hood, two blood red eyes began to glow until they shone brightly. A low growl emitted from this being's throat as he looked away from Vordin to face the creature.

Vordin did not know what to think of this new situation and wondered if this person were friend or

<Zaylyn ><Quest For The Sword Of Anthrowst ><By Katrina Mandrake-Johnston >   <Ch 3> < 17 >

foe. The Killnarin howled defiantly at this man, but did not approach. The man then spun around and seized Vordin in one arm with an inhuman ease and leapt into the air, soaring away from the beast. Vordin watched as it pranced wildly around in anger and frustration below them.

Vordin was being carried high above the countryside as the man held him firmly in his grip. The black cloak flapped in the wind as they sped through the chill night air. He could see the mountain range below that he had been traveling toward and he wondered what intentions his silent captor had for him.

The stars sparkled above them and the full moon was bright. The forest which Vordin had traveled through and where Rasindell's hut lay, looked smaller than it had felt when he had been struggling through it. He followed the road with his eyes and caught a glimpse of Nilnont far behind them. It looked as if there had only been the one creature and Vordin wondered where all the others had gone.

"Perhaps, the beast was a scout of some sort. Maybe to check for survivors or maybe they knew that I had escaped them. But those creatures aren't what I have to worry about right now," thought Vordin, "What is he planning to do with me? Does he intend to drop me to my death or does he have something worse in mind?"

Vordin's legs dangled beneath him. They flew against the wind and as it whipped past them, Vordin found it to be icy cold. They were approaching the mountains and the sight was beautiful. There was snow on the mountaintops, but not much. The night shadows gave the snow a purple glow in places. He had lost track of the road, but he knew it was there, winding its way over the mountains and back down into the valley beyond. The mountains were mainly barren rock, but in places, there were trees and other vegetation. Vordin wondered about the trolls and dragons and where their caves and tunnels might be or if they in fact were just myth after all.

As they continued to fly, he noticed they were now flying at an incline to the mountains and finally they alighted on a mountaintop. The man still held him tightly and Vordin could not struggle free.

There was a dark cave set into the side of the mountain and this is where the man put him. Before the boy had any chance of escape, the man, with an unimaginable strength, rolled a large boulder in front of the cave entrance and Vordin found himself in complete darkness.

Remembering the lantern, he felt around in the backpack until he touched the cool metal of the case. After removing the box, he opened the small door and light filled his tiny prison. He could see that he was trapped within a small area between the boulder and the back wall of the alcove. There was no possible way for him to escape.

Fresh mountain air drifted through a small space between the boulder and the cave wall, and through this, he could see the stars shining in the black sky. He hoped that his captor would return to release him and with good intentions, but feared the worst. Vordin lay on the rock floor pondering the bizarre events that had happened in such a short time. Eventually, he slipped into a deep sleep out of exhaustion.

Lightening flashed and lit up the night sky for a few moments. Thunder roared loud and fierce. A heavy rain, much heavier than the night before, began to fall from above.

***

The tall pine trees, where the mysterious man in black stood now, were dense and made visibility difficult. The Black Shadow looked down at the body of the unknown girl lying on the dark soil. He had lured her out of the village of Dexcsin and into the nearby forest.

She had long beautiful hair, which was of the purest black. She was wearing a thin white gown, and as it became wet, it clung to her shapely form. What blood remained was slowly being washed away by the rain. Her wet, pale face seemed peaceful and it pained him to know she would never awaken.

He averted his gaze, as he could not bear to look at her further. A lump was beginning to form in the back of his throat and he choked it back. He felt guilt, self-hatred, sorrow, pity, frustration, and several other mixed emotions.

He looked up through the treetops to the night sky and let the cold rain wash over his face. He found the sound of the storm soothing and calming. He knew of a place in the forest where he could

<Zaylyn ><Quest For The Sword Of Anthrowst ><By Katrina Mandrake-Johnston >   <Ch 3> < 18 >
find shelter. At sunset tomorrow night, he would return for the boy.

<World of Zaylyn ><Quest For The Sword Of Anthrowst ><By Katrina Mandrake-Johnston ><Ch 4>

CHAPTER 4 =   CANDRA AND DENDROX

Meanwhile, as Vordin lay trapped in his rocky prison and the daylight faded, Candra, a twenty-three year old elf, and Dendrox, a twenty-two year old human, had decided to make their camp for the night. They were situated at the tree line, on the other side of the mountain range in Dee'ellkka Valley, where the grassy plain met the forest. There were small patches of grass here and there that had dared to fight for the sun's rays under the shadow of the tall pine trees. Farther into the forest, the smaller vegetation thrived on the light which filtered down from the treetops. Candra noted that although the majority of trees in the forest were pine and cedar, she could also see a few different types among them where the forest was less dense. She wondered if any of them bore edible nuts or if some of the bushes had berries or roots that they could collect.

Candra had wished that they had stopped earlier in the mountains before the rain had started, but she knew well that the edge of the vast forest, where they were now in the valley, would provide better protection than being out in the open. The cool rain washed against her face as she stared into the night sky. Her straight black hair fell a few inches above her shoulders and was wet along with her clothes. To keep her hair from clinging to her face, she tucked it behind her elfin ears.

The rainstorm eventually drizzled out. The smell of wet earth and pine filled the cool autumn air. A cool breeze, fresh and revitalizing, brought with it the pleasant smell of wild flowers.

She was cold and tired, and the warmth of a fire was what she had been looking forward to since late that afternoon. Now everything was too wet to get a fire started. Her feet, in her well-worn brown leather boots, ached from their long journey through the mountain pass.

"Finally, I might have drowned if the rain had continued like that," Candra said jokingly about the rain after it had stopped.

"Not a bad spot for the night," Dendrox commented about their campsite.

They had a clear view of the road from the trees in which they had made their shadowed camp, and if the need came, they could easily move farther into the forest for concealment against an encounter.

Candra could see the mountain range to the west and the dirt road which made its way down the mountain, across the grassy plain, past their position, and into the dense forest. She had been so thrilled at the sight of thick dark green grass on either side of the road when they had gotten to the base of the mountain, that she had taken off her boots and let her sore feet enjoy the cool rain soaked grass for several minutes.

Dendrox, the shy human boy from her childhood, now a young man, went about his preparations for the night and she thought to herself that she had better get started on hers as well before it got too dark to see.

A short bow was slung over her shoulder. With a sigh, the elf placed it on the ground in front of her. The quiver, which was situated on her back with its strap crossing diagonally over her chest, was next to be removed. Candra was thin and wore form-fitting clothes of a dark green color, the same as her eyes. She found, although not a necessity, that wearing close fitting clothes was an asset to her profession as a thief. Her cotton shirt was sleeveless with a v-shaped neckline and the bottoms of her pants she often tucked into the tops of her boots. At her waist, she wore a belt made of brown leather with a plain square metal buckle. She undid her belt and let it drop to the ground along with the two black leather pouches which were attached to the belt on either side of her hips.

"That feels much better. Now to get these boots off my aching feet," Candra commented pulling the boots off.

Dendrox had dark blue eyes and wore his straight dark brown hair at ear length. He had a pair of black pants as well as a navy blue vest over a plain black shirt with long sleeves. On his belt he wore a collection of throwing daggers.

"Yeah, that hike was pretty tiresome. Better to have traveled it in one day like we did though," Dendrox added as he removed his brown leather backpack. He removed its contents: two dark brown

<Zaylyn ><Quest For The Sword Of Anthrowst ><By Katrina Mandrake-Johnston >   <Ch 4> < 19 >
blankets and an empty water skin. He passed one of the blankets to Candra.

"Thanks," she said to Dendrox, "Hey, remind me to get some new boots when we get to town."

"Okay, sure," he agreed.

Candra spread out her blanket on the ground and Dendrox did the same. They were both thankful that the trees had sheltered the ground partially from the earlier rainfall, making the area less damp. Dendrox tossed the empty water skin back into the backpack and then removed the black leather pouch, which rested at the small of his back, and laid it beside the pack on the ground. He almost never parted with his daggers, even to sleep.

"So what do you think happened at that village we passed?" she asked.

"Don't know. Looked pretty bad though," he answered.

"I think we should have stopped there," Candra told him, "We could have gotten a few supplies. Maybe a few survivors could have told us what happened. Aren't you curious? I should have insisted on exploring the village instead of letting you drag me up the mountain trail like that."

"Come on, you saw it," was his reply, "There wasn't anyone still alive. Whatever happened there was awful and I didn't want to stick around to find out what. We're over the mountains now. We're in the valley and hopefully far enough away from danger. Just forget about it, at least for now, we're going to need our sleep tonight."

Soon they both were sitting uncomfortably on their separate blankets trying to rest their weary bodies.

The tall trees cast their shadows over the barren road. The moon above didn't add much to their visibility, the clouds dulling its light. Sight was not one of the senses they would be relying on much tonight and listening to every little sound would make sleep almost impossible, even though they would be taking turns with watch duty.

She knew the ground absorbed body heat and that having the blanket between her and it was the best thing to do. Packing more than one blanket each into Dendrox's backpack would be awkward and take up the room they needed to store any loot they came across, but still, she wished she had another one to drape over her. Her clothing didn't offer her much warmth on nights like these.

"How much farther to the town of Vackiindmire?" the elf asked.

"We'll probably reach it by tomorrow night, Candra. I can hardly wait," Dendrox said with exhaustion.

As she rubbed at her aching muscles, she said, "Yeah, same here."

He said with a sigh, "Just think… a hot bath, a hearty meal, and a good night's sleep in a warm comfortable bed."

"When we get there, I call first on that bath. I'm a lady after all," Candra said with a sly grin.

"Yeah right, we'll see about that one," he chuckled.

She wasn't sure if he were talking about the first bath or the part about being a 'lady', so she just said, "Good-night, Dendrox."

He gave her an annoyed look as he said, "Hey, I thought you were taking first watch."

"Oh you're such a pain," she said with a smile, "I was just seeing if I could get away with it."

"Hey Candra, while you're up, check to see how much gold we have left," he said as he stretched out on his blanket.

"Well, I'm not up," she said unwilling to move, "and besides, I already know that we'll have to do a little pocket searching when we get there. You can scout out the rich folk while I'm soaking in that hot bath."

"Yeah right. I can see it now. Some guy with a fat pouch smells this horrible stench and looks down to see my grinning face staring up at him, with my grimy hand where his gold should be," he said with a hint of sarcasm.

"Ha ha," Candra teased, "Just get some rest."

She lay watching the stars, imagining the huge feast she would be eating after her bath. Woodland creatures scurried through the brush and she tried to stay alert to every sound in order to detect any sign of danger.

<Zaylyn ><Quest For The Sword Of Anthrowst ><By Katrina Mandrake-Johnston >   <Ch 4> < 20 >

The first snore made her jump, as always, with her hand to her bow in a swift reflex. She groaned slightly and sat up checking the forest and its shadows for any movement and listening for any sounds other than his snoring.

"*With all that noise, it will either attract danger or more likely scare it away,*" she thought to herself with a chuckle.

Candra rummaged through one of her pouches and retrieved her last bit of dried meat.

"*We desperately need to get to a town. We've already gone through Dendrox's water skin coming over the mountains, and like me, he only has a small amount of food in that pouch of his. I think it might be the last of the cheese he has in there. Yes, he's saving it for tomorrow and he'd be really mad if I took a bite or two of it considering that it's probably all he has left. As tempting as it is, I better not,*" she thought to herself looking at her tiny portion of dried meat. "*Well my pouches are empty now of both food and gold. I think he has a couple gold coins hidden away in his pouch, but that won't get us very far. It definitely won't be enough to rent a room for the night. This is ridiculous! We shouldn't have headed out so ill prepared. Sure, we expected to just grab whatever we needed along the road when we needed it, but that idea kind of fell through considering that the last and only village that we passed in the area was utterly destroyed!*" she complained as she slowly chewed the meat and hoped that Dendrox was right about reaching Vackiindmire by nightfall the next day.

Her part of the watch was completely uneventful, and when it came time for his watch, she nudged him gently.

"Oh go away," he grumbled, half asleep.

"It's your turn," she said, poking him again impatiently.

"Already?" Dendrox complained.

"Yes already," she said, now annoyed and frustrated, "I can hardly keep my eyes open. Wake up and quit stalling!"

"Okay, okay, I'm up. Go to sleep," he said with a yawn.

"Oh no you don't! Get up," Candra insisted again.

He grunted and said, "I am. I am."

In an angry tone of voice she said to him, "Remember what happened last time you fell back to sleep on your watch?"

"I never," he protested.

"Oh yes you did. The time we stole those damn scissors. The ones with ivory and gold?" she reminded him.

Dendrox paused a moment in thought before he exclaimed, "Oh yeah, I remember those."

Not convinced with his answer, she continued, "I said to leave them, but oh no, you had to have them. Turns out they were magical or something, and we ended up running all over the countryside trying to get away from all those people hired to retrieve the damn things."

"Oh yeah. Whatever happened to those scissors?" Dendrox asked.

"How the hell should I know? You're the one who got rid of them," she said, this time extremely annoyed with him.

"I did?" he asked with a confused look on his face.

"Well they haven't been able to track us since, so you must have," she sighed, "I guess it's best if you don't remember. Now wake up. I'm going to sleep or at least I'm going to try."

"Oh you're such a pain," he bothered, "It's not going to matter much if we both doze off for a bit. The worst thing that'll happen is some animal will start gnawing at your toes."

"You know, you're a real moron when you first wake up. You say incredibly stupid things," she grumbled. Even though she was exhausted and annoyed, she couldn't help but smile at him.

He smiled also and then said, "Yeah, yeah, go to sleep."

"If I wake up and you're snoring away, I'll skin you alive," she threatened jokingly.

"Good-night already," Dendrox sighed.

Finally, she was asleep. "*Like I snore,*" he thought to himself.

Candra had been his best friend ever since he was a kid. She had always had a fiery spirit, was almost too self-dependant, and was very intimidating even when she wasn't trying to be. The fact that she stood six feet tall, was extremely head strong, and a deadly shot with a bow, didn't help much to make people feel at ease around her either. She loved a good prank and was an extremely good thief. She was the best friend he ever had. Over the years, they had developed unspoken boundaries between themselves and both knew which ones not to cross and how far some of them could be pushed.

"*She should listen to herself snore. It sounds like some dying beast. She'd never admit that she does though. Her snore is definitely worse than mine, if I even snore at all in the first place,*" thought Dendrox.

He brushed off as much debris as he could from his black pants and then he straightened his vest over his shirt as best as he could. He then began fidgeting with one of his throwing daggers waiting for dawn to break.

He looked over at Candra and at her straight black hair lying limply just above her shoulder. He could see at least three leaves and a couple of twigs tangled in it. "*Maybe it is best if she has that bath first, although I wouldn't ever be able to stop her from having one first anyway,*" he sighed. "*Alright, I definitely needed to get more rest than I did,*" he admitted. "*If we keep a low profile in Vackiindmire, we'll probably be able to take the horse drawn carriage that travels between it and the town of Shirkint. Candra would like that. Too bad I wasn't able to take that map with me. Well, okay, let's see what I can remember from it.*"

Dendrox cleared and smoothed out a patch of dirt with his hand. He was thankful that the clouds had dispersed allowing the moon and stars to shine brightly enough for him to see by.

His eyes felt heavy and he yawned sleepily. "*At least this will help me stay awake for awhile. Alright, so this here is the valley.*" Dendrox drew an oval shape in the soil with his dagger.

"*Now on the west side are the mountains we just came over. These rocks will represent the mountains.*" He picked up a few small rocks and placed them on the dirt patch on the edge of the shape he had just drawn.

"*On the eastern side and south edge are high cliffs which act as a barrier between the valley and the sea. These cliffs eventually meet up with the western mountains. The northern edge is the only place where it's open to the sea.*" He picked up a couple small twigs and placed them on the east and south sides of the oval.

"*The forest is quiet large and is situated somewhat in the center of the valley, well just a bit farther south then what would be the center.*" Dendrox grabbed a handful of grass from nearby and placed a bit of it on his map to be the forest.

"*The road goes down from the mountains, through this grassy area at its base, and then continues through the forest. This road would start here, near the southern part of the forest.*" He positioned his dagger near the bottom of his grass pile.

"*We are camped here, on the very edge of the forest, a little distance north from the road, but still keeping it in view. Above the forest, far to the north, are grassy fields and on the eastern side is a lake. A river flows out of this lake traveling south through the forest and then I have no idea where it goes.*" He took his dagger and made wavy lines in the soil to represent the sea, lake, and river.

"*Okay, now below the forest, to the south, is a smaller area of grassy fields before ending at the southern cliffs. In this area, close to the southern cliffs, is the town of Vackiindmire and where we want to go. Oh, and also there is a village, called Dexcsin, and that would be just below the forest, but closer to the mountains than Vackiindmire.*" He placed a couple of rocks to represent the town and village.

"*This road we're about to take, the one that continues out of the mountains, it goes roughly straight through the forest going east for a little more than half way. Then that road will meet up with the main road that runs north up to the town of Shirkint and south to Vackiindmire. There should be a little side road that leads to the small village of Dexcsin just as we come out of the forest on our way to Vackiindmire, but we don't need to worry about that though.*" Dendrox drew the road with his dagger in the dirt.

"*Still have a lot of time to waste, so I might as well fill in the rest of the map.*" He yawned and tried to

<Zaylyn ><Quest For The Sword Of Anthrowst ><By Katrina Mandrake-Johnston >   <Ch 4> < 22 >
keep his eyes open.

"*I think above the forest, at the southern edge of the lake is the village of Leekkar, a road branching off the main road to lead to it,*" he told himself making a line for the road, "*Then if you continue again north along the main road, it branches again and this time to the west back toward the mountains. The village of Torrnell is here.*" He placed a couple of rocks for the villages as he had done with the southern two places.

"*All the way north, at the end of the main road, is the town of Shirkint and beyond that is the sea. I think there is a little side road just before that town which leads to the lakeside and a small boat dock there. I think there's a dock at the village of Leekkar as well. I don't think it's even called a lake when it's joined up like that to the sea. Not really important.*

"*The forest must have been cleared away especially to make the roads, which will make for quick passage through the forest. We should make it to Vackiindmire by nightfall tomorrow, if we keep a steady pace.*

"*Anyway, I have a pretty good idea of what the valley looks like,*" thought Dendrox looking at his completed map, "*I can get us to where we're going. Maybe the maps at Vackiindmire aren't guarded so well against sticky fingers. Perhaps we should forget about trying to steal one and just buy a map. Of course we'll have to steal the money to do so, but that shouldn't be too difficult.*

"*So come morning, we just follow this road into the forest all the way east until it ends and forks north and south. Then follow the road south for awhile until we start coming out of the forest. Then ignore the side road which heads back west leading to the village of Dexcsin and just travel a little more south until we arrive at the town of Vackiindmire.*

"*Okay, that kept me awake for a little while, now what? I really hate watch duty. I don't see the point. If anything happened, we'd wake up in time. Well, maybe not, but still. I just hate being forced to sit here listening to my sleepy brain ramble on about nonsense.*"

The night was a quiet one, with just the occasional rustle of leaves and small night creatures scampering about. Then there was the sharp sound of a twig breaking under a heavy foot. His heart started pounding rapidly in his chest as the adrenalin raced through his body. His eyes frantically searched in the direction that the sound had come from, but saw nothing. He clutched a dagger in his hand. He was quite skilled at dagger throwing, but knew that the darkness would be working against him if an opponent presented himself.

He listened hard for any further sounds of movement for quite some time. Hearing nothing more, he dismissed it as being nothing of importance. He thanked himself for not alerting Candra. He knew that he probably would have never heard the end of it for being spooked by such a trivial thing.

There was another snap of a twig. This time it was closer, but he could not detect any movement within the shadows of the forest. He was getting nervous and the thought of being ridiculed for being a coward by Candra quickly receded to the back of his mind.

"Candra," he whispered frantically.

Her emerald green eyes bolted open with a quick alertness. At seeing the distress in his dark blue eyes, she reached for the bow beside her. She clutched it in her hand, a little disorientated at first, and then took an arrow from the quiver saying, "What is it?"

"A noise from the trees," he said as quietly as he could.

"Where?" she whispered. She moved from the ground up into a crouched position, with bow and arrow in hand, and quickly slung the quiver onto her back.

"There," he said as he gestured toward the trees with his dagger.

"I can't see anything. I can't detect any movement either. Are you sure?" she questioned.

Another snap of a twig sounded. It was closer now and again there was no sign of movement. Candra quickly pulled back the arrow in her bow and held it ready in the direction of the sound.

"Do you think it might be an ambush?" he asked, peering into the forest around them.

"No," she said in a toneless voice, concentrating on the direction the noise had come.

She was well trained in things like predicting the enemy's possible plan of attack, but still he doubted her. He thought to himself, his words dripping with sarcasm, "*It had seemed like a logical*

<Zaylyn ><Quest For The Sword Of Anthrowst ><By Katrina Mandrake-Johnston >   <Ch 4> < 23 >

possibility to consider, but I couldn't question her reasoning, now could I? I wouldn't dare suggest that she may be wrong and should reconsider; I know better than to do that. Candra is way too stubborn to change an idea once it is set in her mind. In most situations she is usually right, having her unspoken reasons why she had made a decision. If you were smart, you'd go along with it and not argue. She says that there's no ambush, so that means concentrate in this direction, but I'm still going to keep an eye out just in case."

He was proud to have her by his side, even though she was often annoying and practically intolerable. He knew she would say the exact thing about him as well. They had a strong bond with each other and that could never be broken no matter how much they quarreled.

"What's taking so long? Where is he, it, she, or whatever the thing is?" Dendrox whispered.

"Be patient," she said in that calm toneless voice again and never let her gaze stray.

Dendrox could see that her fingers were straining to hold the bow ready. He knew she would not break her concentration and hold, no matter what the cost. She was not one to let herself show or accept defeat and failure.

In a low almost inaudible voice she said, "Whoever it is, he's waiting for us to lower our guard. I have to get a better grip. Take the guard for a few seconds."

"Wasn't that what I was doing all this time?" he thought to himself.

It was her way of showing affection for him. She would protect him at all costs to herself. He knew to appreciate this, even though he was well capable of taking care of himself. She was not trying to show incompetence on his part, as most people would probably take it. He knew that he would sacrifice himself for her just as much as she would for him. In fact the reason why they always had trouble maintaining a relationship with someone else, was probably because they were so overprotective of each other. No one could impress 'the best friend' enough to gain approval and could never compete against their friendship. They had a special kind of love for each other.

"Okay, I'm ready again," she said as she stood in her solid stance, with her bow and arrow ready but undrawn. Her fingers ached from holding her bow ready for so long. *"Maybe it wasn't anything at all,"* Candra thought and then she whispered, "If there was someone, they surely would have made their move by now." She looked over to Dendrox and his shorter height of five and a half feet. His hair was a complete mess. She decided, "Whoever it was probably saw that he was no match for us and left."

Dendrox searched his mind for some sort of explanation and then said, "What about someone invisible?"

"What?" she chuckled.

"No, I'm serious. I saw this guy do it once. He was showing off this magic spell he had just learnt. It took him several tries, almost to the point where I thought he was completely nuts, but he did it. It didn't last very long though," he told her.

"You really think so?" she asked as she considered this strange possibility.

"Could be," Dendrox said, "That would explain why we didn't see any movement and why it took him so long to approach."

"If so, he's long gone by now. Check our things. I'll keep watch while you do, just in case," she said in her authoritative voice.

Dendrox nodded and began his search through their belongings as Candra continued to watch for any movement in the surrounding vegetation. "It's not like they'll end up with much," he said to her.

"Just do it," she told him.

"Looks like we'll both have to change our plans. Now there's absolutely no chance of a hot bath, meal, or comfortable bed, no matter how cheap it might be. We've been cleaned out, right under our noses," he reported, "My pouch is gone, along with the last scrap of food which I so carefully had saved for my breakfast, and our last two gold coins."

Candra shrugged at the situation and said, "A couple of thieves getting robbed. How ironic." She tried to hide it, but Dendrox could see the frustration on her face.

He admitted, "Whoever it was, outsmarted us by far and well deserves his prize, but it doesn't make things any easier for us. It's still my watch, so I guess you should get back to sleep."

<Zaylyn ><Quest For The Sword Of Anthrowst ><By Katrina Mandrake-Johnston >   <Ch 4> < 24 >

Dendrox was puzzled that there hadn't been any tracks made by the intruder. He wondered if it were possible for a spell to also hide footprints with magic. There had been no shadow cast by the intruder either, and this he was sure of as he had been watching for fear of an ambush.

They both returned to their blankets. Dendrox wriggled around trying to find a comfortable spot on his blanket that wasn't there. Candra settled back down onto her blanket, a tense look upon her face.

He attempted to lighten the situation by saying, "Oh, and by the way, you do snore."

"I do not," she protested, and he could see the faint glimpse of a smile creep across her pale lips.

<World of Zaylyn ><Quest For The Sword Of Anthrowst ><By Katrina Mandrake-Johnston ><Ch 5>

CHAPTER 5 =   THE ROAD

At dawn, Vordin awoke and began to chip away at the tiny opening between the rock wall and the boulder with his dagger trying to free himself. It was pointless, but he felt he had to try.

Candra and Dendrox packed up their things and made their way back to the road which would eventually lead them to Vackiindmire. They had been traveling in silence for quite awhile now, their leather boots treading on the dirt road at a steady pace.

Candra was the first to speak. "We should have been more alert and we should have known better. We both handled the situation poorly. Maybe if we had…"

Dendrox cut her off by blurting out, "Hey, what's done is done. We can't do anything about it now, and considering everything, I think we both did pretty well. The only thing we can do now is learn from the experience and be better prepared for odd situations like that in the future."

"Yeah, okay," she agreed, "It could have been a lot worse, especially if there had been an attack with such a strong advantage against us."

"Exactly, so don't dwell on it. I'm tired, hungry, and irritable, and you are too," he said curtly. Candra was about to protest but then decided against it knowing that it was true. "I suggest," he continued, "that we just concentrate on the road ahead and when we get settled in the town for the night, we can both laugh over all this. It's not as if we could have gotten anything with the gold we had anyway."

After several moments of silence, she said with frustration, "At least we have the decency not to take someone for all they've got. Not even half a gold piece was left for us."

Dendrox, fed up with bickering, remarked, "Hey, I'm the one who skipped my supper last night so I could have something to eat this morning. I hope the guy chokes on it."

"Dendrox, what's that?" Candra asked, suddenly distracted by something in the distance.

"What?" he asked with curiosity.

She pointed ahead of them and replied, "That shape by the side of the road farther up."

Dendrox strained to perceive the object to which she pointed, but finally said, "I can't tell from here."

As they approached the shape, Candra said with alarm, "I think it's a body."

When they reached the area, they discovered that the shape was indeed a body which was lying face down in the grass beside the road. Dendrox nudged the man in the grey robe and brown leather sandals with his boot. There was no reaction.

"He's dead," Candra stated, "You want me to turn him over?"

"Go right ahead," he said.

Dendrox did not have a strong stomach around death. If he was forced to cause it, that was a different story, but he would make every effort he could to avoid being around it. Candra had said once that seeing it probably made him feel his own mortality a little more than he wanted to.

Part of it was the fact that he wouldn't just see a corpse, but think of who it once was. He would imagine how they had lived their life, their loved ones, what they were like, their thoughts and opinions, and all those things that make a person a person. The thought of all that being able to end so abruptly and easily really bothered him.

There was another reason behind this having to do with his grandfather. He had been a young child and his grandfather had been very ill. Dendrox had been visiting him, and being so young, had

<Zaylyn ><Quest For The Sword Of Anthrowst ><By Katrina Mandrake-Johnston >   <Ch 5> < 25 >

been unclear and afraid of what was happening to his grandfather. His mother and father had left the room briefly to talk privately to each other about his grandfather's condition. Unfortunately, as Dendrox nervously stood beside the large oak bed, his grandfather passed away. He stared at the lifeless body. He put out his small hand to touch the hand of his grandfather, thinking that he could perhaps wake him. This is when his grandfather's eyes bolted open, and with a tiny spark of life that had remained, reached out for Dendrox and then fell limp. Dendrox, only a small boy, had been terrified.

Ever since then, he had a fear of the dead, even though he knew better. In the back of his mind, he kept imagining that the body would suddenly jump to life and reach for him. Almost all of his nightmares were those involving the dead coming to life. There was one reoccurring nightmare in which he was situated in a graveyard after dark. He would walk along, past the tombstones and crypts, and then suddenly the dead would erupt out of the soil attacking him with outstretched claws.

He hadn't mentioned this to Candra, as he knew that she would never understand and probably tease him about it. Dendrox looked away as Candra turned the corpse over.

With surprise, she said to him, "Hey, take a look at this!"

"No thanks," he said without hesitation.

"Don't be so foolish. I think this is the guy. Is this your pouch?" she asked him impatiently and then said with annoyance, "Oh would you just look. I'm not about to pry it out of his hands just to show it to you. Quit being such a baby."

Dendrox glanced quickly at the dead man. This man had short blonde hair and his blue eyes were wide open. In both his hands, he clutched a black leather pouch. It was Dendrox's pouch, which had contained their gold and his stolen meal. Immediately, Dendrox felt terrible for making his earlier comment about hoping this man would choke on it.

"So what do you think?" she asked.

"Yes, it's my pouch, and if you haven't noticed, he has an expression of extreme fright. You realize that this is not a good thing, right?" he said to her with a worried look displayed on his pale face.

"No, really?" she said with sarcasm. Candra tugged the stolen pouch loose from the dead man's fingers and searched around inside saying, "I guess you don't want your breakfast, huh?"

"Did you really have to ask?" he said with a somber look.

Candra handed the pouch back to Dendrox and said, "It looks like everything's here that should be and nothing else that could give us a clue as to what happened. Can you search the surroundings? You're way better at that than I am, so I guess I'll be checking the body."

Although her words had been but a feeble attempt at praise and consideration, Dendrox very much appreciated it. He was in fact better than Candra at searching areas for clues. He could track almost anything, which meant looking for and paying attention to all the small seemingly insignificant details that could very well provide him with the information he needed. He headed toward the trees where he figured the man must have come from, and Candra popped the small piece of cheese into her mouth.

After some time, Dendrox came back after his investigation to meet Candra who was standing a fair distance away from the body now so he would feel a little more at ease when speaking with her about his findings.

"What did you find?" she asked him.

"A couple fresh breaks on branches, trampled vegetation, only a few scattered footprints clearly made by him, and that's all. If the Invisible spell hides footprints, he must have been casting it over and over as soon as it ran out. He must have been running and stumbling in the dark from someone or something, although there aren't any tracks made by his pursuer at all, just trampled vegetation. All I can really tell you for certain is that he traveled through the forest and then emerged onto this road only to die while being extremely frightened of something. Everything else I'm just only guessing at," he said disappointed that there hadn't been any further clues.

"Well all that sounds pretty likely. I didn't come up with anything. I say we get to town as quickly as we can. We might have been luckier last night than we realize," she said looking disturbed.

<Zaylyn ><Quest For The Sword Of Anthrowst ><By Katrina Mandrake-Johnston >   <Ch 5> < 26 >

"I agree," he said, as he nodded toward the road, "Candra, I don't like this. Something just isn't right here."

They continued on their way and walked briskly along the road in silence for some time. Candra seemed as if she were hiding something, but he could never really tell with her. Something had her mind preoccupied though for sure.

The forest had become very dense on either side of the road as they continued their journey. Dendrox figured that the village of Dexcsin was just beyond the forested area now to their right, and he thought, "*It probably wouldn't be that long of a hike to get to the village. It would be more difficult and strenuous than the road of course. Trampling through thick forest in hope of coming to the village, by chance alone, is not very appealing though. Candra is unfamiliar to Dee'ellkka Valley, and right now, it seems to be a good thing. Becoming lost as a result of her blind and stubborn determination is not going to benefit us at all. Seeing that man, and having no clue as to why he came to an end like that, is another good reason to stay on the road. Although, perhaps it isn't a good idea. Why had he been traveling through the trees and not by the road in the first place? There had to have been more to him using the Invisible spells. Surely it was not for the sole purpose of robbing us of a few gold pieces. What could be so horrible to make someone die in fright like that? Why didn't she find any wounds or anything on the body? It doesn't make sense.*"

"Hey, you look panicked. Are you all right?" Candra asked.

He told her, "Yeah, I'm just a little spooked."

"Yeah, me too," she admitted.

If she were, she would never let it show. He wouldn't tell her about the village. If she knew and wanted to go, he would have to follow.

Again, they traveled in silence for quite some distance. Despite his worries, the warm sunshine added some comfort to both his body and mind.

Candra said looking concerned, "Dendrox, don't you think it's odd that so far we haven't seen anyone since we traveled through the mountains?"

"You're right. I hadn't even thought about that. It is strange," he realized, "You would think that we would at least see someone after traveling as far as we have already."

"Except for that dead man of course," Candra reminded him.

"Thank-you so much for mentioning that again," he said with sarcasm and a grave look on his face.

"Sorry," she apologized.

They continued in silence again for a distance, before Candra said to him, "Dendrox, we're only assuming that man was our intruder last night."

With curiosity, he asked, "What do you mean?"

"I hadn't checked the pouch last night, remember? We don't know when it was taken," she stated.

"So you're saying there's a possibility that it wasn't him last night then, that maybe the pouch wasn't taken during my watch?" Dendrox asked with a puzzled expression, "Maybe in your watch then?"

"It's possible, but probably unlikely," said Candra, and then very worried asked, "I'm pretty sure that I didn't doze off, but what if I did without realizing it?"

"That isn't like you at all," he told her.

"That guy looked as if he was the magical type," she commented after further consideration, "didn't he? So he could have been the one last night, right? Casting his spells?"

"I guess so, but you can't really tell. Let's just hope we make it to town by nightfall. There's no way I want to spend another night out here," Dendrox said dreading the thought.

Now there was a slight tone of anger and anxiety to her voice as she said, "You said for sure we would make it by then!"

"Well, I'm not sure how far it is, exactly," he admitted to her slightly apologetic, as Candra walked quickly ahead of him.

"Walk faster!" she said between clenched teeth, "We're not stopping to rest along the way either!"

<Zaylyn ><Quest For The Sword Of Anthrowst ><By Katrina Mandrake-Johnston >   <Ch 5> < 27 >

She was angry and frustrated, which Dendrox recognized as being a front to hide her fear.

By late afternoon, they were extremely exhausted and faint with hunger and thirst.

Dendrox pleaded, "I have to stop. My feet and legs ache."

"So do mine," she said as she sat down on a log by the side of the road.

She pulled off her boots and let her feet enjoy the coolness of the grass. Dendrox repeated her actions and sighed with relief. Dendrox, as he tended to fidget a lot, picked away at the log with one of his daggers.

"You're going to dull your daggers by fidgeting with them all the time like that," the elf warned. He just shrugged and continued. "We're almost there, right?" she asked him.

"I don't know. We should have been there by now. This road we're on now, connects with the road between Shirkint and Vackiindmire. From there, it's not much farther," he explained.

She told him, "I could really use a drink of water right now."

"Yeah, I know. Me too. I guess we could have tried to collect some of the rainwater last night. Aw, never mind," he said, "It shouldn't be that much farther."

Candra pulled on her boots, adjusted the quiver strapped across her back, and stood up. "Well, let's go then," she said impatiently as Dendrox grumbled and reluctantly struggled to get his boots on once more.

After traveling for quite some distance, Candra muttered, "We're not going to make it by nightfall. Are you absolutely sure that this road connects with the main one between the towns?"

Candra noticed the confused tone to his voice as Dendrox said, "Yes, positive. I don't understand. We should have been to town a long time ago and at least have connected with the other road by now."

Dendrox looked around nervously at the forest around them as the daylight began to slowly fade. He then said, still bewildered, "Hey Candra, take a look over there!"

"What?" she asked, unsure of what he was talking about.

"Over there. That log," he said as he pointed to the side of the road, "It looks like the one we had stopped to rest at earlier."

"So," said Candra.

"No, I mean it looks exactly the same," he explained.

"Don't be silly," she remarked, "Keep walking and maybe we'll make it before it gets too dark to see."

Frustrated with her constant impatience, he insisted, "Just hold on a minute. I want to check it out."

She glared at him and said, "If you want to rest that badly, all you have to do is just say so."

Dendrox ignored her and approached the log, so she sighed and said, "Okay, wait for me."

As Candra approached him and the log, he held out a hand to stop her and instructed, "Don't move any closer or you'll disturb the area."

"Dendrox, you're being ridiculous. To think this is the same log is absurd. Besides, it doesn't look like the same one to me." Then she gave in and said, "Okay, just hurry up then."

As Dendrox carefully inspected and studied the area, he commented, "Something is very, very strange here. This can't be possible. Candra, this is the same log. Unless two people with the same size boots as us came to rest at this log here, and decided to peel away some of the bark with a dagger for something to do in the exact same place I had done when we had stopped earlier, something very odd must be going on here."

"You're absolutely sure?" she said with obvious doubt and ridicule.

"Yes," he snapped back at her.

Angered by his foolishness, she insultingly said, "You realize that I'm really starting to doubt your sanity."

"I'm not fooling around!" he yelled.

She realized she suddenly had an unnaturally large amount of violent hatred toward her friend, for no real apparent reason. She quickly composed herself and said, "I'm sorry, Dendrox. Please don't get

<Zaylyn ><Quest For The Sword Of Anthrowst ><By Katrina Mandrake-Johnston >   <Ch 5> < 28 >
mad. Fine, I believe you. So now what?"

"I don't know. It doesn't make any sense," he said, appearing to also have subdued a sudden surge of anger.

Candra, wanting to get everything out in the open, said, "Dendrox, I didn't tell you before, because I didn't want to make you panic more than you were already."

"What are you talking about? Didn't tell me what?" he asked with a testy look in his eye. He was furious that she had kept something from him figuring he was too weak to handle what might have been vital information. He felt betrayed.

Candra found herself feeling a bit ashamed as she confessed what she had kept from him. "When I checked the man's body," she said hesitating a moment, "Well, there were deep slashes and an enormous bite in his torso. There wasn't much blood, which was odd for such a severe wound, but the little that I saw looked as if it had turned to jelly. It was strange. I didn't know what to think. I don't want to even imagine what kind of horror could do that to a man."

"How could you not tell me something like that?!" he said with astonishment.

"I thought we would be in town soon. You panicked at the sight of the dead body. I didn't want to give you anything more that would cloud your mind and judgment more than it already was," she told him.

Dendrox lost control of the excessive anger that was raging inside him, as it amplified to much more than what it actually was. He blurted out with intense fury, "What is that supposed to mean?! You think I'm weak, don't you?! That I can't handle myself?! That I'm incompetent?! Always second best to you instead of an equal?! To you, everything I think or say is foolish!"

The anger he had felt for her a few moments before was completely gone now, as if it had mysteriously vanished from his mind. Dendrox sat on the log and buried his face in his hands. Candra hesitated, not knowing what to say or how to react to his unexpected outburst.

"This is not at all like him," she thought in puzzlement. "Dendrox, I'm sorry," she said as sympathetic as she could.

He remained silent. She sat beside him on the log. She was as frustrated and confused as he was, but it was obviously taking a greater toll on him than her. She placed her hand on his shoulder in an effort to try to comfort him. This felt extremely awkward to her, but she thought it would help. This surprised Dendrox and he looked up to her face. His face displayed a mixture of confusion and anguish.

"I'm sorry. I don't know what came over me. I had all this violent anger inside of me a minute ago, and now it's completely vanished," he said with sincerity, "I almost wanted to physically harm you." He hung his head and ran his fingers through his hair saying, "I don't know what's going on."

When Dendrox finally looked up at her again, he had such an insane and malicious grin displayed on his face, that it greatly startled her.

"Are you going to be okay?" she asked nervously.

"Yes," he said with a mischievous expression.

Cautiously, she asked him in a calm collected voice, "Then, do you want to go now?"

"What's the point? I'm just going to wait here until that creature comes for me. We can't get to town. It's toying with us, waiting for the dark to conceal its attack. Where do you think everyone is? They're dead, and we're next," Dendrox said in a cheerful voice and grinning.

"You're being crazy," Candra said. She then coaxed, "Let's go, okay?" She was getting worried, as she had never seen him get like this.

Dendrox said defiantly, "No, I'm staying here."

"Come on," she pleaded again.

"I said no, and don't make me say it again," he warned with a wicked look.

"I'll scout ahead and then come back for you. Maybe I'll come to the fork in the road," she said, "We should be close, right?"

He remained sitting calmly on the fallen log as if he were quite comfortable there. "You won't," Dendrox said as he took a dagger from his belt and scraped the dirt from under his fingernails.

<Zaylyn ><Quest For The Sword Of Anthrowst ><By Katrina Mandrake-Johnston >   <Ch 5> < 29 >

"Won't what?" she asked carefully.

"Won't find the fork and probably won't be coming back. It'll be dark soon. It's going to find you." He had spoken in such a calm and definite tone and looked at her in such a way, that it gave Candra the creeps.

"Just stop it. Stop it now! What is wrong with you, damn it!" she said partially afraid, "I'm going to scout ahead, alright? Promise me you'll be here when I get back."

"Okay." His voice was that of someone who didn't care anymore about anything.

His eyes had a wild excited look to them and it made her extremely nervous of him. She took off down the road away from him at almost a running pace.

Her mind was racing, *"This is not like him to act this way. Maybe, it's not even him at all? If I'm supposed to accept all these other crazy ideas, like someone invisible, why not that one too? He was out of sight for awhile back at that body. Dendrox could be dead, all the way back there, and the person sitting on that log could be some horrid creature that has taken his place and is toying with my mind and emotions."* She realized how ridiculous her thoughts had become, and she told herself, *"Now you're the one being foolish this time,"* but still she glanced nervously behind her just in case.

He was still sitting there, grinning at one of his smaller daggers as he flipped it over and over again in his fingers. If she were going to scout ahead far enough and get back to him before dark, she would have to run for part of the way. She also wanted to get as much distance between herself and that dagger as quickly as possible.

Candra broke into a sprint, even though her body ached and her stomach hurt with hunger pains. She ran farther and farther, hoping to see any sign of the fork in the road or of another person traveling along this one.

Just when she was about to give up and head back, she saw what looked to be a person on the road some distance ahead. *"Finally, there's someone else besides us,"* Candra thought to herself. She continued to run as her heart pounded heavily in her chest.

As she got closer, she called out, "Hey!... Excuse me!... I need to speak with you!..." The person had shown no sign that he or she had heard her.

When she had approached even closer, she called out again, "Hello!... I need to speak with you!..."

The man slowly turned around and she cleared the distance between them. Staring at her with wild eyes and with an overly expressed grin, was Dendrox. "No... How could it be? No, it can't..." she stammered, backing away from him.

"Well, I was right, wasn't I? You're right back where you started. Now do you believe me? But don't worry, when it comes for us, I'll protect you," Dendrox told her as he walked back over to the log again. "Come," he said to her, "Sit with me and wait, Candra." He gestured toward the log with both hands and he still had the huge grin on his face.

"No! Listen Dendrox, if that's really who you are, you had better stay away from me. Leave me alone! I'll defend myself if I have to," she said threateningly as she pulled an arrow from her quiver and the bow from her shoulder. "Stay away from me," she insisted.

Dendrox merely sat down on the log and said, "You're the one who's talking like you're crazy. What are you talking about? Of course I'm me. Who did you think I would be? I've just accepted the fact that we're stuck here, and whatever is doing all this, isn't going to get the satisfaction of watching me stumble through its little games. I'm no fool, and I'm not going to be toyed with. If it wants to play, it'll have to do it with my daggers stuck in its gut. Candra, come and sit. All we can do is rest and wait for it to make its move. In the morning, if we still can't get to town, I suggest we travel through the forest to try to find the village of Dexcsin. It should be somewhere on the other side of this part of the forest. If not, at least we'll be close enough that we should be able to find it eventually. We should make our camp for tonight. While you were gone, I piled together some wood. I found quite a few dry pieces. Some are a little damp still in places from last night's rain, but it'll have to do. I think we

<Zaylyn ><Quest For The Sword Of Anthrowst ><By Katrina Mandrake-Johnston >   <Ch 5> < 30 >

should go together to find food though. There's probably a rabbit out there somewhere close. I thought I saw one a bit earlier."

"Are you finished?" Candra said angrily.

"What's your problem?" he asked defensively.

"A village? You just thought to mention that to me now!" she shouted.

"Sorry, I guess we're even," Dendrox said calmly.

She was not satisfied with his complete lack of guilt, but she found it fair enough. She was grateful that the wild frantic look had subdued and his concentration was now focused on the tasks ahead for making camp. The thought of a warm blazing fire was appealing. "You start the fire, and I'll get dinner," she told him, "There won't be enough light to see by if we go together. I'll yell if anything happens, okay?"

She didn't like the idea, but her empty stomach wouldn't let her reconsider her decision. She was still nervous of him and thought it would be a good idea to not go along with his plan, even though it made sense if there was some creature lurking around causing all this as Dendrox thought. "*If tonight is going to be as strange and confusing as today has been,*" she thought, "*maybe following what's logical isn't the best thing to do.*"

She found a rabbit easily and loosed an arrow into it. She was pleased to see the small fire to welcome her back.

"That was fast," he commented, taking the rabbit from her.

Candra spread out her blanket by the fire and collapsed onto it exhausted. Dendrox prepared and cooked the rabbit, as she removed her boots and equipment and began rubbing at her tired aching muscles. The fire felt wonderful. She only wished that it could warm all sides of her at once. She hated to have one side warm while the other side remained away from the fire feeling icy cold.

***

Vordin, in his solitude, had taken a small stone and made it glow indefinitely by applying a few drops from the lantern's flask. It served him no purpose other than to pass the time. When he had become bored with it, he placed the stone into one of the small outside pockets of the backpack.

He had given up on trying to dig his way free. The rock that formed the cave wall was extremely hard and he had only managed to chip away a very small amount. Vordin had spent the remainder of the day listening to the birds singing outside and longing for the freedom they enjoyed. He had watched the daylight fade as the sun set below the horizon. Vordin lay down on the hard rock floor and tried to sleep, as there was nothing else he could do.

<World of Zaylyn ><Quest For The Sword Of Anthrowst ><By Katrina Mandrake-Johnston ><Ch 6>

<u>CHAPTER 6 = THE CREATURE</u>

Dendrox looked over at Candra, who was sitting on her blanket by the fire, and said to her, "Do you see what I mean, Candra? We can't do anything about being stuck here, so we might as well make the most of it. Panicking isn't going to help things. I already tried that and it didn't work. We have to stay focused and level-headed." She knew his words were really meant for himself rather than her.

"You're exactly right," she reassured him, "I'm starved. Is it almost ready, the smell is making my mouth water."

She watched the roasting rabbit meat cook over the fire. Dendrox had skinned the carcass, stuck a fair sized stick through it, and propped it over the fire. He was sitting in a relaxed position with his forearms resting just above his knees. The firelight illuminated the thick tree trunks around them. Candra could see the road from their camp. To her, it looked so barren and empty. She wondered if they would ever make it to town or see anyone else but themselves. The smoke from the fire billowed up in-between the treetops of the large pine trees into the night sky.

"Be patient, you're always in such a rush. No wonder every time you cook, the food's half raw," he teased.

"*This is a good sign,*" Candra thought, "*He seems to be more like himself than before.*" She questioned, "So whose watch is it tonight?"

<Zaylyn ><Quest For The Sword Of Anthrowst ><By Katrina Mandrake-Johnston >   <Ch 6> < 31 >

"Mine," he said.

"You did the last watch last night though," she stated.

"You're either really confused, or you still think I'm not me. We go by who does first watch, remember? We argued about it practically all night once until we settled on this. You did first watch last night, so I do it tonight," he said and shook his head.

Dendrox sliced off a chunk of meat for Candra with his dagger and tossed it to her. She devoured this as quickly as she could and wiped the grease from her lips with the back of her hand. Soon the carcass had been picked clean between the two of them. Dendrox looked as if he were pondering something.

Candra broke the silence between them by saying, "You know Dendrox, I think this is the most we've ever fought. I know we both have our differences, but we've never acted like this before ever, even considering everything that has happened. I had such an intense anger toward you before that I could barely contain it and there was no apparent reason for it either."

"That was exactly what I was just thinking. Something strange is going on," Dendrox said still deep in thought.

"I'm just saying that I'm really sorry about the way I've been acting," she said with sincerity.

"Yeah, same here, Candra," he told her.

They sat in silence for awhile and then, from behind where Candra was sitting, there came a noise from the trees. As Candra turned around, one of Dendrox's daggers flew past her head and sunk deeply into the shiny black flesh of a huge and hideous creature. It staggered back on its six legs from the pain; each leg on its thick torso equipped with long sharp claws. Dendrox had just saved Candra's life. The creature's large oval eyes were solid black and were set on either side of its huge salamander-like head. Its eyes appeared to be staring at everything all at once, and its short stocky tail moved slowly from side to side.

Candra frantically scrambled along the forest floor to get an arrow and her bow. The creature opened its oversized mouth filled with grotesque teeth covered in a yellowish slime. It howled an unearthly wail that sent shivers down Candra's spine. She now had her weapon. She could see Dendrox reaching for another dagger, and as she turned her upper body up from the ground to face the creature, it lunged toward her. She could never have fired her bow in time... Despite her fear, with the arrow in hand, her aim remained steady, and she drove it deeply into the left eye of the creature. A murky fluid began to drip from it, and as the beast reared up on its back four legs with a squeal and began to scratch at its head around the eye and the protruding shaft of the arrow, another dagger flew through the air to sink into its torso just below its thick short neck.

It now swung viciously at Candra with its clawed front paw, which she desperately tried to dodge. She managed to avoid what surely would have been a fatal blow, but suffered a deep wound to her arm. Blood gushed from the deep gash in thick sticky streams. She winced from the pain but forced herself not to cry out, releasing only a slight whimper. Dendrox threw another dagger into the creature as Candra tried to push herself backwards away from the beast as best as she could. It howled and dropped back down again to all six of its legs and Candra felt the ground shudder beneath her from the weight of the monster. Two more daggers sunk into the beast.

Dendrox could tell that their attacks on the creature so far had been futile. The loss of its eye appeared to only be a mere inconvenience to this creature. It seemed to him that it was waiting for them to become weaponless, so it could hunt them further throughout the forest, enjoying their fear and anguish. *"This has to be its plan,"* he thought, *"because it could have killed us both so easily if it truly wished it. It had been toying with us earlier, I just know it."*

Candra was incapable of firing an arrow in her bow and he only had one dagger left. He decided his only hope was to strike the creature in its remaining eye in hope of blinding it. He thought that at least this would give them a better chance for survival. He could tell that the creature was about to attack again, locking its jaws onto Candra in one deadly thrust of its massive body. He aimed and threw the dagger, hoping it would find its mark and save her.

<Zaylyn ><Quest For The Sword Of Anthrowst ><By Katrina Mandrake-Johnston >   <Ch 6> < 32 >

When the creature roared over and over in a panic, he knew that he had blinded it. Candra was incredibly weak and dizzy from the loss of blood, but on top of this, her vision had begun to blur and she could hardly move. All she was able to do was crawl slowly along the ground trying to desperately get as far away from the creature as she could, as it now stomped wildly about and very easily could crush her to death. The beast stopped, made a guttural sound, and then moved its head back and forth as if it were somehow searching the area. To their horror, it seemed to lock in on them, letting loose a vicious snarl in their direction.

Candra watched with a pale face as Dendrox grabbed a thick burning branch from the fire. As he ran straight at the creature, he drove it into the throat of the beast like a stake. It screamed one last gurgling howl and collapsed finally in death. The foul stench of the creature's scorched flesh made them both gag.

"Candra!" he said in a panicked voice, rushing to her side.

"I'm fine," she said weakly, "It's dead?"

He could see that she was not at all fine. She was always too proud to admit injury and the need for help to the point of being irrational sometimes. "You're bleeding quite a lot, and I don't know what to do," he said frantically.

"I'll be okay. We should get away from this thing," she said weakly, as she fumbled to grab an edge of her blanket and then pressed it to the deep slash in her arm.

"Damn it, you're not thinking clearly! And should you be doing that? What about infection? The blanket is filthy," he said in a panic.

"I have to… stop the bleeding," she said struggling to remain in a sitting position. She looked past him to the road, her vision getting worse, and asked, "What's that… that light?"

Dendrox searched in the direction with his eyes and saw what he thought to be the light of a lantern in the distance.

"It looks like someone's traveling along the road. Wait here," he told her. He ran up to the road and called out, "Hey! Is anyone there! We need help!"

< World of Zaylyn >< Quest For The Sword Of Anthrowst >< By Katrina Mandrake-Johnston ><Ch 7>

CHAPTER 7 = WEENA

"Is someone there?" a female voice called and the light from a lantern moved to shine in his direction, "I heard horrible frightening noises a few minutes ago."

"Over here. We need help. We were attacked," Dendrox urgently said as a woman hurried toward him.

She was dressed in loose greyish-blue robes that were collected and tied at her waist with a yellow sash. A small cloth bag hung from a cord, which sat loosely above her hips. On her small feet she wore a pair of leather sandals. She was roughly the same height as Dendrox and of an average weight. She had high cheekbones with a small nose and a rounded chin. Her blonde wispy hair fell just below her chin and her eyes were of a bright blue color.

The woman said to him, "I'm so glad I've found someone. I saw that dead body back there and figured I had better get to town as quickly as I could, even if it meant traveling through the night."

"Listen, my friend was wounded by this hideous creature. We killed it, but she's bleeding heavily," he explained to her.

"Dendrox?" Candra called out to him weakly and they both ran over to her.

"My name's Weena," the woman told them, "Can I take a look at your arm?"

Candra removed the blood soaked edge of the blanket from her arm. Surprisingly, the bleeding had slowed and now was oozing from the wound in thick gooey clumps. The elf looked nervously to Dendrox, her vision fading in and out.

Weena continued by saying, "I know magic, although I'm not an expert. I've actually just begun learning it not that long ago. Would you like me to try my healing spell?"

"I don't really… have a choice," Candra said bluntly. Dendrox looked very worried and Candra realized the wound was more serious than she had first thought. Candra looked at Weena apologetically

<Zaylyn ><Quest For The Sword Of Anthrowst ><By Katrina Mandrake-Johnston >   <Ch 7> < 33 >

and said in a kinder tone of voice, "Please, I'll be grateful… for anything you can do."

Candra could no longer hold herself up, the world seeming to swim about around her, and she collapsed backwards to the ground as Weena rushed in to kneel beside her. Weena's bright blue eyes got a vacant look to them and then she began to mouth strange inaudible words. She placed a trembling hand on Candra's arm. Candra felt a burning itch besides the original pain and almost pulled her arm away.

"There, that's the best I can do," Weena told her when the spell was finished. Candra examined her arm, amazed that the bleeding had stopped completely and that the gash had closed slightly. "Here, let me bandage it for you," Weena offered. She removed the yellow sash from the waist of her robes and bandaged Candra's wound as best as she could. Her robes fell loosely now about her as the only thing holding her clothing in place was the cord holding her cloth bag about her waist.

"I'm Candra and that's Dendrox. So, you said your name is Weena?" Candra asked weakly, trying to not give in to the incredible nausea she was feeling.

"Yes," she said, "I'm trying to reach the town of Vackiindmire. You two are the first people I've seen for a long while. There was a man back there who looked as if he had been killed by some strange creature. When I saw that, I decided to travel through the night as well, instead of stopping. Not to mention that entire village back across the mountains. Oh, it was horrible," she said putting a hand to her mouth trying to stifle the emotion, "I didn't think it would be so dangerous to make this trip, but now, I realize I should have paid for an escort." She paused and then added sheepishly, "Well… if I had that much gold, I probably would have. I'm just really relieved to see someone else out here. It was so frightening traveling all alone in the dark, especially after all I've seen." Weena picked up her lantern and as the light shone on the corpse of the creature, she almost dropped it. "Is that it?" she gasped, "This is the creature you spoke of?"

"Yeah, I've never seen anything like it," Dendrox said and then asked, "Have you?"

Weena stepped closer to the beast in curiosity and said, "No. What do you think it is? You're sure it's dead, right?"

"It better be," Candra said as she tried to stand, then decided against it, "Could you retrieve my arrow for me Dendrox, if it's undamaged?"

"Yeah, sure," he said, but he hesitated not knowing how to go about it at first. He grasped the arrow and pulled until it came loose. More of the murky liquid oozed from the creature's eye. He wiped the arrow clean on the grass and tossed it to her. He then retrieved and cleaned his daggers in the same way.

"Thanks," Candra said trying to focus on him as he placed the six daggers back on his belt.

"You okay, Weena? You look a little ill," he commented.

"I'm fine," she said as she held up her lantern for him, "This must be the creature that killed the man and probably had something to do with the massacre of that village. You know… this could be a demon, or a least that's what they've been called."

"You've seen one before then?" Candra asked in amazement.

"Well no, but I've heard stories. This is what they've been said to look like. It's said that they sometimes use magic spells on their prey. Spells such as Confuse, Hallucinate, Hate, and perhaps more, I think."

Dendrox commented, "That would explain our extraordinary day."

"Makes sense," Candra agreed, feeling a little better, "We've been trying to get to town all day, and then found we were traveling the same segment of road over and over and arguing the whole time. Well more than usual. All those insane looks and grins, those weren't natural."

"I have no idea what you're talking about," Dendrox said honestly, "Is that why you were acting so strangely? You were seeing things?"

"Well anyway, I'm glad all that is over now. I didn't know what was real and what wasn't, for the longest time. So, we can all start to think rationally again, right? No more crazy situations?" Candra said looking extremely pale and tired, "I can't handle not being able to trust my instincts."

"You don't think there are more of these things about, do you?" Weena asked them nervously.

<Zaylyn ><Quest For The Sword Of Anthrowst ><By Katrina Mandrake-Johnston >   <Ch 7> < 34 >

"I hope not," Dendrox said, "We almost didn't survive our encounter with this one."

"Do you know how much farther it is to the town, Weena?" asked Candra.

"I've never been there before, but I don't think it would be very far," she answered.

"That's good enough for me. You ready, Dendrox?" Candra said with a strong will to not let her wound inhibit her actions in any way.

"Are you okay to travel?" Dendrox asked with worry.

"I guess we'll find out. I really don't want to stay around here any longer than we have to," Candra said and then struggled to stand.

Weena rushed over to support her. Candra at first was going to refuse her charity, not wanting to appear weak in character, but found herself submitting completely and without protest. Dendrox packed up his equipment and Candra's as well. Then he helped her into her boots, while Weena tried to balance her. Dendrox put on the backpack, then swung Candra's quiver over his shoulder, then her bow, and finally strapped her two pouches to his waist as best as he could. He kicked some dirt onto the tiny fire and stomped it out. Dendrox then walked beside the two women as they all made their way up to the road.

"Dendrox, here, would you be able to take my lantern as well?" Weena asked holding it out to him with her free arm as Candra leaned weakly against her.

"Sure," he said accepting it.

Dendrox walked ahead of them holding the lantern up to light the way. As they traveled, Dendrox was pleased to see that the scenery they were passing was new.

"How's Candra doing?" he asked after they had traveled some distance.

"Not too well. I think we should stop so I can take another look at her condition," Weena suggested.

Candra moaned as if she were extremely ill. As Dendrox shone the light on her, he could see that her face had taken on a sickly pallor. Weena helped her to sit upon the dirt road and she then checked the wound.

"The wound looks like it should heal well. It doesn't look like there's an infection starting, but she has a fever and her color isn't right," she commented.

Candra coughed and thick mucus sputtered from her lips. "Candra examined the dead man when we had come across him. She had said that his blood looked as if it had turned to jelly," he stated, the distress showing in his dark blue eyes, "This is what's happening to her, isn't it? Her blood, it had begun to look odd just before you healed the wound. What do we do? You have to be able to do something! We have to save her, please!"

"Oh, let me think. I came across something like that in my studies once. I think the magic spell Poison might have that effect. I do know that the spell doesn't have the effect natural poisons have, so it could be," she said.

"Could it be that Candra has just lost a lot of blood?" he asked her.

"No, I think it's more than just that. I really do think she might have been poisoned by that creature. You didn't get cut did you?" she asked him with a look of worry.

"No. She's getting worse by the second. Is she going to be okay?" Dendrox asked, truly fearing for his friend's life.

Weena looked at Candra and then to Dendrox saying, "I don't think so."

Dendrox could feel the anger and frustration build up inside him. He felt absolutely helpless and that was something he hated. If it were a physical danger, at least he could do something, but with this he couldn't.

"*At least Weena had been honest about it to both of us,*" he noted to himself, as this was something he greatly respected in a person. The feeling of triumph he had felt after the beast was slain had vanished, as he realized that even in death it might succeed in killing one of them. He wished that he had been the one injured instead of Candra, that way she would be safe.

"I do know a Cure spell, but I don't think it will work. All of my spells are pretty weak. I'm surprised my healing spell even worked at all and on the first try too," she explained to him.

<Zaylyn ><Quest For The Sword Of Anthrowst ><By Katrina Mandrake-Johnston >   <Ch 7> < 35 >

"It's better than nothing. Why didn't you try before? Hurry, before she gets any worse," Dendrox insisted.

"I'm just saying to not get your hopes up. I'll try my best," she said.

She placed her dainty hand to Candra's pale forehead. Weena got the vacant look in her eyes again as she mouthed the strange words of the spell. Dendrox could see Candra's cheeks miraculously get their color back. The glossy look to her eyes faded and her brilliant green eyes sparkled up at him as Weena ended her spell.

"How do you feel? Did it work?" she asked Candra.

"My arm hurts…" she replied, as her head began to clear and her vision gradually started to return to normal, "but that's to be expected from the wound. Nothing else though, except for feeling extremely weak. Thank-you," Candra said to her savior, truly grateful, "You know, I think I'm going to need a couple minutes."

"Yes, of course, you shouldn't push yourself like that," Weena told her, brushing Candra's hair away from her face and checking her temperature.

Weena stayed close by Candra's side until the elf felt well enough to travel once more, and then the three of them continued along the road in the darkness. Candra now walked on her own, but occasionally still needed support from her new companion. She insisted on taking back her equipment from Dendrox, who was glad to be relieved of the extra weight but remained concerned about this. Dendrox still carried Weena's lantern, lighting the way for them as he walked a few paces ahead of the two women.

***

At first Vordin thought the mountain was collapsing around him, but then realized that the huge boulder was moving away from the entrance. Moonlight illuminated the man in the black flowing cloak. He had returned. Vordin, knowing he could not escape this being, waited with fear for his fate to be decided.

"I mean you no harm," said the man in a soothing voice, "I am The Black Shadow, but please, do not fear me."

Vordin did not know what to do. *"If this really is The Black Shadow, I am in the presence of an extremely powerful and dangerous being,"* he thought to himself nervously, *"He's evil, isn't he?"* Vordin just stood there in the cave, afraid to do anything.

"Come," The Black Shadow said to him, "I shall take you into Dee'ellkka Valley."

The Black Shadow came toward the terrified boy, picked him up as he had done the night before, and leapt into the air to fly down from the mountaintop into Dee'ellkka Valley. Vordin could see a trail as they flew above which led down from the mountain to become a road. The night air was cool and refreshing, and by the moonlight, he could see that this road was flanked by deep green grass on either side near the base of the mountain before eventually entering into a dense forest.

They soared over the treetops for some distance before they stopped, landing with their feet upon the dirt road. "There," he said to Vordin, pointing to an area in the trees just off the road.

Vordin was released, and The Black Shadow walked with him over to the area he had indicated. Vordin found the remains of a small campfire and looked to the man confused.

"Over there, in the trees," he said pointing once more.

Upon discovering the body of the creature Dendrox and Candra had fought with, he exclaimed, "This is the kind of creature that attacked my village?"

"Yes," The Black Shadow answered.

"This is the same one that found me along the road?" Vordin asked, remembering the night before and the fear he had felt.

"Yes," he told him, "and it would have killed you. These creatures can be killed, but it rarely happens. This one underestimated its prey. A foul wizard named Dranngore rules over these creatures. Whole villages are being slaughtered at his instruction. Nilnont was the first. Another is under attack tonight. If this lunatic is to be truly stopped, the only means to do so is to slay him with the Sword of Anthrowst. I will not intervene, as it is not my place to do so."

<Zaylyn ><Quest For The Sword Of Anthrowst ><By Katrina Mandrake-Johnston >   <Ch 7> < 36 >

Before Vordin could say a single word, The Black Shadow had him in his grasp again and took flight to soar above the treetops once more. Vordin saw a small light ahead on the road below them, and as they approached closer, he could see that there were three figures traveling along this road carrying a lantern to light their way. They continued to fly through the air, well past them, and eventually Vordin and The Black Shadow came down to land at a fork in the road.

< World of Zaylyn >< Quest For The Sword Of Anthrowst >< By Katrina Mandrake-Johnston ><Ch 8>

CHAPTER 8 =   THE CROSSROADS

The Black Shadow pointed in the proper directions as he said, "Directly to the north is the town of Shirkint and the sea. The sea comes into Seedelle Bay at the northeast edge of the valley and there are high cliffs to the east and south. Because there are high rock formations on three sides of the valley, I magically keep the valley from being cast in almost constant shadow. The village of Leekkar is at the southern edge of the bay. The village of Torrnell is farther north and west, near the mountains and surrounded by grasslands. South along this main road and back west is the village of Dexcsin in a secluded area on the southern edge of the forest. Directly south is the town of Vackiindmire. I must leave now. Rasindell, the storyteller, has used my potion well. Trust her."

"You mean that spider creature, Lorenta? I left her back at Rasindell's cabin," he told him.

"You have a stow away. Trust her," The Black Shadow said as he rose up into the night sky leaving Vordin behind.

Vordin sat down on a large rock by the road. He removed his backpack and looked inside, but found only his lantern. He decided that he would wait for the people he had seen to reach his position.

He had been waiting for only a few moments when someone grabbed him from behind and held a sharp dagger to his throat. A raspy voice whispered frantically, "Give it to me! I want your magic. I need your magic. I've got to have it. You don't understand! Say the words. Say the words! Give me your magic. Give it to me now!"

With the blade pressed dangerously at his neck, Vordin managed to say, "I don't know what you mean! What magic?!"

"You fool! Just give it to me! I need it!" the raspy voice insisted again. Then the man hesitated, the blade still at Vordin's throat, and he looked to his left saying, "No, it's you! You have the magic. You! Give it to me now!" he demanded and the man released Vordin.

Vordin could now see that Lorenta had indeed hidden inside his backpack and must have crawled out when he had been speaking with The Black Shadow. She was standing a few feet away beside a large oak, and before Lorenta knew what was going on, the man had her in his grasp and held his dagger to her throat.

"Now I've got you! You are the one. You will give me your magic now, or you will die! Give it to me! I need it! Do you understand?" he screamed at her.

The man's once white robes were dirty and in shreds. His reddish-blonde hair was dirty and askew. His eyes were wildly insane and full of desperation for this 'magic' he craved so badly. Vordin also noticed the man wore a medallion on a gold chain around his neck. It consisted of a large red jewel encircled by braided gold and silver.

Vordin stood and took a couple of steps toward them, wanting to somehow save Lorenta, but the man said, "Stop! I'll slit her throat! Don't move! I want my magic!" Then to Lorenta he continued, "You're going to give it to me. I need your magic, and I need it right now! Say the words!" Lorenta had an expression of terror and utter confusion on her pretty face. The man reached up and clutched her plump left breast with his grimy hand. He whispered in her ear, "Maybe you'll give me your magic now?" He pressed his body up against her, as he touched and fondled her, and he whispered, "Maybe you think you're going to keep your magic, but I need it. You have to give it to me." He ran his hand down the front of her body to rest on her inner thigh as he continued to press up against her excitedly, while all the time still holding the blade at her neck. "You must have lots of magic. I know you do. I can feel it. You must give me your magic," he whispered again and continued to touch her body. Vordin was desperately trying to think of a way to save her, but was afraid of what this awful man

<Zaylyn ><Quest For The Sword Of Anthrowst ><By Katrina Mandrake-Johnston >   <Ch 8> < 37 >
might do.

Two gigantic spider fangs erupted slowly and silently from Lorenta's cheeks and sank into the man's arm, the one that held the dagger. He screamed in astonishment, fear, and pain. The dagger fell from his hand and landed harmlessly on the ground. She retracted the fangs back into her face and resumed human appearance once more. The man staggered around clutching his injured arm for a few moments until he collapsed dead in the grass beside the road.

She stared at the dead man in wonderment. She looked at Vordin in confusion and said, "I think he was trying to mate with me. Why?" After a moment's hesitation and thought, Lorenta then said, "I was frightened. He was trying to kill me. I've never killed anyone before. I never knew that I could do something like that."

Vordin didn't know what to say to her about this, but he was glad to see her safe. He asked, "How is it that you were able to travel with me all this way? In the cave, when I was searching for my lantern, why didn't I find you then?"

"I don't think this is the appropriate time to be asking trivial questions like this," she said staring at the dead man with a fearful look in her eye, "It's Rasindell's backpack, remember? There's a hidden magical compartment in it that was made especially for me to travel in. You were going to leave me behind. I didn't want to be alone anymore and so I am seeking adventure. I was hoping to do so along side you, but if need be, I will do so on my own. Actually, I'm finding the world a little more harsh than I had hoped, but I will not return to that horrible old hut again."

They heard voices not far off, coming from the eastern road, and saw the approaching light from a lantern. "Please," Lorenta begged, "Help me hide the body."

"There isn't time," was his reply, and as he looked at the man, he noticed that the jewel in the medallion had turned mysteriously from a vibrant red color to pitch black.

"Then please hide me! I'm an ugly and now murderous monster! Do not let these people discover me! This is what Rasindell feared! Please!" she said to him quickly and then suddenly melted back into spider form.

Vordin opened his backpack, holding it so she could crawl in. As soon as she had made it safely inside and he had replaced the backpack onto his back once again, Dendrox, Candra, and Weena came into view.

Dendrox exclaimed as he saw the fork in the road by the light of the lantern, "Candra! It's the fork in the road! We've finally been able to reach it!"

Weena said to her new companions, "I think I see someone standing there."

Candra stated, "Another dead body," as they met Vordin's position. "Who are you?" she asked with suspicion.

"Vordin," he answered nervously.

Weena questioned him in a soft voice, "Where did you come from, and what has happened here?"

"I came from over the mountains. My village was destroyed by some terrible beasts. Was it you that slew the one along the path?" he said not really knowing what to say to these people.

Dendrox eyed him cautiously, "Yes, we killed the beast. Tell me how you came to know this."

"I..." Vordin stammered.

"Tell me how you came to pass us on the road without us seeing you, and how you managed to arrive here so quickly," Dendrox demanded.

"Well..." Vordin said trailing off. He felt his face get hot. He hated this unfeeling interrogation and he knew if he told them the truth that they would never believe it.

"Tell me how this man came to die. Did you kill him? Who are you really?" Dendrox questioned impatiently.

"The Black Shadow brought me here," said Vordin.

"Oh really?" Candra said with a sarcastic smirk.

"He carried me through the air and showed me the dead creature, telling me that these horrible beasts were ruled by an evil lunatic named Dranngore. He said this person could only be slain by the

<Zaylyn ><Quest For The Sword Of Anthrowst ><By Katrina Mandrake-Johnston >   <Ch 8> < 38 >

Sword of Anthrowst. A fairy queen also told me this," Vordin explained as best as he could, "I saw the three of you from overhead. I had been at this spot for only a few moments when this insane man attacked me from behind. He was insisting that I give him my 'magic'. What he meant by this, I have no clue. After a struggle, he met his end. That medallion he has around his neck is a peculiar object though; the jewel was bright red, but when he died, it turned black." Vordin felt ashamed now at how he had doubted Lorenta's unbelievable story so harshly back at Rasindell's cabin.

Weena was the first one to speak, after Vordin had finished his speech, saying, "I've heard something of this."

"Of what?" Candra asked her, astonished that Vordin's bizarre story might hold a bit of truth.

"There is a contest that a group of master wizards hold. Most people are wise to its evil nature now though. When a contestant would prove himself to be highly skilled in magic, he would be awarded an object. In this case, it appears to be this medallion. This object would increase the potency of all the person's magic spells. Then after a few days, the object would start to drain that person's magic. The wizard of this guild, who awarded the poor fool his prize, would slowly gain his or her existing magic spells until all the magic was depleted and then the object would start to drain the very life out of the person's body. The only way the person is able to stay alive is to attack others that have magic ability and drain them of it, killing them in the process. These cursed objects can never be removed from these unfortunate people unless in death. No one must ever possess this medallion or they shall meet the same fate and take several lives with them. The more spells and life these objects collect, the more these wicked and malicious wizards will gain."

"I had no idea. I thought this man was just ranting in his insanity," Vordin commented.

Candra glared suspiciously at Vordin asking, "So what spells do you know?"

"Well, none," he answered nervously.

Weena spoke up quickly in his defense. She suggested, "This man was probably so desperate that he was willing to attack anyone in hope that they knew a spell or two."

"So what's this nonsense about a fairy queen and The Black Shadow bestowing a quest upon you?" Candra said curtly.

"They just told me about him," he protested, "They couldn't possible want me to attempt to slay Dranngore, could they? I'm not a warrior."

"So where is this Sword of Anthrowst supposed to be?" Dendrox asked him.

"They didn't say. I don't even know why they told me. I would have been killed by one of those monsters had The Black Shadow not rescued me," Vordin said to them, his voice wavering with emotion.

Weena looked at him kindly and said, "Why don't you come with us to Vackiindmire. You look like you've been through a great ordeal, whether or not your amazing story is true. This is Dendrox and Candra, and my name is Weena."

Relieved to hear this, Vordin said, "Thank-you so much. I promise not to be much of a burden. Is it alright with the two of you?" he added as he addressed Candra and Dendrox who both wore distrusting expressions.

They looked at each other for a moment and then Candra said, "I don't mind. If you start trouble I can dispose of you in an instant," she teased, but Vordin saw that it was also meant as a very real threat.

"Alright then, Vackiindmire shouldn't be much farther from here," Dendrox said to them all.

"Wait. We have to bury the body," Weena said with a somber face as she looked down at the man.

"But why?" Candra said impatiently, "Let's just go to town. I'm starved, exhausted, and sore."

"The medallion," she reminded them all, "We can't let anyone find it. If anyone puts it on, they'll kill many innocent people and probably end up dying themselves. As soon as they come across someone who knows even just a single magic spell, they'll lose all control and frantically try to absorb the spell into this medallion. Don't you realize that this man would have attacked and killed me if Vordin had not vanquished him?"

At seeing the great importance that this had to Weena, they all proceeded to perform the long and strenuous deed. They dug with their bare hands into the dark soil.

<Zaylyn ><Quest For The Sword Of Anthrowst ><By Katrina Mandrake-Johnston >   <Ch 8> < 39 >

After a few hours, the morning sun rose above the horizon, but they were not nearly finished.

"Is all this really necessary?" Candra asked with a sigh and stopped to rest as her wounded arm throbbed with pain.

"Yes. We're saving lives by doing this," Weena said to her with a smile.

Candra realized that she didn't really care as long as it wasn't her own life that was being put in danger. She wondered that if her own life had traveled a different path, if she would have ended up being more like Weena. She found herself resenting the tough shell she had formed around herself. Her attitude of self-preservation and well-being seemed shallow and selfish when she compared herself to Weena. She had not seen herself as power hungry and bitterly unemotional, as she had heard others joke on occasion, but she saw it now and wondered if it were possible to change. Those characteristics weren't what she wanted to be defined as or known for. It was not who she was.

Candra found herself enjoying the fact that Weena had accompanied them. She didn't see her as being intrusive as she found most other women to be. There was something about being around Weena that made her feel alive and whole. She had noticed the way Weena and Dendrox often exchanged shy glances, and Candra found herself approving.

By early afternoon, the man was laid to rest several feet under the ground. They stomped on the grave to pack the dirt and gathered stones, twigs, and leaves at Weena's suggestion to help hide the grave.

"If we hurry, do you think we might make it by nightfall?" Weena asked Dendrox hopefully.

"Not now, but I think we'll be safe enough being not far off from the town. Besides, there's a horse drawn carriage that travels this road," Dendrox told her and smiled reassuringly.

"Does anyone have any gold?" Candra asked, remembering that they did not have enough even for Dendrox and herself.

"I have a few gold pieces. Unfortunately, I'm afraid it may not be enough for a room and a meal as I had hoped," Weena replied.

"I haven't any," Vordin said with disappointment, but then remembered the glowing rock he had made. He took it out and held it out to them in a closed hand. "I do have this though," he said as he opened his hand and revealed the glowing stone.

"You could fetch a fair price for that, I suppose," Dendrox told him.

"We could be a lot worse off. I guess we shouldn't really complain," Weena said as she considered their situation.

"Let's head out then," Candra said starting off down the road toward Vackiindmire as the others followed, "I'm sure Dendrox and I can scrounge up enough coin for us all from some of the townsfolk there at Vackiindmire." With this being said, both Weena and Vordin realized that the two of them were in fact thieves.

They all traveled in silence, as they were all exhausted.

Vordin exclaimed, as they approached a fork in the road, "Where does that road lead?"

"It probably leads to the village of Dexcsin," Dendrox told him, "Straight ahead is the town of Vackiindmire."

They stopped to rest a moment at this second crossroad where a smaller road branched back west off the main one between the two towns.

Weena had been looking down this new road, when she said, "Hey, look," and pointed. They all turned their eyes toward the road. There was a figure in the distance who was coming toward them.

"We should continue to the town before it gets dark," Candra suggested.

All of them, extremely weary and hungry, agreed to this, and were about to leave, when they heard a man's deep voice calling out to them, "Wait! Please wait!" This burly man who had short, thick legs was now running slowly and awkwardly toward them.

"Come on, whatever he wants can't be very important. Let's just leave," Candra blurted out cruelly.

<Zaylyn ><Quest For The Sword Of Anthrowst ><By Katrina Mandrake-Johnston >   <Ch 8> < 40 >

Weena glared at her and said, "Well I'm waiting here. If you are really so uncaring of others, you can leave without me. Just remember that if I had said the same thing when you were in need of my help, you would not be standing here now." She turned away from Candra with an expression of disgust.

Candra just shrugged and started walking toward Vackiindmire. As she walked, she noticed that Vordin and Dendrox were not following. She continued her stride, miffed that Weena was yet again trying to manipulate the group's decision to what she wanted to do. Candra expected Dendrox to eventually come after her and join her on the way to the town, but he had not moved from his position.

"*I can't go alone! I can't leave him...*" Candra complained to herself with frustration, "*His expression, could it be that he's ashamed of me? Why should he care what she thinks? We helped her to bury the man with the medallion. My debt to her has been repaid. Now we should be on our way to town. We don't owe her anything. Who cares if she's disappointed? So what? We're all going to go our separate ways once we get to town. Why would her opinion be of any importance?*"

But as she continued to walk, Candra knew that she wasn't going to convince herself otherwise. Weena's opinion of her meant more to her than she had realized, and apparently it meant a lot to Dendrox as well. Candra, swallowing her pride, turned around and headed back.

Candra could see that her companions were crowded around a dwarf who was gasping for air after running to meet them. This thirty-seven year old dwarf stood four and a half feet tall and his curly reddish-brown hair was tangled and loosely tied to hang just below his broad shoulders. His scruffy beard ended at his collarbone, hiding his thick short neck. Above his bushy mustache was a large bulbous nose and his two round eyes were a deep brown.

He wore a pair of brown leather boots and dark brown pants. The dwarf also wore a leather jerkin over a light brown shirt, the sleeves ending in a close fit at mid forearm. His strength clearly was found in his stout barrel chest and muscular arms. His short legs contributed to his balance and sturdiness rather than speed. A medium-sized brown leather pouch was attached at his side and a large battle-axe was strapped to his back.

Candra, arriving at their position, came to stand beside Dendrox.

The dwarf had a frantic expression on his broad face, as he said to them all urgently, "Please, I fear that I will not make it to Vackiindmire and back to Dexcsin in time. These terrible creatures attacked there last night killing many of the villagers. My party has remained to protect the survivors. Several of my friends have already died in the attempt. I left to seek reinforcements, but I fear I may already be too late, as night approaches soon. Please, I beg of you, come with me to Dexcsin to try to help these innocent people." He winced in pain and clutched the thigh of his left leg. His brown pant leg was stained reddish-brown as the result of a large gash.

As Weena looked to Candra with a calm expression, Candra offered, "I'll assist you and your companions, to save these villagers."

A smile spread across Weena's pink lips at this. Candra had longed to see Weena smile again at her, as she had feared that she had lost this indefinitely. Dendrox also smiled at her.

Vordin looked worried and he asked, "What kind of creatures were these that attacked the village?"

The dwarf's dark brown eyes looked now to Vordin as he replied, "I'm not sure. I've never seen such horrid beasts in all my life. One of the foul things slashed at my leg, but I had managed to get in a couple of good blows to the beast."

Vordin admired the large and heavy battle-axe that was strapped across the dwarf's back over the leather jerkin. His boots were caked with dried blood and mud. "*The Black Shadow said another village was under attack last night. And this dwarf, he actually fought his way past them! Candra and Dendrox also battled one. Maybe this other village can stand a chance against them if we come to help,*" Vordin thought with hope.

"Did they have six clawed feet and shiny black skin?" Dendrox questioned. Dendrox was glad that he and Candra had not ventured in that direction earlier.

"Yes, but what are they? Do you know?" the dwarf asked.

<Zaylyn ><Quest For The Sword Of Anthrowst ><By Katrina Mandrake-Johnston >   <Ch 8> < 41 >

"We encountered one. We killed it, but I was wounded and poisoned," Candra replied and then gestured toward Weena, "Weena healed and cured me, to which I am eternally grateful."

"You managed to kill one? It seemed near impossible even to cause these creatures the slightest bit of harm. Well this is excellent. It may give us some sort of advantage against them. Are all of you with me then?" the dwarf asked with a hopeful twinkle in his eye and everyone nodded.

"I guess introductions are in order. My name is Nodwel," he said extending a burly hand toward Dendrox.

"I'm Dendrox," he said shaking the dwarf's hand.

"I'm Candra," the elf told him.

"Weena," said the wizard in the greyish-blue robes.

"And I'm Vordin," he said extending his hand to Nodwel and at the same time being careful not to greatly jar the backpack in which Lorenta remained hidden.

"We should leave as soon as possible," Nodwel urged, and the group began the journey to the village of Dexcsin.

<World of Zaylyn ><Quest For The Sword Of Anthrowst ><By Katrina Mandrake-Johnston ><Ch 9>

CHAPTER 9 = DREAMS IN THE NIGHT: VORDIN

The group traveled quite a distance in silence. Their eyes would stray from the road and occasionally gaze into the dense forest on their right, across the grass covered fields to their left to the high cliffs, and also to the mountain range in the distance ahead.

Darkness was approaching and it was some time before Nodwel reluctantly stated, "We'll have to make camp for the night. There's no chance of making it to the village before nightfall. It will be too dangerous to continue in the dark. This spot here looks as good as any. We'll need a fire and a big one. I want to see these beasts if they decide to make their way over to us. It's doubtful they'll travel this far away from the village, but there's always a chance that they might. I'll start gathering wood for the fire."

"I'll help you," Dendrox offered.

After they returned and the fire they built was burning bright and hot, everyone rested their weary bodies. They were off the road a little way into the forest where the trees were sparse. Grass blanketed the ground and there were a few large rocks scattered about the campsite. The fire was a few feet from the dirt road, so the camp had a good view of the road and fields.

Both Candra and Dendrox had wondered whether this had been a wise choice, for anyone or anything approaching could detect their camp with ease. They did not voice their concerns, however, as they were both tired and confident in their abilities. Also, if a danger presented itself, there were several options for the two of them to make an escape, even if it involved sacrificing some of their newfound companions to do so.

Nodwel eased himself down to sit on one of the boulders beside the fire. It was obvious that his leg was still giving him pain. Everyone else chose to relieve themselves of some of their gear and stretch out on the grass, warming themselves around the fire.

"Do you feel ill or weakened?" Weena asked Nodwel with concern. Nodwel gave her a puzzled look. "Your leg…" she continued, "Candra was poisoned by the wound she received. I was just wondering…"

"Oh, no, not at all. I guess I was lucky," Nodwel replied with a warm smile, "It's pretty shallow. It shouldn't give me too much trouble."

After awhile Nodwel discovered that not any of the others had food or water with them, so he distributed his entire supply of rations among them and they were graciously received and eaten by all.

"I fear for my friends and those poor people," Nodwel said speaking in a solemn voice, "I believe that they are engaged in battle with these creatures at this very moment. I just hope they somehow are able to survive, and that when we arrive, we are able to defeat the creatures or at least drive them away."

"All we can do is try," Candra added.

"I've seen the devastation these creatures are capable of. Across the mountains, my entire village

<Zaylyn ><Quest For The Sword Of Anthrowst ><By Katrina Mandrake-Johnston >   <Ch 9> < 42 >

was slaughtered by these beasts. I was able to survive, so perhaps they have a chance as well," Vordin said trying to inspire a little hope back into the middle-aged dwarf.

Nodwel smiled at him, but Vordin could see the despair that lay behind it. Nodwel, favoring his wounded leg as he sat on the boulder, threw another piece of wood into the fire.

Weena asked him, "Would you like me to try to heal your wound with a magic spell?"

"Well…" the dwarf said hesitating, clearly nervous of magic.

"Oh please," said Weena, "I just want to see if I'm able to. I need the practice, and besides, it probably won't work anyway."

"Oh I guess, it would be all right then," submitted Nodwel.

"Thanks," she said and everyone watched as she held her hand over the wound. With a vacant look in her eyes, she mouthed the strange words of the spell. "Well?" said Weena when she had finished.

"Not a thing," the dwarf answered.

"Oh no. I'm sorry," Weena exclaimed with sympathy.

"Just try it again," Vordin suggested.

Weena shook her head and told him, "I can't use this spell again right away. I have to wait. It's as if the energy used to cast the spell has depleted itself and then it needs time to recharge."

"Oh, I didn't know that," Vordin admitted.

"Weena, that's quite alright that your spell failed," Nodwel said to her and then explained to all of them, "The pain and inconvenience of a wound is a major part of battle. If you have to take the time to endure your injuries, in the next battle you will have learnt to avoid them better. I received this injury because I failed to anticipate my opponent's attack. If magic is always used to heal injuries, your battle skills will never increase. You'll have no motivation to learn to avoid them better."

"Yes, that does have some truth to it," Dendrox agreed.

Weena had been proud of herself when she had saved Candra's life, but now she felt her magic skills weren't of such importance anymore. *"How often does a life or death situation arise like that? Without my magic skills, I am nothing,"* she thought to herself, *"I can't even protect myself if I need to. That horrid man that we buried would have easily killed me. I would not have been able to do anything at all in my defense. Even that complicated Shield spell I have, would not have done any good. And in this case, the moment it was cast, the medallion would have absorbed it, even if it had failed, which it most likely would have. Maybe if I were more like Candra, I would be able to put up some resistance if I were attacked. Maybe what Nodwel had said has a larger truth to it. Maybe I am just a weak and feeble person who is just hiding behind my magic, impressing people with the magnificent show it displays when my spells work. What good is that? Without my magic, I am useless. Even if I were an expert mage, what happens if I have to wait for a spell to recharge? I would be slaughtered if I were in the middle of a battle. I could buy amulets and potions to assist me, but without them I would be helpless. Maybe one of my new companions will be able to teach me to use some sort of weapon. Maybe Dendrox will teach me to use daggers. I like that idea. That will give me an excuse to spend more time with him. I have to admit, he is very handsome. The way he looks at me with his dark blue eyes makes me feel as if my whole body is blushing. Why I find myself so infatuated with him is a mystery to me. He's a thief. We have nothing in common. Candra would be a better match for him, but it appears their relationship is more like that of a brother and sister than of a couple. It's really a shame."* Just then, Dendrox gave her a shy glance and then looked back to the dancing flames of the fire. *"Well, maybe not,"* she thought blushing.

Nodwel addressed the group saying, "We're going to need our rest. We can't allow for a slip in reflexes because of a lack of sleep. I'll volunteer for the first watch."

Nodwel watched over them as they slept. Both Candra and Dendrox were lying on their blankets, while Weena and Vordin were asleep upon the thick grass.

"What am I doing?" Nodwel thought to himself, *"I'm most likely leading these poor people to their deaths. At the first sign of danger, I'm getting these people to safety. I'm not going to be*

<Zaylyn ><Quest For The Sword Of Anthrowst ><By Katrina Mandrake-Johnston >   <Ch 9> < 43 >

responsible for their deaths. Apparently they have already been through quite a lot. Hopefully my friends have everything secured and the villagers will be ready for escape when I return with these meager reinforcements. Hopefully my efforts and those of these generous people before me, will not go unrewarded. I feel as though I am betraying my friends by being here though. Here I am safe from harm or at least so it appears, while at Dexcsin, they are probably at this very moment struggling for their very lives and for the lives of those helpless villagers. I am returning sooner than I would have if I had gone all the way to Vackiindmire, but still I fear that it will not be soon enough."

As Vordin slept, a dream came to him…

He was sitting on a large rock in the middle of a deep and dark pond. Black swirling masses lurked in the depths. Trees loomed around him, surrounding the entire pond.

Tiny sparks of light came at him from the trees. Vordin thought they meant to attack him, but they stopped just in front of him to hover over the water. The fairy queen was among them.

"You must find the Sword of Anthrowst," she whispered, "You must defeat Dranngore, the evil wizard behind these creatures. You must…" Her words were cut short. She and all her tiny subjects met their deaths in the jaws of one of the creatures as it leapt up from the murky waters.

The beast snarled and glared at Vordin, as its claws dug into the stone of his tiny rock island. There wasn't anywhere for him to escape to. The creature's teeth were dripping with drool and fairy blood.

Just when he thought he would join them in their fate, someone grabbed him from behind. It was Lorenta. With incredible strength, she lifted him high into the air above her head and walked along a thin strand of web from the rock to safety among the trees…

He awoke briefly to see Nodwel keeping watch over them like a parent protecting its young. Vordin then drifted off into sleep once more.

<World of Zaylyn ><Quest For The Sword Of Anthrowst ><By Katrina Mandrake-Johnston ><Ch 10>

CHAPTER 10 =   DREAMS IN THE NIGHT: WEENA

As Weena slept, a dream came to her…

She was back in her home village. It was winter and Weena was ten years old. The cold wind beat against the shutters of the schoolhouse. She sat at her small desk with books piled in front of her. She scribbled and drew silly pictures on a piece of paper, not wanting to attend her studies. Weena had been forced to come early to the school as punishment. Her teacher was a drunk and had slipped out to the local tavern for a few drinks. What he had told her was that there were several urgent 'errands' he had to attend to before class. Even he didn't want to be forced to sit here as she was. She had to finish all her assignments and tend to the fire so the schoolhouse would be warm for when the class started. She felt she were being unjustly punished, especially when she couldn't even remember what for. There was a large snowy hill at the back of the schoolhouse and Weena had brought her sled. She tapped at the wood of her desk and then glanced over at her sled.

"I'll just write a bunch of fake answers and then copy off someone else," she decided, "That fat, stinky, old teacher of mine will be filling his gut with ale right up until class starts. He won't bother to check until later anyway."

She glanced longingly at her sled again. She scribbled down some answers as quickly as she could. When she was done, she almost bounced with excitement over to her sled and thick dark blue cape. Weena threw her cape over her shoulders and held the sled in her hands.

"Oh damn, the fire will burn out and they'll know I was gone. I'll get in so much trouble. Remember what your brother said: Weena, if you get into trouble again at school… ah well, I can't remember the rest. Anyway, it doesn't matter because I won't get caught."

She stuffed several armloads of wood into the fire. Then she searched throughout the room and threw an assortment of things into the fire as well, anything she thought would make the fire last.

<Zaylyn ><Quest For The Sword Of Anthrowst ><By Katrina Mandrake-Johnston >   <Ch 10> < 44 >

Then Weena skipped gleefully out of the schoolhouse and out to the hill. *"This is the one even the boys are too chicken to go down. Too bad I won't be able to brag about this."*

She followed the course with her eyes: over the many slopes of various sizes, the tricky turns, and then the tiresome hike back up to the schoolhouse. The latter would be worth it though.

Down she went, shrieking with excitement. She flew over the hilltops with the icy wind whipping through her hair. Each turn sent a cloud of powdery snow into the air.

Finally, she stopped. Her breath came out in short pants. The thrill was amazing. She wanted to try it again. Weena grabbed her sled and started to run back up to the school.

She only made it a short distance before realizing it was a lot farther than she had hoped and that walking through snow slows your pace incredibly. She was halfway there when she saw the students entering the schoolhouse. *"Oh well, I'll just say I heard a strange noise outside and went to investigate or something,"* she said to herself.

Weena was nearing the school now, when she smelt a strange odor in the air. Then the school burst into flames. She heard screams and smelled scorched flesh.

She ran toward the school. The doorway collapsed as she reached it. She heard desperate cries for help coming from inside. The windows were foolishly bolted and barred to prevent vandalism. They were trapped. Foul smelling smoke billowed out from everywhere.

"I did this. They know it was me! The fire... maybe something I put in it. I don't know. But it was me! I did it!" she thought in terror and shock. There were more cries for help. *"What can I do?! I'll get blamed for everything!"*

Weena panicked and ran. She hid in the woods, curled up behind a tree. She cried until she couldn't muster the strength to do so anymore.

She didn't know how long she had remained hidden there sobbing. She was frightfully cold and she wrapped her cape around herself with numb fingers. *"Surely I can go back now,"* she told herself, as she was now far too cold to care about any consequences.

As she walked through the trees and neared the schoolhouse, she could see a crowd of people around the remains. She stayed out of sight within the trees. One man was naming off a list of the dead and each name struck her heart with sorrow and guilt. Her brother, her only surviving relative, was named last. He apparently had died looking for her within the burning building during a brave rescue attempt...

Weena awoke with a tight empty feeling inside. Nodwel was warming his hands by the fire. Occasionally, he added more wood from the pile he and Dendrox had gathered earlier. He wore a worried look on his face. The fire crackled and sparks fluttered about in the air.

"Do you want me to take watch?" she asked him.

The sound of her words startled him at first, his hand reaching defensively toward his battle-axe. He then relaxed and said, "Nah, go back to sleep, sweet lass."

At first she thought that the dwarf felt she couldn't do the job, but then realized he had meant nothing by it. He had a lot on his mind and sleep probably was the furthest thing from it right now. "They'll be okay," she told him and rolled over on her side to get back to sleep.

"Thanks," Nodwel said as he tossed another log into the fire.

After a short while, Weena woke again, and this time, Nodwel agreed to let her take over the watch. The dwarf made his way over to the base of a large tree and slumped down against it.

<World of Zaylyn ><Quest For The Sword Of Anthrowst ><By Katrina Mandrake-Johnston ><Ch 11>

CHAPTER 11 = DREAMS IN THE NIGHT: DENDROX

Dendrox began to dream...

He stood in a forest glade. The sweet fragrance of wild flowers filled the air. The sunlight filtered down through the trees. He could hear birds singing as they fluttered from branch to branch, and there

<Zaylyn ><Quest For The Sword Of Anthrowst ><By Katrina Mandrake-Johnston >   <Ch 11> < 45 >
was the sound of a nearby waterfall.

Just then, something darted out from behind a tree to hide behind another. Dendrox caught a glimpse of pale blue.

Again the person came into view, as she leapt from one tree to the next. Her robes flowed around her as she moved.

Dendrox tried to approach her, and as he did, she giggled and darted away. He tried to follow her, as she danced from tree to tree in an illusive game of chase.

Finally, he lost sight of her. The sound of the waterfall was nearer now, and Dendrox headed toward it. As he approached through the trees, he could see a small lake. Water splashed over a high rock cliff to meet the lake in a bubbling spray.

She was there. Dendrox remained unseen within the tree line. It was Weena. She was beautiful. She gathered her robes about her and bent down to gracefully dip a hand into the water of the lake. She stood up and brushed her blonde hair, which hung just below her jaw line, away from her face to tuck it behind her ear.

She lifted her robes up over her head revealing a thin, blue, gossamer undergarment. He could almost see the smooth creamy skin of her body beneath. She tossed the robes to the ground and waded into the water. There, Weena tilted her head back to wet her hair. She closed her blue eyes, as she enjoyed the coolness of the water.

Dendrox crept down to the lakeside to get a better view. He could see her pale form beneath the water, as it moved back and forth to stay afloat.

Suddenly, she opened her eyes, caught sight of Dendrox, and a smile crept to her lips. Dendrox suddenly felt ashamed for invading her privacy and prepared himself for a proper scolding. Instead, she simply said, "Hello."

Weena glided through the water toward him until she could stand on the lake bottom. Then walking along it came closer and closer to him. Each step she made, revealed more and more of her body, the undergarment clinging to her shapely form. He could see that the water had been quite cold.

She now stood before him on the grassy lakeside. She smoothed back her wet hair. Her creamy skin glistened with moisture. Her bright blue eyes sparkled with excitement. Her soft pink lips parted in a warm inviting smile.

He wanted to touch her, to kiss her; to take her in his arms and hold her close. He thought to himself, "*How can I? How could someone so beautiful, so perfect, be attracted to me? I'm a thief. I'm scum. I take what I want. What do I have to offer her? An empty pouch? A broken heart? She doesn't want me. How could she?*"

She stepped closer until she stood in front of him. Her presence so close made his body ache. He felt his heart quicken and his body grow warm.

Weena ran her fingertips down the length of his arm, and where she had touched him, tingled and felt incredibly hot. Her eyes looked into his, and he felt hypnotized by them.

Then to his amazement, she kissed him. It was a soft, moist, and gentle kiss. Then she put her arms around him and kissed him again, long and hard, with a fierce passion for him that he never imagined could exist.

He held her tightly against him and stroked the small of her back. She was warm despite the chill of the lake, and she was soft. Each kiss from her sent shivers of pleasure down his body. He could feel her warm breath on his skin and it felt wonderful. Every movement she made screamed desire. She looked into his eyes and gave him a sly little smile.

"*She is so beautiful. This can't be happening,*" he said to himself. He ran his hands along her back and kissed her hard again and again.

Then she pulled back and away, making him think that he had done something wrong.

"Hello," said a voice from behind. It was Candra wearing a mischievous grin.

"*Candra, I'm going to kill you,*" he thought with an embarrassed chuckle.

"So, what's going on? Or do I already know?" Candra asked with a cunning smile.

"*I really hope you're enjoying this now, because I'm really going to make you suffer later.*

<Zaylyn ><Quest For The Sword Of Anthrowst ><By Katrina Mandrake-Johnston >   <Ch 11> < 46 >

There's no way I'm going to let you get away with this one," he sighed to himself.

"Oh, don't mind me," Candra said with her ridiculous grin, "I'm just here for the view. Really, there's the lake, the waterfall, and the trees. It's quite nice," she said almost breaking into laughter at the torment she was putting him through.

"Don't you have somewhere to go?" he asked her, his words showing every bit of annoyance and frustration that he felt.

Candra's smile widened, "Oh no, I've got plenty of time and nowhere to go." She paused a moment and then said, "Thank-you for asking though. You know how I hate to be late."

He thought with a frustrated growl, "*I am really going to hurt you for this, Candra.*"

"I'm not interrupting anything, am I? So what were you two doing?" she asked with that same mischievous grin.

"*Candra, please shut up and go away! Of course you won't, you're enjoying this torture way too much,*" Dendrox thought with frustration.

He looked to Weena. "*How am I ever going to apologize for this?*" he asked himself.

Weena smoothed Candra's hair away from her face as she had done when Candra had been injured and poisoned. It had been a simple motherly act before, but now it seemed to be more than that.

Weena turned to him and said, "Dendrox?"

"What?" he asked.

She looked at him with a puzzled expression saying, "Dendrox, wake up."

"What are you talking about? I am," he told her, not wanting to admit that this was a dream.

"Dendrox," she said again.

He grabbed on to her and held her tightly, not wanting to let go, but he felt himself waking up…

"Dendrox… Dendrox…" Weena called sweetly.

He opened his eyes to see Weena's pretty face looking down at him with concern.

"You were breathing pretty heavily. Were you having a nightmare?" she asked innocently.

"Ah, yeah," he said, but couldn't stop the wide grin that spread across his lips. "I'll keep watch if you want to get some sleep," he offered, "You can use my blanket."

"Thanks," said Weena as she accepted the blanket and laid down wrapping it around her. She fell quickly into sleep.

Dendrox sat by the fire. He could see the black starry sky above. The fire crackled. The dwarf was snoring loudly in sitting position against the bark of a large tree. Candra was sprawled out on her blanket, and Vordin was curled up with his backpack beside him.

<World of Zaylyn ><Quest For The Sword Of Anthrowst ><By Katrina Mandrake-Johnston ><Ch 12>

CHAPTER 12 =   DREAMS IN THE NIGHT: CANDRA

As Candra slept, a dream came to her, her memories surfacing…

She was home. She was a small child of nine years. Her father was there. His dark hair was pulled into a short braid at the base of his neck. He was roasting meat over the fire in the hearth. It smelled wonderful. They were a poor family of two, despite how hard her father worked himself in the crop fields. This meat would have to last them the next couple of days. He smiled at his young daughter, his bright green eyes sparkling in the firelight. He was a tall man for an elf.

"Tell me about elves again, father," Candra asked. She loved to hear him talk, even though he would ramble on and on.

"Well, my dear, some elves are very small, anywhere from three to four feet not unlike a lot of the fairy folk I've told you about. Some elves are of a little larger size, anywhere from four to six feet like most humans. And then, some are very tall, anywhere from five and a half to seven feet, like us. The eyes are either slanted or oval and all elves have pointed ears. Some ears are longer than others, but you can always tell if you're looking at an elf by the ears. Well, actually, I think some of the fairy folk have pointed ears as well. Now that there is definitely a race with a lot of variety. With the fairy folk, some

<Zaylyn ><Quest For The Sword Of Anthrowst ><By Katrina Mandrake-Johnston >   <Ch 12> < 47 >

have wings and many are no taller than one or two feet. Candra, you know, I have heard stories of tiny fairies that live in the forests. They're supposed to be so tiny that they appear as little sparks of light. They're also supposed to be awful pranksters, but I think the people that tell these stories drink too much ale and then blame these tiny fairies for their own clumsiness. Or, perhaps people simply see fireflies and are just hoping to see something more, something rare and magical. I think at one time, most of the fairy folk and even our kind used to dwell in the forests, mountainous caverns, in burrows underground, and even on and in the lakes and ponds. Now, so many just live in the towns and villages. It's sad in a way that so many have lost the magical and mysterious quality that we had in our past. Zaylyn is never short of its mysteries, and its strange and exotic people. I would have loved to have the chance to just travel the world and see even a small amount of the wonders it holds, maybe even discover a hidden civilization or who knows what. Alas, all the excitement and adventure I'll ever get to see is an odd-shaped potato in the field. Ah, the meat is done. Could you get the big knife so I can cut it?"

Candra went to the small cupboard, which was almost completely bare, and retrieved their only knife. She placed it on the small rickety wooden table for her father.

"Oh, I need that big plate too," he realized.

Candra went again to the cupboard and retrieved their only plate. She placed it on the table, and her father placed the tiny roast onto it.

"Oh that's hot!" he exclaimed.

He picked up the large knife and was about to carve the meat, when the door burst open. In stepped two burly men. They were covered in filth and smelled foul.

One of them blurted out, "I thought I smelt somethin' good cookin' in 'ere." He pushed his companion aside and stepped up to the table. Then he grabbed the roast with a large dirty hand and bit into it like an apple.

Candra's father stood there in utter astonishment, still holding the carving knife in his hand. Candra immediately despised these crude and selfish ruffians. She yelled angrily at them, "What do you thing you're doing?! Put down our food and get out of our house! Now!"

The two men just laughed at her. The one holding the roast took another bite of the meat with what few teeth he had. The other man, the one with greasy black hair, laughed again and said, "Who's gonna stop us? Not you, little girl, and definitely not this weakling over here." Still laughing cruelly, he asked her father, "Where's yer valuables?"

Her father remained silent. The only thing of value they owned was her mother's necklace. It was the only thing left that they had of hers, and they would not give it up to two selfish scoundrels.

"Y' look like yer hidin' somethin'. Everyone values somethin', whether it be worth money or not. I think ya have somethin' of both, don't you?" the black haired man said with a sly grin of rotting teeth.

"Leave us be," her father spoke up, keeping his voice strong, "We have nothing you want. Your friend here is eating our only thing of value."

"Ah, now I know you be hidin' somethin' for sure now. Beat the girl. That'll get 'im to talk. Then we'll know, won't we?" he smiled wickedly at her father's worried face.

The brown haired man dropped the meat on the table and grabbed the thick wooden club which hung at his side. She would fight back. The man was coming. His club was raised.

The black haired man called, "Don't kill 'er, at least not right away. Just make 'er squeal."

Her father came to her rescue, not by giving the location of her mother's necklace, but by stabbing his daughter's attacker in the back. Neither of the men were expecting this. The large knife had been driven deeply into the man's torso, so far that only the handle protruded. It was not the instantly fatal wound that her father had hoped to inflict, but the man lost the ability to wield his club and Candra was saved.

The black haired man pulled the knife out of his companion's back and snarled angrily at her father. The horribly wounded man made his way over to the door, closed it to any curious eyes, and slumped down against it, wincing in pain. The black haired man still held the carving knife which was dripping with his friend's blood.

<Zaylyn ><Quest For The Sword Of Anthrowst ><By Katrina Mandrake-Johnston >   <Ch 12> < 48 >

"You'll pay for this!" he bellowed. With the bloody knife he stabbed at her defenseless father, striking him in the stomach. Snarling, he then pulled his club from his side. This man's club had sharp metal spikes protruding from the head of the weapon. Then he raised his spiked club and began to beat her wounded father to the ground. He swung again and again.

Candra tried to stop him, but he gave her a vicious kick that sent her small body across the room. She was breathless for a few moments and then each breath after gave her pain. All she could do was sit there as the man continued to smash the very life out of her loving father.

The man had finished. Her father lay dead in a pool of blood.

He searched the house until he found the necklace. He held it up triumphantly and said, "I've found it. This is some prize! Come on, we'll get you healed up."

He helped his companion up and out of the door, slamming it closed behind them. Candra was alone. She made her way painfully across the floor to where her father lay. She couldn't even recognize him. His skull had been smashed open from the heavy and repetitive blows. His face was nothing more than a pulpy mass. She could see the knife that had been thrust into his gut. Several of his bones had been broken as he had tried to defend himself, his body misshapen and bloody. She could look no more.

A dark fury burned inside her. She wanted revenge. She wanted to make them suffer like no other ever had. Her father had taught her to use a bow. She wasn't very good, but she didn't care. She took her bow and a handful of arrows.

Candra left the house and started the hunt for her father's assassins. Her chest ached incredibly. It was definitely bruised and perhaps a couple of ribs had been cracked. The pain just fueled her rage like an internal fire. She would have her revenge.

She thought she had known the direction they had gone, but now she wasn't sure anymore. She had some tracking skills, knowing what sort of signs she should be looking for, but they never did her any good, usually leading her in the wrong direction. She entered the woods at the bottom of the hill.

"Hey you," said a small human boy. He was a year younger than her.

She thought to herself, "*Oh no, it's that annoying kid again.*" She said to him, "Go away! Can't you see I'm busy?" Her words were choked with emotion.

"Don't you want to play?" he asked.

"*He'll ruin everything. I don't have time to play hide-and-seek. I'm on a mission. Besides, he always manages to find me, no matter where I hide,*" she thought. Candra replied, "No, I don't." This time she tried to put more strength into her words, but it didn't work.

"Why not? What are you doing?" he asked her.

"Two men killed my father, and I'm trying to find them. When I do, I'm going to send a million arrows into each of them. Then they'll wish they never came near us," she told him, her words angry and forceful, but her voice trembled.

"Oh…" was all he could bring himself to say.

She thought for a minute and then said, "Dendrox, you're good at finding people. You know, like hide-and-seek. Can you help me find them?"

"I don't know. They really killed your father? This isn't some sort of game?" Dendrox asked, amazed at the thought.

"Yes," Candra replied, this time starting to cry.

"Won't they kill you too if you follow them?" he asked hugging her the way his mother did when he was sad.

"I don't know. They took my mother's necklace too," Candra told him.

"I thought you said that you were really terrible at using a bow. How are you going to send a million arrows into them, if you can't even hit the targeting board?" Dendrox asked her. She sobbed and sobbed. Dendrox offered, "Why don't you come live at my house. I'm sure my mother and father will say it's all right. Then we can practice every day together. I'll come help you, okay? You can practice your bow, and I'll practice my daggers. Then when we're really good, we'll go on adventures. We'll find those two men and then you can fill them full of arrows, and I'll throw some daggers into

<Zaylyn ><Quest For The Sword Of Anthrowst ><By Katrina Mandrake-Johnston >   <Ch 12> < 49 >
them too, okay?"

She nodded, and then drying her tears said, "I thought your mother wouldn't let you play with daggers."

"Well no, but I still do sometimes," he smiled at her, "Anyway, I have to go now. Come on, we'll go practice until we're good enough to beat them. We'll be able to find them eventually."

Dendrox took Candra by the hand and led her to his house. She got to use the spare bedroom across from Dendrox's. She remembered how his parents fussed over her for weeks and how every day they had practiced.

Her dream shifted. It was now years later and they had left for adventure on their own. Visions of the hardships and dangers they went through to gain information about the two men, flashed through her mind until her dream focused on when they had eventually found them.

She had taken her revenge. Their tortured screams filling her ears until it finally gave her a sick feeling of satisfaction. She did not want to be that person she had become that day. It made her shudder each time the memory surfaced of what she had done to them. Both she and Dendrox had been surprised that the two men had kept the necklace all those years.

Candra remembered how they returned to their home village soon after. This was the first and only time she had visited her father's grave. She dug a small hole beside the grave and buried the necklace there. Candra said good-bye to both her parents and headed back to the road to adventure with Dendrox by her side.

They had become thieves themselves and experts at it, as this had been the best way to eventually track the two men down. They needed to associate with the same people, become accustomed to the same kind of life, and with the places they would frequent.

"Had seeking my revenge really taken over both our lives so completely? Have I, in turn, become exactly what they had been? No, I will never be like them." Yes, she and Dendrox were thieves, but for them, it was somehow justified in their minds, as they would only steal from the rich who had plenty to spare. There was never a time they had taken from the poor.

Another dream came to her now, and Candra found herself in the middle of a vast and extremely dense forest. Dendrox was beside her as always.

"Where do you think we are?" she asked him.

Dendrox remained silent. "Dendrox?" she said trying to get his attention.

He started to walk off into the forest, completely ignoring her. "Hey, where are you going?" she asked, as she tried to walk beside him. She found that the trees grew too close to do so, and she was forced to walk behind him.

As Dendrox walked, he would push the branches out of his path, and as he passed, the branches would then fly back to hit Candra in the face. "Hey, Dendrox, watch it," she told him, as she pushed away the offending branches.

Dendrox continued to make his way through the forest, not speaking a single word to Candra. "Is something wrong?" she asked, "Where are you going?" Another branch snapped back at her.

Forest obstacles seemed to appear out of nowhere to bar her path. She made her way over logs, inched her way past brambles, pushed branches out of her way, and stumbled over the rough and rock strewn ground. Dendrox, however, seemed to have an easy path and continued farther and farther away from her. She had to put all her effort into trying to keep up to him.

"Wait!" she called, "Dendrox, please wait! Let me catch up! Dendrox, wait for me!" If he had heard her, he made no acknowledgement of it as he moved farther and farther away. Candra feared that she would lose sight of him and become lost in this terrible forest that seemed to be holding her back and away from him.

She would not lose him! She struggled to catch up to him, but it seemed that the more she struggled to catch up to him, the more strenuous her path became. "Dendrox, please wait!" she called to him, "Dendrox, I'm falling behind! Where are you going?! Wait for me, please!"

Soon she lost sight of him altogether, but she continued on and on. Finally she came to a small

<Zaylyn ><Quest For The Sword Of Anthrowst ><By Katrina Mandrake-Johnston >   <Ch 12> < 50 >

clearing. She stood on one edge of the forest, while Dendrox stood beside Weena on the other.

"Dendrox, why didn't you wait for me?" she asked, quite out of breath. Both Weena and Dendrox had expressionless faces and seemed to stare right past her as if she didn't even exist. "Weena? What are you doing here? Where are we? Do you know? Where are we headed?" Candra asked in confusion.

Weena said nothing. She turned her back on Candra, and so did Dendrox. Then they started into the forest holding hands. "Wait for me!" Candra called in desperation, and she started to cross the grassy clearing to follow them into the woods on the other side.

Suddenly the ground began to shake, and she struggled to keep her balance. The earth in front of her opened up, creating a wide chasm to block her way. There was no way for her to get across. Even if she found a way, it would be too late to find them.

Candra sat down on the grass, knowing that she was helpless. Dendrox was gone. Weena had taken her best friend away from her. She was bitterly alone. She didn't care about holding back her emotions, not here, and she allowed herself to cry. She cried in great heaving sobs. She cried about everything; everything she had held back. She had lost her mother so long ago, and then her father was taken brutally away from her. And when she had taken her revenge, she had lost a bit of herself. Now Dendrox, he had left her too…

Candra awoke. Dendrox was digging at a piece of wood with the tip of a dagger.

"You know, if you keep fidgeting like that, you're going to ruin your blades," she commented.

"Oh, hey," Dendrox said looking down to Candra who was resting on an elbow, "You feel like taking watch now? I'm beat."

"Sure, I don't think I can sleep any longer anyway," she replied.

"Oh, Candra, can I borrow your blanket?" he asked, "I lent mine to Weena."

"Then take it back if you need it," she snapped, the fears from her dream surfacing.

Dendrox gave her a sour look.

She gave in saying, "Okay fine, take mine then."

Dendrox lay down with Candra's blanket and fell asleep. Candra looked from Dendrox to Weena and wondered what might happen to their friendship should their flirtations increase. Candra took her place by the fire.

<World of Zaylyn ><Quest For The Sword Of Anthrowst ><By Katrina Mandrake-Johnston ><Ch 13>

CHAPTER 13 =   DREAMS IN THE NIGHT: LORENTA

Lorenta, still hidden in Vordin's backpack, also dreamt…

She found herself back in Rasindell's hut. She was alone and in human form. The place gave her an empty and lonely feeling. Then, Lorenta heard the cry of an owl.

The wood of the roof began to splinter, and then she could see the talons of a gigantic owl. The massive bird tore the roof off the hut as if it had been the lid of a box. A giant yellow eye peered into the room. The owl let out a deafening shriek and tried to widen the opening it had made in order to snatch up its prey. Lorenta was terrified.

Her hand, the one with the severed fingers, was grabbed by someone. It was Vordin. He led her out the door and away from the owl to safety. Her ability to change form had made it possible for the wound to seal itself in both her forms, and Lorenta wondered if there were any other mysteries about herself she was unaware of.

She and Vordin were standing by the side of a road, and there were trees on either side. Before them was the corpse of the man she had killed. In his stiff white hand he clutched the cursed medallion.

"This was not right," she said to herself, *"He was cursed, but I had to act in self defense as anyone would. Rasindell told me stories as a child. Some were of love and romance. That's what I want, not to be groped like some worthless plaything. It's like being poked at with a stick for fun. Eventually, you fight back in self defense, and that's what I did here."*

<Zaylyn ><Quest For The Sword Of Anthrowst ><By Katrina Mandrake-Johnston >   <Ch 13> < 51 >

When she turned around, Vordin had vanished. Then she heard a familiar voice, one she had not heard in a long time. "Lorenta… Lorenta, my child. Come sit by the fire with me. I have another story for you," the voice called to her. It was Rasindell.

She wandered through the forest searching for him. "Lorenta…" he called again. She tried desperately to follow the voice. "I'm here my child… Over here by the fire," he called to her.

She looked and looked but could only see dense and dark forest. She was becoming frantic. She would not lose him again!

Suddenly she fell through a deep hole in the ground and landed in the arms of her father. She was a little girl again and in the warm and cozy home she had known growing up. Rasindell smiled down at her and said, "There you are. I've been waiting all day to see you again."

"I've missed you father," she said and felt tears welling up in her eyes.

"What's the matter, dear? You look as if you are about to cry," he asked his daughter with concern, as he smoothed her dark brown hair. She just shook her head, not knowing what to say. "Okay, I have the perfect story for you tonight. Have I ever told you about how the human-dragons came to be? There are two different kinds: Dragonites and Avygons. Have you heard this one before?" She shook her head. "Okay, now where should I begin? There once was a dragon, long, long ago. She would often fly near the humans, as she was always intrigued with their way of life. Of course, she was always careful not to be seen on her ventures. If she were spotted by the humans, she would be attacked for sure, or at least scare the humans away from where she could watch them."

As she usually asked quite a few questions throughout his stories, Lorenta asked Rasindell, "Why would the humans attack her?" Maybe that's why he kept his storytelling short and simple when he told them to her. With Vordin, his stories were long and elaborate; Vordin usually didn't ask so many questions.

"Why? Well, they were afraid of her," he tried to explain.

"But why were they afraid, if she meant them no harm?" she asked.

"Well, I think it's not a matter of whether she wanted to harm them or not. It's more that she was capable of doing harm," he told her.

Lorenta looked solemnly up at her father's kind face and said, "So, they don't care what her intentions are? If she's dead, there's no possible way for her to do harm? This is their reasoning?"

"I'm afraid so, at least in this case," he told her sadly.

"So, just because I might be able to harm a human, they would want to kill me too? Even though I would never do so? The few times you've taken me with you in the backpack, I've seen horrible things, father. Creatures that could never even threaten a human, being tortured and killed by them as they laugh and make fun. Even the children do it. You can't tell me different, father. If someone saw me in my true form, whether I was capable of harm or not, they would try to kill or injure me. And, they would do this just for the fun. Even a small child would. Humans are horrid things. I don't want to be one." Lorenta was crying now and holding on tightly to Rasindell.

"Dear, I am human. Not all of us are like that. I have to admit a lot of them are, but not all. Don't cry. Come on, let me finish the story. There's a good message in it, and I think it will suit you," Rasindell tried to comfort her.

"Okay," she said wiping the tears away.

"Alright, now where was I? Okay, so this dragon, she would watch the humans from time to time. She would always remain hidden, which was a hard thing to do for a large dragon as she was. Over the years, her random viewings of the humans became more frequent and narrowed to one particular man. She found that she couldn't stand to be away very long. A dragon had fallen in love with a human, as bizarre as that may sound.

"She couldn't stand it any longer. Her dragon heart burned with passion for someone who could never love her. He did not even know she existed. She felt so empty inside. Knowing that she could only watch him from afar, made her sadden more and more each day.

" *'There must be a way,'* she thought to herself, *'If the other dragons knew that I have feelings for a human, they would probably banish me for being insane. But my heart knows different, and I can no*

<Zaylyn ><Quest For The Sword Of Anthrowst ><By Katrina Mandrake-Johnston >   <Ch 13> < 52 >
longer deny it.'

"The dragon had heard tales of an old witch who had strange and powerful magic abilities. She flew to where she was rumored to live and searched for many days by air until she found the small hovel. She landed in front of the entrance. She was afraid, but she did not care. If this was her one chance at the happiness she had imagined each day since she fell in love, it would be well worth it to risk the danger.

"An old woman hobbled out of the dwelling. The witch looked up at the dragon towering over her and called, 'Hey, you up there. What do you want? I don't have much time for visitors. If you have nothing of importance to say, be off with you. You wouldn't be here for any particular reason, would you?'

"At first the dragon was astonished that the witch had spoken to her as if she would a human. She wanted to be human. Then, maybe she could live out the rest of her life with the one she loved. This is what she told the witch.

"A wide, toothless grin spread across the wrinkled face of the witch and she said, 'This is an interesting request. Usually people come to me with small problems. Spoil this man's crops or give someone a headache for three days straight. I won't do anything nasty of course; just things that can be taken as being coincidence, that's all. I don't want anyone hunting me down for who knows what.

" 'But in your case, that would really test my abilities. You truly want this? You do realize that if the transformation works and you become human, that he many not take a liking to you. Just because you love him, doesn't necessarily mean that he will love you.'

" 'I'm willing to take that chance,' the dragon told her.

"So the witch went to work on the task of finding a way to transform the dragon into a human, while the dragon waited patiently for the results.

"Finally, after many days and nights the witch came to the dragon and said, 'I've done it. However, the spell will not last forever. From the moment you dust yourself with this powder, you will become human. You will have five years to remain that way. That's exactly five years, so remember the day and the hour. Hold out your hand, and I shall place the bag of powder into it. It would be a long walk for you to be human now. Good luck.'

"After the witch gave her the powder, she flew gleefully back to her home, clutching the precious bag in her claw. She had to find clothing for when she made her transformation, so that night she swooped down into the village and grabbed a full clothesline.

"When she returned to her cave in the mountains, she waited patiently until early morning. Then the dragon made the transformation, put on some of the clothing, and headed toward the village. There was a small pond along the way, and this is where she viewed her new appearance. Her long hair was a reddish-brown and her eyes were emerald green. Her wings and tail had vanished. She was tiny and frail. Pale smooth skin had replaced her scales. She was human at last.

"As she approached the village, she realized that they would wonder who she was and where she came from. *'I'll say that I had been captured by goblins or Garcs and held captive by them. Then, that I escaped and made my way down here. It will have to do,'* she decided.

"In the village, she told her story and was accepted into their community. As she had hoped, she eventually caught the eye of her beloved. A romance followed and eventually they married.

"Over the years, she almost allowed herself to forget that she was in fact a dragon and that one day she would have to leave her life here and the one she loved. The end of the five years was drawing near. She did not want to tell her beloved that she had to leave. She couldn't bear the heartbreak of telling him why. Even if she could, he would not believe her. She decided it was best just to leave. She would have to go back to watching him from afar.

"The time came to go. She waited for him to leave their home. She had sent him to the market for eggs. She rushed out and started the strenuous climb to the mountaintop where she could make her transformation unseen. Unknown to her, her beloved had seen her leave and, wondering where she was going, had followed her.

"She waited for the change before a steep cliff. It would be perfect for her to take flight from in her

<Zaylyn ><Quest For The Sword Of Anthrowst ><By Katrina Mandrake-Johnston >   <Ch 13> < 53 >
dragon form. Her beloved came up the path.

" 'What are you doing? Is something wrong? What's going on?' he asked, not knowing what to think.

" 'Oh no, please,' she begged, not wanting him to see her true form. She wanted him to remember her the way she had been and the wonderful years they had together. Him seeing her as a dragon, would ruin the memories. 'Please, go back home. Hurry! Please, I beg you, do not stay here!'

" 'What are you talking about?' he asked confused, and he came to face her.

"It was too late. The transformation had begun. It was slow at first and then rapidly increased until she was a dragon once more. Her poor beloved, so astonished, backed away from her until he was right near the edge of the cliff.

" 'It's me. This is what I really am, but I am still the one you loved,' she pleaded desperately.

" 'No… How can this be? You're… You're a monster… Keep away from me…' he said staring up at the massive dragon before him.

"She took a step toward him, wanting him to accept her, wanting to comfort him, and afraid of what might happen. Her beloved backed away from her with fear and fell over the edge of the cliff to his death. She could do nothing now but return to her old cave in the mountains."

Lorenta asked, "Can dragons speak the way we do? How could she have told him that it was still her after she had transformed? I can't talk when I'm a spider."

"I suppose I should have mentioned that," Rasindell chuckled, "Dragons speak with their minds to each other and can easily penetrate the mind of a humanoid being with their words if they wish to speak to one. I'm sure this also added to his fear, to hear her voice speaking to him from within his own mind.

"So, anyway," Rasindell continued, "She did not leave her cave for many days, and then it was only out of desperation for food that she did. After some time had passed, she realized that a bizarre miracle had taken place when she had been in human form. She had become pregnant and was pregnant still as a dragon. This became her new joy in life.

"When the time came, she laid her eggs and mothered them with the greatest of care. She had not returned to the dragons after her transformation. They would never accept her young and what she had done.

"The eggs hatched and two different types of offspring emerged. One appeared completely human except for having the wings of a dragon. They grew to become an arrogant race, rarely associating with anyone but themselves. Very few have seen this race, and they are known as Avygons.

"The other type was wingless and also appeared human except for being hairless, having the scales of a dragon, a tail, and claws. Actually, they have normal smooth skin but there are patches of scales scattered randomly along their flesh. I've met a few before. It's hard to describe them really, and their varied eye and skin color are usually more like that of dragons as well. They grew to be a compassionate race and were accepted as a sociable race among the world's population. They are known as Dragonites or human-dragons as they are sometimes called.

"There are a great many wonders in the world and a great variety of people. I've met dwarves, elves, fairies, Garcs, goblins, centaurs, and Dragonites, to name a few. I don't know if my story will help you, child, but a least it made you sit still for once. Okay, run off and play now."

Lorenta hopped off her father's knee and went through the cabin door.

Her dream shifted, and she stepped out into a village. She felt as if she were floating. She moved throughout the village until she came across a crowd situated around a small building.

"We have the foul beast trapped!" one man said triumphantly.

"Burn the evil thing!" someone said angrily.

"It's unnatural! It shouldn't exist! Get rid of it once and for all!" one woman said.

"Who knows what it's capable of? We could all be in danger!" somebody said nervously.

Lorenta could hear a soft sound coming from inside the building. She floated closer. It was singing. The song, which was meant to be a happy cheerful one, held such sadness that it brought tears to her eyes just by listening.

<Zaylyn ><Quest For The Sword Of Anthrowst ><By Katrina Mandrake-Johnston >   <Ch 13> < 54 >

She touched the wall of the building in sympathy and found that she could pass right through it. The villagers continued to rant, as they held their torches and makeshift weapons.

Inside, Lorenta saw a figure sitting on the floor of the small one-room building. The villagers now had set fire to the roof and walls of the place. She could hear cheers and vicious hateful words coming from outside as the building began to burn.

The figure rocked back and forth. It was a woman with a black hooded cloak wrapped about her with the hood drawn up. She had a bundle of something in her arms. Her sad song continued, broken by comforting words whispered to the bundle. Lorenta's heart ached for this poor woman.

She heard a horrible garbled noise coming from the bundle. "Shh, it will be okay. Hush now baby," the woman whispered, but her words were filled with grief.

Smoke began to fill the room. The flames eagerly devoured the wood of the roof and walls. More cheers could be heard. "Burn, you foul thing! Burn!" an old woman cackled.

The heat from the flames was becoming unbearable. Lorenta approached the woman through the smoke-filled room. As she did so, she caught a glimpse of the baby. It was human except for having four bulbous eyes, eight hairy legs, and large curving fangs. Then the woman, her face wet with tears, lifted her head to look up at Lorenta. Lorenta saw her own face beneath the hooded cloak, and then the flames engulfed the three of them…

Lorenta awoke to the darkness of the backpack. Then she drifted back to sleep, realizing that she was no longer truly spider and would never be truly human.

<World of Zaylyn ><Quest For The Sword Of Anthrowst ><By Katrina Mandrake-Johnston ><Ch 14>

CHAPTER 14 = NODWEL'S DREAM

Nodwel also began to dream in his slumber, remembering the events of the day before…

Nodwel stood in the small village of Dexcsin. His companions, tired and hungry, had gone in search of food and lodging for the night. Asdella, Narr, and Dimwar had gone to the general store to buy supplies. Nimdor and Borin had gone to find shelter for the night for them all. There had been no sign or word of the illusive wizard.

Nodwel walked through the village toward the designated meeting place: the well at the center of the village. The forest edged the village to Nodwel's right. He and his companions had made a strenuous journey through those very trees all the way from the road to end up at the village. To his left, past the village crops and animal pens was a grassy plain with high cliffs towering above beyond it. Behind him stretched a road that most likely joined with the one that connected the two towns, Shirkint to the north and Vackiindmire to the south.

Vackiindmire had been their original destination, being the closer of the two, before the wizard had disappeared into the forest. The villagers stared and smiled as he passed them on his way to the well. They obviously didn't get many travelers here, as the village was in an isolated location. One little boy, a human, ran up to Nodwel.

"Are you a dwarf?" he asked, his green eyes wide with excitement.

"That I am," Nodwel replied with a warm smile.

"Can I see your axe?" the boy asked.

His mother came to fetch him. "Come on, honey, don't bother the nice man," she said as she ruffled her son's tawny blonde hair.

"Aw, mother," he protested.

The woman took the boy by the hand and said to Nodwel, "Sorry, I'm sure you're busy," then to her son, "Come on, dear, we have to go home for dinner."

"Oh it's no bother. Good-day ma'am," he said with a nod, and he continued down the dirt street of the village.

When he reached his destination, Nimdor and Borin were there already, obviously successful in their task of finding suitable lodgings. Nimdor waved a welcome to the dwarf. "Any word about our

<Zaylyn ><Quest For The Sword Of Anthrowst ><By Katrina Mandrake-Johnston >   <Ch 14> < 55 >
newly recruited wizard? Has anyone seen him?" Nimdor asked.

"No," Nodwel replied, "What about tonight?"

Borin answered, "We've secured a place for tonight and meals too. Compliments of the village leader and his wife."

"Yes, Bren and Kreasa are their names," Nimdor told him as he leaned on his wooden staff, "The others aren't back yet, but they should be able to get enough supplies to last us until we reach Vackiindmire."

Nimdor was an elf. He was an older man of fifty-five years and his hair, which was as white as bone, hung to his shoulders. The pointed tips of his ears showed through his straight wispy hair, which he always wore loosely about his face. He wore dark green robes, a pair of brown leather boots, and his wooden staff had ornate swirl-like designs carved into it. Nimdor stood five and a half feet, and the features of his face were thin and elongated, especially his nose and chin. His bright blue slanted eyes reflected his patience and wisdom.

Although there were no ranks among this group of friends, the entire group looked to him for leadership. He was adept in Natural magic, but he also had some skill at casting a few Black and White magic spells. Also he was a skilled fighter, and despite his age, Nimdor's thin form was still agile and swift. He could knock a weapon out of a hand or sweep someone off their feet with that staff of his in an instant. Nimdor preferred to use his spells over physical combat though, and probably liked the awe he inspired among his friends every time he cast a spell.

Borin was a thirty-nine year old human and a big man, standing at almost seven feet. His hair was short, black, and had the early signs of greying. His round tanned face had high cheekbones, an average-sized nose, a rounded chin, and had the stubble of a beard starting. Borin's grey eyes always seemed to have an adventurous spark to them, and he always had a large wide smile when he laughed.

For clothing, he wore a light grey cotton shirt with its sleeves ending at his elbows, a brown leather vest with crisscrossing leather strips up the front, and a pair of black pants. His leather backpack was strapped loosely to his back, and at his sides, he had a short sword and a hatchet.

He was more of a woodsman than a fighter. If he hadn't been there to guide them through the forest, they probably would have gotten hopelessly lost. Borin had lost track of the wizard almost immediately, which was strange; it was almost as if he had vanished.

Shortly thereafter, the others came into view. These three humans each were carrying two small sacks of supplies.

Dimwar stood six feet tall and had short auburn hair. His squarish face was clean-shaven and had a prominent jaw line with a cleft chin. He had a small flat nose, a small mouth with full lips, and his eyes were light brown.

He wore a chain mail coat over a black full-sleeved shirt. His black pants had patches of thick leather sewn into them for added protection to his thighs and calves. He found that this added greatly to the ease of movement much more so than the heavier chain mail leggings he used to wear. Dimwar also wore a pair of brown leather gloves and black boots.

Dimwar was an excellent fighter, trained in many different styles and techniques. Oddly, his favorite choice of weapon was a spiked flail, and he could wield it in a most deadly fashion. He also wore a long sharp dagger at his side and a brown leather traveling pouch. His small iron shield, that was plain except for the large spike in its center, was slung over his shoulder by a leather belt.

Asdella was dressed in brown suede, but barely. She wore only a halter-top and a pair of high-cut shorts. Her feet were bare, but she didn't seem to mind the rocky dirt roads of the village. Her skin was tanned, and she had short reddish-blonde hair. She was twenty-six years old and tall for a human, standing near six and a half feet. She had a pretty face, but there was a hardness to her dark brown eyes. There was a light spray of freckles along the bridge of her small nose and cheeks, and under her small mouth was a v-shaped chin.

Asdella was clearly muscular, especially in her arms and legs, but not unattractively so. Her firm stance was always daring and defiant. The only possession she carried was her bare bladed sword. Usually someone else would have to hold on to her food and water, as she refused to carry anything but

<Zaylyn ><Quest For The Sword Of Anthrowst ><By Katrina Mandrake-Johnston >   <Ch 14> < 56 >
her sword.

Narr, a slender twenty-eight year old man, wore a sly smile across his lips, as usual, as he approached the group at the well. He always appeared to be aware of some joke which no one else knew and usually had some snide remark to share. He had a rounded face and stood just over five feet tall. He had eyes of blue and short blonde hair which had a slight wave to it.

Narr always seemed to be annoying at least one member of the group at any given time. Knowing the pride a male dwarf takes in his beard, one of Narr's many torments for Nodwel would be to start bragging about how soft and silky his own hair was. He'd go on saying how the ladies always love a man with fine hair, being able to playfully run their fingers through it. Then he would tease the dwarf about whether or not he would even be able to run a comb through his tangled beard without getting it stuck. Narr would joke about all the different kinds of birds that would just love to use it as the perfect nest, and he would pretend for hours that they were secretly being followed by a whole flock of birds determined to make Nodwel's beard their home. Nodwel knew that all his talk was just in fun to pass the time; otherwise Narr would wake up completely bald and with a black eye or two.

Narr was always joking and talking. It made a long journey seem shorter, which was a blessing, but only to a point as he often got quite annoying. He also had his 'words of wisdom' about how things are or should be and all the silly little things that sound as if they make sense until you think about them.

For clothing, Narr wore a pair of plain dark brown pants and a leather jerkin under which he wore a white long-sleeved shirt. At his waist was a short sword. He wasn't especially skilled with it, but he could manage all right. He was better fighting with his fists after too many drinks were in him. In this, he had a lot of practice, as his mouth and ego tended to get him in trouble quite often.

Nodwel's dream shifted, and he found himself seated at a long, crowded wooden table. The village leader Bren, his wife Kreasa, their two young sons, Nodwel, and his companions all began to eat a hearty meal of roast lamb and vegetables.

Near the end of their meals, a chilling scream was heard through the open window. Everyone fell silent.

Dimwar was the first to react. He stood up quickly from the table, his square jaw continuing to work at a mouthful of meat. His chain mail glistened with the light from the fire. He hesitated a moment. Another strangled cry was heard. Dimwar quickly donned his leather gloves, took up his spiked flail and his small shield, and looked to his companions. He had a worried look in his light brown eyes, and then Dimwar yanked open the door and strode quickly into the night in the direction of the screams.

Asdella got up from the table with a wild excited look in her eyes. She grabbed her sword and standing there in her leathers, which barely covered what needed to be, said to them all, "Someone or something needs to be gutted. I can't let Dimwar have all the fun, now can I? You boys coming?"

"You know I'd follow you anywhere. Who could resist such a view?" Narr said to her with a playful smile.

The others quickly grabbed their gear and headed toward the forested edge of the village. Panic-stricken villagers raced past them trying to herd their family members to safety. When they approached Dimwar's location, they beheld a fearsome sight.

The bodies of at least five villagers were strewn about on the ground. A black six-legged beast was stomping about not knowing what to make of Dimwar. The creature's gaping tooth-filled mouth drooled a slimy liquid.

It took a swipe at Dimwar who blocked the blow with his shield. The force of the blow sent Dimwar staggering back. He swung his flail, striking the beast in a downward motion to the base of its skull. The creature paused a moment, only slightly dazed, and Dimwar got ready for a second attack.

The group was almost at his position, weapons drawn. The beast reared up on its back four legs, and one of its front clawed paws lashed out toward Dimwar. He swung again with his weapon with obvious strength behind it to smash the beast towering over him in the jaw. The flail's blow appeared harmless, and the beast's attack did not falter. The dagger-like claws of the creature slashed clean through Dimwar's neck in one swift and fluid motion.

<Zaylyn ><Quest For The Sword Of Anthrowst ><By Katrina Mandrake-Johnston >   <Ch 14> < 57 >

The group watched in horror as Dimwar's severed head rolled toward them, his body collapsing before the beast. The creature howled in triumph.

Asdella screamed a battle cry and started slashing her sword wildly in the air, and then she leapt forward ready to run at the beast in full fury.

"Asdella! No!" yelled Narr and grabbed her sword arm with both hands, "You'll be killed!"

"Not if I kill it first! Let go of me!" she snarled and wrenched her muscular arm out of his grasp. Borin and Nodwel also grabbed her, and Narr once again attempted to hold her sword arm. "Let go!" she screamed.

Narr, with the help of the other two men, was finally able to pry the sword out of her hand. Nimdor stood nearby ready to cast a spell if the creature attacked them, but the beast seemed to pay them no notice. It gave Dimwar's headless body a swat and pranced idly about. More screams and howling shrieks could be heard elsewhere in the village.

Asdella was dragged away from the scene, as she screamed and struggled. She kicked and even bit her so-called companions. Eventually, they were able to get her back inside the home of the village leader.

Narr bolted the door once they were inside, mainly to keep Asdella from running blindly into battle. Sadly, Nodwel wasn't sure if the insane rage she had shown here was the result from a desire to avenge Dimwar's death or because she had been kept from battle. She seemed to desperately crave battle and confrontation as if it were a necessity of life. Nodwel's dream seemed to pause as he thought about her.

She possessed such a rage, and although she was unpredictable and hard to manage sometimes, she usually proved herself a worthy ally in battle. Asdella tended to go overboard with the number of blows she dealt to her opponent, usually continuing to strike well after the enemy had been slain, completely berserk. Sometimes, she would try to take on an entire group all by herself in a battle that she usually had provoked. She would refuse any and all help from her companions, pushing them away from combat, purely so she could have the thrill of the kill.

She acted as though she were completely invulnerable, but that of course was untrue. Oddly, she seemed to enjoy pain, almost hoping for injuries. Once Nodwel had seen her smearing the blood of the recently slain all over her body in an almost sexual ritual and then go racing into further battle against incredible odds, laughing insanely and grinning maliciously.

Asdella was clearly mad. She was definitely distracting to her opponents as she would enter battle practically unclothed which would especially affect her male enemies, if only for a vital second or two, enabling her to deal a deadly blow. Also, because she made herself so vulnerable without any armour of any kind, she placed doubt in her enemy's mind of exactly what kind of defenses she possessed, perhaps magical abilities or something other that they should be wary of. Of course, she had no protection other than her sword fighting abilities.

Most people are cautious when engaging in a fight, usually feeling out the situation, weighing the odds against them, and so on. Asdella would just lunge in, screaming a battle cry and with that crazy grin of hers. This tended to give her a slight edge, as most were a little shocked by her, not expecting such a ferocious attacker.

Anyone that knew her, quickly realized that one needed to be constantly wary of her and to always be ready with some sort of defense in case out of boredom she decided to give someone a painful jab with her sword. Nodwel had known her for a few years now, and every time he had traveled with her, the time was never an uneventful one, especially if they ended up at a tavern. She loved her ale and was even more violent and nasty when drunk, if such a thing can be imagined.

Nodwel wondered if she even cared that Dimwar had been killed and if she were at all concerned about what was happening outside to the innocent villagers of Dexcsin. What Narr saw in her, Nodwel couldn't tell. Narr was so persistent in his pursuit of her and it was clear that she was definitely not interested in anything other than being comrades in adventure. He would continue to taunt her with his silly little remarks, and she would bicker back. But they seemed to enjoy it, almost a verbal battle between them.

<Zaylyn ><Quest For The Sword Of Anthrowst ><By Katrina Mandrake-Johnston >   <Ch 14> < 58 >

Nodwel often wondered if she considered the individuals in their group as her friends or as just convenient battle partners. One thing he strongly felt though, as crazy as she may be, was that he could trust her, even with his life if the need came.

Nodwel's mind drifted back to the events happening around him.

"They're gone," Borin stated, "Bren and Kreasa with their children."

Nimdor suggested, "They must have fled or more likely are trying to provide some direction in all this insanity being the head figure in this village."

"What are we to do?" asked Nodwel.

Asdella, still being held by Borin and Nodwel, seemed to be calming down. "If I give your sword back, are you going to stick any of us with it?" Narr asked her.

"No," she answered reluctantly and with a glare.

He handed back her sword, and she stood up after the others had released her. "You know, Asdella," Narr smiled at her, "when I dreamt of the day your lips would be pressed up against me, I didn't think it would be so painful." He rubbed at his arm where the red imprint of her teeth could be seen.

"I can't believe Dimwar's gone," Borin exclaimed as he rubbed at his leg where Asdella had given him a nasty kick, "One minute we were all here eating dinner, and the next..."

Narr said, "We have to do something. We can't just stand by while these people are being slaughtered."

"But what the hell is that creature we saw?! I've never seen anything like it before!" Nodwel exclaimed.

No one had an answer.

"I don't really care. Once I kill the lot of them, I'll let you examine one, alright?" Asdella told them, anxious to shed blood.

Borin asked, "Nimdor, what should we do?"

"Well," said the elf, "there are definitely more of these creature about in this place than the one we encountered. We'll need a plan of attack and a plan of defense for these villagers."

"Yeah, hack the things to pieces and tell the villagers to stay out of the way. That's a good enough plan for me," Asdella blurted out.

Finally, out of frustration with her, Borin said sternly, "In case you haven't noticed, Asdella, Dimwar is dead. You know that he was a damn good fighter, probably better than most of us put together. These creatures can't be taken lightly!"

"Do not worry," Nimdor added, "I'm not about to let Dimwar's death be in vain. He was a good man and my friend. I will miss him greatly. We are going to save as many of these people as possible, and then concentrate all our efforts on destroying these terrible beasts, whatever they may be."

Nodwel could see the tension and grief growing in Nimdor's light blue eyes. The elf paused a moment looking down to straighten the cord about his waist on which several small cloth pouches were tied. His action was mainly to hide his emotion from the others. He composed himself quickly and held his staff in front of him, leaning on it slightly with both his hands as he often did.

"Alright then," Nimdor continued, "It didn't seem to be too concerned with us earlier. Therefore, instead of rushing into battle, I say we concentrate on getting these people together and to safety. Having them running around in a panic just makes them easy prey. After that, we can figure out some sort of strategy. Everyone agreed?"

Everyone nodded, including Asdella reluctantly.

Nimdor went on to say, "Okay then, we'll split up. Direct villagers to the center of town. I remember someone saying at dinner that there is a large building used during festivals that is situated around there. It shouldn't be very hard to find. I'll be there. Try to get a rough count on how many of these beasts we're dealing with and try to return as quickly as possible to help build up some sort of resistance against these creatures. I'll use spells to protect and defend in the meantime. I'm not sure how long I'll be able to keep the beasts at bay and unaware of our activities, but I'll do my best. I'm not expecting the villagers to be much help in battle, but we won't know until we get everyone together and

<Zaylyn ><Quest For The Sword Of Anthrowst ><By Katrina Mandrake-Johnston >   <Ch 14> < 59 >

focused. These people are frightened and need direction. If we don't provide all the help we can, they'll be doomed. Alright, let's go. Remember, do not engage in battle if you can help it. We'll have a better chance if we attack together."

Narr added, "Don't worry, I'm not going to go near those things. Look what one of them did to Dimwar and in a single slash from its claws. I don't even want to think of what they could do to us with one of their bites."

Nimdor said to them, "Let's just focus on the plan, alright, for all our sakes. We can't just abandon these people. We at least have some battle experience." He hesitated mournfully a moment before adding, "Besides, it's what Dimwar would have wanted."

Everyone nodded their agreement.

<World of Zaylyn ><Quest For The Sword Of Anthrowst ><By Katrina Mandrake-Johnston ><Ch 15>

CHAPTER 15 = NODWEL'S DREAM: NIMDOR'S PLAN

The dream shifted as he continued to relive the events of the night before. Nodwel found himself standing on a village street with his battle-axe ready. People were screaming and scattering about, dragging their loved ones to what they hoped was safety. He heard children crying and a dog was barking somewhere in the distance.

"Everyone!" Nodwel bellowed, "To the center of the village! We'll try to protect you!"

"Where's my son!" one woman screamed.

Nodwel tried to calm her as best as he could, but she was hysterical. She would draw one of the beast's attention very quickly. As much as he wanted to help the woman, he couldn't afford to start a search for her lost child.

"Find him and get to the center of the village, otherwise we can't help you," he finally told her. He was unsure if what he told her even registered. He didn't have the time to deal with her; it meant more lives would be lost because of it.

When Nodwel finally headed there himself, he had several villagers following him. Several men of the village were determined to fight; anything to protect their families. Some of the women carried small children crying in their arms. Many of the frightened people, unable to locate their missing family members, hoped to find them at the center of the village alive and well. It was heartbreaking, but Nodwel knew he had to keep these people focused. He had to be firm and strong. These people saw him as their only hope right now. Everyone was looking to him for their own strength and for direction.

His dream soon brought him to stand outside the building Nimdor had chosen near the center of Dexcsin. It was a little way north of the village well and its doors faced in the direction of the forest. It was a large community hall that they would use during their festivals and other events. There was a large fire pit here, and as it was a wide spacious area, with the moon bright overhead, visibility was fairly good here. The group had led as many of the villagers they could find still alive into the building.

As the group was directing the last of the villagers into the building, one of the foul creatures saw through Nimdor's deceptions and discovered them. It ran toward them on four legs, its head held high with its two front clawed limbs ready to strike. Nodwel held his axe, and Borin had both hatchet and sword in his hands. Narr, holding his short sword, managed to close the double doors after the last villager had entered and then turned to face the creature along with his companions.

Nimdor and Asdella were closest to the beast, being farthest from the building. It was the elf that the creature decided to attack. It leapt straight for him. He was ready for it, and so was Asdella.

Nimdor cast a ball of fire directly into the face of the creature that was bearing down on him. It stopped, shook its head slightly, and as its solid black eyes became fixated on him once more, it let out a growl from deep within its throat. Asdella's sword struck the beast's side repetitively, as she yelled and screamed in an insane fury. It simply swatted her aside, and then pounced on Nimdor, knocking him down.

Everything happened so fast that Nodwel, Borin, and Narr had no time to react, not that it would have made a difference. Asdella rolled from the ground into a crouch, then ran at the beast and slashed at it again and again, hacking bits of flesh from its torso. Once again seeming to ignore the onslaught

<Zaylyn ><Quest For The Sword Of Anthrowst ><By Katrina Mandrake-Johnston >   <Ch 15> < 60 >

from Asdella, the creature stomped its front leg hard into Nimdor's chest. Bones cracked. The malicious creature howled triumphantly at this and leapt away, escaping down a village street. Asdella, in her unstable anger, started to venture after the beast until she heard Nimdor urgently utter a word.

"No," he managed to say to her.

Asdella stopped, staring off in the direction the beast had gone, and then came to his side, as did everyone else in the group.

"I'm dying friends," he coughed. It was clear that each gasping breath he managed caused him great pain. Foamy blood sputtered from his lips. "Someone… go for… help… Save… these…" he uttered before he died.

"Damn it! No!" Borin yelled with hatred for the horrid creatures.

Narr said frantically, "We're all going to die! First Dimwar, now Nimdor. These things are picking us off one by one! Who's going to be next?! They were our best chance against these things, and they took them both out like they were nothing! I mean, I'm all for trying to help these people, but I say we get the hell out of here now! To hell with the plan! We can't beat whatever these creatures are! Let's run and take as many villagers as we can with us."

"We can't now," Borin said to him, "They'll never make it. You know that! Our best bet is to keep these people together and try to protect them as best we can. Of course, it will be only a matter of time before they tear that building apart, and if that happens, again, we'll try our best to protect them. So like Nimdor said, someone has to go for help. We can't do this on our own."

Nodwel suggested, "We should get inside before another creature comes this way. We don't want to draw too much attention to this place."

"What about Nimdor? Are we just going to leave him here? Shouldn't we bring him inside?" Narr asked.

"We can't. We're trying to give these people hope, remember?" Borin said, his voice cracking with emotion.

At the sound of another howl, Nodwel said, "I really think we should get inside and quickly."

"Let them come! I'm ready," Asdella said defiantly.

"We're not losing you too. Come on!" Nodwel demanded.

"Please," Narr pleaded, "don't do this."

"Alright, fine. I'm coming," she told them.

"Rest well, my friend," Borin said with tears in his eyes.

They all entered the building leaving Nimdor's body where it lay as they had done with Dimwar's.

"Everyone, calm down, please," Borin told the frightened group of villagers, "Try to stay quiet, everyone. We don't want to draw attention here. We are sending someone for help."

Nodwel looked at all the pale faces staring helplessly at them.

"We're all going to die!" one man wailed.

"My son, why isn't he here?! I have to find him! He's still out there somewhere! Let me out! Let me out…" one woman cried as others held her back and tried to calm her, trying to give her hope.

One man, cradling a woman's head in his arms, called out, "My wife, please someone help her! She's losing a lot of blood! Someone, anyone, help her! Please! I'm losing her!"

Children were sobbing along with several of the women and men. Others were just staring blankly in front of them, grief-stricken and paralyzed with fear and the shock of what was happening.

"Where's the elf?! The man with the white hair, the green robes, and staff. Where is he?!" one woman asked, "He's dead, isn't he? He must be dead! Who's going to save us now?!"

Nodwel asked, "Who's going? How far is the nearest town?"

"I'm staying to fight and to kill these horrible things," Asdella said through clenched teeth.

"No," Borin said, "It has to be fair." He took a small piece of string from his backpack and cut it into different sized pieces using the blade of his sword. "Okay, whoever picks the smallest piece goes for reinforcements."

Borin held the pieces up for everyone, and they all chose until he was left with the last. Nodwel had the shorter piece of string.

<Zaylyn ><Quest For The Sword Of Anthrowst ><By Katrina Mandrake-Johnston >   <Ch 15> < 61 >

"It's decided. Good luck old friend," Narr said to him with a pat to the dwarf's shoulder.

"Good luck to all of you," Nodwel told them, "I'll see you real soon, and we'll beat these things."

Nodwel left them and made his way through the village to the beginnings of the road. Just when he thought he would be able to make his escape, Nodwel felt a sharp pain in his leg and stumbled forward. He recovered quickly, however, and turned with his axe ready to strike. The front claw of the beast before him dripped blood... Nodwel's blood.

Its black eyes stared down at him as if daring the dwarf to attack. Nodwel swung his axe and it imbedded itself into the beast's neck, biting into the creature's shiny black flesh. The beast howled in rage. The dwarf swung again. He would not let it beat him. He swung again and again, with as much force as he could muster.

Finally the creature decided to wander off in search of easier prey. Nodwel headed down the road away from Dexcsin, trying to ignore the pain his wound was giving him. He would not let them down. He would return before it was too late... Nodwel felt himself waking up.

<World of Zaylyn ><Quest For The Sword Of Anthrowst ><By Katrina Mandrake-Johnston ><Ch 16>

CHAPTER 16 =   THE ROAD TO DEXCSIN

Nodwel awoke anxious to return as quickly as possible to the village. At dawn, as soon as there was enough light to see by, they headed once again in the direction of Dexcsin. Nodwel led the way, walking in front of the group at a swift and steady pace. Candra and Vordin walked slightly behind him, with Weena lagging behind beside Dendrox.

"So, if time allows, do you think you might be able to show me how to use a dagger?" Weena asked hopefully.

Dendrox smiled at her and nervously brushed his hair back behind his ear. "Yeah, sure. I guess."

"That would be great," she said with enthusiasm.

Dendrox thought a moment to himself and then asked, "Why do you want to learn how to use a plain ordinary dagger when you know how to use magic? Isn't that far greater than any physical weapon?"

"Well yes, sometimes," Weena said and then after hesitating for a moment added, "I just feel as if I'm helpless. My magic isn't as reliable as I would like it to be. Besides, I don't have any offensive spells, and all I have is one defensive; a Shield spell. I guess I'm still bothered by the thought of that man with the medallion. If things went differently and he had attacked me, my magic would have been completely useless to me. Candra can face danger, deal with it, and then not give it a second thought. At least that's how it seems. I don't have that kind of courage. If I knew how to use a weapon, at least I wouldn't feel so insecure," she explained.

Candra smiled to herself at Weena's compliment, as she was listening to Weena's conversation with Dendrox.

Weena's bright blue eyes sparkled up at him, as Dendrox said, "Oh, I see. Well I guess I could teach you a few things. It will take a lot of work and a lot of practice, and even a greater amount of patience. These things don't come easy."

"Don't worry, anyone who has ever been able to learn a spell knows well about patience and the frustration of trying to learn something new. Most give up during the first three days and nights of continuous study, usually giving into sleep. The fourth and fifth days are the worst; trying to concentrate is almost impossible. Oh and there's the really creepy fact that you start to see things out of the corner of your eye. Dark shapes that you can never really get a good look at, but can feel lurking about. It gives me shivers just to think about it. People rarely speak of such things, but I'm sure it's been the reason why a few people I know have quit learning spells all together. They would rather not be aware of mystical creatures which people rarely glimpse, and I know exactly how they feel. You're usually alone when it happens and whether you sense good or evil from whatever being you happen to glimpse, it's very frightening either way. People just say that your mind starts to drift off into dream now and then when you're awake because of the incredible lack of sleep, but I think it's something

<Zaylyn ><Quest For The Sword Of Anthrowst ><By Katrina Mandrake-Johnston >   <Ch 16> < 62 >

more. It could be that part of learning magic is learning to alter your perception of things and to be aware that within and around us is magic that just needs to be manipulated in order to use it. Whatever these beings are, they are connected to it all on some greater level somehow and therefore can only be seen when the perception of things is altered. Well, at least that's what I suspect to be true. Or, the incredible lack of sleep could just be making people go crazy, who knows? If I start to think about how a spell is actually working itself, it just doesn't happen. I guess it would be similar to trying to consciously control your heartbeat. You would have to be concentrating so carefully and the beats would surely end up irregular. Casting a spell is like that. If you try to understand what is happening and concentrate on casting the spell, it just doesn't work right and most often not at all. You just have to relax, clear your mind and sort of let the spell unconsciously work itself. Anyway, what was it that I was talking about?" Her face had grown flushed and hot with embarrassment. "Um, sorry, yes, I'm prepared to work at learning to handle a dagger and would appreciate whatever you can teach me," she said sheepishly, "Sorry, I tend to ramble when I'm nervous." "*Oh yeah, admit that he makes me nervous. That will make a good impression,*" her mind told her sarcastically, "*What's the matter with you? Bla, bla, bla! You're so scared of not having anything to say that you end up talking everyone's ear off.*" Weena hesitated before adding, "You know, with all this impending doom and all, it doesn't really put my mind at ease."

Dendrox commented, "I know what you mean. I sure wasn't expecting all this when we first decided to head out to Vackiindmire."

"Why did you travel out this way?" she asked.

He answered with a sly smile, "Let's just say it was a professional necessity. The place we were in started to become less and less tolerant of us and our trade. We had to leave rather quickly."

Candra chuckled to herself at this.

"Oh," Weena said quietly, again being reminded that he and Candra were criminals. She found that this was something that kept slipping her mind.

Vordin was fascinated with the determination Nodwel had shown. "*He clearly has a good heart and is willing to put his own life at risk for another. Well, I guess we all are,*" Vordin thought to himself as he walked with his new companions. Vordin admired the large battle-axe displayed on Nodwel's back once again and tried to imagine the dwarf swinging it madly with his thick and muscular arms at a fierce Killnarin. "*The creature would slash toward his broad chest covered by his leather jerkin and Nodwel would skillfully maneuver out of the way and bury the double-bladed axe deep into the evil beast,*" thought Vordin trying to visualize it in his mind.

Vordin let his gaze fall onto Candra: her creamy white skin, her black hair falling gently about her face, her sparkling emerald green eyes... He found her to be a very beautiful woman. He thought to himself, "*She's like a rose. Beautiful, but if you get too close you'll probably get pricked by the thorns.*" Candra still had Weena's yellow sash tied around her arm as a bandage for her wound. Vordin counted eight arrows in her quiver which was strapped tightly to her back. The leather strap of the quiver lay on an angle across her chest between her small breasts. The points of her elfin ears could be seen through her hair. She appeared to Vordin, from what he had seen, as being a cold and heartless person, but he hoped this was not entirely so. He would have to rely on her and the others to protect him when they encountered danger.

Candra looked down at him from the corner of her eye, and Vordin realized he had been staring at her for quite some time now. Annoyed by this, Candra asked abruptly, "Did you want something?"

Vordin, not wanting to admit that he was just admiring her beauty, quickly thought of an excuse and said, "Oh, I was just wondering how your arm is doing. That is where you were wounded by the creature, isn't it?"

"It's fine," she said sharply and returned her gaze to the road ahead.

Vordin, feeling rejected, slowed his pace slightly until he was walking beside Weena and Dendrox.

Weena's clothing fell loosely around her body, as her sash was being used by Candra. Her leather sandals patted against the dirt road and the small cloth pouch at her waist swayed back and forth as she

<Zaylyn ><Quest For The Sword Of Anthrowst ><By Katrina Mandrake-Johnston >   <Ch 16> < 63 >
walked. In her left hand, at her side, she carried her lantern.

Noticing that Vordin was glancing at her more frequently as they walked, she felt the need to say something to break the uneasiness this was creating. "Hello," she said, as she tucked a loose piece of her hair behind her ear.

"Hello," Vordin replied looking into her blue eyes and then said attempting to make conversation, "So, I heard you say you were thinking of learning to use a weapon?"

"I thought it might be a good idea," Weena commented.

"You're lucky, I guess. I don't know how to use magic or a weapon," he told her, and in doing so, felt extremely awkward and foolish.

"That's okay," Dendrox told him, "We were going to use you as bait anyway. Also, if we have to run, you'll slow the creatures up." Dendrox chuckled to himself, as a confused and panicked look crossed Vordin's face. "Relax, I'm kidding," he added, but then thought, *"That's exactly what we might have to end up doing to you. Not that I would want to, but if you get in the way and endanger the rest of us, getting rid of you might be the best thing to do. Candra would leave you here by the road, tell you where to find a town or village, and just walk away. Even if you proved to be of some use to us, she still would rather get rid of you. She's a loner who can't stand to be truly alone. I guess that's my role, to be a loner with her. I'm surprised she hasn't said anything much to insult Weena. Usually, she's fiercely aggressive toward women I take an interest in."*

Vordin decided to walk to the front of the group and converse with Nodwel, since he was feeling insecure and hoped that the dwarf would be more receptive of him. "How much farther is it?" Vordin asked him.

"We should be there fairly soon I hope," Nodwel replied.

Dendrox was showing Weena how to hold a dagger properly as they walked, and Candra began to feel slightly rejected. *"I know I'm not jealous. It's only Dendrox. He's like a brother to me. He's my best friend. I like Weena. She's a good person. Still, I feel threatened by her… Dendrox would never trade in our friendship for her, right? Besides, she doesn't seem selfish enough to try to ruin such a strong friendship. Weena's already getting all of his attention as it is. He's hardly said a word to me. Plus, he hasn't shown any interest in attempting to catch up to me and include me in their conversation. He would rather walk behind me, and with her. I'm not going to lose him. I'm not going to be cast aside. I know that I'm not perfect, but that's why we're inseparable. We're thieves. We thrive on adventure and danger. We rely on our skill and cunning to survive,"* Candra thought to herself and then slowed her pace until she was beside Dendrox.

"Hi Candra," Weena said grinning.

Candra looked at her with an expressionless face and said calmly, "Hello."

To Dendrox she said cheerfully and in a joking manner, "So, you two are really getting along well. Maybe some day you'll get a little cottage, have a couple kids, maybe do a little farming… Of course I'll visit from time to time as Auntie Candra when I pass by in my travels. I'll bring by some of the loot, maybe part with a couple of jeweled trinkets for the kids and a couple adventure stories." Candra knew this would shock him back to his former self.

Dendrox stopped smiling and his face grew somber. Candra knew he was deep in thought and this pleased her. She told them, "Well, I'll leave you two alone. I'm going to walk ahead and ask Nodwel how much farther the village is." Candra walked quickly to meet Nodwel and Vordin. "How much father is it?" she asked without any real interest in the answer.

Nodwel replied, "We're almost there now."

"Thank-you," she said and resumed her position just ahead of Dendrox and Weena so she could hear what they were saying.

"So, Dendrox, am I holding the dagger right?" Weena asked him.

"Yeah," he said without even a glance toward her hand and the dagger.

"Oh," Weena said with such a sadness and disappointment that Candra felt guilt sneaking up on her.

"Why did I do that?" Candra asked herself, *"I put distance between Dendrox and Weena. I hurt*

<Zaylyn ><Quest For The Sword Of Anthrowst ><By Katrina Mandrake-Johnston >   <Ch 16> < 64 >

them both, destroying the happiness they were feeling by spending time together. I'm the one that's selfish. I'm the one who has to have all the attention I can get from him. That's the reason why I feel threatened by her, and it's a terrible one. I like her, and I didn't want to hurt her or Dendrox. I did though, and I can't take back my words. If they start a relationship, it wouldn't really matter. I would be included as a friend to both of them. Also, if she decides to join up with us, the addition of magic to our adventures would be a great asset and a profitable one as well. As long as she learns to be inconspicuous, that is. What he'll do now is just play her for a fool and leave her behind with a broken heart. I couldn't allow him to do that to her, especially now that I know he would be disregarding his feelings about her to do so. He doesn't act like this toward someone where his interest in them is purely physical. I have only been able to have unfeeling and short relationships when I take the time to begin one, but if Dendrox is able to have something more than that and be happy, I'm not going to hold him back."

"So you said that your village was annihilated by these same creatures?" Nodwel asked Vordin.

"Yes," he answered, "Killnarin are what they're called, but that's all I really know about them."

"So the things have a name… What was it again?" inquired Nodwel.

"Killnarin," Vordin answered disheartened, "An evil wizard named Dranngore is supposed to control them and has to be defeated by the Sword of Anthrowst."

"Really? How did you come to know something like this?" Nodwel asked amazed.

"A fairy queen, no bigger than a few inches tall, told me this after I had escaped my village, and also I was told this by The Black Shadow," he answered.

"I wouldn't joke about such things," Nodwel said seriously.

"No, it's all true! I swear!" he told the dwarf.

"Alright, calm down, lad. I believe you," Nodwel assured him.

There was an awkward silence between Vordin and the older dwarf for a few moments, and then Nodwel questioned, "What was the name of your village?"

Vordin was glad that the dwarf was taking an interest in him and not finding him an annoyance and inconvenience as he imagined the rest of the group did. "Nilnont," Vordin replied.

"And that was the village on the other side of the mountain range?" the dwarf asked with a hint of a smile which seemed to welcome Vordin into further conversation.

"Yes. You're the first person to ask the name of my village or anything about it since it happened. I'm the only one left. No one else survived," said Vordin.

"Really?" exclaimed Nodwel with surprise.

"Do any of the others even care about what happened to Nilnont? They know what happened there," Vordin thought feeling hurt, *"Shouldn't they be more sympathetic toward me? I mean, I've lost everything. Everyone is dead. Maybe they just don't know what to say. That must be it. What can anyone possibly say anyway? Any words will just be hollow. Words cannot take the pain I feel away. Words can not undo what has happened."*

"What was your village like, and the people that lived there, what were they like?" Nodwel asked combing his stubby fingers through his beard.

"Well, the village had a few fields of crops. There was corn… several other types of vegetables and grain. Umm, there were several animals: sheep, horses, pigs, and others that I can't think of right now. Quite a few people had cats or songbirds as pets. It was a small village. A lot of people made pottery. There wasn't really anything special about my village or the people in it… Ah… My father… he worked as a butcher and my mother worked at the general store there," Vordin paused with emotion but continued after a few moments, "I didn't have many friends… My best friend growing up was an old hermit who lived in the forest near Nilnont… During the many years after he died, I spent most of my time with my parents and doing puzzles and other little projects like that by myself."

"Interesting… You know, you should be proud of where you come from. Even more so now, since you are the only person remaining to keep those memories alive," Nodwel said to him, "Exactly how did you survive such a brutal onslaught?"

Vordin ignored Nodwel's most recent question, as he had been pondering a disturbing thought.

<Zaylyn ><Quest For The Sword Of Anthrowst ><By Katrina Mandrake-Johnston >   <Ch 16> < 65 >

Vordin abruptly asked, "How exactly did you and your companions arrive at Dexcsin? This is the only road leading to it that I saw, and Vackiindmire would have been a lot closer than this small village. Why would your group travel all the way down to this remote village in the opposite direction of your destination? You were headed to Vackiindmire, weren't you? Weena was the one that first suggested we follow you. Candra, when did you meet her?"

Candra answered, her suspicions growing as well, "Along the road just after we defeated the Killnarin."

Vordin continued, his fear growing, "What if I'm caught in some elaborate lure to dispose of the two thieves that had become a threat to them and me as well being the one that escaped them at Nilnont. Maybe I'm just being paranoid, but I have a good reason to be, and it's nothing personal about you or Weena. If it's true, I shouldn't really be telling you this…" Vordin added slowly backing away from the group.

Candra pulled an arrow from her quiver, and Dendrox seeing her actions, took a dagger from his belt.

"What is it?" Weena asked Dendrox in a frightened voice.

"Be quiet," he said sharply. "Candra, what's going on?"

Candra explained, "Weena and Nodwel might be some of the creatures in disguise leading us into an ambush. Revenge against us and taking care of unfinished business with Vordin, if you know what I mean. Then again, we can't even be sure about him either. How likely is it that they would let someone escape? Nodwel, I could see maybe, but not Vordin. He's unarmed and unskilled; it's too suspicious. Weena came out of nowhere, just when it was convenient for us. Helping me to survive could have been just to gain our trust. Who was that man we buried? It was Weena that had insisted on it. Why was she so eager to trust Vordin? I don't like this one bit. I said we should go straight to Vackiindmire, but she said to follow Nodwel. We are heading to a small village, that would be out of the way and pointless for any group of travelers to go to, and especially when a larger town is closer. There's one road that leads to Dexcsin, right? Why would Nodwel and his traveling companions go there? What do you think, Dendrox? If you are in fact Dendrox."

Everyone was now standing in the middle of the road staring at each other in confusion, and there were also several suspicious and mistrusting glances exchanged. Candra and Dendrox still had their weapons ready. There was a long silence filled with suspicion throughout the group. Vordin wished that he had kept his mouth shut and didn't have such a vivid imagination. He had created chaos.

"This isn't going to get us anywhere," Nodwel exclaimed, "What man are you talking about that you had to bury?"

"Don't change the subject. Who are you?" Candra demanded. She drew the arrow back in her bow and pointed her deadly weapon directly at him a few feet from his face.

"You don't trust anyone, do you?" Nodwel chuckled nervously as he backed slowly away from the arrow, his hands held up to show he didn't want a fight.

Candra replied calmly, "I trust Dendrox." She then hesitated a moment and added, "When I know for sure that it really is him. Damn creatures, I can't trust my own senses or instincts!"

Weena was amazed at how cold Candra could abruptly become, even toward Dendrox which had shocked her the most.

Nodwel explained, "We originally were traveling along the same road leading into Dee'ellkka Valley, probably some time before any of you did. One person in our group, who had just recently joined us, went into the woods when we had made camp. In the morning, when he still hadn't returned, we started to search for him. Someone said that he had heard him muttering something about a pair of scissors. The guy must have been completely insane."

"Go on," Dendrox said, at hearing something about a pair of scissors, and then thought to himself, *"Maybe we're not free of those cursed things. I wish I could remember what I had done with them. Why can't I remember?"*

Nodwel continued, "We looked for him. We couldn't find him and eventually came across the village of Dexcsin, where we all had planned to stay for the night, until the village was attacked by

<Zaylyn ><Quest For The Sword Of Anthrowst ><By Katrina Mandrake-Johnston >   <Ch 16> < 66 >
these creatures. The rest I've already told you."

"We found your friend. He was killed by one of those creatures after stealing my pouch," Dendrox told him.

"I'd hardly call him a friend; we just met him. He just happened to be traveling the same road with us," Nodwel added.

"*Oh, how could I have forgotten? I had hidden them in the lining of my pouch! That must be why he had gone for it!*" Dendrox exclaimed to himself, "*Things make better sense now. I'll have to check later. Maybe I can find out what's so special about them. It must be something magical.*"

"What about you, Weena?" Candra said pointing her arrow toward her now. Weena's magic ability made Candra nervous, not knowing what to expect from her.

Weena protested, clearly afraid of what Candra might do, "Everything I've told you has been true! I've been completely honest with all of you!"

"And you?" she said to Vordin, "Your story was odd to begin with. You're the one that instigated all this paranoia."

"I haven't lied to any of you," he protested.

"How did you escape the creatures?" Nodwel asked once again.

"I hid inside a hollow tree," he told them.

"Why?" Weena asked curiously.

"Rasindell told me to. Well, he really just had just told me a similar story when I was little. Rasindell was an old hermit I used to visit," he explained.

"Rasindell?" Nodwel said pondering the name, "Rasindell… Why does that name sound so familiar?"

"Okay," Candra said putting the arrow back into the quiver and the bow over her shoulder, "This is ridiculous. I'm becoming so paranoid, I can't bring myself to trust my own judgment. I'm even starting to doubt Dendrox's identity again. And I just can't grasp all these crazy illogical happenings with all these weird magic spells and creatures and everything. I'm just going to assume everyone is who they appear to be. And if any of you aren't, I'll just have to kill you. Deal?"

"Yeah," Dendrox chuckled, replacing the dagger back onto his belt.

The group all started toward the village again. After some time had past, Candra was pleased to notice that Weena and Dendrox had resumed their flirtatious manner toward each other once more.

<World of Zaylyn ><Quest For The Sword Of Anthrowst ><By Katrina Mandrake-Johnston ><Ch 17>

CHAPTER 17 =   DEXCSIN

Nodwel described his companions to the group, so they could recognize them if they found them, along with stories about them just to pass the time. More and more he feared for them as they neared the village. He found that the more he worried, the more he talked. The others were thankful for it, as it kept their minds from imagining what they would find when they reached Dexcsin.

When they finally entered the village, they immediately noticed the eerie and unnatural silence. As they viewed the destruction and carnage before them, Vordin's mind raced with images of his own village's demise. He found that he had started to form an outer shell toward all the blood, strewn entrails, and the stench of death. It was not that he didn't feel for these people, he just wasn't letting his emotions cloud his mind. He told himself that there was plenty of time to feel for these people later when he wasn't in danger. Perhaps it was the fear that there might still be Killnarin here that kept his emotions at bay and his body alert. In this, he felt he could identify with Candra.

"*Candra's feelings must be buried so deeply that no one can seem to find them. I wonder how she came to be like that? Perhaps total cold-heartedness just comes with being a thief. I really shouldn't be so hard on her. She isn't such a bad person. I'm actually quite fascinated with her,*" Vordin thought. Vordin couldn't fool himself any longer and a cold lump began to form in his throat, as he viewed his surroundings. He had feelings of panic and anguish. "*We shouldn't be here. We're in danger. Not again! I can't be here! I can't see this again!*"

The whole group was just standing there silent and astonished. None of them, except for Vordin,

<Zaylyn ><Quest For The Sword Of Anthrowst ><By Katrina Mandrake-Johnston >   <Ch 17> < 67 >
could have expected the extent of the slaughter before them.

"Oh…" was all Weena could gasp as she witnessed the horrors that had taken place here.

"Hey Candra, and I thought just one dead man was bad, and he was intact," Dendrox said, his face extremely pale as he tried to hold back his nausea.

"Damn it!" Nodwel exclaimed, a look of anguish and helplessness on his broad face. A tear escaped his eye and ran down the side of his bulbous nose and into his reddish-brown beard.

Candra's stomach wanted to violently empty its contents, but she was able to calm the nausea by searching the debris with her eyes for something else to focus on.

Nodwel took charge of the situation finally, and said to them, "Help me search for survivors. It's almost dark. Salvage anything you can find that might be of use to us should the beasts return. We'll have to find some sort of shelter. The creatures may very well decide to return, and I don't think we should assume otherwise."

"If we split up, we'll cover more ground," said Candra.

"I don't want to go alone," Weena commented weakly. She looked to Dendrox with anticipation.

"I'll go with Candra," Dendrox decided.

Candra could see the effect that this decision had on Weena. Candra knew that it was she, not Weena, he would want to be with during this. Candra was kind of an emotional crutch for him. She thought to herself, "*I would never be able to explain that to Weena without making him seem weak. He has an exceptionally strong character, stronger than most people, just not in this aspect. Everyone needs someone to turn to in some way or another when they're faced with a weak point. Even I have times like that. I thought for a long time that I was turning into myself in times of need. Then I realized that I was actually turning to my dead father and finding solace in knowing that his spirit was with me. Then I realized that Dendrox had become very important to me in that aspect as well. I would be devastated beyond capability if anything happened to him.*"

"I'll go alone," Nodwel told them, "I'll try to discover if any of my companions are still alive. I'll know the places they're most likely to be."

"I'll go with Weena," Vordin offered.

"What if something happens? What if we're attacked?" Weena asked filled with worry.

"You have your magic capabilities," the dwarf stated. Nodwel sighed to himself and added, "Use extreme caution. You'll probably find that we won't be far off. It's a small village, so if you two get into trouble, just run," Nodwel instructed Weena and Vordin who both wore expressions of helplessness and despair. He hated to have to say that to them, but he couldn't afford to coddle them. He didn't know how much time they had until another attack, and he feared there would be, as the beasts had obviously attacked two nights in a row so far. He assumed their attack would be at nightfall, as was the first invasion. Also, he didn't want to argue with the thieves trying to get one of them to go with Weena and Vordin, as that would waste more of their precious time to find any survivors and secure themselves for the night. Nodwel said to them all, "There's a well at the center of the village. We'll meet there?"

Everyone agreed. Nodwel left them quickly and headed toward the center of the village. Candra and Dendrox decided to head left to search the south end of the village. Weena and Vordin went right and toward the forested edge of the village to the north.

Weena had made the suggestion that it might be safer for them in that direction. She decided that if they were in danger, they might be able to climb a tree and call for help or signal the others somehow. Weena felt that there was safety among the trees; she felt protected there. She could hide, being blanketed by the foliage. She felt that it was a far wiser decision than being vulnerable out in the open. Vordin had been unsure about this, but went along with her decision.

<World of Zaylyn ><Quest For The Sword Of Anthrowst ><By Katrina Mandrake-Johnston ><Ch 18>

CHAPTER 18 =   YARIN

Nodwel rushed to the building where he hoped to find the surviving members of his party and the remaining villagers. Nimdor's plan had failed. The walls had been broken through. He was slightly relieved to see that his companions were not among the dead that he could see, and that the number of

<Zaylyn ><Quest For The Sword Of Anthrowst ><By Katrina Mandrake-Johnston >   <Ch 18> < 68 >
villagers slain wasn't as large as he had dreaded. There was still hope.

"*They must have escaped and hopefully with some of the villagers,*" thought Nodwel, and he tried to think of where they may have fled to. He would look for the general store.

"I'm sorry, my friend," he whispered to the wind as he passed the place where Nimdor had fallen and still lay. "*I should have gotten here sooner… I'm not sure if the help I brought will be of any use. I've probably led them here to meet their doom as well. I don't know what to do, old friend. Where is the hope now? Is there even anyone still alive here? I've failed. Everyone was relying on me, and I've failed them. What was Borin thinking in having a fair pick? Damn him and his bits of string. Send the dwarf, the one with the shortest legs? Now there's a great idea,*" he said to himself sarcastically, "*Oh yeah, he'll be able to cover the distance in no time. Damn it, I could have done a hell of a lot better if I had stayed here. I should have insisted. Narr should have gone. He's the weakest fighter out of all of us and could have traveled a lot faster than my stubby legs could have taken me.*" Then he said to Nimdor, "And you'd have something wise to say to me now, wouldn't you?" Nodwel continued, "*If Narr had gone, the beast that attacked me would have attacked him. I survived, where Narr most likely wouldn't have. Then there would be no help for these people. Well, here's the help, as meager as it is, and there's no one left to save that I can see. The village of Dexcsin is now a graveyard and nothing more. The poor lad, Vordin, he shouldn't have to be seeing this, not after what happened to his own home.*"

Nodwel could still see in his mind the frightened faces of the people that had been huddled together in the hall. All of them had looked to them for help and for some sliver of hope. It was he they were relying on. He was their one chance. He was the one that had been sent. "*Don't worry,*" he imagined them saying, "*We just have to hold on a little longer. Nodwel is coming with help. We'll be saved. We just have to hold on.*" The dwarf wept heavily. He recognized some of the faces within the remains of the building, now cold and lifeless. The worst was seeing the children. Nodwel couldn't remain any longer.

"Nimdor, if there is anyone still alive here, I will save them. That includes the people I've brought here as well. You have my word. I won't let you down. And when all this is over, I shall return and lay your body to rest."

He started walking in the direction of the general store where he hoped he would find some clue as to what happened and where the survivors, if any, might be. His mind continued, as he tried to ignore all the blood and the occasional corpse along his path, "*And don't worry, Nimdor, it will be a funeral as is custom with your elfin kind. Your body burned with that of trees, so the two become as one in the flames, and the ash returns to nature on the wind to watch over it, or something like that. I know it's supposed to be all lengthy and poetic and all that, but I'll do the best I can. For us dwarves, it's mostly centered around the earth rather than trees. You know, from the earth, nourished by the earth, for most housed in the earth, and in the end, back to the earth with burial in it. It's basically the same thing if you think about it, all with having to do with nature, having respect for it, and knowing that everyone is connected to it. And yet there are always arguments started where one race figures that another should abandon their ways and customs and adopt the ways and beliefs of the other. It's silly, really. Nature is made up of many different elements. Why should it be any different when it comes to its people? As for Dimwar, I'm not sure what to do for him. Humans have so many different customs; they really don't have one they call their own. Some bury their dead as the dwarves do, or follow the ways of the elves with fire and scattering of the ashes, or some even send their dead out to sea. I'm sure that there are plenty of customs and beliefs that I have yet to hear of as well. As for your daughter, Nimdor, I don't know how I'm going to bear telling her what has happened. Dimwar had a sister. He told me once the name of the town where she lived, but I cannot seem to remember it…*"

When Nodwel finally reached the general store, he found the door slightly ajar. When he pushed on it, Nodwel found that a feeble attempt had been made to barricade it. With a couple good shoves, he made his way into the small store.

Nodwel now stood inside and saw that a cabinet had been used to block the door. There was a gaping hole in the roof and four bodies were sprawled out on the floor. The counter had been toppled

<Zaylyn ><Quest For The Sword Of Anthrowst ><By Katrina Mandrake-Johnston >   <Ch 18> < 69 >

and various goods were scattered about. One of the dead here had been one of his friends. A Killnarin must have torn through the roof and made its departure the same way. "Rest easy, my friend," he said with grief.

From Narr's head, a large pool of blood had formed. His skull had been smashed in, and Nodwel could see the bits of brain that had been exposed. He had to look away; it was too much for him.

Nodwel closed his eyes, *"Narr, old pal, you could sure make people laugh in rough times. I know you did your best to protect these people and made them smile even though they were facing inevitable peril... I should have been here for you. This is not how it should've ended for us..."* He blinked away his tears and took in a deep breath trying to compose himself.

There was a young woman with long black hair and wearing a light yellow dress. Her left arm had been severed, and she obviously had bled to death. An older man, in a shabby grey robe, bald and with a long white beard, had been disemboweled from a large gash across his belly.

"This shouldn't have happened. The village of Nilnont, if that was even the first, and now Dexcsin. These people were defenseless and innocent. What mad reasoning is behind this? Why? What possible motive could this wizard Dranngore have? This is just pointless death and destruction; chaos," Nodwel commented to himself sadly and with an angry frustration.

A small brown haired boy in a dark blue shirt and grey leggings, was sprawled out beside the old man. The boy had lost both his legs in what looked to be a single bite from one of the creatures. Nodwel thought despondently, *"The poor kid appears to have been crawling toward his mother. This is awful!"*

He looked away and tried to concentrate on finding supplies for the approaching night. He searched the shelves and found enough provisions to last the group at least a day or two. He put the food into two small sacks, which he had found beside the front counter of the store. In a small box, he found five candles that he placed in his own pouch along with a length of rope. Nodwel had hoped to find a flame box, a magical box that produces a small flame each time the lid is removed, but he was unable to find one.

He went over to the cabinet, bringing the two small sacks of food with him. It was made of solid oak and was beautifully made with dragons carved onto the cabinet doors. Nodwel attempted to open the cabinet. The doors opened slightly and then, to his great surprise, were pulled right out of Nodwel's hands to slam shut again.

He again tried to open the doors and this time with more force. The cabinet doors flew open to reveal a small boy shielding his face with his arms and trembling with fear. Greatly surprised and relieved, Nodwel said to the boy, "It's alright. I'm here to help you. I'm a friend." *"Narr, you did it. Your sacrifice has not gone in vain. I won't let you down. I'll get him to safety,"* he promised.

The boy put his arms down and said, "I... I thought you were one of them. One of those monsters."

Nodwel could see that he was an identical twin to the dead boy on the floor. Immediately, he was suspicious of this, but then he thought better of it. Over his thin frail form, the boy had a light grey shirt and brown shorts which came to his knees. A pair of dark brown shoes were on his tiny feet.

"Come on, let's go outside," Nodwel coaxed with a wide friendly grin.

The boy hesitated nervously and then agreed, "Okay," and stepped weakly and cautiously out of the cabinet.

Nodwel knew that the boy would see the death in front of him, but it couldn't be helped. The boy remained silent as he walked slowly out of the store, his head down. The dwarf followed, and once they were outside, Nodwel sat down on the wooden bench there, as did the boy.

"My name's Nodwel. What's yours?" he asked in a friendly manner.

"Yarin," he answered. His eyes were red and swollen. They were brown, the same color as his hair.

Nodwel thought, *"He must have been crying right up until I entered the place. Poor kid."*

"Narr said someone was going for help. Is that you?" Yarin asked.

"Yes, I'm the one that went for help. I'm with some others, and they'll be meeting us soon up by

<Zaylyn ><Quest For The Sword Of Anthrowst ><By Katrina Mandrake-Johnston >   <Ch 18> < 70 >

the well. One's a powerful wizard. Her name is Weena. Another also escaped the creatures as you did, and his name is Vordin. His village was also attacked. The other two, a man named Dendrox and a female elf named Candra, are expert… 'fighters'," he decided, not wanting to say that they were thieves even though he had heard Dendrox hint at it in his conversation with Weena.

"Oh," Yarin said, as if all Nodwel had said didn't really matter.

"The poor kid. Here I am trying talk up the others and for what? The help I've brought is far too late to save his family. What we needed here was an army, not a handful of adventurers," he thought with a sigh.

Yarin was staring blankly out into the silent village, and Nodwel decided it was best not to attempt further conversation.

<World of Zaylyn ><Quest For The Sword Of Anthrowst ><By Katrina Mandrake-Johnston ><Ch 19>

CHAPTER 19 = ASDELLA

Candra and Dendrox walked side-by-side in-between the buildings. There weren't many bodies visible in this part of the village which Dendrox was thankful for. Dendrox offered to stand guard while Candra checked the houses and shops, but Candra knew the real reason why he had suggested conducting the search in this way. Everywhere she went, she only found the mutilated bodies of innocent people.

She wondered if Dendrox knew. *"Does he realize how much seeing… Does he think it doesn't bother me?! Just because I shelter him as best I can from it, doesn't mean all this death doesn't greatly effect me too. I just have to remain strong…for him…for myself…"*

They soon came across a large Killnarin, dead in the middle of the street. A woman, scantly clad in brown leather was collapsed over the beast. She still clutched the sword that had been thrust into the creature's chest.

Candra thought to herself, *"She doesn't leave much to the imagination dressed like that. It would prove to be most distracting in battle against a man. It certainly would give her an edge. This must be Nodwel's companion, the warrior woman he spoke of. "*

Candra knelt down and put her elfin ear to the woman's back. Her skin felt cold. She heard a faint heartbeat. "She's alive!" Candra exclaimed, "I don't want to move her. She doesn't have much time. I don't know what to do. Damn it, where's Weena."

"There's no time to find her," said Dendrox. He placed a hand on the woman's back in an effort to comfort her in her last moments of life.

"Am…" breathed the woman to their surprise. They hadn't thought that she still had it in her to speak, and they realized that she was using her last reserves of energy to do so. "Am… u… let…" she painfully forced out.

Dendrox looked frantically around using his skills to determine where she might have come from to battle the beast before them. He reasoned, *"It must be nearby for her to ask for it."* He turned to Candra saying, "Wait here, Candra." Dendrox then sped away into one of the houses close by.

"It's alright," Candra said stroking the woman's back, "Don't worry. You're strong. You'll make it. Fight and you'll live. Don't give in to death. You're stronger than that."

Dendrox found the body of a small girl lying face down in the house he had entered. An amulet was next to her outstretched hand and deep slashes were in her back. *"If the amulet does have healing properties, those foul beasts made sure that this girl couldn't get to it,"* Dendrox thought with further hatred for the beasts.

He snatched up the amulet and ran back to Candra and the dying woman. He held it in his outstretched hand not sure of what to do, and then said, "Ah, here," and placed the amulet on the skin of her back. To his astonishment the green jewel set into the amulet began to glow. Dendrox immediately was reminded of the cursed medallion and the man they had buried, but he hoped that his thoughts were misled.

When the glow subsided, the woman weakly stood up and the thieves watched in amazement as a large gash in the woman's torso closed, rapidly healing itself until the wound had completely vanished.

<Zaylyn ><Quest For The Sword Of Anthrowst ><By Katrina Mandrake-Johnston >   <Ch 19> < 71 >

Then the woman weakly said to them, "This means the girl is dead, and that the amulet is useless now." She threw the amulet across the street and then looked into the faces of the two thieves saying, "Thank-you. It was the strongest healing spell I've ever seen, but I never expected that I would be the one it would be used on. Once again, thank-you both for saving my life. Did Nodwel send you?"

"Yes, we're with him," Candra replied.

"Wow, you're completely healed. I can't believe that you were seconds away from death just a few moments ago," said Dendrox, amazed at the miracle that had taken place.

"So the girl, she is dead?" she asked him.

"Yes," he replied with sorrow.

"Damn it. I had given her the amulet as a good luck charm. I didn't know what else to do. She was frightened and so I had promised to keep her safe," the woman said. Her words were filled with anger and frustration, but it appeared that she felt only a sense of failure and not really any grief or sorrow for the child. Then her show of anger abruptly stopped as if a switch had been turned off, and she said calmly and plainly, "Even if the amulet had healed her, she would have died soon after anyway."

"I'm Candra, and this is Dendrox," Candra told her.

"Asdella," she said and then spoke with enthusiasm saying, "So Nodwel's around here somewhere, is he? Let's find him. Narr is still alive, as far as I know, and is protecting several of the remaining villagers. Borin might be as well. I have no clue as to how many villagers are still alive or where they might be though. Everyone got separated in all the bloodshed that took place last night. It was a glorious battle. It was a good thing that we sent Nodwel for help the night before last. I'm alive now because of it. After the horrendous struggle for survival that night and the one last night as well when the creatures attacked a second time, well, things looked pretty hopeless. We thought about making an escape during the day, but we soon found out that the creatures were merely lying in wait within the forest. They wouldn't outright attack in the daylight, well, that is unless anyone attempted to leave the village. But less talk and more action. Follow me. Nodwel has probably gone already to the general store. Let me guess, you're meeting him at the well, right?"

"That's right," Candra said with a nod.

Asdella's dark brown eyes had the look of a fierce and unpredictable warrior. Candra and Dendrox both had no problem at all imagining her madly screaming a battle cry and charging wildly into battle, as Nodwel had spoken of during their journey to the village.

Asdella grasped the hilt of her sword, positioned her bare foot against the shiny black skin of the beast, and pulled until the bloody blade withdrew from the corpse. She grinned triumphantly.

She headed toward the well, with Dendrox and Candra following her lead.

<World of Zaylyn ><Quest For The Sword Of Anthrowst ><By Katrina Mandrake-Johnston ><Ch 20>

CHAPTER 20 = THE WOLVES

Weena and Vordin saw death everywhere as they walked.

"It looks like the creatures came from the woods," Vordin commented, "You see here, where it borders this side of the village? At Nilnont, my village, the houses and buildings were burnt to the ground. Nothing was left. Why didn't they do that here?"

Weena suggested, "Well, if they did in fact come out of the forest, it would make sense that they would avoid setting fire to the village. The trees and brush would catch flame as well and destroy their hiding place." She realized that her plan to search this side of the village was perhaps not as wise as she had thought.

"Do you really think that they would even consider that?" Vordin asked her.

Weena replied, "Well, didn't you say that these creatures are controlled by an evil wizard? Anything is possible when magic is involved, at least to some extent. I suspect the creatures are intelligent though. I highly doubt the wizard is in total control of their every action."

"That's frightening," he said, "I mean, right now, they are following whatever horrible plan the wizard has for them, but what if he loses control or they decide to turn on him? Can you imagine these

<Zaylyn ><Quest For The Sword Of Anthrowst ><By Katrina Mandrake-Johnston >   <Ch 20> < 72 >
creatures running loose all over Zaylyn?"

Weena, not watching where she was going, tripped and fell, landing on the hard gravelly dirt which made up the streets within the village. Looking back, the sight of what she had tripped over made her frantically crawl away in revulsion.

She could see the glazed, sunken eyes of the dead man staring straight at her. His lips were dried up against his gums making his teeth more pronounced than they should be. A swollen tongue protruded slightly from his mouth. His skin was a greyish-white. Intestines trailed from a large wound to his gut. Dried blood was on the ground around him and various fluids had seeped out of him. Flies buzzed around and on him, attracted by the putrid stench emitted by his body.

"The beasts must have done something to promote such accelerated decay, as it is definitely unnatural. He must have been one of the first people to die here, so close to the forest... Oh my stomach..." Weena thought just before she vomited again and again.

Vordin helped her up, when she had finished, and led her away, approaching a building which appeared to be some sort of shop. They were about to walk around to the front to find a door, when they heard a noise.

As Vordin peered around the corner of the small building, he saw what looked to be a wolf or perhaps a large dog nudging and licking the exposed leg of a young girl. "Wait," he whispered to Weena.

"What is it?" she whispered to him as she also peered out from behind the corner.

They heard the wet tearing sound of flesh being ripped from the bone. The wolf looked up from his meal and sniffed the air in their direction. Its snout was stained red with blood, and it slowly licked its jaws. They feared that they would be discovered, but then it continued to rip the muscle from the girl's leg.

Vordin could see that the girl had been a victim of the Killnarin, as she had large puncture wounds in her torso made by the teeth of the foul beasts. He whispered this to Weena, but it did not seem to put her at ease in the slightest.

"Look what it's doing to that girl's body, that could very easily be us," Weena said and then retched again, but there was nothing left to be emptied, "Let's get out of here before it sees us."

Another wolf, much larger than the first, now approached the body from out of the woods. A deep growl resounded from the throat of the first wolf, as it did not want to share its gruesome prize. The second wolf suddenly looked to the corner of the building where they were, perked up its ears, and growled.

"He's seen us!" Weena whispered frantically, "We'll never be able to out run them, not both!"

The smaller wolf now looked up in their direction. The second wolf seized its opportunity and snatched the little girl's arm attempting to drag her away in his direction. The first wolf, realizing what was happening, snarled at the larger wolf, threatening to attack. It returned a deep growl which made the smaller wolf back away slightly, but it was determined not to give in to the second and clamped its jaws around the bare bone of the leg trying to tug the body away from its rival.

"Come on, let's go," Vordin whispered, "Quickly, but don't run. We don't want to draw attention to ourselves."

Weena nodded, and they both headed toward the center of the village with Weena mentioning that the behavior of the wolves seemed odd somehow.

<World of Zaylyn ><Quest For The Sword Of Anthrowst ><By Katrina Mandrake-Johnston ><Ch 21>

CHAPTER 21 = THE WELL

"So Yarin," Nodwel said to the boy, "shall we head toward the well then? My companions should be heading there by now."

"Sure," Yarin said without emotion.

Nodwel led the small child toward the well at the center of the village, and as they walked, they both tried to keep their eyes from the awful sights around them.

"So, how old are you? I'd guess ten, maybe eleven, years old?" said Nodwel trying to break the

<Zaylyn ><Quest For The Sword Of Anthrowst ><By Katrina Mandrake-Johnston >   <Ch 21> < 73 >
uncomfortable silence surrounding them.

"I'm nine," Yarin answered plainly.

The dwarf couldn't think of anything else to say to the boy. He was trying to pick his words carefully for fear of saying something that would upset the boy any further, as Yarin was already in a very tender and unstable state.

"I like the way the setting sun glints off your axe," Yarin said.

"Yeah?" Nodwel said pleased that he had spoken. *"Yarin's right,"* he thought with worry, *"the sun is setting. We don't have much time left until dark. I hope the others are well, and on their way to the meeting place."*

"We'll be dead by dawn," Yarin stated calmly.

"Don't say that. We'll make it," he encouraged, but he thought, *"You're probably right kid."*

When they arrived at the well, Nodwel exclaimed, "Oh no, what's this?"

Strewn across the ground were several dead spiders. They were huge creatures. Alive, they would have stood about four feet high. Their bodies were about the size of a small child. Each leg was at least two to three inches thick. Nodwel counted four of them. Beside the well and the bodies of the giant spiders, were three dead villagers in front of a small building.

"Stay close to me," Nodwel told Yarin.

"Okay," he said meekly.

Yarin remembered seeing a similar looking spider in one of his picture books. His mother had given the book to him and his brother on their last birthday. She had traveled all the way to Vackiindmire to purchase it for them at a bookstore there.

These spiders looked similar to a tarantula, only much larger. He noticed the tiny brown hairs all over their bodies, almost giving the appearance of fur. Yarin had read that these hairs enabled the spider to sense vibrations. This was how the spider could hear approaching prey and predators.

The numerous eyes of each spider were tiny in proportion to the rest of it. The eyes were clustered close together in a tiny area in the center, positioned over the two large fangs. Being as large as these spiders were, each eye was a little smaller than an egg.

Each spider, in addition to its eight legs, also had two smaller legs in the front that it could use almost like hands to manipulate its food and feel around.

The fangs were tucked neatly under the front of each spider. Yarin thought to himself that the front of the spiders looked almost like two furry fingers that had been curled into a fist, the eyes being between the two knuckles and with the smooth, black, claw-shaped fangs curling underneath at the second knuckle.

Yarin could remember how he and his brother had been fascinated with spiders and insects. That time had passed.

Being wary of the spiders, Nodwel and Yarin approached the small building. It was a home belonging to one of the villagers. Nodwel peered inside the house through the open door and discovered two dead women. He entered and saw that he was in the first of two rooms. This was the kitchen and living area of the home and the second room was a bedroom.

He dragged the bodies out of the house and laid them beside the others, while Yarin watched. After seeing the pale look on the boy's face, he realized, *"Maybe this wasn't such a good idea... Well, he would have seen the bodies anyway when we went inside. I guess I could have told him not to look or something. But then where was he supposed to look? There's death all around us, and now giant spiders added to the mix. I mean, he probably knows more than half the people here in some way or another, but what am I supposed to do? What can I possibly do?"* "Yarin, you okay?" he asked.

Yarin nodded, but he looked terrible and was trembling slightly. His eyes were wide with fear, and he kept looking nervously about, and up to the sky and the quickly fading light.

"Let's get inside, alright? We'll stay here for now and wait for the others," Nodwel said, and then upon further observation of their surroundings, stated, "This house has been somewhat barricaded against the creatures. It looks like Borin's work. Of course, I could be mistaken... Are you sure you're all right?" Nodwel asked with concern.

<Zaylyn ><Quest For The Sword Of Anthrowst ><By Katrina Mandrake-Johnston >   <Ch 21> < 74 >

Yarin just nodded.

The bedroom, which Nodwel could see clearly, was bare except for a bed with a heavy wooden frame. The bed had been raised up to block the only window in the room and could be removed quickly enough in an emergency. In the front room, a large brown couch was turned over and upright against the wall next to the door for use as a barricade if the need came. There was a small wooden chair and table with a few eating utensils scattered about the room.

Nodwel eased the couch down to the floor so Yarin could sit upon it. The boy sat, curling his legs tightly up against his chest until his knees were almost to his chin. Yarin waited silently and patiently, staring out the open door.

Nodwel mentioned, "I can see well in the dark; something I inherited. I'll be able to see if anything comes for us, and we'll have time to escape if we need to. Don't worry, okay?"

Nodwel stood at the doorway and watched for his companions and for any signs of danger. He dreaded the fact that night would soon fall upon them all and that the creatures might return once again.

Nodwel's mind was racing, "*Where are they? They should have been here by now! Okay, I'm getting carried away here. There's still plenty of time before the sun passes below the horizon... But who knows if these creatures are even going to wait until that time? They could be upon us any moment, if they wanted to. Perhaps they are already here? No, I can't be thinking like that. We'll have time. I have no idea how we are going to go about preparing for whatever awaits us during the night, but we'll do our best. If anything, my main goal is to protect Yarin and the others as best as I can.*"

Soon Weena and Vordin came into view. "Over here!" Nodwel called out to them.

When Weena saw the spiders, she cried out suddenly, "Oh! They're huge! They're not alive, are they?"

Keeping their distance, Vordin and Weena began to edge toward the spiders, nearing the house where Nodwel was waiting for them. "I've never seen spiders like this before," Weena told Vordin, as she clutched his arm tightly, "I didn't think ones this big even existed... I can't stand spiders. They're absolutely hideous. I squash even the tiniest of them... Would you just look at the fangs on them!"

Vordin felt Lorenta stir in the backpack, as Weena's words had made her uneasy. Weena's grip was intensifying more and more, as they slowly approached where the spiders lay. "They're dead, Weena, relax," Vordin told her.

"Of course they're dead. I can see that," Weena snapped defensively, trying her best to sound brave, "If I thought they were alive, I'd be fleeing in the opposite direction."

"*Let me guess. Right now she's imagining one of them coming to life, and is about ready to explode from the terror,*" he thought to himself with a silent chuckle.

"Do you really think I'd even get this close to these things if I knew that they could just jump up and..." Weena started to say and then let out a muffled whimper and made a frantic dash for the safety of the house.

When she reached the doorway and the dwarf, she suggested, "They must have also attacked the villagers."

Vordin eyed the villagers as he passed them and joined his companions in front of the house. "No," Vordin told her, "Looks like the Killnarin got these ones."

"Still..." Weena said.

Nodwel greeted them with a firm handshake and ushered them both inside. "This is Yarin," he told them.

"Hello," Yarin said looking up at them.

"I'm Vordin," he said with a slight wave to the boy.

"My name's Weena," she told him kneeling down to Yarin's eye level. "You must be the bravest little boy I have ever met," she said with a smile and got the beginnings of one in return.

<World of Zaylyn ><Quest For The Sword Of Anthrowst ><By Katrina Mandrake-Johnston ><Ch 22>

CHAPTER 22 = REUNION

<Zaylyn ><Quest For The Sword Of Anthrowst ><By Katrina Mandrake-Johnston >   <Ch 22> < 75 >

Candra, Dendrox, and Asdella reached the well, and then, locating their companions, entered the small dwelling.

Nodwel, upon setting eyes on Asdella, exclaimed, "You're alive!"

"That I am," she said with a smile.

Nodwel's expression showed joy and relief at discovering at least one of his friends was still alive.

Weena thought to herself, "*I'm so glad for him. It had seemed like he was feeling somehow responsible for the deaths of his friends. No one can be responsible for everyone. No one can protect everyone all the time. He shouldn't put himself down for the loss of his friends...*" then scolding herself she thought, "*Wake up, Weena! Why don't you follow your own advice? You didn't start learning magic for no reason at all. You still feel useless. I can't bring those kids back. They died. I could have done things differently. Maybe if I had acted more quickly instead of hiding in the forest while the school burned, I might have been able to save someone at least, probably more. My brother would still be alive today, of that I'm certain. It was all my fault.*" Tears started to well up in her eyes and then she told herself, "*Oh please, this is not a time to start getting all emotional over the past. Don't show that you're weak, Weena. Be strong like Candra.*"

Asdella gave Nodwel's beard a playful tug and said, "I thought you'd never get back. You missed all the action. I killed one of the beasts. I told you I would."

"You did? And managed it without a scratch, eh? You sure are a fierce one aren't ya?" Nodwel said and nudged her shoulder gently with one of his large fists. This actually looked quite comical, since Asdella was taller than the dwarf by a fair amount.

"I still say the axe is better than a puny sword," he teased.

"Oh really? And why is that, old fool?" she questioned in a playful manner.

"Well," he said pulling out his axe and balancing it in his hands. "Yes," he said grunting to accentuate that the weapon had a fair weight to it. "This here is, I think, about the best weapon there is. It can be used as a bludgeoning weapon to crush a man's skull, or perhaps that of an obnoxious warrior woman," he said with a smile directed at Asdella. "And, it can slice clean through an offending limb, say one holding a puny sword," he added with a wink and continued, "granted the user of the axe has incredible strength in his arms, say that of a handsome dwarf."

"Ah, well, I see little man," Asdella said with a smirk, "But you see, with a sword, I can slice through all the major tendons before that clumsy piece of metal could be wielded, especially if the user of the axe has to chase after me with stubby little legs."

"Really?" he said to her. "*That's Asdella. I'm glad she's as happy to see me, as I am her. Most of the time I don't have the faintest idea of what's going on in that muddled head of hers. Maybe that's a good thing. To tell the truth, I thought she might turn on me, blaming me for not returning quickly enough and for Narr's death and perhaps Borin's too wherever he may be,*" Nodwel thought slightly nervous.

She ignored him now and said, "I'm Asdella," to the unfamiliar faces.

"Oh, I'm sorry," Nodwel apologized, "Introductions are in order. Everyone this is Asdella..."

"I already said that," she interrupted.

He gave her a smirk and continued, "As I was saying, this is Asdella. This little boy here is Yarin. I found him hiding in an oak cabinet at the general store. Do you think that's similar to the way you survived Vordin?" he asked him.

"I don't know. A hollow tree was how I escaped them. The wood cabinet might have had the same effect. I really have no clue," Vordin replied.

The dwarf continued his introductions, "Anyway, this is Vordin. This fine lady is a powerful wizard or sorceress or whatever you want to call it, and her name is Weena."

Weena was about to protest the part about being a 'powerful' wizard, but on second thought, she just politely nodded a greeting to Asdella.

"Yarin, the lady elf there is Candra, and over there is Dendrox," Nodwel told him.

Yarin said meekly to the new arrivals, "Hi." Then he looked up at Asdella and said innocently, "Aren't you cold? Where's all your clothes?"

<Zaylyn ><Quest For The Sword Of Anthrowst ><By Katrina Mandrake-Johnston >   <Ch 22> < 76 >

At this, all she could do was laugh and smile at him. Asdella then noticed that Vordin was intensely studying her nearly naked body and she snapped angrily at him, "What are you looking at?!"

"Oh come on," Nodwel stepped in quickly, "He doesn't mean anything by it and you know it."

Her mood suddenly and drastically changed as she joked, "Well, I guess I can't really blame him. I am extremely beautiful. Oh! And this body is simply exquisite!"

Candra saw that there was a pain buried deep in this woman, surfacing now and then briefly in her words and expression. Candra wondered, "*Could she have been abused? From what Nodwel told us of her on our way to Dexcsin, she seems to treat her body as a tool, a distraction to be used in battle, as if it were separate from herself. This insane rage, that Nodwel spoke of, must stem from somewhere. I haven't seen her in battle, but I can sure imagine. She certainly is interesting, but already I'm assuming too much. I really don't know anything about her.*"

"Nodwel," Asdella said suddenly somber, "about what you said."

"What?" he asked.

"I killed the beast, but I would be dead now if not for these two passing by," she said gesturing toward Dendrox and Candra. She continued, "I used the amulet. The one that Nimdor used to have. We decided to take what we could and split up, each of us taking a group of villagers. We took what magic items we could find off Nimdor's body, as it was nearby. I took the healing amulet. When the beasts found out where we were, they all attacked together tearing down the very walls to get at us. We figured that we would have a better chance separately as trying to take on all of them together would have been suicide. All those under my care got slaughtered except for a small girl. I had given it to her for protection while I was in battle against the creature that had been following us. I hadn't expected to live and was hoping that she would. It's really good to see you, old friend. Really, it is."

"I see," said Nodwel.

There was a short pause of silence before Dendrox broke in, "Does anyone know where all those dead spiders came from? They're gigantic!"

Asdella shrugged her reply.

"Don't know," Nodwel commented, "It was like this when I arrived here with Yarin."

"Any helpful hints on how to kill these creatures?" Asdella asked them.

"We've discovered that these beasts have a name. They're called Killnarin," Nodwel told her.

Weena added, "Apparently, a wizard named Dranngore summoned them. Whatever purpose he has for these creatures, we are clueless to it. Why he would have them attacking helpless villages is beyond me. Perhaps, the slaughter is simply a reward for the creatures. Or maybe to prepare them for something larger."

Vordin added, "One thing for sure is that the creatures are thorough in making sure no one is left alive to talk about it."

"So, there is a good chance that they'll be back tonight then?" Dendrox asked.

Vordin said, "Well, they did send a scout out after me. They must have come back to Nilnont. I don't know. Maybe they caught my scent or just happened to be searching for anyone that might have escaped them. It found me, and if it weren't for The Black Shadow, I would have been dead for sure."

"The Black Shadow?" Asdella scoffed with disbelief.

Vordin explained, "He brought me over the mountains, showed me the Killnarin that Candra and Dendrox had killed, and told me of Dranngore and the Sword of Anthrowst. A fairy queen also told me of the wizard and the sword."

"You're saying that you met The Black Shadow, that he actually saved your life instead of taking it," Asdella snapped accusingly at him, "and that he spoke to you, and then on top of that, that you met some ancient fairy queen who is thought to exist only in myth and legend?"

"Well, yes, but no one believes me. I didn't think what happened to me would be such a rarity," Vordin admitted.

"Well it would be, if it were true," Asdella snapped in response.

"It is!" Vordin protested, "Why would I lie? What would I have to gain by it?"

"I don't know. You tell me," she continued.

<Zaylyn ><Quest For The Sword Of Anthrowst ><By Katrina Mandrake-Johnston >   <Ch 22> < 77 >

"I…" Vordin started.

"Asdella, leave the poor lad alone," Nodwel told her.

"Okay, yeah, I believe you," she said to Vordin, eyeing him suspiciously, and then her lips spread into a sly smile, "I was just testing you. Maybe it is true. Strange unbelievable things have been known to happen now and then."

"Come on, we have work to do," Nodwel commanded.

"This is our camp for tonight?" Asdella asked.

"It'll have to do. What do you think? Borin's work?" the dwarf asked her.

Asdella eyed the barricaded room and then said, "Could be. He did head off in this direction, last I saw of him. You find his body?"

"No. I did find Narr's though," he said gravely.

"Oh," she said without emotion, but her eyes betrayed her as the sorrow began to build. She finally had to look away from him in an attempt to hide it.

Nodwel was furious with himself, *"Damn it. Think before you blurt things out! You're getting clumsy you old fool. Narr and Asdella had been close. You always saw them teasing each other, flirting every once in awhile. It never amounted to anything, Asdella being so reclusive in her emotions when it came to things like that. But still, there was a certain something between them. Nodwel, you're a damn idiot. She didn't need to know that about Narr. Oh sure, she seems like a killing machine without any emotions whatsoever, but she is still a person and has to have some sort of feelings, even if they are buried way down deep. That's where it's going to hurt her the most."*

Yarin bravely spoke up to the group, "Narr was the one who helped to protect my family. They all were killed, but I survived."

"Well kid," Asdella addressed Yarin, "I guess in the end, Narr and I were more alike than I thought. I was going to be dead for a kid too, but I got a second chance. He didn't." Yarin was confused and wondered if she were still speaking to him or not. She continued, "We used to have many great arguments about things like that, you know? I mean, in what situations we'd be willing to die. Well, I guess you win this one, Narr. I am like you. I do care about something. There, I've said it." She paused and looked around the room. "I'm going for a walk," she decided abruptly.

"Are you crazy?! It's dark now. If those creatures are out there already, you might be killed!" Dendrox told her.

"I am going for a walk," she repeated, and then with a threatening glare, she pushed past him and out through the door.

Nodwel mouthed the words 'Let her go' and then thought, *"See even Asdella has a heart. A cold and icy one, but still it's there. Poor thing. The persistent flirtations from Narr probably was the closest to love she had allowed herself. Nothing can be done about it now. Damn, why didn't I keep my mouth shut. She's probably gone to find him. She needs the visual confirmation; words aren't enough for her. Well, if trouble starts, at least I have a good idea of where she might be. Please, please, let this be a peaceful night."*

Yarin was fascinated by these so-called 'warriors' as the dwarf had called them. A few of them seemed just as weak and frightened as he was, but because of them, he had been saved from the bitter loneliness and helplessness he had felt when hiding in the cabinet. The time he had spent there seemed like an eternity. He felt as if there was hope now, even though he had seen several strong 'warriors' fall before the vicious Killnarin.

Everyone in the party needed sleep, but they all were experiencing the restlessness that fear and danger brings. Nodwel distributed the rations he had collected and discarded the two small sacks. He put Asdella's portion into his own pouch for her when she returned. Everyone ate slowly and silently, except for Yarin who just stared blankly at his share of the bread and cheese.

"Honey, aren't you going to eat something?" Weena asked Yarin.

"My belly feels like it has a big lump in it. I don't want to eat," Yarin said on the verge of tears.

"None of us feels like eating right now, but we need to keep our strength up," she told him.

"I want my mother. I want my brother. I want everything to go back the way it was. I want to be

<Zaylyn ><Quest For The Sword Of Anthrowst ><By Katrina Mandrake-Johnston >   <Ch 22> < 78 >
able to go home," Yarin cried.

Weena took him into her arms and tried to comfort him as best as she could. "Dendrox? Could you pack his food away for him?" Weena asked, "He might feel like eating later."

"Sure, I guess," Dendrox answered.

"*Great, now she's got him babysitting. We're all going to get killed,*" Candra muttered to herself.

Vordin removed his backpack and placed it gently in the corner by the door, where he hoped Lorenta would be safe from clumsy feet. He was unsure whether the magical compartment would protect her against such things. He then sat down beside Yarin and Weena on the couch.

Nodwel motioned for Candra and Dendrox to join him over by the bedroom door. They did so, and Nodwel whispered to them, "As we all well know, those three won't be any help in battle. If anything, they'll just get in the way. These creatures are far too dangerous. For us to be worrying about those three while in battle, might distract us enough to lose our own lives."

"So what do you suggest?" Dendrox whispered.

Candra said coldly, "Just forget about them. If they're of no use and liable to inhibit our own attacks, we don't need them. If they can't fend for themselves, well that's just too bad."

"No one gets sacrificed," Nodwel said angrily, "I wasn't suggesting that. I would never even think of something like that! The whole purpose of us coming here was to save the innocent."

"I don't care anymore," Candra blurted out, "This is insane. We're all going to get slaughtered. If everyone can't make it on their own, good riddance. I'm not about to get killed because I'm coddling someone who's hanging all over me to protect them."

"Well I'm sorry you feel that way. We'll just have to remember that when one of those beasts is gnawing on your leg, okay? We'll just stand there and watch," Nodwel snapped angrily.

"Listen, there's no use in bickering like this. We're all frightened," Dendrox told them, "There's no need for panic." Candra glared at him. "Yes, you're frightened too, Candra," said Dendrox, "even though you won't admit it. We all need to stick together in this or we won't have the slightest chance of survival, Candra, and you know it."

"Okay, fine. So what do you think we should do about them?" Candra asked Nodwel.

"Thank-you. Now as I was saying, they won't last very long if the creatures attack. Yarin survived in that cabinet, but no one but him is small enough to hide in there. We'll have to somehow make our way back to the general store though."

"So, hide the boy. That sounds good. What about the other two?" added Dendrox.

"Well, that's where I need some suggestions," Nodwel said. Then, a guilty look spread across his face as he noticed that Weena, Vordin, and even Yarin, who had reduced his crying to a teary-eyed sniffling, were staring at them blankly. They had apparently heard every word despite their hushed tone.

Weena took Yarin by the hand and walked over with Vordin to where the others were standing. "So we're expendable, Candra?" Weena said in a hurt voice.

Candra didn't let her gaze falter.

"Weena, it's just fear talking," Dendrox told her, trying to keep peace between the two women.

"It would be nice to be able to have some say into our own fates," Vordin told them.

<World of Zaylyn ><Quest For The Sword Of Anthrowst ><By Katrina Mandrake-Johnston ><Ch 23>

CHAPTER 23 = LORENTA EXPLORES DEXCSIN

Meanwhile, Lorenta had escaped the confines of the backpack and crawled out through the open door unseen. Once outside, against the wall of the building and away from the door, she transformed. Lorenta looked up at the moon with human eyes and felt the chill night air against her human skin.

She left the group to their quarrels and walked silently away from the building to explore the village. She knew it would be dangerous, but the excitement led her on. Just being somewhere other than the dreary old hut and woods she had lived in all her life was a thrill. As she wandered, she saw numerous bodies.

The stench of death was everywhere. She covered her nose with her hand and was reminded of

<Zaylyn ><Quest For The Sword Of Anthrowst ><By Katrina Mandrake-Johnston >   <Ch 23> < 79 >
her encounter with the owl at the sight of her missing fingers. In her spider form, it was her wounded front leg with its missing tip and another leg which formed together to create this human arm, so only a thumb and forefinger remained now on her right hand. It was becoming a constant reminder of how lucky she was to be alive and how precious life is.

"*Why,*" she wondered, "*did these creatures kill all these people? It's obvious that they weren't meant for food. It's as if they were killed purely for their entertainment, playing with these people's lives. It goes against the laws of nature. I've seen enough. I'm going back.*"

When Lorenta returned to the area near the well, she saw for the first time the bodies of the giant spiders strewn across the ground. She had been curious about them ever since she first heard the others talking about them, but was nervous about what she might discover. She crept closer to one of the spiders and knelt down beside it.

"*He's huge! I've never heard of a spider reaching this enormous size. My size as a spider increased when I gained my human form, but this is amazing. Where could they have come from?*"

Upon further examination, she noticed a wound along its abdomen. "*This slash was made from a sword! No, this is what I was fearing! The humans attacked them! Why? I didn't see any of the bodies with evidence of spider attacks.*"

Just then she saw a long hairy leg reach up from the well. Then another leg appeared and then another. Lorenta stood up. A giant spider was now standing on its eight legs in front of the well. Spiders aren't usually tolerant of another spider within their territory and most often see the invading spider as being either a threat or food, or both. But she was here as a human and not as another spider. She didn't know what to expect. The spider padded over the earth toward Lorenta.

She stood motionless, afraid of what might happen. It touched her lightly with one of its front legs and then began nudging her toward the well.

Then Lorenta felt as if there were a heavy weight settling into her mind. At first, she was going to fight this invasion into her mind, but then gave in and let it envelope her. To her astonishment, she heard a voice within her head which said, "The creatures… It's safe in the well… Go… Hurry…"

Suddenly an arrow flew through the air, sinking into the abdomen of the spider.

<World of Zaylyn ><Quest For The Sword Of Anthrowst ><By Katrina Mandrake-Johnston ><Ch 24>

CHAPTER 24 =   DISCOVERING LORENTA

Lorenta collapsed to the ground, screams of agony and fear filling and echoing within her head. The spider recoiled from her mind, leaving Lorenta confused and disorientated.

"Damn arm. So much for my aim. Now I'll have to fire yet another arrow just to finish it off," Candra muttered to herself as she pulled another arrow from her quiver.

As Lorenta stood, she could see Candra standing in the doorway of the nearby building. The room behind the elf was filled with the light from Vordin's magical lantern, as it was now dark. Lorenta recognized its strange glow. "*They must be conserving the fuel of Weena's lantern. Good idea,*" she commented to herself.

Her head still felt hazy and it took her a moment to realize what was happening. Candra's sleek form, illuminated by the light behind her, aimed her bow in Lorenta's direction. A slender arrow was between the elf's nimble fingers. The string was held taut, ready to loose the arrow.

"*No… The spider…*" she realized. Unsure of what exactly had taken place during the peculiar communication between herself and the spider, this was the first time that she really noticed the arrow protruding from the creature. She hoped desperately that it wasn't too late to save him.

"No! Don't!" she screamed and leapt in front of the spider. She wasn't sure if this would stop the thief from firing, but she had to do something. She also hoped that Candra had enough control to still have a choice in whether she fired or not, as stopping the arrow with her body wasn't something that Lorenta really wanted.

"What the… Hey! You stupid villager! Can't you see I'm trying to save your pathetic life? Get out of the way!" Candra barked at her.

"What's going on?" Nodwel asked as he stepped into the doorway.

<Zaylyn ><Quest For The Sword Of Anthrowst ><By Katrina Mandrake-Johnston >   <Ch 24> < 80 >

"What is it?" Vordin asked with curiosity as he poked his head into view.

Candra explained as she lowered her bow, "I could have killed the thing with one shot, if my wounded arm hadn't affected my aim so. I would have been able to put more strength behind it too. Looks like it will have to suffer a slow death because of it. I think a mercy kill is definitely in order here, but this damn villager I found keeps getting in the way." Seeing the look of terror on Lorenta's face she told her, "Oh calm down, I wouldn't have hit you. My aim's not that bad, even with my arm in this state."

"Vordin! Do something! Stop her!" Lorenta pleaded, desperately trying to protect the wounded spider.

"Lorenta?" he exclaimed in surprise, as he thought she was still hidden inside the backpack. "What are you doing?" he asked her, coming out of the house.

"Hey, what's going on out there?" Dendrox called from inside, "Yarin's panicking. I don't want to leave the kid."

"It's okay," Vordin called back.

Candra replaced the arrow into her quiver and swung the bow over her shoulder. "Okay, what is it this time?" Candra said giving Vordin a distrusting look.

"How can you possibly know this woman?" Nodwel asked him. His face was stern. "That spider doesn't look as if it will cause us much of a threat anymore, so explain away."

Vordin realized that attempting a lie wouldn't be very useful. He assumed that they would see right through him if he did. He wasn't even very good at telling the truth. "Her name's Lorenta. She's my companion. She's been traveling with me for awhile now. She's a shape-shifter of sorts and she's been riding along in my backpack. Being different, she thought it best that she remain hidden, especially with everything going on like this. Don't worry, we can trust her. At least hear what she has to say," Vordin said with a pathetically hopeful look on his face.

They looked at Lorenta expectantly. Dendrox came to the doorway with Yarin holding on tightly to his hand. Weena peered out from behind Dendrox, deathly afraid of the giant spider.

"Hey, that thing's still alive. You want me to take it out?" Dendrox asked the group.

"No," Lorenta said frantically, "Please, listen! This spider here, he was trying to warn us!"

"Warn us of what?" Candra said in a threatening tone, showing that she wasn't one to be toyed with.

"We must help him!" she begged, "He was trying to lead us to safety! The others were trying to do the same, but were attacked." Lorenta felt hot tears welling up in her eyes as her words seemed to fall on uncaring ears.

"Enough with this nonsense! Candra just saved your life. This is your gratitude? To fabricate this insane story?" Nodwel said to her unkindly. The stress of the past few days had taken its toll on the dwarf who was usually quite friendly.

"No, please. I don't know how, but he spoke to me through some sort of telepathy. Please believe me! We have to help him! Can't you see he's dying?" Lorenta pleaded.

"I've heard enough," Nodwel said with a stern look of intolerance. He crossed his arms and remained in his firm stance. His distrusting gaze did not falter.

Lorenta found herself becoming more and more wary of Vordin's companions. *"What if they find out my true identity? Will they treat me in the same manner as this spider here? Kill first and ask questions later? It seems to be human nature to do so. Just look at these others. They were just trying to help these villagers, to take them to safety. Their kind gesture was met with bloodshed. Suddenly I don't feel so bad about my encounter with that 'magic stealer'. He got what he deserved... No, I can't think like that. If I do so, that makes me no better than them. I have to stay in human form as long as possible around them. My life would be in grave danger if they knew. But when daylight returns, I have no choice in my form. What will I do then? I'll just have to overcome that obstacle when the time comes. Oh no, here comes that berserk warrior woman!"*

<Zaylyn ><Quest For The Sword Of Anthrowst ><By Katrina Mandrake-Johnston >   <Ch 25> < 81 >

CHAPTER 25 =   KILLNARIN OR GIANT SPIDERS

Asdella came into view, walking slowly toward them.

"Asdella!" Nodwel called to her raising a hand to greet her. "Well, Lorenta, or whoever you are," he said to her unkindly, "Looks like your precious spider is done for now. As soon as she sees that thing, she'll slice and dice until nothing's left. We no longer have a say in it. Go ahead, try to stop her. It will only get her to attack you as well."

"Please… He said that there's safety in the well. They must have an underground lair of some sort," Lorenta said to them.

Asdella approached them calmly and said, "Looks like a trap and she's the lure, but I'd rather face a bunch of giant spiders than those foul demons."

"She must be taking Narr's death worse than I thought. To pass up a battle? Even a wounded and dying creature wouldn't have invoked mercy from her before," Nodwel commented to himself.

"So who's this?" Asdella asked.

Candra repeated what Vordin and Lorenta had told them.

Lorenta pleaded with them again, "We have to hurry! He said the beasts are coming! Who knows how close they are… We have to get down into the well! We have to help him… We can't just leave him here to be killed!"

"We can put it out of its misery," Nodwel told her.

"No! We have to help him!" she protested.

"Looks like we're taking it with us," Asdella commented. Lorenta was surprised to be getting help from the one she expected the least.

"There is no way I'm getting close to that thing," Weena said, her fear showing through, "And I'm especially not going to help carry it down into a well with its fangs so close to my skin."

"Will no one help?" Lorenta asked desperately.

Vordin shook his head. He too was afraid, agreeing with what Weena had said.

Dendrox added, "We'd end up falling down the well ourselves trying to maneuver down a ladder with such a huge load. We aren't even sure if there is a ladder."

"You wouldn't leave one of your own here. You'd find some way of making the journey," Lorenta said with frustration.

The others stood silent.

"Okay, looks like I'm taking the spider down myself then," Asdella spoke up. "Bunch of scared wimps," she joked.

Lorenta felt a wave of relief at Asdella's words. Asdella picked up the giant spider awkwardly, trying to take the weight on her back and keep an arm free as well. She finally got the spider positioned so its wounded abdomen was behind her head, the front of the spider was resting on her lower back, and its many legs were dangling weakly about her. Asdella's left arm was behind her trying desperately to hold the spider in place at its mid-section.

Lorenta had the strength to carry the spider herself, but she didn't want to have to try to explain that to them. Also she never had to climb in human form before. This would be a new and awkward task for her.

"Lorenta, see if someone has a rope and then strap this thing onto me. I think I can manage the climb," said Asdella.

"Sure. Does anyone have a rope?" Lorenta asked timidly.

Nodwel chuckled slightly at the awkward display of Asdella and the giant spider. "You really intend to carry that thing down into that well, don't you?"

"What does it look like?" she said with a mocking smile, "You're the sort to have a rope. So hand it over."

"It just so happens that I found a rope, so here you go," the dwarf said to Asdella, as he took the rope from his pouch and handed it to Lorenta. "You do know that I think you're making a big mistake," he continued to tell Asdella, "That thing's going to bite you, especially where it's wounded and all."

<Zaylyn ><Quest For The Sword Of Anthrowst ><By Katrina Mandrake-Johnston >   <Ch 25> < 82 >

"Yeah, I know, and when has that ever stopped me before? Where's your sense of adventure? You can't have a little adventure without some danger, now can you?" she replied.

Lorenta wrapped the rope around the spider and the woman, at the same time trying her best not to aggravate the wound. She wanted to remove the arrow but feared she would do more harm than good if she made the attempt.

"There," she said as she finished tying the last knot, "But I'm not sure if that's going to hold."

"Well, it's the best we can do," Asdella told her, "Let's go." Asdella peered into the well. It was very dark but she could see that there were metal rungs set into the stone forming a ladder. With Lorenta's help, she lowered herself into the well with the spider. "Someone better have a lantern," Asdella grumbled, "Oh and Nodwel? You found rations, right? Could you grab mine then? Unless you want me stealing yours."

Lorenta lowered herself into the well, after Asdella and her burden.

The remaining group hesitated quite awhile before deciding.

"They're walking into an ambush," Dendrox said, "Even if Lorenta is on our side, she's clearly being tricked."

"We can't just let them face a battle alone," Vordin said to them, "Asdella may be an excellent warrior, but how well can she fight with that spider strapped to her back? Not to mention how quickly the venom will affect her if it bites her. She probably won't be able to survive a bite from that thing. What was she thinking? Does she have a death wish or something? We'll need her in battle if the Killnarin attack again."

"That's Asdella. There's usually no reasoning behind her thinking that I can see. I'm not about to argue with her about her decisions either. I would have better luck trying to move a boulder with a blade of grass," Nodwel told them, "I agree with Vordin though, we can't let them face an ambush alone."

"How well do you know Lorenta anyway? Are you sure she's trustworthy?" Dendrox asked Vordin.

"Well, I haven't known her very long actually, and I know not much more about her than I do any of you. The Black Shadow said to trust her though," answered Vordin.

"Well, that can't be good," said Candra, "But I'm not about to start turning on people again like before. Asdella seems to trust her, and I definitely don't want to make that woman angry by arguing about it." Candra stepped over to the well and called out, "What do you see down there? Does it look safe?"

Asdella called back, "What do you think I see? It's pitch black down here! You're the ones with the lanterns, aren't you? Hurry up! I feel a draft down here. Could be a tunnel."

Yarin pulled at Dendrox's arm. "What is it?" he asked the boy.

Yarin's eyes were wide with fear. "I hear them," he whispered, "The beasts are returning! Quick, we have to hide!"

Nodwel cursed, "Damn it, this is insane! We're wasting time! We'll all be trapped down there! How are we supposed to defend ourselves halfway down a ladder and in the dark? Vordin, give me that magic lantern of yours and hurry." Vordin did what he was asked. "Alright," Nodwel said as he went over to the well and held the lantern over it, "Can you see anything now?"

"Hurry, I hear them too," Vordin said beginning to panic, "It's them. It's the Killnarin for sure. We'll all be killed! Hurry! Are we going into the well or staying here?!"

"Just wait," Nodwel demanded. "Asdella!" he called, "Can you hear me? Can you see anything now with the light? Are you sure that there's a tunnel down there?"

"Yes, I'm sure. I can't tell where it leads, but it does lead somewhere," she answered.

"We should all stick together in this, which means down in that well," Nodwel decided, "Damn it. I still think this is a bad idea."

"I agree that we'll have a better chance fighting off a horde of giant spiders than even a few of the Killnarin," said Candra.

Between spiders and the Killnarin, the well did seem a better choice, but not by much. Everyone

<Zaylyn ><Quest For The Sword Of Anthrowst ><By Katrina Mandrake-Johnston >   <Ch 25> < 83 >
collected their supplies, and Weena lit her lantern with the flame box from her cloth pouch. Then as the howling sounds of the Killnarin began to close in on their location, they all followed Lorenta and Asdella in their descent into the well by the light of the two lanterns.

<World of Zaylyn ><Quest For The Sword Of Anthrowst ><By Katrina Mandrake-Johnston ><Ch 26>

<u>CHAPTER 26 =   THE SPIDERS</u>

Soon they could see the well water beneath them. Also a few feet above the water, they could now see what appeared to be an opening in the rock wall of the well.

"Hey," Asdella called out to the others, "I'm heading into the tunnel." She awkwardly made her way into the opening, being careful of the spider strapped to her back.

"What do you see?" Lorenta asked.

"It looks like a tunnel to me. There's enough room to stand, and it seems wide enough for at least two people to walk side-by-side. It's pretty dark though; I can't tell much from here. If it is a tunnel and if it stays like this for the length of it, we'll have no trouble traveling along it. And if we have to battle some horrible beast, it won't be so difficult to maneuver. Come on, I think it's safe," the warrior woman yelled out to the group and then waited for them to join her.

They discovered that the tunnel they were now in, sloped slightly downward. As they traveled along it, Vordin was reminded of the dream he had back in Rasindell's hut where Lorenta had betrayed him and sent millions of tiny spiders to engulf him. They eventually found themselves in a large chamber with many passages leading off in all directions. Including the short tunnel leading back up to the well, there was a total of eight passageways.

"Untie the rope," Asdella demanded, "I'm getting this thing off me."

Lorenta removed the rope and helped Asdella lower the spider to the stony floor of the cavern. "At least he'll be somewhat safe here. I wish there was something more we could do for him," said Lorenta.

"Besides put it out of its misery?" Dendrox added.

Candra said to Lorenta, "It is cruel to let the thing suffer like this, but I guess its fate lies in your decision. I'm not going to decide for you, when you've become so attached to it. You are a strange one."

Asdella looked around at their surroundings and said, "Okay, now what?"

"Doesn't look like this place is a natural formation," Weena said as she moved her lantern around trying to see better, "Perhaps some of it is, but several tunnels appear to have been cut into the rock. Could be that an ancient civilization once lived here in these underground passages."

The light from the two lanterns only dimly lit the large chamber. She stepped a bit closer, trying to examine the construction of one of the tunnels. "This is such an incredible find! Aren't any of you even a little bit interested? Do you think any of the villagers knew about this place?" she asked the others.

"Ah, curiosity… It can be a deadly thing sometimes," Nodwel muttered. His eyes darted nervously from tunnel to tunnel. Occasionally, his wary gaze fell on Lorenta, who was squatting next to the spider and whispering comforting words to it. *"I don't like this situation one bit,"* Nodwel thought, *"I feel that we may have been led into a trap, even more so now than before we descended into this eerie place. I just have a really bad feeling about this."*

"Oh… See here? In places where the soil and rock has crumbled… It's been repaired and the weaker points have been strengthened. It appears that this place gets regular maintenance. This is exciting," Weena said getting bolder with her exploration of the chamber.

Dendrox called quietly to her, "Weena, it would be wise not to get away from the group."

"Yeah, okay," she replied, but made no apparent effort to follow the advice, at least not right away.

Yarin was clearly afraid. His eyes were wide as he looked all around him, his fear keeping him alert. Yarin's heart pounded hard and fast in his chest. His ears almost hurt from trying to be aware of every tiny sound. He looked to Lorenta and the giant spider and didn't know what to think. All he knew was that he wanted to be safe and that's not what he felt here. To Yarin, both Asdella and Candra appeared calm and collected, and it was clear that they had not let their guard down, not even for a

<Zaylyn ><Quest For The Sword Of Anthrowst ><By Katrina Mandrake-Johnston >   <Ch 26> < 84 >
second. He could tell that Dendrox was on edge and so was Vordin. The dwarf wore a worried expression and Weena seemed to be oblivious to the fact that there could be danger here.

As Vordin did not want to cause the others to have further mistrust in Lorenta, he said to her only in his mind, with some part of him wishing that she could actually hear him, "*Lorenta, I hope you know what you're doing. To trust these spiders just because they say we should is probably not a good idea. You might have only seen what you wanted to see and not the reality. Perhaps this voice you hear inside your mind is there just because of some desperate need to be accepted. If that's the case, we are dead for sure.*"

Weena called out to them, "The tunnel repairs seem to be held and strengthened with some sort of strange substance. I think it's... web. A lot of it..." Weena quickly realized that this was the last place she wanted to be. Fear led her back to the safety of the group. "We really should get out of here as soon as possible. Maybe it's not as bad as we think up above. We should go back. We really should. We're in a whole nest of these giant spiders!" Weena urged with fright.

Candra told her, "Just relax. There's no immediate danger, at least not yet. Did you find out anything at all? Any bit of information could be helpful."

"Didn't you hear what I said? We are in a large nest of these huge spiders!" Weena explained in disbelief of the elf's words, "The webbing used to fortify the passages, the new and recently laid, suggests that there has to be quite a lot of them! We won't be able to escape! We can't possibly fight our way out, not after they find us! So, before they discover us and realize that dinner has stupidly walked right into their snare, we should leave! Right now! Come on! Please, I can't go all by myself!"

"First you have to calm down," Candra said to her with an annoyed look, "I'm not going back up to the surface, especially if there are Killnarin up there. So what do we know about these giant spiders, besides being large and creepy, with fangs and everything else?"

"I don't know!" Weena began, but then quickly changed her tone noticing the angry glare starting in Candra's eye, "It's peculiar behavior. Spiders don't live in colonies like ants and bees do, at least not that I've ever heard of. When baby spiders emerge from an egg sack, there are a lot of them that scatter, but that clearly isn't the case here."

"What else?" Candra asked.

"Why do you keep asking me all these questions? We're wasting time! We have to get out of here!"

"For one, she's trying to calm you down and stop you from drawing attention to us," Dendrox explained and then added, "Maybe we're dealing with some kind of advanced form of spider. They don't seem like ordinary ones, as we know them. Maybe the spider did communicate with her somehow." He asked Lorenta, "Sorry, what was your name again?"

"Lorenta," she answered remaining in her solemn state. She wasn't pleased with the way the spider, in his critical state, was being ignored. He was most likely their savior, and they were treating him as if his fate didn't matter one way or another. Lorenta added despite her feelings, "Yes, I agree. It is odd behavior."

"I want to leave! I have to get out of here! We all have to get out of here!" Weena said still in a panic, "We are in a nest of giant spiders! Hairy and hideous spiders with fangs the size of daggers, dripping with venom... I feel itchy, like tiny ones are crawling all over me! I have to get out! Which tunnel leads back to the well?"

"Shut up!" Asdella snarled, "Before I make you!"

"I'm sorry, it's just that..." Weena started, shocked at Asdella's intolerance.

"What's that noise?" Yarin asked, his voice choked with fear.

They all paused a moment in silence, trying to hear what Yarin had heard.

"I hear it. It sounds like... like... I don't know, like a drumming sound of some sort, like rain on a rooftop or something like that," said Dendrox.

Candra said, "Whatever it is, I don't like the sound of it."

A moment passed before Lorenta told them, "It's footsteps."

"What?" Vordin asked her.

<Zaylyn ><Quest For The Sword Of Anthrowst ><By Katrina Mandrake-Johnston >   <Ch 26> < 85 >

"Footsteps. There is web within the tunnels, allowing for easy movement through them. What you hear is the sound of footsteps padding along the webbing. There are quite a few of them, and they're coming from all directions." She was able to feel the vibrations of their movements even in her human form. Here, in this, she was more aware of her surroundings as she did not have only her ears to rely on. Lorenta then added, knowing that these next words would be ignored, "I'm sure they mean us no harm."

"Yeah, right," Candra laughed uneasily as she got ready for battle, as did the rest of the group, whether it was to run or fight.

The soft drumming of the footsteps gradually got louder as the spiders approached the chamber.

<World of Zaylyn ><Quest For The Sword Of Anthrowst ><By Katrina Mandrake-Johnston ><Ch 27>

CHAPTER 27 = SPIDER CONFRONTATION

"If they are part of some strange telepathic community, they aren't going to take it lightly that we have one of their members wounded and dying beside us. And it doesn't help that we're responsible for making it that way either," Nodwel said lifting his battle-axe from his back and holding it ready in his muscular arms.

Illuminated by the lantern light, at least one giant spider could be seen at the entrance to each tunnel. Several also came around to guard the short tunnel leading back up to the well, blocking their escape. Their party was surrounded and outnumbered. The spiders did not approach them, and once again there was silence.

"Ambush… This should be interesting," Asdella said with a grin.

"Tell me something," Dendrox asked her, "Which is it? Do you have a death wish? Do you think you're invincible? Or are you just plain nuts?"

"Maybe all three," said Asdella, "Maybe I just got bored and decided to create a situation full of awkward and dangerous obstacles just to see what happens. You know, see if we survive or not. It's all in fun. Don't you find this thrilling enough? We could always throw in a twist. Maybe see what happens if we hack up their friend here a bit. That would make it more interesting, you think?" Her sword was positioned so the blade tip was on the ground and she rested her hands on the hilt. She appeared to be just calmly waiting for something to happen. Dendrox wasn't sure if she were joking or not, so he just left it alone.

"Lorenta," Vordin said as he held the small dagger he had taken from Rasindell's hut, "can't you tell them we come in peace or something?"

"I can't talk to them. I'm not one of them. Even when this one was speaking to me in my mind, I was unable to speak back to him. As far as I know, they can only talk to us or maybe only to me. I don't know," she told him, "I wish I had the answers. I'm just as scared as you, you know. I have no idea what their intentions are."

"Oh great! You could have told us that before!" Dendrox snapped angrily, "You led us all to believe that you could somehow talk to the damn thing!"

"I didn't. I said that he spoke to me, and I told you what he said. I never said that I could speak to him," Lorenta protested.

"It doesn't matter now," Nodwel said to them, "We all made our decision to come down here, whether we had our suspicions or not."

"I'm sorry. I never knew what their intentions were when I suggested we follow," Lorenta apologized, "I just thought that maybe… I wanted to trust them… I wanted to believe that there was some hope, that all was not lost… I do know what the intentions of those 'demons' are, though. They kill and destroy. I'd rather be here with these spiders who perhaps have good intentions than to be slaughtered by those foul beasts."

"I agree, I like our odds better here than up there," Vordin added.

"Are you blind?! Have you not looked around us at the situation here?!" Candra said with a grim face, "We have chosen one death over another. Our odds are better here of receiving a quick and less painful death than above, where I'm sure those creatures would prolong it and torture us as long as

<Zaylyn ><Quest For The Sword Of Anthrowst ><By Katrina Mandrake-Johnston >   <Ch 27> < 86 >
possible before letting us die."

"What are they doing?" Weena managed to say, "Why are they all just standing there?"

Several moments passed. Then, what felt like a heavy weight tried to settle into each person's mind.

"What's going on?" Candra demanded.

"Don't fight it. They're trying to communicate with us. Let them into your mind," Lorenta told them.

"So they can take control and do whatever they want with me? Turn us against each other, so they can watch us kill each other? I'm not going to give up my mind to them," said Candra, "I'm keeping my wits about me and I think I speak for everyone too when I say that."

"I'd have to be pretty trusting to allow something like that, and right now, I am everything but," Nodwel commented.

Dendrox said, "We don't even know what their intentions are, and even if we did, I wouldn't agree to it."

Vordin added, "Yeah, they might be seeking revenge on us for their wounded member. If they want into my head they'll have to force their way in. Sorry, Lorenta."

Yarin crouched down on his knees holding his head, trying to keep them out. Weena placed a hand on his back to comfort the frightened boy.

Weena suggested to them all, "Try to imagine an empty room, and the force trying to enter as one of the walls. Push with your mind against this wall as hard as you can and hold it back. That works for me at least."

"Alright, I'll try that," said Asdella.

"Lorenta? Are you going to let them in?" Vordin asked her.

"I have to try. It's our only way of finding out anything," Lorenta told him, letting the weight settle and envelope her mind as before.

A long silence passed while the spiders spoke to Lorenta, while the others, still wary of a possible attack, waited nervously for a response.

Finally, Lorenta addressed them. "They spoke of the creatures that attacked the villagers. Several spiders came to the surface last night to make an attempt to save some of the people by dragging them down into these underground passages. They were attacked and killed, as we saw, and not by the beasts. The Killnarin continued their attack upon the people and nothing more could be done. A further attempt to help the people was decided as a lost cause, and that no more lives should be lost to their ignorance. This spider here went above tonight against the wishes of the others. He found us, and almost died, and probably will, for his brave and selfless rescue. They really don't trust us."

"They have good reason not to," Weena said.

Lorenta continued, "Anyway, they want us to drop our weapons. We're to go with them and wait until a decision has been made. Apparently their telepathic capabilities have enabled them to evolve into a prospering community much like you would find in any town or village."

"That's all very interesting, but there's no way I'm parting with my weapon," Asdella told her, "I never do."

"Neither am I. I'm the one that shot their friend here with an arrow, remember? As if I want to be weaponless when they learn that little bit of information," Candra said giving Dendrox a nervous glance.

"Well, I'm putting my pathetic little dagger away. It probably won't be of much use to me anyway in a fight," Vordin said tucking the dagger back into the side pocket of his backpack. He looked to Lorenta saying, "I'm hoping that this will be sufficient enough for them. I don't want to part with my only tool and means of defense."

"Don't look to me," Lorenta told them, "I'm just relaying their message."

Several moments passed in silence as the party stood there ready for action. Then, as if from nowhere, thick and sticky net-like webbing dropped down from the ceiling onto all of them. Everyone

<Zaylyn ><Quest For The Sword Of Anthrowst ><By Katrina Mandrake-Johnston >   <Ch 27> < 87 >
was instantly ensnared and the more they struggled, the more helpless they became, eventually falling to the floor of the chamber like wriggling worms. Luckily, Weena's lantern was extinguished in the process, eliminating the possibility of the webbing catching fire.

Several of the giant spiders, obviously the ones that had released the trap, descended down a series of narrow ramps that led from several small platforms near the ceiling of the chamber to the floor.

The spiders then proceeded to separate the struggling adventurers. Vordin's magical flask continued to light their way, although it was of little help to them as they couldn't discern one thing from another, as the spiders were now rolling the tightly bound captives toward the tunnel opposite the one leading up to the well.

Eventually, they stopped in a smaller but spacious chamber. Except for being incredibly dizzy, no one in the group was hurt except for a few minor bruises. Weapons and accessible belongings were stripped from the prisoners and placed in the center of the room. Then each person was pushed into separate alcoves in the rock wall. The alcove openings were sealed by use of the same thick and porous net-like webbing that had been used to capture them. All of the spiders then exited the chamber except one, who remained as a guard at the tunnel entrance which also happened to be the only exit.

Vordin's lantern was on the very top of the pile of their belongings, lighting the room in a dim glow. Vordin was thankful that the flask had not been broken, and found himself wondering if it even could be broken, as it had taken quite a beating. The clasp locking the metal door of the case to its side had held firmly, keeping it open, which he was also thankful for. The last thing he wanted, was to be in the dark as well during all this.

After some time, everyone managed to struggle free as the strength of the web had diminished greatly and most of the webbing had been removed when their weapons and items were taken. Asdella still had her sword, as the spider would have had to free her completely to remove the weapon from her.

Vordin, within his alcove which was only about three feet deep, looked around the circular chamber through the webbing. He could see that there were tiny holes in the ceiling, which let in light and fresh air. These were about the size of a rabbit hole, so they offered no hope of escape. He wondered if small animals ever fell through these holes and decided that this was probably so and partially how these giant spiders obtained their food.

"*Perhaps foolish adventurer for dinner and clumsy woodland animal for dessert. How did we get ourselves into this? What was the point of surviving my village? Instead of going somewhere safe, I foolishly agree to travel down to another village which I know is being attacked by the same creatures that slaughtered mine,*" he said to himself, "*And now I'm here awaiting my death, just as I did in that damn tree! And what about that poor kid? We take Yarin from the one place he might have been safe and drag him down here. There must be a way to escape. I won't just wait here! I have to figure something out.*"

"Is everyone all right?" Nodwel asked.

"I'm scared," Yarin said, his voice full of fear, "What's going to happen to us? Are they going to eat us?"

"Well, that ambush was sneaky, but they're obviously not too smart. This little bit of webbing they've celled us up with can't hold us. I'll have you all out in a second," Asdella said. Her first attempt to break through the webbing was with her sword and then in frustration with her bare hands. She found that she couldn't break the web, no matter how hard she tried. "What's going on? This isn't right!" she exclaimed.

They all tried to free themselves and their efforts had similar results.

"It can't be," Weena exclaimed in amazement, "but it's the only thing that could make sense."

"What?" Candra asked.

"It has to be a spell of some sort. It's the only explanation," she answered.

"How can they possibly cast spells or even know magic in the first place?" Dendrox muttered.

"I don't know. What are they going to do to us? I don't want to die…" Weena said as she started to cry.

"So what? We just wait here and accept whatever fate they decide for us?" Vordin said in

<Zaylyn ><Quest For The Sword Of Anthrowst ><By Katrina Mandrake-Johnston >   <Ch 27> < 88 >

frustration, "Can't you do some sort of counter spell or something, Weena?"

Weena replied between sobs, "I'm nothing. How many times do I have to tell you people that? I'm an amateur. So I got lucky twice. So what? I'm useless. I can't do magic. Not the way you want. Nothing that can help us."

"There has to be some way of escaping," Vordin said.

Dendrox said to him, "And then what? Brave a million giant spiders with all their strength, venom, and speed? Even if we fight our way through, then what? Back up the well to face who knows how many of those foul Killnarin? We have a better chance of survival if we just wait and see what options arise. I have no intention of going out without a fight."

Nodwel added, "What we need is a plan. We need to find out more about these spiders and what their intentions are. Any ideas? Lorenta seems to be our best bet at getting us through this. I agree with Dendrox. There's just too many of them to battle our way free."

Asdella announced, "I'm no good at plans. You know that Nodwel. I'm going to catch some much-needed sleep." Then she said calmly, "Oh and Weena?"

"Yes," she replied, still sobbing.

"Do shut up. I thought you were supposed to be somewhat intelligent," she said to her in an annoyed tone.

Weena tried to stifle her tears, mainly out of fear of angering Asdella.

"Nodwel," Vordin tried to whisper to the dwarf, "How can she take a nap at a time like this?"

"Don't ask. I have no clue either," he replied.

<World of Zaylyn ><Quest For The Sword Of Anthrowst ><By Katrina Mandrake-Johnston ><Ch 28>

CHAPTER 28 =   THE SPIRIT

Of course, Asdella could not sleep. Sleep had merely been an excuse to be left alone. She sat upon the cold rock floor with her tormented thoughts of Narr and his horrible death. Even though she tried not to think of him, she couldn't stop herself.

"What did he expect from me? That I would eventually fall in love with him, if he kept pestering me? Sure, he's the type that grows on you after awhile, even to the point where you start to take him for granted. I guess I got used to having him around, that's all. I'm just expecting to have some annoying remark or aggravation from him to put up with, nothing more. Now that he's gone, it doesn't feel right. All the unwanted attention he kept giving me, most of the time I couldn't get rid of him. I should have just given him a good punch in the nose every time he bothered me. I don't know why I could never bring myself to do that. I can't possibly miss him. I just need to get used to the peace and quite of not having him around, that's all. Could I have loved him? Even if I could have brought myself to feel something, then what? A kiss, a touch, for him to be near me... The only emotions I'll ever feel regarding that are hatred, disgust, and a feeling of violation. I would end up hating him. What we had was fine. It was comfortable. But I realize now that it wasn't. I find myself longing for something more now, wishing that there had been something more than the awkward but comfortable distance that I accepted for so long. I'm such a fool. Comfortable? What, that I didn't have to admit that I felt something for him? I should have tried. But it would have ended horribly and I would have lost one of my closest friends. I know it would have ended that way. But can I even call him a friend? I don't really allow myself to have friends, now do I? If you have friends and people close to you, they can be used against you, tortured and killed until you can bare it no longer. Then they win and you lose. But I have lost. What they did to me... What they did to the others... And now my heart is cold, and I am alone even when I am among people I call companions. But for that slim chance that it may have worked somehow for Narr and me... that this ball of hatred might have melted just a little bit... that someone might be able to connect with the inner me, the one that was lost to me so long ago... Perhaps it might have been worth the risk to let him get close. If I could feel something more than this cold and aching hollowness... If there was anyway that I could have somewhat of a normal life... It would have been worth it. I know that now. And now it's too late... I do miss him... And even more now that I can imagine that we could have had something more, like he wanted. I'll probably hate

<Zaylyn ><Quest For The Sword Of Anthrowst ><By Katrina Mandrake-Johnston >   <Ch 28> < 89 >
myself forever for this, for letting my chance slip by."

Figures I have to die for you to finally notice me.

"Who said that?" Asdella said as she instinctively raised her sword.

"Who said what?" Candra asked, "No one said anything just now."

"We've given up on the plan making for now. Everyone needs rest. Get some while you can," Nodwel added.

Asdella ignored them both. She was sure that she had heard someone speak to her.

Looks like you're just replacing one excuse to be miserable with another. You can't love because of your past and now you can't love because the only person you cared about is dead. Is that your excuse?

"Show yourself," she demanded.

"Nodwel, is she okay?" Weena asked.

"Asdella?" Nodwel bellowed, hoping that she was merely talking in her sleep and that he would wake her. She made no reply. Then he realized, *This might be the only way for her to deal with Narr's death: to sleep it off. I shouldn't wake her.* He told Weena, "I think it's best to leave her alone."

After hearing the voice twice now, Asdella was alert and defensive.

You can hear me? Asdella, you can really hear me? It's me! Don't you recognize my voice?

"Of course I do. That's why my weapon is drawn. You are not who you pretend to be, and you will die horribly for your choice of disguise. Narr is dead. I saw for myself," she whispered under her breath.

I know it must be hard for you, and I'm sorry, but it's me! I can't explain it. I think I might be a ghost or something. It's crazy, I know. You're the only one who can hear me. I can remember dying, I think. You can't see me, can you? Narr's voice said to her.

"No, I can't," she whispered very quietly, "You're not one of those damn spiders are you, because I didn't mind any of you much until you tried getting inside my head and started suggesting I part with my sword."

No, it's actually me, he tried to convince her.

"You do realize that I want to believe you're real. So… I will accept that by some strange miracle you actually are somehow," she decided, and then made sure her very real and serious threat was made extremely clear to him, "But, you better hope that I don't discover otherwise or my revenge will be violent and messy."

"*I can hear your thoughts,*" Narr told her, "*Maybe it would be a good idea to just think what you want to say, instead of saying it. I think you're making your new companions uneasy.*"

"*Alright,*" she agreed and asked within her mind, "*What's it like then?*"

"*Well, it's hard to explain,*" he told her, "*I don't have a body, so that's bad luck for you, eh?*" Then realizing that his attempt to lighten the situation was an utter failure, he said, "*Yeah, well, everything that has to do with a body is gone, like sight, smells, touch, taste, and things like that. Well, I don't need to eat anything ever again, so I guess my loss of taste won't bother me too much. Okay, it's weird, and I don't really know how I can do this, but I can experience these senses through others. What I think, is that somehow my energy can slip into someone and sort of share experiences. I can hear their thoughts, see through their eyes, experience their emotions, feel what they feel, maybe even taste what they taste. I have yet to try that one. I can sense things. That's how I see and feel. I really don't know how to describe it to you. You know, if you close your eyes and walk towards a wall, you get a weird feeling just before you hit it, and you just somehow know it's there? It's kind of like that. Well, I guess some would hit it without sensing it first, but you know what I mean, right? And I can sense a person's energy. Like if there is someone standing behind you, and you can tell there's someone there and maybe even who it might be without even looking? It's like that, only on a larger and more complicated scale. So far you're the only one that can hear me, or more likely, feel what I want to say. Maybe it's because I have a special connection with you. Can't hide from me now,*" he laughed, "*I can read your every thought. No more cold shoulder treatment for me this time. There's no*

<Zaylyn ><Quest For The Sword Of Anthrowst ><By Katrina Mandrake-Johnston >   <Ch 28> < 90 >

getting rid of me. Oh come on, what do I have to say to get you to smile?"

"It's just that all this is a little hard for me to accept," she admitted.

"How do you think I feel?!" he exclaimed, *"This is much harder for me to accept than it is for you! I'm dead! Is this even supposed to be happening to me? I don't have a body, I'm scared, I... I..."* Then Asdella could hear him let out a big breathy sigh inside her mind as he tried to calm himself. He finally said, *"I'm just relieved that I don't have to be alone in this anymore."*

"Lucky me," she thought sarcastically and not very kindly, *"I'm glad you're still alive in a way, but can't we talk later? All this talking within my head is starting to make it ache terribly."*

"Hey, sorry, but this is pretty frightening for me, alright?" he said starting to get upset with her, *"Plus, I'm thinking my thoughts at you, rather than speaking them, so I'm sorry if I'm rambling on and on. This is all new to me. You have my full attention now, I mean, who else am I going to talk to? No one else can hear me!"*

"Okay fine. If you need to talk, I'll listen. Just try not to overwhelm me," she allowed.

"Sure, Asdella," Narr agreed, trying to subdue the tension he was feeling and keep it from affecting her mind. *"Hey, I'm going to try something,"* he said with a mischievous hint to his voice, *"Tell me if you can feel this."*

An electric-like shiver ran along the length of Asdella's arm. *"Oh wow, was that you?!"* she exclaimed in astonishment, *"I could almost feel a hand run along my arm."*

"Who says it was my hand?" he joked.

"Oh stop it," she blushed and the corner of her mouth turned up in the beginnings of a smile.

"Ah, it worked! I knew I could cheer you up," he chuckled.

"It's good to have you back. So, tell me, how exactly do you move about?" she asked.

"Well, you know how I said I can sort of sense the presence of other people. I can move within the spaces, but like I said, I can't see things the way you do anymore. Imagine a dark room and everyone in it with a light around them. And I figure that like vision gradually adjusting to the darkness of a room, I have a feeling that as I become more accustomed to my new state, things will become clearer for me. My abilities have already improved quite a lot since I first died. At first, I was completely blind to everything; I couldn't sense or feel anything or anyone. Then I gradually became aware that Yarin was still alive. I'm glad Nodwel was able to find him. Asdella, I just want to stay with you for now, riding in the back of your mind where I feel safe. Alright? I felt so lost before: no one could hear me, no one could see me, no one could touch me. I'm also afraid that if I discover too much about my state, that I might move on to something different and lose you again. You're so incredibly tired, Asdella. Get some sleep. As far as I can tell, things seem safe enough for now."

"Alright," she thought to him, as she tried to get as comfortable as possible on the hard rock floor. Then to her surprise, she felt ghostly arms wrap around her, and she felt a sense of comfort that she had not felt since she was a very small child.

<World of Zaylyn ><Quest For The Sword Of Anthrowst ><By Katrina Mandrake-Johnston ><Ch 29>

CHAPTER 29 = YARIN'S DREAM

Meanwhile, Yarin, sitting as quietly as he could on the rock floor of his cell, listened to all that was happening around him. Everyone had their attention drawn elsewhere, and Yarin didn't mind, as he didn't want everyone fussing over him. He wanted to be alone.

"How did all this happen? A few days ago everything was fine. I was happy. My mother and brother were with me. This is like a horrible nightmare... Maybe I'll wake up soon... I want my mother... I want to see my brother..." Yarin cried trying not to make much noise, as he didn't want the others to hear. His head ached. His face was wet with tears. And, even though he fought it, he dozed off for the first time in two days.

He began to dream...

His mother and brother were standing beside him in an open field of green grass. The sky was clear blue, and the sun was shining brightly.

<Zaylyn ><Quest For The Sword Of Anthrowst ><By Katrina Mandrake-Johnston >   <Ch 29> < 91 >

Then suddenly he felt himself falling backwards. He was falling down a hole in the earth. As he fell, he could see his family reaching out to him from the top of the hole. Darkness surrounded him as he fell farther and farther away from his mother and brother.

He landed on wood. Large cabinet doors closed in front of him blocking the vision of his family. He pounded on the cabinet doors trying to break them open and to somehow get back up to his family. The doors wouldn't budge.

He heard a voice shouting. It was Narr. He was back in the store. His mother and brother were just on the other side of the heavy wooden doors. He heard the beast tear into the room.

Narr was shouting for them to get back, as he was going to try to hold off the beast. Yarin couldn't see anything. He had to get the doors open! He couldn't let it happen again! He pounded as hard as he could on the doors, but they wouldn't move.

The old man that had been with them let out a painful cry. Then his mother was screaming. A beast was snarling. Narr was shouting. Yarin heard objects breaking. He heard the sound of claws on steel. His brother let out a horrible sound and then there was the sound of something hitting the floor.

Soon there was silence. Narr was dead. His family was gone and so was the old man. Just the beast remained. Yarin could hear its heavy and raspy breathing as it searched for him. Its heavy feet pounded on the floor as it walked. It was close now. Yarin could feel its breath through the doors, it was so close. It was searching for him; it wasn't going to let him escape.

Claws suddenly ripped through the cabinet doors as if they were paper. The creature lunged at him viciously with huge teeth dripping in blood… and Yarin woke up screaming.

<World of Zaylyn ><Quest For The Sword Of Anthrowst ><By Katrina Mandrake-Johnston ><Ch 30>

CHAPTER 30 =   THE TRIAL

"Yarin, are you all right?" Weena asked with great concern.

"I just had a bad dream. I'm okay," he told them.

The spider that guarded the entrance suddenly moved from its position. Another spider entered the chamber and came to stand in front of the cell containing Lorenta.

"I think it's talking to her," whispered Dendrox.

Everyone waited impatiently, and after some time, Lorenta said to the others gravely, "It has been decided, that if the one who was shot with the arrow dies, so shall the one who shot him." Lorenta looked to Candra with a worried look.

Having relayed its message to them, the spider departed, and the guard took its position in front of the tunnel once more.

"Hey, Weena," Candra called, "Can't you use some sort of magic to get us out of here?" Even though she tried to hide it, there was a hint of panic to the elf's voice.

"I know three useless spells: Heal, Cure, and Shield. And they don't work properly," Weena explained, once again on the verge of tears.

Vordin told her, "Use the Heal spell to heal the spider. Why can't you just do that?"

"Yes, do it," Candra said, "Sooner or later they'll discover that it was me that shot the spider."

"There's a slight chance it might work," she replied, "but I'm so incredibly frightened of them. If I have to walk out there, vulnerable and afraid, there is definitely not any chance of the spell working. It takes a lot of concentration to do a spell you know, and the only thing I'll be concentrating on is keeping myself alive."

"I thought you said you have to let a spell work itself or something like that, that you didn't have to concentrate. You told me that it will fail if you try to concentrate on how a spell works," said Dendrox.

"No, that's right. What I meant was, I wouldn't be able to clear my mind enough even to make a feeble attempt at casting it!" she explained, "It's not exactly easy when there is danger everywhere I look!"

Vordin asked, "Well what about that Shield spell? Can't you use it and be protected that way?"

"Okay, say I go out there. What if my Heal spell doesn't work? And it won't, because I won't be

<Zaylyn ><Quest For The Sword Of Anthrowst ><By Katrina Mandrake-Johnston >   <Ch 30> < 92 >

able to concentrate," Weena said in a hurried voice, "The point is, they don't know how slim the chance is of it working. They'll kill me thinking that it's some sort of deception. And if my Shield spell works, all they have to do is just wait until the spell wears off to get at me."

"Lorenta," Nodwel said, "tell them that it's a weak spell. All she can do is try, nothing is guaranteed. I will accompany Weena to provide protection for her."

"I can't speak to them. I can only understand them. I've explained this before," she told them, "In spider form, maybe, but even then I probably wouldn't be able to since I'm not one of them. They behave very differently and speak to me through some kind of mind ability. When I feel them trying to enter, I simply don't resist them. I have no reason to. Then a voice fills my mind."

"Okay, we understand. So you're saying you can change into a spider then?" Dendrox asked, "Vordin said that you were some sort of shape-shifter. So you can change into any form you wish, including a spider?"

They had made their feelings on spiders clear already, but Lorenta didn't care what they thought of her anymore. She was angry, and she refused to hide who she was any longer. Besides, come morning she would not have a choice in the matter. "No, at dawn I will turn back into my true form. I am just the same as these beings you despise. I am a spider who at night can change into a human. I know now, that this has to be a curse. Humans are cruel. Why should you treat me any differently than these spiders here? Just because I appear human to you now? I don't want to pretend anymore. If it means anything, I think their decision is beyond fair. They show mercy now after all the pain and suffering that the villagers gave to them, and they still continue to show mercy to you, Candra. All they want is our help to save the wounded one. Anyway, these spiders truly act more human than they do spider, just without the cruelty and prejudice."

"I don't trust her," Nodwel told the others.

"Oh who cares," Asdella spoke up, "Lorenta's not the threat here. Just use gestures to show that you mean them no harm and that you want to help. Don't seem threatening, and don't show fear. Animals hate that. It makes them nervous. I guess that goes in this situation too. If you don't try, Weena, they'll most likely kill us all, so where's the harm in trying then? Maybe you'll get lucky and save us all, who knows? Of course, there's always the option of fighting our way out, but even I have to admit that the chance of victory trying that, is less than measurable."

Nodwel was surprised, as he had never seen this side of Asdella before and he was sure that not many people had. She was actually weighing the odds of a battle beforehand and giving encouragement to a fellow companion. It was not like her to do so and especially not in the manner she had.

"Don't show fear?" Weena asked letting out a weak laugh, "Yeah right, that is definitely not going to happen." But then Weena said reluctantly, "But I will try. I guess I'm our only hope, right?"

Weena patted the web to get the spider's attention. She put her hands to her breast and then held them outstretched in hope that it would be interpreted that she was willing to help.

As the spider moved slowly toward her, Weena pressed her back up against the back wall of her cell, trembling with fear. The spider began tearing down the web to Weena's prison. Weena whimpered and squealed, her face fear-stricken and with tears running down her cheeks. Vordin was worried that she would faint before she was free.

When the webbing had been removed, the spider stood aside and waited for her to step out. She clung to the back wall, frozen with fright.

"I can't do it," she managed to choke out, "I'm too afraid. It's right there. Right beside me. I can see its fangs… its hairy legs… It's looking right at me with all of its eyes. Help me. Somebody help me," she whimpered.

"He's not going to hurt you. Come on, just go," Lorenta told her.

"I can't move," she hissed at them, "Do something! Keep it away from me! Help me…"

The spider moved one of its front legs slightly, and Weena frantically attempted to clamber up the rock wall behind her in a desperate panic.

The spider moved away from Weena and waited over by the tunnel entrance, giving Weena some much-needed space. Weena calmed down slightly, but not much.

<Zaylyn ><Quest For The Sword Of Anthrowst ><By Katrina Mandrake-Johnston >   <Ch 30> < 93 >

"I can't do this. Please don't make me do this," she whined.

"Weena," Vordin called, "take my lantern with you or else you won't be able to see."

"I'm too afraid to move," she told them again.

"It will be okay," Nodwel said to her, "We're all counting on you."

"He's not going to hurt you. They want you to help, remember?" Lorenta added.

"What happens when I fail? They'll kill me," Weena said.

"No, they won't. They'll bring you back here," Asdella told her, "They said if the wounded one dies, that the one who shot him is going to pay. That means Candra. Isn't that what they said?"

"Oh great, thanks a lot," Candra tried to snarl at her, but her fear was showing. "Weena? Don't fail, okay?" Candra said to her with desperation in her voice, "You can do this, alright? Please do this, and hurry! You're wasting time! The thing's going to be dead before you even get out there, which means so will I!"

"*Damn it, why doesn't she move! It's going to be too late!*" Dendrox screamed at her within his mind and then pleaded, "Weena, don't let this happen. If you're not even going to try…" There was anxiety in Dendrox's voice. "They're going to kill Candra for sure! Most likely all of us!"

"Okay, I'll do it. I'll try," she told them.

She tried to give herself the strength to do what needed to be done. "*I can't let this happen. I sat by, too afraid when the school burned, while my brother… There was time to warn them… to get them out before it was too late. I saw the signs that something was wrong. I smelt the strange odors and knew it had to be something I added to the fire. I could have saved my brother. I could have saved everyone, and all I did was hide and let it happen because I was too scared to do something about it. Even in my dreams I alter what really happened. I try to fool myself into believing that I had no time to help, that I didn't know what was happening, that I didn't know that my brother had gone in to look for me, and worst of all that I wasn't entirely sure of what I had put into the fire. I didn't intend for anyone to get hurt, just to maybe get back at them a little for all the teasing they did and that damn teacher who kept picking on me. I was just angry, that's all. I didn't mean to… But whether I meant to or not doesn't matter. Everyone died and because of me. I can't let that happen again. I have to try and I have to do it now…*" and Weena pushed herself away from the wall and into the room.

She edged slowly toward the pile of their belongings, her eyes falling on all the weapons she couldn't wield. She spotted the box with the glowing flask inside. She retrieved it from the pile, her eyes ever-watchful of the enormous spider and its fangs.

With great effort, Weena forced every reluctant step, bringing her slowly toward the exit and the spider that awaited her.

"*All their encouraging words, and all of them trying to show confidence in me and my abilities. All I see is fear,*" Weena thought to herself, "*I am in this situation alone now, and I will be relying only on myself. All their words are just words without any meaning other than to give me false hope. They all are counting on me. I don't want this responsibility, not when lives are at stake.*"

She hesitated, looking at her imprisoned companions, and Weena was then pushed gently with a hairy leg urging her toward the tunnel entrance. She cringed, a shiver jolting down her spine. She held Vordin's lantern close in front of her with both hands, and held the metal case so tightly that her knuckles were turning white.

Rigid with fear, she slowly entered the tunnel. Words of encouragement continued to be called after her as she walked, and Weena could hear the sound of the spider's many feet patting along the tunnel as it followed her.

When Weena exited the tunnel, she found herself once again in the larger chamber, and by the magical light of the lantern, she could vaguely make out the other passageways that led away from it. Her eyes searched from tunnel to tunnel, longing to find the one leading to the well and her freedom, but she knew being surrounded by numerous spiders as she was, meant there wasn't any chance for escape. She could feel the fear building up inside her to the point where she thought she might actually explode from it. She wanted to run… to escape. She counted four of the spiders between her and one of the tunnels, and she figured that this must be the one leading to the well. Her complete focus was now on the tunnel before her. Each time she weighed her chances, her mind kept pushing in favor of running. Deep down she knew that the fear was keeping her from thinking rationally.

"*Don't run. Don't run! Whatever you do, you can't run,*" she commanded herself, "*You will be killed, if you run. You can do this. Don't run. The others are counting on you.*"

The one that had led her from the prison nudged her again. Weena jumped and a frightened screech escaped her lips. Some of the spiders around her shifted position slightly, but they did not attack as she thought they might.

She moved forward until she could see the wounded spider. Weena tried to focus on the single spider and the task that lay before her. She would have to concentrate in order to keep the fear from taking her over. Weena approached and she desperately tried to ignore all the spiders that encircled her now with their many eyes watching her every move so intensely. She found that she could not simply ignore their presence and the sound of her heart began to pound loudly in her ears.

Weena tried to compose herself and knelt down beside the wounded spider, making sure to be as far away from its fangs as she could. As she did so, one of its legs twitched and brushed up against her robe. Her whole body jolted with terror and she let out a shriek, which she immediately and desperately tried to muffle.

"*If my spell is going to have any chance of working, I have to get over this fear and fast,*" she commanded herself as she tried to hold back the almost unbearable panic which was erupting inside her. She placed the lantern beside her, noticing how terribly her hands were trembling. "*Okay,*" she told herself trying to remain calm, "*Imagine that in reality the spiders are actually the remaining villagers. They were somehow turned into spiders and have come here to hide from the beasts. It's plausible. There are odder things happening all around, like Lorenta for example if she truly is a spider as she says. Anything is possible, right? They are intelligent and they have a village-like community down here. It makes sense. That's why they are so incredibly different from regular spiders and this would explain their bizarre behavior as well. They must have been human once. This spider here before me could possibly be a small child… an innocent little boy perhaps, with his mother and father standing by terribly worried about him. It is obvious that they are worried for him. His family is depending on me to save him. Why would these 'people' want to hurt me? They were trying to help us and this poor boy was almost killed for doing so. It's our fault and we must help. I am our only hope. I am this child's only hope.*"

A spider nudged her from behind, as she had been kneeling motionless for some time now. This time, it wasn't as frightening for her as before. She saw them as people now and not just a tangle of hairy legs, fangs, and eyes. She found herself, in some part, actually believing her scenario, at least enough to keep herself from going into an uncontrollable panic.

Weena drew in a deep breath and tried to let it out slowly. Her breath quivered as she did so. This was not good, as fear still had her firmly in its grip.

She drew in another breath and tried to focus. She released the air quickly with determination and in that same instant placed her hands around the wound to its abdomen where the arrow was protruding from it.

She closed her eyes, concentrating on what she was trying to do, and then let her mind relax. The spell began to take form. She felt the magical energy bubbling up inside her and then flowing outward as she mouthed the silent words of the spell.

She kept her eyes shut tight, afraid to see whether or not her spell was working. "*This has to work. It's going to work. It needs to work!*" Then she heard the sound of the arrow hitting the rock floor.

Her eyes bolted open in surprise. "*It worked! It worked! I actually did it! I saved him!*"

She watched as her spell slowly closed and healed the wound until just a small bald scar-like area represented the spot where the arrow had struck. Several of the spiders approached her, and after Weena had snatched up Vordin's lantern once more, they led her back to the prison chamber.

A guard came to stand in position at the entrance, and one spider came to stand in front of the cell containing Lorenta.

"Weena?!" Candra asked with worry, "What happened? Did you do it?"

<Zaylyn ><Quest For The Sword Of Anthrowst ><By Katrina Mandrake-Johnston >   <Ch 30> < 95 >

"I healed him! I really did it!" she replied with a grin, although it quickly faded as she looked nervously over at the spider speaking to Lorenta. Weena asked, "What do you think they're going to do with us now? I mean, now that they don't need us to do anything for them."

After the spider was finished communicating with Lorenta, it left the room. The guard stood motionless in his position, forever watchful.

"Well, at least they didn't lock me up again," Weena commented, "That's a good sign, isn't it? Perhaps they will let us go."

"What did it say?" Vordin asked Lorenta.

"Well, they give thanks for saving the life of their wounded member, but they're afraid that if they release us, that they will be attacked," Lorenta replied.

"So, then what's going to happen to us?" Candra asked her, "They can't just leave us here!"

"Most likely they'll use us for food," said Dendrox.

"Don't say that," Nodwel snapped, "Think of the boy!"

"Well it's true. Why shouldn't they?" retorted Dendrox.

"But I helped them. I healed the spider. Why would they want to kill us after we helped them like that," Weena added, nervously rubbing her hands together.

"Nobody helped them," Dendrox answered, "We made the problem, and now we've just undone it to the best we can. They don't owe us anything. Don't you realize that? Did you ever think that they might decide that we are somehow responsible for the deaths of the spiders above as well simply because we are human? What then? We don't know how these things think! You even said it, now that we're of no use to them, now what? We'll all be food for these things, that's what!"

"But I don't want to die," Weena whined, as tears welled up in her bright blue eyes, "Isn't there something we can do?"

"If everyone would just calm down for a minute," Lorenta spoke up, "I have more to tell you. They're going to remove the webbing, but we must stay in this room until they decide what to do with us. If we provoke them, they will defend themselves. They also want to attempt to teach me to speak as they do. I'm going to try to learn, if I am even physically capable of doing so. If I am able to speak back to them, it will be of great help to us."

Nodwel said to them all, "So, I guess all we can do now is wait."

It was only a few moments before a group of spiders came into the chamber and started to remove the webbing.

"You think we should attack? It may be our one and only chance. What do you say?" Asdella asked.

"For one, you're the only one with a weapon right now. Even if we all did have weapons, we wouldn't stand a chance and you know that," Nodwel explained to her.

"No, please don't attack them," pleaded Lorenta, "You'll ruin any chance of us getting out of this alive. Just let me go with them and see if I can learn anything from them. I may be able to save us. You just have to be patient."

Once everyone was free from their cells, Lorenta was escorted out of the chamber.

"Good luck," Vordin called after her.

<World of Zaylyn ><Quest For The Sword Of Anthrowst ><By Katrina Mandrake-Johnston ><Ch 31>

CHAPTER 31 = DARK THOUGHTS

After Lorenta was out of sight, and a spider had taken position as guard in front of the entrance once more, Weena exclaimed, "Why did they release us? That is what they're going to do, right? I mean it's not dinnertime for them, or anything like that, right? I saved that one; they must be releasing us."

"Who cares, at least we're out of those tiny alcoves. Me, I'm getting my weapons as quickly as possible," Dendrox said heading over to the pile of their belongings, as did both Candra and Nodwel right away.

Nodwel, ever wary of the spider, after picking up his battle-axe, next retrieved his pouch.

<Zaylyn ><Quest For The Sword Of Anthrowst ><By Katrina Mandrake-Johnston >   <Ch 31> < 96 >

"My arrows are scattered all over the place," Candra remarked, clearly annoyed.

"Yeah, well so are my daggers, alright?" Dendrox said to her, "Just get your stuff as fast as possible, okay? I don't trust these spiders, and I at least want to have my weapons if I need to defend myself."

The guard watched them with its many eyes as they rummaged through the pile in search of their belongings.

"It appears that it will be quite awhile before Lorenta returns. We should eat now, as we may not get a second chance depending on what they decide for us," the dwarf suggested.

They all agreed and sat down to eat the remainder of their food in silence, by the magical light of Vordin's lantern.

***

"I can still see her blood on my hands, even though it has been cleansed long ago. The taste of her blood on my lips is still vivid in my memory.

"I told her to leave. I couldn't stop myself. I tried to warn her. Why didn't she leave?

"I shouldn't have pretended to be something I'm not. I can't possibly have a normal life. I can't have love… only fear and hate. I am a danger to everyone. The closer someone gets to me, the greater the risk to their life. I am a fool to think I can have the simple things in life.

"I am a monster. I can't control these evil urges. The closer I get to love or even a simple friendship, the greater the desire to destroy it. The more I try, the stronger the hunger grows within me.

"I've tried feeding only a little from several people to take the place of the one or more whole victims I claim in a night… somehow trying to reach some sort of equivalent in hope of sparing lives. I even took the time to heal their wounds and to erase the memory of the attacks from their minds. I've managed to spare a few lives here and there in the past. But when I do this, the hunger is worse than ever, and it's so hard to hold back and stop myself before it's too late. The hunger is never satisfied, and when I try to resist it, the need to feed is almost constant.

"Is there any hope that I can be good? To somehow repay the people for the suffering I cause? How can I possibly? There is no way of justifying what I am. I could save lives, stop criminals, punish the wicked. I do sometimes, but that doesn't make a difference when it's weighed against my past deeds.

"I have been named many things: God of gods, Bringer of Death, Monster, Demon… There are so many," he sighed, "I am The Black Shadow.

"I frighten even myself sometimes knowing what I am truly capable of. That is why I can never lose total control over myself and my evil nature. I must always care. I have all this power and could destroy the world with a single thought if I wished. But what kind of life would I have if I used the full extent of my powers? Is there even a limit to what I can do?

"All this power and I can't have love. Maybe it's best if I am denied it. If I love someone, it will give people a way to actually hurt me. They would take out all their fear and rage on her because they can't get to me. But that's not the point.

"I can't handle love. For someone to get close, it would be unbearable. The scent of her skin, the warmth of her touch, the soothing rhythm of her heartbeat… the beast in me wouldn't be able to resist. I would take hold and drain the life out of her until there was nothing left. I would try so desperately to hold back, but the hunger wouldn't let me. She would fade away in my arms. I would be alone again and by my own doing. How can someone ever put trust in me when I can't even trust myself?

"Such a stupid girl. Couldn't she see that she was in danger? I warned her to leave. It was her choice to stay. It was her fault that it happened. No, I can't allow myself to blame her. I am the monster, not her.

"Why didn't she go! Would that really have mattered though? How far would she have gotten? Her scent had excited me. I would have hunted her down no matter how many unsuspecting prey came between us.

"What was I thinking? That somehow, in some way, that she could have loved me being the horror that I am? It would have been over as soon as she discovered what I really am. Just my name strikes fear into people. She would have never gotten that close if she had known the full truth… seen the evil

<Zaylyn ><Quest For The Sword Of Anthrowst ><By Katrina Mandrake-Johnston >   <Ch 31> < 97 >
surface beyond a simple feeding…

"What kind of life could I have given her? One of death and isolation? Living in constant fear that the one she loves could suddenly lose control of himself and take her life away? Well, that's what happened, didn't it?" A tear ran down his pale cheek under the hood of his dark cloak.

"I didn't have control. I thought I did. I thought I could control the urges. But the smell of her skin, the warmth of her touch… it was too much for me. The sound of her heartbeat pounding in my ears getting louder and louder, until I couldn't resist any longer, to the point where all I could do was bury my face deep into her warm flesh. And then… bite down and drink long and hard… until she became limp and lifeless in my arms...

"Why do I try to have something more? I have to be alone! It's what I deserve!

"I should just feed. There is no other reason to come in contact with the people of Zaylyn other than to do that. There's no use in trying to prolong the inevitable. All that happens is that I end up just toying with the victim, trying so desperately to have something more. Whether it be trying to gain affection, friendship, or whatever... when someone gets close, they get hurt. I can't stop it. I've tried.

"Am I truly evil? I must be. All the good I try to do doesn't make up for any of it. It can't. Should I just give in and play with these helpless beings as I see fit? Assume that they exist merely for my pleasure? That wouldn't be right.

"But so many of them, if they were in my place, would relish in the pain and destruction they could cause. All the suffering… and to them it would be mere fun. Enjoying it because it wouldn't affect them. They wouldn't stop once to think about things from the perspective of the victims.

"I know I've caused a lot of pain in the past, but I truly want to help these people now, beyond what I am already providing for those in the valley. I owe it to them. But I have vowed not to use my higher powers and I must keep to that vow.

"But, I cannot stand idle while this insane man slaughters entire villages. I feed from these people. I must make sure that my supply doesn't run short. No, that is not the real reason, I can't think like that. I could stop him myself, but I won't. Instead, I will guide the group toward this mad man's defeat. At least it will be more interesting this way. Perhaps I should get more involved with them than I have, or perhaps not."

From his perch in a large oak tree, he glided down to the ground. Like a shadow moving across the earth, he silently crept to the nearby cottage. He climbed up the wall of the cottage, a sleek creature of the night, and slipped quietly into the open window. Camouflaged in the darkness of the room, he spied the sleeping figure lying in the bed.

"What does your mind tell me… Your children sleeping downstairs… You beat them almost to death… More often now than before… You blame them for your drunk of a husband leaving you… You never even wanted your children in the first place… They were just a tool to be used against him to make him stay… I think your sister should have your children instead of having you beat them into their graves. At least this will be doing your children some good whether they realize it or not. But who am I to judge? Is it right to deprive children of their mother, even one as horrible as you? You could change. Things could be different… Stop wasting time!" his mind screamed at him, "Feed before you lose control of your actions! You'll slip into a feeding frenzy and end up killing her, the children, and anyone else unfortunate enough to be nearby!"

He reluctantly approached the bed. "Perhaps feeding only when it's absolutely necessary is not as wise as I thought. Sure, less people die, but the risk of losing control is greater, and if that happens, the death toll would be much more than a little restricted feeding here and there could ever balance out. Just listen to me, I'm talking about people's lives as if they were meaningless! Like a balancing of numbers and ratios could make it any better. Life is precious, and each individual is unique. I can't just ignore that, slap a number on them, or figure that somehow they deserve it. Saving the lives of three won't make up for the death of one. Nothing can make it somehow all right. The only ultimate solution is my own death. I've even tried that too, unsuccessfully. Am I truly invincible? The least I can do, if I am forced to feed, is try to do some good for the people of Zaylyn as a result of it."

There was a sharp pain in his gut and the hunger intensified. He was starting to lose control. The

<Zaylyn ><Quest For The Sword Of Anthrowst ><By Katrina Mandrake-Johnston >   <Ch 31> < 98 >
woman lay before him, unaware that she was in grave danger.

"I'm sorry," he whispered and drained her of her blood and her life.

<World of Zaylyn ><Quest For The Sword Of Anthrowst ><By Katrina Mandrake-Johnston ><Ch 32>

CHAPTER 32 =   ANGER

They idly wandered about the chamber, waiting for Lorenta to return. The spider at the tunnel entrance, who had remained motionless for quite some time now, began shifting its position as if it had become agitated by something.

"Nodwel, what do you think is going on?" Asdella asked calmly.

"Don't know. I say, just be prepared for anything," he answered.

Asdella let out a bit of a snort. "I'm always ready for battle you silly dwarf."

"Do you think we can leave now?" Yarin asked in a meek voice, "I want to leave now."

"So what do we do?" Vordin asked.

"Easy, we wait," Nodwel said calmly, "We simply wait to see what happens, lad."

The guard returned to its motionless state at the tunnel entrance, and the group continued to wait patiently for Lorenta to return as it seemed they had no choice but to do so. Through the small holes in the ceiling of the chamber, they watched the night sky gradually turn to dawn and then high noon. Lorenta still had not returned.

Weena asked, "What do you think they're doing?"

"I have no idea. I just wish they would hurry up," muttered Dendrox, scuffing his boot along the rock floor.

Candra commented, "Yeah, it's pretty near unbearable just sitting here not knowing."

More time passed as they waited impatiently. It was now late afternoon, and there was still no sign of Lorenta.

Suddenly, to everyone's surprise, Asdella put both hands to her head and winced in pain.

"What's wrong?" Weena asked concerned, "Does your head hurt?"

Asdella's pulled at her short reddish hair, clenched her hands into fists, and screamed in rage.

"What the hell's wrong with her?" asked Candra with an insulting look.

"Shut up!" Asdella screamed, "Shut up, shut up, shut up!"

"Who is she talking to? One of us? What the hell did we do?" Dendrox asked defensively.

She bellowed out in rage, "You will never control me! It's my mind! I'm in control. I'm in charge!" Then she ran over to the rock wall and started banging her head against it, the whole time screaming, "Get out... of my... head!"

Nodwel exclaimed, "Asdella! No! What are you doing? Stop! You're going to hurt yourself!"

"Shut up!" she said refusing to stop.

Dendrox muttered, "One too many nuts in her fruitcake."

"What?" Candra snapped at him, "That is the most ridiculous thing I've ever heard!"

"Asdella, I'm just trying to help," said Nodwel.

She stopped banging her head and turned to him, giving him a disgusted look and saying between clenched teeth, "I'm not talking to you! I'm talking to them!"

"To who!" Nodwel demanded as his patience with her was diminishing fast.

Dendrox, insulted by what Candra had said, now said in defense, "Sounded good at the time."

"No it didn't!" the elf said with a scowl.

"To the voices, fool!" Asdella yelled at Nodwel. "Who else?!" she said looking at him as if he were a complete idiot.

"Voices? You know damn well there aren't any voices. Listen, I've had quite enough of your craziness!" Nodwel yelled at her, "I always stick up for you, telling people that you're not a complete lunatic, that all they have to do is get to know you. But it looks like I'm the fool for thinking it. There isn't a sane bone in your body, is there? You treat your friends like enemies, acting like you're so tough, when in reality you are the biggest fool I've ever seen!"

Yarin exclaimed, "Hey, how did that little spider get over there by Weena?"

<Zaylyn ><Quest For The Sword Of Anthrowst ><By Katrina Mandrake-Johnston >   <Ch 32> < 99 >

Vordin and Weena both had been watching the others argue and had not noticed much else. Weena looked down beside her and, in seeing the spider so close to her, immediately reacted in fear by stomping her foot down toward it. Luckily, Vordin reacted quickly. As soon as Yarin said this, Vordin instantly knew what Weena's reaction would be. He shoved Weena as hard as he could, knocking her down just before her foot connected with the spider and was able to save Lorenta's life.

"Hey, why did you push me?" Weena blurted out, and then seeing Vordin's glare, realized what she had almost done. "Oh... I can't believe I almost... It was simply a reaction; I wasn't thinking... If you hadn't been so quick... I can't believe... Hey, wait a minute, why didn't she change to human form? Why'd she sneak up like that?! Of course I would have reacted like that! What was she expecting?"

"It's not night yet! She can't change during the day," Vordin told her, "That doesn't matter. You could have killed her! There's no excuse! Especially after all she's done to try to help."

"Candra," Dendrox said in an annoyed tone, "you always snub everything I say."

She rolled her eyes and hissed at him, "If you didn't say such stupid things, I wouldn't have too."

Nodwel continued, "Running around like that with hardly a scrap of clothing on, bare feet most of the time even! Putting everyone else in danger, running blindly into battle without caring who else gets hurt as a result of it! You don't even care about yourself, and it ends up that it's us that has to do all the reasoning for you and pull you out of certain death situations. Oh, and then you fight us as well for saving you, don't you, as if you want to die! That's it, isn't it?! You crazy lunatic! You want to die, and you don't care who you end up taking with you, friend or foe! Well, I've had enough!"

Sunset had arrived, and Lorenta transformed. The green flames engulfed her spider form and her human form rose up out of it as the flames subsided. Her expression was one of utter hatred.

"You tried to kill me you horrible woman!" she said staring down at Weena who was still on the ground, "What were you going to say? 'Oh oops, sorry' and be done with it?! 'Miss all high and mighty' with your spells, thinking you're better than everyone and most of all me."

Weena stuttered, "No... I... I don't... I didn't mean..."

Lorenta snapped viciously at her, "Oh shut up, you whining insect," and she took a slight step toward her, "You tried to kill me," and she took another step, "The other wizard tried to hurt me."

"What other wizard? The one with the medallion?" Weena asked, her fear growing.

Lorenta continued, "I killed him, and it was so easy too, and he deserved it, the filthy beast. Try to crush me under your shoe?!" She took another step toward Weena who was starting to tremble. "Try to crush me, like I'm nothing?! You horrible self-centered whining bitch! I'll kill you too!"

Vordin grabbed Lorenta and tried to hold her back saying, "Lorenta no! It was an accident! What are you doing!"

"So you're saying that you're perfect, Candra?!" Dendrox glared at her, "Should I recall some of the times you supremely messed up opportunities for us? Gee, there's so many I don't know where to begin."

"Oh, and Asdella," Nodwel continued, "You can carry your own damn supplies, or, you can see how your belly likes going empty."

Candra replied to Dendrox, "You would be dead so many times over if I wasn't there to save you."

"Oh really?" the thief said, "If you weren't always getting in the way..."

"Me?! Ha! That's a laugh," she snapped.

Dendrox gritted his teeth in anger, "Yes, you! I don't need you to protect me! It's you that needs to think that, so you can feel as if you are somehow above me. It's all in your head!"

"Yeah, whatever," she said waving her hand at him as if she were sweeping him and his words away.

This made Dendrox even more furious. "How about I show you how well I can defend myself by pounding your smug arrogant face into a bloody pulp!" he yelled at her raising his fist.

"I'd like to see you try. I'll have you on the ground begging for mercy so fast you won't even know what happened. Oh, and I'm not feeling very merciful right now, so try not to bleed on me too much," she said with a sneer.

<Zaylyn ><Quest For The Sword Of Anthrowst ><By Katrina Mandrake-Johnston >   <Ch 32> < 100 >

"Let go of me, Vordin! You know I'm stronger than you, don't make me throw you off me! I've never been so furious in all my life! She has to pay for what she tried to do to me!"

Weena blubbered, "I didn't mean it... I'm sorry... Keep away from me!"

Nodwel continued to yell angrily at Asdella who was just staring at him in silence, but it was clear that there was a mountain of rage bubbling inside her, and it didn't seem like she was going to hold it back for much longer.

"You're just going to put the rest of us in danger!" Nodwel yelled at her, "We enjoy life, we want to live, and if there's a chance to get out of here alive, we're going to fight for it! I'm not going to let you jeopardize that! Hell, you want to die so badly, let me help you along!" He took his hefty battle-axe into hand and it was certain that he actually meant to fight her.

"You!" Asdella burst out with hatred, "It's all your fault! We should have never trusted you to go for help! You, with your uselessly short stubby legs. You didn't even try to go for help. You just brought back these useless fools, and you took your sweet time about it too while we all were risking our lives! I tried to avenge Dimwar, when that beast took his damn head off, and you pulled me back! You let Nimdor die! You didn't even try to help when he and I were in battle with the other one! You wanted him to die so you could play at being the leader. The girl I tried to save would be alive if you had done your job!"

And her next words were filled with such malice that it almost made Nodwel shudder. "Narr was killed because of you. And the boy he saved was dragged down here into this hellhole. And instead of getting us out, the little tiny speck of a dwarf decides to make his big manly decision to simply wait here for our deaths! Well let me hurry yours along, because the rest of us are done waiting," she snarled pointing the blade of her sword toward his face taunting him to make the first move. "Come on," she barked at him, "You made your little speech. You have the guts to say it. Lets see how much you have to say after I spill them. As I once called you friend, I'll let you take the first move," and then she dared, "The question is are you foolish enough to do it?"

The spider guard, more agitated now than ever, hurried down the tunnel leaving them to their quarrels.

"Look!" exclaimed Yarin with excitement, "The spider is letting us go."

Everyone was too caught up in their own arguments and barely even heard Yarin. The small boy started to edge slowly and nervously toward the tunnel. "Come on! Don't fight. We're free! Let's get out of here," Yarin tried to convince them.

As soon as Yarin reached the tunnel, a Killnarin burst from the shadows of the passageway and clamped its massive jaws onto his frail little body in one fluid snap of the creature's thick muscular neck. All anyone could do was just stare in shock. All their prior heated words instantly became meaningless, their ears filled with the small boy's screams and the sickening sound of his bones snapping within the creature's jaws.

The beast stomped into the chamber, as Weena let out a horrified protracted wail. The beast turned to them and let what was left of Yarin's body drop to the ground in a crumpled heap of mangled tissue, the tiny boy's innocent face white and blood-splattered.

<World of Zaylyn ><Quest For The Sword Of Anthrowst ><By Katrina Mandrake-Johnston ><Ch 33>

CHAPTER 33 = KILLNARIN INVASION

The Killnarin howled defiantly. It swung its head back and forth, gnashing its teeth together, daring the astonished group to attack.

Six spiders immediately rushed into the chamber after the Killnarin and surrounded the creature. The beast was down on all six of its legs and the yellow fluid, which dripped from its deadly teeth, was streaked red with Yarin's blood. As the Killnarin tried to approach the rest of the group, the spiders came to stand between it and the adventurers. Their front legs were raised defensively with their fangs clearly displayed to the beast.

The creature snorted in frustration at this. It quickly reared up and simply batted one of the spiders away with its clawed forepaw. The spider was thrown through the air hitting the wall to the side of the

<Zaylyn ><Quest For The Sword Of Anthrowst ><By Katrina Mandrake-Johnston >   <Ch 33> < 101 >

beast where it fell in a crumpled heap near Weena. The Killnarin howled in triumph and started to approach, ignoring the spiders around it and intent on spilling more blood.

By this time, Candra had been able to get an arrow ready, and taking aim, fired it with great speed. Dendrox also threw a dagger toward the beast. Nodwel and Asdella did not approach the Killnarin but had their weapons ready. The attack by the thieves didn't seem to affect the creature except to startle it slightly.

The spiders, taking advantage of this, quickly crawled up onto the Killnarin to bite the creature repeatedly, trying to release as much of their venom into the beast as possible. The Killnarin began thrashing about, knocking the spiders to the ground where the creature could bite and claw at them. One spider was mashed between its huge teeth. Another was crushed under a heavy foot as the creature stomped and thrashed about. It took a forceful swipe at another but managed only to graze its abdomen. This spider, even though it was wounded, still tried to crawl back up onto the Killnarin.

Candra asked them, "Should I let loose another arrow? It seemed to have no effect."

"No, you'll hit one of the spiders," Vordin said to her, "Look, it's working. The beast looks like it's about to collapse."

The creature staggered about until it slumped to the floor, but was still very much alive. The Killnarin, even in its weakened state, still tried to bite and claw at the remaining spiders as they began to hurry out of the room. The wounded spider, however, collapsed just before the tunnel unable to follow and quickly died soon after.

Nodwel and Asdella ran up to the Killnarin and hacked, slashed, and stabbed at the beast's thick resilient hide as they avoided its flailing limbs and vicious mouth of slimy teeth.

While the two warriors fought the beast, Lorenta smiled at Vordin and said, "Vordin, looks like you saved my life again and intentionally this time. First from the owl and now from Weena," and then she apologized to Weena saying, "I'm sorry about what I said earlier."

"I understand," Weena said, knowing what the Killnarin were capable of with their spells.

"It's the beasts," Dendrox added, "They did the same to me and Candra earlier. They make you hate. They don't make you say things you don't mean, just things you normally wouldn't say. They create chaos, destroy friendships, turn people against each other, and try to create as much suffering as possible before they kill you." His voice was sorrowful but was also filled with great hatred of the beasts and a desperate need for vengeance against them all. "All the arguments we just had were all part of its plan to kill Yarin first, as it knew that his death would cause us the most suffering and grief."

"You don't know that for sure," Candra told him.

"After all you've seen?" Dendrox snapped, "You know it's true. And why are they so strong? The ones Nodwel's group encountered were apparently much stronger than the one we killed and so is this one."

"Why won't you die!" Asdella screamed at the beast as she continued to stab at its black oily skin.

"I can't believe he's gone," Weena sobbed, "I can't even bring myself to look." As she said this, she glanced over to where Yarin had fallen. Still upon the ground, she drew her legs up about her, hugged them tightly in her arms, and began to rock back and forth, sobbing miserably.

Lorenta told Vordin, "I learnt to communicate. Well, only a bit. The spider teaching me got distracted suddenly and left saying something about the demons finding a way in, and that is when I returned here to warn everyone. But, I ah, got distracted." She felt ashamed and knew that what Dendrox had said was true, in some way she had meant what she had said. "*I might have had time to warn everyone of the Killnarin, if I hadn't given in to my anger. I might have been able to save Yarin. Now it's too late.*"

Nodwel took another swing with his axe at the beast and then dodged the beast's claws as it took a weak swipe at him.

"This isn't right," Weena sobbed, "How could this happen... I can still hear his voice... He can't be dead... We were trying to save him... Everything was going to be okay... I told him everything was going to be okay... He looked up to me... This can't be happening... This can't be real..."

The Killnarin was finally slain. "It's finished," Nodwel announced, and then as he stared at Yarin,

<Zaylyn ><Quest For The Sword Of Anthrowst ><By Katrina Mandrake-Johnston >   <Ch 33> < 102 >
his axe fell from his hand.

Dendrox and Candra retrieved their arrow and dagger, but dared not look at the boy. To Candra's disappointment, she discovered her arrow to be broken. Nodwel picked up his axe; he knew there would be more of them.

"I… No… I was just talking to him; he can't be gone…" Weena sobbed, "It's not right… It can't be real… Yarin, the entire village of people… all gone… All dead… It just isn't possible… Why didn't we listen to him? If we had been paying more attention… We should have made sure that he was safe. He can't just be gone… He just can't be dead, and that's it… He's a little boy. He didn't do anything to anyone…"

Asdella came over to her and shook her violently. "He's gone! Get up and deal with it, or you'll be dead too!" she snapped at her unkindly.

Weena reluctantly got up from the floor and managed to reduce her sobbing to a mild whimpering.

"We've got to get out of here. Right now, or we're as good as dead," Dendrox spoke up.

Weena re-lit her lantern with the flame box from her pouch, and soon everyone was racing down the tunnel with the two lanterns held high lighting the way. To their surprise, the large chamber was empty except for the sticky remains of one spider.

Vordin commented, "This is probably the spider that was guarding our chamber. The two spiders that survived the battle, where do you think they took off to? I'm sure there must be more Killnarin down the other passageways."

Candra said, "The Killnarin had us trapped back there. If it weren't for the spiders and a large amount of luck on our side, we wouldn't have made it out of that room. They could ambush us very easily down here, especially if they attack together. You saw how hard it was to kill that thing, even with the spiders' help. We have no idea where this maze of tunnels leads, or if there even is an exit other than the well."

Lorenta knelt down beside the dead spider and said, "Thank-you for trying to keep us safe. We shall not forget your sacrifice, as well as the others that gave their lives today."

"Should we make an escape through the well then?" Nodwel asked them all.

"We can't just leave the spiders to perish," Lorenta exclaimed, "You were all so eager to risk your lives for the villagers, but when the spiders need your help, you just flee and leave them to fend for themselves?"

"Their only chance is to flee as well," Vordin told her, "You saw how many spiders it took to take down that one Killnarin, and they weren't even able to kill it. If you can tell them to escape, or better yet, ask them if there is an escape route somewhere…"

Weena, who was slowly backing up and staring wide-eyed toward one of the tunnels, interrupted, "We can't go through the well, because here comes one of them through it!"

The others turned their attention to the tunnel that was on the far side of the large chamber.

"I don't see…" Nodwel started.

"Shh, listen," Weena whispered loudly in fright.

A few moments of silence passed as the group listened for what Weena had heard. Then they heard a faint scraping sound and the light sound of pebbles and dirt falling.

"Do you hear it?" Weena whispered, "It's coming down the well. We have to get out of here, now!"

Candra made a dash for her missing arrow, the one that had been shot into the spider, and retrieved it from the floor of the chamber. She held it ready in her bow. Dendrox slipped a dagger into his hand.

Weena said urgently, getting frustrated that they seemed to be ignoring her, "We can't fight it! We have to go! Quickly before it gets into this room! You're wasting time!"

"Where are we going to go?" Asdella barked angrily at her, "At least we know what's here in this room. Do you want to walk into another ambush?"

Nodwel thought to himself, "*Asdella's sure acting strange. She normally runs about, madly trying to kill everything in sight. She's actually making decisions based on reason and not just blind rage. I don't know what it is exactly, but something's very different about her. Ever since she went to see*

Narr's body. Could it be possible that she is somehow under the control of the Killnarin? That would explain how they managed to find us. No, that can't be it. I know it's silly, but it's almost like she's taken on a bit of Narr's personality. I can definitely see it in her now and then. And more so now since the attack of the Killnarin. Could his death have affected her more than I can possibly understand? I don't know. It must be my imagination. I miss him terribly, as I do the others… Nimdor, Dimwar, Borin… and Yarin. How could we have failed so miserably? How could I have failed so terribly? Was Asdella right about what she said? The beasts bring out the worst with their Hate spells, but what we say is all true. Well, at least what we are feeling deep down inside and little things that annoy us from time to time... things we normally wouldn't say because they hurt. Damn beasts mess with you even after they're dead, the evil things."

"Nodwel? Nodwel? You okay? What should we do?" Dendrox asked.

"How am I supposed to know?" the dwarf snapped back and thought, *"Don't look to me as if I have all the answers. I never wanted to be a leader in all this."*

"Well, I just thought…" said Dendrox.

Weena said to them all in an anxious tone, "Listen, you don't want to leave this room for fear of an ambush? Well look around! We are in a room with who knows how many passages all leading into it. We are standing in the very spot where an ambush would be perfect, am I right?" She paused to see if they were listening to her. "From all sides," she added.

"The wizard's right," said Lorenta, "It would be smart to leave this place. If the creature can communicate with others of its kind, as soon as it sees us, it will alert the others to our location. Others could be on their way already."

"Can you talk to the other spiders?" Vordin asked, "Find out if there is a way out of here?"

"No… I don't know… Maybe. I learnt how to receive messages which was easy, and he explained how the whole things works and a little bit about their history, but we only just started the lesson on how to send out messages to others. He was saving that for last, as it was the longest and hardest to learn. He wasn't even sure if I were going to be physically capable of doing it, but where I have this shape shifting ability, he thought that I might be able to by channeling that magical energy and expanding it."

"Lorenta, just try it! There's no time!" Vordin said to her as he heard a large thud and the scraping of claws on the rock floor.

"It's in the tunnel!" Weena screamed, "We have to run!"

A single spider rushed into the chamber. "Did you call him?" Vordin asked with amazement.

"No, I didn't. But he says for us to get out of here now, as there are more of the creatures and they are slaughtering everyone," Lorenta answered.

The Killnarin walked slowly into the chamber. Its black eyes and skin glistened in the light from the lanterns. It opened its mouth showing its many grotesque slime-covered teeth to the adventurers. The spider rushed to their defense. Lorenta screamed, "No! Don't!"

But it was too late, even if the spider had been able to understand her words. The Killnarin batted the spider aside as if it were nothing. The spider skidded across the floor from the force of the blow and lay broken and dying in a crumpled heap. The beast snarled and returned its focus to the adventurers.

"I think we should run," Asdella said to Nodwel's surprise, as he was expecting her to rush into battle with the beast and endanger them all.

"I hear more of them in the tunnels and they're coming this way," Candra reported.

"Which one do we take?" Weena asked hurriedly.

"Asdella, Borin is here! Take the far left tunnel. Hurry!" Narr said in her mind.

CHAPTER 34 = BORIN

"Follow me! Run! Now! All together!" Asdella commanded, and she darted toward the passageway with Lorenta following right beside her.

"Go! Don't get separated!" Candra yelled and ran after them, pulling Weena along by the hand

<Zaylyn ><Quest For The Sword Of Anthrowst ><By Katrina Mandrake-Johnston >   <Ch 34> < 104 >
with Dendrox running after.

Nodwel and Vordin also headed for the tunnel behind the two thieves and Weena. This is when the creature decided to leap toward them shrieking, as if it had been waiting for the group to make their move. Now it had become an exciting chase and exactly what it wanted. It scurried after them on all six of its legs, snapping its massive jaws in eager anticipation.

"They like fear! They're definitely getting what they want!" Vordin called back to Nodwel.

The dwarf was falling behind. His short legs were holding him back. Nodwel, realizing that there was going to be no chance of him being able to outrun the beast, shouted ahead to Vordin, "Run boy! I might have to hold this thing back!"

"As long as you keep running," Vordin panted, "it will want the chase," he breathed, "If you fight… try to slow it down… it will just kill you swiftly… in order to continue the chase… after the rest of us… Come on…" he encouraged, "We need you… Run! Don't give up!"

Vordin was beginning to lose sight of Dendrox and the others, as he also was starting to fall behind. "*I'm so glad that Nodwel's here. At least he can fight, maybe slow the beast up a little,*" Vordin thought to himself. "*What can I do? Maybe it'll choke on one of my bones,*" he tried to joke with himself, but all he could think about was Yarin and how easily the creature killed him.

Yarin's screams haunted him as Vordin pushed himself to run faster, but he felt his exhausted body refusing him. The light from Weena's lantern was beginning to disappear from sight as the others got farther and farther away. Vordin began to feel the hopelessness and despair take over, and his pace faltered even more so.

"You'll not take me! Not now!" someone bellowed from farther up the tunnel.

"Borin!" Asdella called out at the sound of his voice.

"Borin?" Nodwel exclaimed with surprise, between heavy breaths, and his pace quickened slightly.

The warrior woman bolted ahead and emerged from the passage into the small chamber where she could see Borin engaged in battle with one of the beasts. It was reared up on its back four legs as it slashed madly at him with its claws. The large middle-aged man, wielding both a short sword and hatchet, was a welcome sight to the warrior. She raised her sword and then screaming in a fierce fury at the creature, joined Borin in battle.

His leather backpack was missing and had been replaced by a small leather pouch at his side. His short black hair was wet with perspiration and clung to his round face. His grey shirt and brown leather vest were caked with mud, as were his black pants. His pant leg was torn and a bloody gash on his muscular leg could be seen.

There were torches wedged into crevices in the rock around the room, which Borin must have placed there. The chamber had four passages leading from it. At the north tunnel, Asdella and Borin fought with the Killnarin as it bore down on them both. Lorenta emerged from the east passageway followed by Candra and Weena with Dendrox close behind.

"Be prepared to use your spells," Candra told her breathlessly, "We'll need every advantage we have."

"Yes, I know," the wizard panted heavily, trying to breathe. "*I can't believe anyone could run that fast!*" Weena said to herself, "*No more sweets for me, that's for sure. I guess Candra and Dendrox are used to making a quick get away being thieves and all. Asdella being a warrior and Lorenta a spider, I guess they all can move pretty quickly. Candra practically had to drag me the whole way. Oh, my side hurts. I can hardly breathe. Why did she care so much? I thought her thinking was, if you couldn't keep up, you get left behind. It can't be that she's expecting my magic to work. I'm expendable in her eyes, aren't I?*"

"Dendrox!" Candra commanded, "Asdella and the other will have to battle on their own. We have the creature behind us to worry about! Get ready!" She drew an arrow and pulled it back aiming into the darkness of the tunnel.

"Wait for the others!" Weena yelled in a panic, "You'll hit them! Where are they? They were right behind us, weren't they?"

<Zaylyn ><Quest For The Sword Of Anthrowst ><By Katrina Mandrake-Johnston >   <Ch 34> < 105 >

"I won't miss," Candra said calmly.

Vordin came stumbling into the room and collapsed into Weena's arms, almost knocking her over. His breath was coming out in desperate gasps, but he managed to say, "Nod…" followed by an enormous gasp for air and then, "wel…"

"I see the dwarf," Candra shouted to Vordin's relief, "The creature's right behind."

She loosed her arrow. It flew right past Nodwel, so close that he felt the air rush past his ear. The arrow punched deep into the creature and it howled in pain and rage.

Borin dodged the claws of the attacking beast at the northern tunnel and struck with a well-placed blow to its thick throat. It made a choking noise and stepped back a bit.

Nodwel emerged from the east tunnel and ran right over to join Asdella and Borin in their battle, hoping that the others could hold back the other one at least for awhile.

"Borin!" Nodwel panted, "You're alive!"

"There's an escape tunnel to the west," Borin told them, "The spiders are trying to come up from the south to escape through it. We have to hold this thing back."

"One followed us. We have two to worry about," Asdella told him.

Their creature gnashed its teeth together and dropped down to all six of its legs. Then it came at them viciously with its powerful jaws.

Nodwel came down with his axe on the beast's head, dealing it a mighty blow. All this did was distract it for a second, but it gave enough time for Asdella to ram her sword through its eye and into its skull. Its body twitched and collapsed.

Before they could feel any sort of relief, she yanked her sword free and shouted, "Here comes another behind it!"

From the southern tunnel, a group of five spiders entered the room. They stopped and watched as the warriors engaged in battle with yet another creature from the north passage. Candra shot another arrow and Dendrox managed to throw two daggers at the approaching creature from the east passage, but both were unsure if they had succeeded in wounding the beast.

"Go! This way!" Lorenta shouted, both in speech and in her mind while pointing over to the west tunnel, hoping that they would understand her. The spiders quickly moved over to the west tunnel and disappeared down it into the darkness. "They say they're the last," Lorenta reported.

"Good," Borin shouted, "Follow them. There's another room where we can hold these things off better."

Weena, Vordin, and Lorenta ran after the spiders down the west passage. Dendrox threw yet another dagger at the beast but missed terribly and, having only a few daggers left, ran shortly after. Candra also followed, stopping only twice to loose an arrow toward their beast.

"Go Nodwel, we can handle this one," Borin told him, trying to block the clawed arm with both his short sword and hatchet as the arm bore down on him from above.

Nodwel, knowing that he was slower than the rest, didn't argue and started for the tunnel.

"Next chance we get, we'll go, okay?" Borin said to Asdella.

"I can take this thing. You go," she argued, "This one's not as strong as the first one for some reason."

"We have to go," he told her again.

"*Asdella go! Please! Go and live! Before the other one decides to attack,*" Narr pleaded with her in her mind.

She slashed her sword across the Killnarin's head. It didn't flinch; it just growled at her.

Borin yelled, "Go now!" and they both ran for the tunnel.

The beast they were fighting shrieked at them and climbed over its dead sibling to meet the creature who now emerged from the east passage. Two of Candra's arrows protruded from its left shoulder. Borin looked back as he headed down the tunnel and could see that many more creatures were piling into the room, all eager to pursue them.

Borin stopped, took an amulet from his pocket, and rubbed at it furiously.

"What are you doing?!" Asdella barked at him, "Come on, if you want to flee so badly!"

<Zaylyn ><Quest For The Sword Of Anthrowst ><By Katrina Mandrake-Johnston >   <Ch 34> < 106 >

"It's a Camouflage amulet. I'm hoping it will disguise the tunnel and give us some time," Borin told her. He dropped the amulet on the ground and continued down the passage.

"I see the exit!" Asdella said to him, "The others are there waiting for us."

When they reached the rest of the group, Borin told them, "There's too many. The spiders saved my life, dragging me down into the well before the Killnarin could finish me off, so hopefully, I'll be able to save their lives in return. I owe that to them, especially after all they've told me. If there is any chance that I might be able to trap these creatures here, if only for a short while, it might be enough to save all of you and the spiders as well. Please, you must escape and find a way to defeat these things." He took a bottle from the leather bag at his hip.

"What's that?" Nodwel asked, "What are you going to do?"

"There's too many, friend," he answered, "They'll follow and kill you all. I have to stop them. This is a Blast potion. Nimdor had it. It will collapse and seal the tunnel, maybe even kill a couple of them. Well, at least I hope it will."

"You'll never be able to survive that!" Weena exclaimed.

"I know. Now go," he commanded.

"You can't just kill yourself! There has to be another way! Can't you just throw the potion at them?" Weena asked, extremely upset.

Borin explained, "There's no other way! I have to make sure this works. If I throw it, there's too great a chance of something going wrong. We only have one go at this. I've made my decision. This was my plan before I knew you all were here, and it's definitely not going to change now, now that your lives are at risk as well. Go, please. There's no time to argue about it." The howl of a creature came echoing down the tunnel and it was nearing their position. "Go! The magic of the amulet won't confuse them for long," he yelled as he uncorked the potion, "I'll try to wait until the last moment. Make sure you're all clear."

"I am not going to leave," Asdella said calmly.

Borin said sternly, "Damn it, Asdella, go!"

Candra called to her as she started to shove Vordin and Lorenta out of the tunnel, "Asdella! He's made his decision. Do what the man says!" The sky had already begun to brighten with the coming dawn. The elfin thief turned to Borin and said, "Thank-you. You are an honorable man."

"There has to be another way," Vordin protested.

"Are we just going to abandon him like this?" Lorenta asked.

"Come on," Candra called to the rest, "There's no sense in all of us dying!"

Dendrox and Nodwel made their way reluctantly toward the exit.

"Are you sure you want to do this?" Nodwel asked Borin.

"Nothing you can say will make me change my mind," was his reply.

"I... I could take your place..." Nodwel suggested.

"No! Now take these people out of here!" Borin demanded.

"Weena, come on," Dendrox said to her.

"Asdella," Nodwel said, "Let's go!"

"I'm not leaving him to die! I can save him!" she screamed with fury.

"Now is not the time to have a change of heart, Asdella. Go. Save yourself," Borin told her, "These things have definitely found their way through the magic of that amulet by now. There is no time to argue."

Borin held the bottle ready and waited for the creatures to come. He could see them now. The two wounded creatures were at the front of the group and held up the others in their slowed pace.

"You all go," Weena said to them, "I think I can convince her to follow. If not, I'll leave too."

"You sure?" Dendrox asked her, the deep concern showing in his eyes.

"Yes go," she answered, although she was unsure if this was the right thing to do.

They exited through the opening, and Weena, Asdella, and Borin stood alone as the Killnarin grew nearer and nearer.

"I'm not going to leave him," Asdella said angrily through clenched teeth.

<Zaylyn ><Quest For The Sword Of Anthrowst ><By Katrina Mandrake-Johnston >   <Ch 34> < 107 >

Weena did not want to leave Borin to his death any more than Asdella did, but there was no sense in all three of them getting killed.

Weena, seeing that one of the creatures was moments away from bursting through the tunnel at them, cast her Shield spell hoping that it would be able to counter the Blast potion's magic.

Borin could wait no longer and shattered the bottle. A blinding light filled the tunnel and the force of the blast shot Weena and Asdella backwards out of the tunnel in their protective shield bubble. The spell had been able to absorb the energy of the explosion and saved them from harm, but ended abruptly and they both landed hard on the ground. Weena watched, by the early morning light, as the tunnel entrance collapsed in on itself.

"*We're safe for now,*" Weena said to herself, hugging the ground in utter exhaustion, "*I did it. Asdella's alive.*"

"No! Borin!" Asdella wailed.

Asdella's mind screamed at her, "*Dimwar, Nimdor, Borin… Narr… even Yarin! They're all gone! Why didn't I do something! I'm the one who should have died! I'm expendable, not them!*"

"*I'm so tired,*" Weena's mind said weakly, "*When they said that extending the spell to include another takes a greater toll on the mind and body, they weren't kidding.*" She closed her eyes and let herself rest. "*How could Borin sacrifice himself like that? He's dead. Yarin's dead. This can't be happening! This isn't real…*" and then Weena passed out lying on the rocky ground with a trickle of blood from her nose.

<World of Zaylyn ><Quest For The Sword Of Anthrowst ><By Katrina Mandrake-Johnston ><Ch 35>

CHAPTER 35 =   SORROWFUL CAMPSITE

Nodwel, Dendrox, Candra, and Vordin all raced toward where Asdella and Weena had fallen. They had been waiting anxiously for the two women to emerge, worried for their survival.

Lorenta was at the bottom of the hill, trying to console the group of agitated spiders.

The tunnel entrance was completely collapsed in on itself; a heavy amount of rock and forest debris barring the passage. If any of the approaching Killnarin survived the explosion, they were now trapped within the spiders' lair.

The tunnel had been situated near the top of a rocky hill and from here they could tell approximately where they were. From the top of the rocky hill, they could see that they were a little way into the western edge of the forest, as the mountain range could be seen not too far away from their location. They could also see that the forest seemed to thin out and that the land eventually turned into grassy plains not far to the south.

"We should get everyone into the cover of the forest," suggested Dendrox, "I feel vulnerable up here in the open like this, especially when those creatures are just on the other side of this rubble."

"I doubt if anything could have survived that blast," Nodwel commented, "including Borin."

"Candra, how's Weena?" Dendrox asked.

"She's alive, but unconscious as far as I can tell," was her answer.

"Do you think she'll be okay?" Vordin asked, greatly concerned that yet another companion might die.

Candra answered, "She'll be fine. Asdella won't say a thing to me, all she'll do is glare."

"She's fine," commented Nodwel, "I agree with Dendrox about getting down into the trees. I say we make camp though and give Weena a chance to recover. I've heard of wizards going through something like this. She's not injured is she?" Candra shook her head. "Yeah, then it must be the magical strain put on her. Saving both herself and Asdella took a lot out of her. Something, by the way, which could have been avoided if someone hadn't been so damn stubborn. Asdella, you both could have been killed! If Weena's spell hadn't worked…"

"Yeah, well Borin's still dead. Just leave me the hell alone," and saying this, she got up, sword in hand, and stomped off into the woods.

"Should she be off all by herself like that?" Vordin asked, "What if something happens?"

"It'll be a good idea just to let her be. She'll find us well enough when she's ready. Let's get

<Zaylyn ><Quest For The Sword Of Anthrowst ><By Katrina Mandrake-Johnston >   <Ch 35> < 108 >
Weena to a safe spot," said Nodwel.

"Lorenta?!" Vordin called suddenly realizing that she wasn't in sight anymore, "Where did she go? She was here a moment ago, wasn't she?" Then realizing, he said, "Oh, it's morning already, she must have changed back into spider form. Yeah, there she is," he said pointing to a smaller spider in among the larger ones. Confused, Vordin asked them all, "How is it possible that it's already dawn?"

No one had an answer for him, but Nodwel told him, "Let's just be thankful for it. The Killnarin seem to be more active during the night. There's only one person that comes to mind when I think of how this is possible, and I'd rather not speak of such things."

Vordin nodded saying, "The Black Shadow."

Nodwel and Dendrox carefully carried Weena down the rocky hill and laid her gently on a soft bed of moss. Then they proceeded to clear an area suitable for making a campfire. Candra and Vordin offered to look for food and headed off into the forest together.

A total of twenty-six giant spiders had been able to escape out of a community of almost two hundred. Lorenta and the group of spiders went off into their own secluded area, and Lorenta once more began her lessons on learning the communication ability.

Nodwel remained silent as he gathered wood for the night. His mind was clearly not on his task, as his face was grief-stricken. He was thinking about friends lost and the boy that would have given their deaths some sort of meaning. But Yarin was gone. Their efforts to save the villagers, the deaths of his friends… it was all for nothing.

"Hey Nodwel?" Dendrox said, but Nodwel was lost in thought and did not hear him at first. "Nodwel?" Dendrox repeated.

"Sorry, you were saying something?" the dwarf asked.

"I was just thinking," he said, "Do you really think it's safe to camp here? You're obviously planning to stay here all day plus the night, right? I mean, sure the tunnel has collapsed in on itself and the creatures probably won't be able to get through, but what's to stop them from still coming after us? Dexcsin is a little way to the east and probably not very far away. They could just come up the well or out another way. We don't know how many went into the tunnels. Several could have remained out in the forest."

"I don't want to move Weena," the dwarf told him, "We all need some recovery time. You saw how much trouble the beast had coming down the well; they'll have the same trouble going up. Besides, I don't want to walk into one of their traps again, especially when they have the ability to manipulate our minds. Yarin's death proves how cunning and effective they can be. It'll be better to camp here."

"Yeah, I agree. It's just that I'm feeling kind of helpless," admitted the thief.

The two men continued their task in silence once more. Dendrox now started to collect kindling, and Nodwel began to chop a fallen log into smaller pieces with his axe. He hated to use his battle-axe in such a manner, but if they were going to be safe during the night, they were going to need a large fire. It wouldn't matter if the blade was a little dull from chopping wood if the creatures caught them unaware because of poor visibility. Besides, he had a whet stone in his pouch. It was about time he tended to its edge anyhow.

Dendrox asked him, "Do you think all this trouble is over us?"

"What do you mean?" asked Nodwel tossing another chunk of wood into their growing pile.

"The Killnarin," he explained, "Do you think they came down into the spiders' lair after us?"

"I don't know. It seems silly to send a whole army of the beasts after the likes of us, don't you think?" replied Nodwel.

"Yeah, it does seem unlikely. So you think invading the tunnels and the village were part of a bigger plan? What would they want with the tunnels?" Dendrox asked.

Nodwel suggested, "Great place for the creatures to hide, prepare for something larger perhaps?"

"Maybe. Then they'll probably want to send a couple after us, just to make sure we can't warn anyone of what this wizard is doing," added Dendrox.

Nodwel chuckled, "Doesn't need to. No one would believe us if we did tell. I think we are just

<Zaylyn ><Quest For The Sword Of Anthrowst ><By Katrina Mandrake-Johnston >   <Ch 35> < 109 >
more of an annoyance than a threat."

After several hours, Candra and Vordin returned. Candra carried two large rabbits and several good sized sticks in order to make a spit once a cooking fire was started. Vordin had a collection of berries and nuts nestled in the front of his outstretched shirt.

Candra wore a triumphant grin on her face as she announced, "We've done well, as you can see. We'll have somewhat of a feast this morning, eh? It's not much of a breakfast, but it's a lot more than we've been getting these past few days."

"How's Weena doing?" Vordin asked.

"Still recovering," said Dendrox, "She could do with some water. You find any?"

"No," Candra answered.

"Hey Vordin, you better let me check that stuff, just in case. Candra's terrible at picking out the poisonous from the good," Dendrox told him.

"Yeah, I'm not so good either," Vordin admitted transferring the berries and nuts to Dendrox's lap.

"You see Asdella at all?" the dwarf asked.

"We sort of went off in the other direction," answered Vordin, "We were kind of nervous about running into her, to be honest."

Candra asked, "Hey Dendrox, you think any of the creatures are going to come this way?"

"I was just talking to Nodwel about that," Dendrox said as he examined a dark purple berry.

The elf said, "By the luck we had with the hunting, it looks like we're safe at least for the moment. I'm pretty sure those damn creatures would scare every living thing out of the area for quite a distance."

Weena opened her eyes and tried to sit up but still felt a bit groggy. Nodwel was busy trying to get the fire started. Vordin went over to Weena and sat down beside her on the moss-covered ground. He held her hand to steady her and felt her forehead.

"I'm fine, just a little dizzy," she told him, "Asdella? She's okay?"

Vordin nodded and said, "She took off on her own for awhile though."

Weena took her hand back as she was feeling better. "How long was I out for?" she wondered.

"Hours. It's still a few hours before noon though," he told her.

Nodwel went about getting the fire started, arranging the wood and with the kindling between. Candra grabbed a dagger from Dendrox's belt as she sat down next to him with one of the rabbits. Dendrox tossed a couple of berries into the trees and then proceeded to examine another handful.

"Oh, Nodwel, I have a flame box. I didn't think of it before, but wouldn't it be a lot faster and easier to use it to light the fire?" Weena said as she took it from her pouch and offered it out.

"Yes, I was about to ask to borrow it actually. I never really liked getting fires started much. I always let someone else do it," he explained. She walked over to the dwarf and handed him the tiny box. "I see you've recovered quite quickly," Nodwel said with a smile.

"Oh, I feel fine now," she told him.

"Really? I've heard that most don't for a day, sometimes two. That's great though, means you're stronger than you think. Here, why don't I show you a few things about starting a fire," he offered.

"*I already know plenty about getting a fire started, don't I?*" she thought with a hollow feeling, forever haunted by the memory of the fire she caused at the school. "Sure. Thanks Nodwel," she said with a weak smile and knelt down beside him in front of what was to be the fire. She was glad it was to only be a small fire, meant for cooking the meat. "*A small one. But that's what my fire was supposed to be at the school, wasn't it, and look what happened there...*"

"See how I've arranged everything here? Now you want to light it in these places and that should get it going," Nodwel instructed, "I'll watch to see if you need any help."

They all remained silent as they went about their tasks, thinking about recent events and about all the many lives that had been lost. Occasionally, Vordin would check Weena's condition but each time she insisted that she was perfectly all right.

After a long drawn out silence, Vordin, no longer able to stifle his emotions, choked out, "Yarin should be here with us."

Everyone had been thinking about the loss of their young companion, about all the innocent people

<Zaylyn ><Quest For The Sword Of Anthrowst ><By Katrina Mandrake-Johnston >   <Ch 35> < 110 >
from the two villages, and the members of Nodwel's group that had given their lives.

"None of this should have happened," Nodwel said.

Candra said, "First Vordin's village, then Dexcsin, then even the spiders' lair. Why? So much death… It doesn't even seem real. I don't even know how to react to all this. I'm just in a state of constant shock."

"He was like me," Vordin said, his face wet with tears, "He was the last of his village… a survivor. He beat the beasts, just like I had. We both escaped them. He should be here. Saving at least someone was the only reason we even went to Dexcsin in the first place. I can't… All I can think is just who's going to be next to die and how much longer I have to live. Whether or not this will be the last time I'll ever hear a bird's song or even feel moss beneath my fingertips like this. Every moment is precious no matter how small. I know this now. I miss my mother and my father. Everyone I ever knew in Nilnont. I just can't take anymore."

Weena had a tear in her eye, "We've all lost people we've cared about. You must be feeling the worst, but everything's going to be okay. We can't lose hope."

"My mother, my father, everyone I've ever known," Vordin sobbed, "And now practically everyone I meet ends up dead as well. At least with Yarin around, I wasn't alone. I'm useless! I can't fight these creatures! At least with Yarin, there was someone like me; someone who had gone through the same thing."

"I'm still amazed that we escaped at all," Dendrox commented, "I didn't think we were going to survive the spiders. But we did. And when the Killnarin attacked, I thought we were all trapped and were surely going to be killed, but we survived. We should be thankful of that."

"And because we are the only ones still alive," Nodwel told them all, "we should do our best to try to prevent anyone else from dying because of those beasts. We owe everyone that much. We may not succeed, but we have to try. We're the only ones that have encountered the Killnarin and lived to talk about it. I hate to say it, but we're probably the only ones that have even a slim chance of stopping these things. Anyone else wouldn't know what they were up against; they wouldn't know what to expect. We can't just sit by while innocent people are in danger, hoping that someone else will defeat them."

"The only way we have any hope of stopping them is to defeat the wizard behind them," said Vordin, "Dranngore was his name. Even if we could kill all the Killnarin, what's to stop him from summoning more?"

"You mean, the ones we killed, the ones Borin gave his life to kill, it could all be for nothing?" Candra asked with shock as she stood up, her face tense with frustration.

"Now can you see why everything seems so hopeless?" Vordin said.

"I doubt the blast did them any harm," commented Asdella, "Nimdor, our friend, cast a fireball at close range right into a Killnarin's face and it didn't even faze it at all."

"No!" Candra said pacing back and forth in front of the fire which was now lit, "It can't be like that! It can't all just be for nothing! We have to get rid of this wizard and end it all!"

"How are we going to do that? We don't even know where he is," said Dendrox.

Candra was getting more and more upset, and she told him, "Well, then we find out where. We have to do something. No one else is going to believe us. It's up to us. And like Nodwel said, we have to at least try. I can't just admit that it's hopeless and that hundreds more are going to be slaughtered."

"Do you think the spiders may know something?" Weena asked.

"We'll have to wait 'till nightfall for Lorenta to change," Vordin told her as he dried his eyes with the back of his hand.

Dendrox asked him, "You're the one that told us about Dranngore. Something about a sword?"

"Yeah, the Sword of Anthrowst. I was told that the wizard can only be defeated with it, if we're going to stop the Killnarin," he answered.

"Well, there we go. We find out as much as we can about the sword and any information there is about the wizard," Weena said trying her best to sound cheerful, but her heart was heavy.

"Alright," Candra said propping a rabbit over the now roaring fire, "So we sort of have a plan now.

<Zaylyn ><Quest For The Sword Of Anthrowst ><By Katrina Mandrake-Johnston >   <Ch 35> < 111 >

Travel to Vackiindmire then, and find out information. Sounds good to me." She picked up the other rabbit and began to prepare it for the fire as well.

Dendrox wondered if she were going to hold up to her heroic words when they finally reached Vackiindmire. She was not the type to willingly put herself in danger for someone else if she could help it, and neither was he.

Everyone sat grieving, absentmindedly watching the crackling fire and the cooking meat. Dendrox passed around the nuts and berries.

"I'll save a share for Asdella," Nodwel offered, remembering his harsh words to her when they had been under the spell of the Killnarin in the spiders' lair and feeling regretful of them.

Candra, who was finished with the second rabbit, stuck it on a stick and positioned it over the fire as well. They all ate the nuts and berries in silence waiting for the meat.

Once all the meat was cooked, passed around, and eaten, it was near noon.

Weena had been trying so hard to be strong, but tears were starting to well up in her eyes once more. Vordin noticed this and decided to start up a conversation with her to get both their minds thinking about something other than the tragic deaths and the shock and fear of their escape.

"So what's it like to do magic?" he asked her.

She looked at him with tears in her eyes and he could see that her hands were shaking. "It's pretty complicated," she said softly.

"I'd like to hear," Vordin urged.

"Um, well, the words of a spell have no sound," she told him, calming slightly as she tried her best to explain things to him, "It's as if the sound the words would have made are instead replaced by a magical power. You have to will the words into being. The words themselves are more feelings than actual words. Anyone can speak the syllables, that's easy. You have to feel the sounds in your mind and project the energy they create in you. It's hard to explain, like I said. You have to will the magic to work by concentrating your emotions into what you want to do. Just saying the sounds in your mind isn't enough, you have to put a bit of yourself into it."

Vordin was glad that he was able to get her mind off the recent horrors, even if it were just briefly. "So what are these words? Are they actual words or just magic nonsense words?" he asked.

"It's actually an ancient language. Probably the first language or more likely the language of the spirits or a combination of both perhaps? Anyway, these words have power. It's not language like we define and use today in our speech. It's more meanings than definitions and labels. In language, we have so many labels for one thing. A woman, for example, has the label woman, but also mother, daughter, sister, grandmother, female, person, human, and the list goes on and all these words mean the same individual. Okay, this is more difficult and complicated to explain than I thought. There are words for certain emotions and for objects, but it's not as specific as we have in our language where things have many names and classes for the same thing. Most common examples are 'you' and 'I', and 'physical body' and 'soul'... These are all rough translations of course. Umm... 'hot', 'cold', 'love', 'hate', and different degrees of these. It's all too complicated for me to explain, but in a way, it's simple at the same time. I'm still trying to learn the basics and the whole concept of invoking the feeling and a bit of myself behind these words. The sound of the words are highly tied in with their meanings and purpose. As in with the word 'hate', it will have a harsh sound. The word 'love' will have a soft sound for example. The translation is hard to explain too. Our words are very specific in what they mean, where the words used in a spell are more general and have a broader meaning. A single word can have various meanings depending on how it's used and most importantly the feeling put behind it. Oh, and the way the words are written express both sound and meaning within the strokes and shape of the symbols."

Vordin was having difficulty understanding exactly what she meant, but he was glad for the conversation and it seemed to be helping Weena to calm her emotions. "What made you choose to learn the spells you did?" he asked her.

She answered, "I don't know. I thought they would be something good to learn. That way I could help people, I guess."

<Zaylyn ><Quest For The Sword Of Anthrowst ><By Katrina Mandrake-Johnston >   <Ch 35> < 112 >

"Maybe that's why you've been having such good luck with your spells," he suggested, "When it's really necessary and someone really needs your help, that's when your spells really come through for you."

"I don't know, maybe I should just give up," she sighed, "I'm never going to be a proper wizard. It takes so much effort and patience. I mean, I've studied so long and hard already and haven't even gotten a single spell mastered to where I can rely on their abilities when I need them, and that's with simple first level spells. It takes a lot of skill to perform a spell, and it's not guaranteed to work every time. Wizards usually have magic items along with them and when they need to perform a spell and happen to fail at casting the magic themselves, they can just use a magic item in place of the spell to get the same effect."

"What do you mean?" Vordin asked confused.

"Potions, amulets, powders, globes, things like that. Some wizard I am. I can hardly do a simple spell and can't afford to buy the pricey magic trinkets to back me up. And, I have been put in situations that even the most highly equipped and experienced wizard couldn't have anticipated," she said looking even more upset now than she had before.

"You made it through. You came through for us. You saved lives," he told her.

"Not Yarin's. Not Borin's. If I were a proper wizard, I would cast my spells properly and I would have magic items with me for emergencies," she said with tears in her eyes. Vordin's success at maintaining a pleasant conversation had ended. Weena continued, "How can you say we made it? We came to Dexcsin to try to help the villagers. We found the only person left, an innocent child, and we couldn't even save him. Sure, we survived, but he should have been the one. I would have taken his place if I could have."

"I know what you mean," Vordin said remembering how he had felt when he had returned to his village. Seeing the dead children had given him a horrible hopeless feeling and a feeling of guilt that he had remained safe and alive while they had been forced to suffer. He knew that Weena was probably feeling the same way, as he too again had this same feeling. But he knew that he had to fight it and that Weena had to fight it as well. They had to move on, all of them had too. Many of Rasindell's stories had been meant to teach him this and now he realized this to be true. They couldn't dwell on things that couldn't be changed, not if they were going to stop Dranngore and the Killnarin. "That's the way it happened though, so the most we can do is try to do some good," he said hoping that he could reach her, "We survived, while the others died. Borin sacrificed himself. Don't let it be in vain. We can't just give up. How many other innocent people will perish if we do that?"

"I… I think I need to be alone. I'm going to take a walk," she decided.

"It's not safe, you should stay here," Vordin protested.

"I'll yell if I get into trouble. I'm not going to go far," Weena assured him, "I just need to go."

"Weena, be sure not to wander. Stay close to camp," Nodwel cautioned, as Weena headed off into the forest.

She didn't stop until the campsite was just out of sight. She sat upon the forest floor and let the tears run down her face. *"Why couldn't we save Yarin? Maybe he could have survived if we hadn't come,"* she thought sobbing.

The sun was filtering down through the treetops. The air was cool and crisp, and there was the faint smell of damp earth and pine. Everything was still and quiet. She stood and inhaled a deep breath, but the ache in her chest did not subside. Vegetation surrounded her like protective walls shielding her from everything and everyone.

She had been thinking about what Vordin had said. *"What if these are the last moments we will be alive? Do I really want to be worried about every little thing or do I want to be enjoying what time I have left?"*

A small brown and black bird, not seeming to notice her at all, fluttered down from the sky and landed on the branch of a nearby tree. Its small black eyes darted around its little world and then it opened its black beak and sang a sweet happy song. She watched and listened, and the beginnings of a

<Zaylyn ><Quest For The Sword Of Anthrowst ><By Katrina Mandrake-Johnston >   <Ch 35> < 113 >
smile started to cross her lips. The bird knew nothing of her feelings and of her life, but it seemed to care and to be concerned for her. The bird jumped to another branch and continued its song. Her smile grew, but the ache was deep in her heart and could not be removed so easily. The bird spread its little wings and flew high up into the sky.

Weena stood, and brushing the debris from her robes, stepped away from where she had been sitting and stepped onto a narrow overgrown trail. She didn't think of where it might lead. She moved a slender branch full of lush green leaves aside.

The silence was calming, and she walked slowly along the trail. Her feet moved quietly over the rocks and gravel. Weena took her time, enjoying the natural beauty of her surroundings and she tried to take in every detail. She stopped to touch a leaf, her fingers caressing its surface. She then noticed a fuzzy little caterpillar on the branch of the tree. As it inched along, its body rippled with every movement. She plucked it from the branch and placed it gently in her hand and smiled as its many feet tickled her. She was simply enjoying the fact of being alive. She wondered briefly if this might be a rarity to find one during the early autumn, and then replacing the caterpillar carefully and gently on the branch once more, she continued along the path.

After awhile she stopped, opened her small cloth pouch, and took out her mother's ring. The gems sparkled in the light and Weena slipped it onto her finger. She hadn't worn it for a very long time. It gave her the comfort she needed, and then deciding that she was getting too far away from the camp, she turned around and headed back.

<World of Zaylyn ><Quest For The Sword Of Anthrowst ><By Katrina Mandrake-Johnston ><Ch 36>

CHAPTER 36 = ASDELLA AND NARR

Asdella had been sitting upon a fallen log for most of the morning now.

"*I wonder what they all think of me? That I'm crazy? That I talk to myself because of Narr? That I might turn against them? That I can't be trusted? Wait a minute, since when did I ever care of what they might think? I don't feel like myself anymore. I don't like it. It's Narr… he's invaded my mind and somehow is changing me. At least I think he might be. I hate this. I can't escape him. He's always swimming around in my thoughts… in my private thoughts... Watching my every move. It's not right. Sure, he helped get us out of the tunnels; found Borin to be still alive and told me how to find him. Didn't really matter in the end though, as he's dead now too. I wonder if I'll start hearing him too inside my head. No, I don't think so. But it must have been Narr. He must have been influencing my decisions. It was like I was being held back. I wanted to kill those beasts, make them pay for what they did. Hell, I just wanted to kill something and make everything go away.*"

"*Asdella,*" Narr's voice said in her mind.

"No, go away!" she yelled out loud.

"*What's wrong?*" he asked, "*I discovered Borin, told you, came with you all in your escape, and then I've just been exploring the forest trying to learn more about this whole ghost thing. No sign of the creatures in the forest, so that's a help. I've come back to keep you company, if that's okay. I don't like being out there all alone with no one to connect to, at least not like I can with you.*"

"Oh joy," she said sarcastically, "You've been staying out of my inner thoughts like you said you would, I hope."

"*Of course I have. I said I would, didn't I?*" he said defensively.

"You know Narr, you don't seem to joke around as much as you use to," she told him.

"*Yeah, I know,*" he said, "*It's just that I'm trying really hard to adjust to this new ghostly state and it's really confusing and frustrating. There's so much that I wanted to do and wanted to say to people, and now I can't. Well, unless I share the experience through someone else I guess. But it's not the same… it will never be the same. I know so much more than I did before about myself and others now, and I would be able to live my life to the fullest, savoring every moment whether it be good or bad, if I only could.*"

"Okay, I think I liked you a lot better when you didn't try so hard to figure things out," Asdella thought to him, "*Maybe you're not supposed to. You used to be so carefree before. What's with all the*

<Zaylyn ><Quest For The Sword Of Anthrowst ><By Katrina Mandrake-Johnston >   <Ch 36> < 114 >

regrets now? You used to be happy. Sure, you used to let loose a couple of snide remarks now and then in fun, but now you're simply just depressing and annoying. And you didn't talk as much. You tend to ramble now. But that could be just because it's thought and not speech. I find that I ramble on a lot when I talk to you in thought. I'm starting to sound like Weena. And why are you so desperate to tell me all these romantic feelings you have for me? It's getting to be really overpowering. I know you're going through this 'analyze your whole life stage' or something like that, but please, give it a rest. You have the rest of eternity probably to do it."

"*Sorry,*" he said, sounding truly hurt by her words.

She asked, "So is Borin around too?"

"*If so, I can't see him or talk to him, but I'm sure he's about somewhere in our world. He had a younger brother. If I were him, that's where I'd be,*" he told her, "*I guess that's why you should make the most out of the time you do have around the people you care about. I've been thinking. You know how ghosts are said to remain about because they have some unfinished business?*"

"Yeah sure," she said, letting her voice show that he again had started doing what she had just complained about.

Narr ignored her tone and continued, "*I don't think that's entirely true. Well, from what I've been experiencing, I think I might have it figured out. Everyone has a soul, and I mean everyone, including the animals, plants, insects, birds, and so on. They live their lives and eventually die, some sooner than others of course. I seem to have two parts to my consciousness. One is me, Narr, the life I just lived recently. The other part is a larger consciousness, like a higher being too large to fit inside a body completely. I see this as my soul, not me Narr as you know, but the entire me, a being existing beyond time and living many, many lives. My soul, my pure self, is judging Narr, the life I lived. I have to explore myself and come to terms with the life I had with this higher knowledge that my soul possesses. When that happens, and I become at peace with myself, I carry on into another life, starting out fresh and renewed. Of course it will be quite awhile for this, and I guess this transition period could seem to be either extreme torment and frustration, a hell of sorts, or as joy and happiness, depending on how you lived your life and how you look at it. I would have liked to have children. I could be watching them grow and experience life right now, living on through them. I have a lot of things in my life that I'm pondering, and there is a lot that I have yet to deal with.*"

"So I'm finding out," she commented impatiently, trying not to think any of the sour remarks she had for him and his non-stop thoughts, because she knew that he would hear her. She had become wary of making him angry, as she was uncertain of what he was capable of. She was worried that he may be able to take complete control over her body and that she would be trapped in some kind of limbo.

Narr continued, "*I'm able to see things from aspects I never thought possible. I can't explain it. I find my happiness in you, Asdella. I'm frightened and alone right now. I need you. Please don't shut me out. I watch you. I feel you. I feel your pain, your sorrow. I want to make you happy. I want to be a part of your life. I can't watch you from afar. The fact that you can hear and feel me just shows how much you really do need me too.*"

"I don't need anyone. You know that. I can handle things myself," she told him, and then as an after thought, "*Except maybe a ghost in my head.*"

"*Just be thankful that I'm just roaming around in your head, although if you would prefer other parts of your body to be haunted, I could arrange it. In fact that sounds like it might be fun. I have some places in mind that could be very interesting,*" he said with the same slyness that Asdella so well remembered.

"Being molested by a ghost isn't my choice in fun," she said with a smirk.

"*At least you couldn't punch me,*" he said with a laugh.

"Lucky you," she said.

He then said in a serious and caring tone, "*Listen, Asdella, part of you is reaching out desperately for help, and so here I am. It's the only explanation for why I can contact you like this as if I was right here beside you. You can't live your whole life hiding from the pain, denying yourself love. I haven't pried into your memories. Those I'm leaving for you to share if you wish on your own accord. But I*

<Zaylyn ><Quest For The Sword Of Anthrowst ><By Katrina Mandrake-Johnston >   <Ch 36> < 115 >

feel that you blame yourself or have this self-loathing for some reason, and all I can say is that you can't punish yourself like this. You don't deserve this isolation no matter how much you think you do. I love you, and I'm not going to let you push me away like you did when I was alive. I'm not trying to force myself on you. I'm just saying that I am here for you. Talk to me if you need to. It's all unconditional. You can tell me anything, and I'll try to understand and help, if you want me too. Besides, it's not like I can go and tell anyone else what secrets you've told me."

"Please just get out of my head. I want to be alone right now. Am I forever cursed now to never be alone with my own thoughts? To have you constantly swimming around in my head? Telling me what to think and forcing your opinions on me all the time? At least before, I had the choice of whether not I wanted to share something. Now you're in there eavesdropping on my inner most thoughts and feelings," she said unkindly, "Am I never to have privacy again?"

"*That was not the reaction I expected,*" Narr said. He was clearly hurt and frustrated by her. "*Figures though, I pour my inner most feelings out to you, and you shoot me down, getting all defensive,*" he said to her, his temper rising, "*Fine. It was hard enough for me to finally open up to you about things. If you think I'm annoying and that I'm violating you, then I will leave you alone! What was I thinking?! I guess everyone was right. You are just a crazy nut! No one can reach you! I was a fool to think that you could feel. Your heart is as cold as ice and as hard as a stone. All that time and life I wasted trying to pursue some sort of affectionate response from you. You aren't capable of it, not even now!*" Asdella simply shrugged. "*Do you even realize how selfish you are? Everything is about you and how things will affect you and you alone. Think about it, you'll see that it's true. Do you even care that that kid died? Was Borin expendable?*"

She refused to provide him with any sort of reaction.

"*I'll be around. If you ever come to your senses I might decide to visit you again. Don't expect me to come crawling back.*"

She slid her bare calloused foot over a smooth stone.

"*Things don't exist for your amusement, including people and their feelings. A friend is not just someone who is useful in battle and amusing at times, although you seem to think otherwise. You can't just brush people off and expect things to return to normal when you need something from them. I know you don't care, and you think that you're alone, and that you don't need anyone, and that you don't need to depend on anybody for anything. I have to say this, that one day you will be utterly alone; you will have hurt everyone that has ever cared about you. You'll realize that although you thought you could take on the whole world by yourself, that you can't, and no one will want to help you. I know, you're a fierce warrior and all that hate and anger feeds your strength and your fury. To let that go, would make you weak and vulnerable, or so you think. Realize that this is all you're going to have left inside. You'll be a bitter old woman talking about how fierce and ruthless you were in your younger days and find that no one cares except for other angry people that wish that they could vent in the same violent manner and without the consequences as you did. There are always consequences. You're losing yourself. Do you feel it? You must. You figure you'll die young in battle and won't have to deal with it all later. Surprise, I am dead. You don't just vanish. You'll be dealing with it all, and for you it will be torture. Your soul will feel the regret, sorrow, and loneliness, even if you choose to ignore it all your life. It will be a bitter and painful hell for you, Asdella. You know what, I think I've said enough. You need to wake up and take a good look at the world around you. I'm sorry, but if you truly want to suffer alone, so be it. I care about you, more than that, but it seems that this means nothing to you. Like I said, I'll be around. Good-bye, Asdella.*"

Asdella shifted her position on the log. Her mind was clear; he was gone. But what Narr had said had hurt her deeply. A tear rolled down her cheek to fall onto her bare knee making a clean spot in the dirty film covering her body. She wiped the tear away angrily.

"A tear? How often do I see one of those? What's wrong with me? Narr's not real. I don't want to be crazy anymore. I don't want people to call me that anymore. It's not like I care. Why should I? Others should be allowed to determine their own opinion about me before the 'crazy' label is suggested to them by someone. Why am I creating Narr's ghost? I don't want to lose my sanity. I know that it

<Zaylyn ><Quest For The Sword Of Anthrowst ><By Katrina Mandrake-Johnston >   <Ch 36> < 116 >

can't be real. Why can't I make it stop? Who am I really? I thought I knew, but now I feel as if I'm an empty shell even more so. I can't even be alone with my thoughts, because even my thoughts are tainted. Why can't I tell what's real anymore? Even if the things my ghost says are true, so what? I can't change the way things are, not now. I can't change the past. I can't just forget about things as if they never happened. I can't start fresh. I can never regain my old self... But what if somehow I could? My innocence, my sanity... Shut up. I don't want to think anymore. My own mind won't leave me in peace."

Another tear ran down her cheek, which she wiped away in disgust.

"Get a grip, you miserable wimp! What? Are you going to start crying like a little baby now? Boo hoo, things aren't perfect, my life is horrible," she mocked herself, "So what! That's the way things are! I do miss Narr, but as a ghost, he's just not the same anymore."

<World of Zaylyn ><Quest For The Sword Of Anthrowst ><By Katrina Mandrake-Johnston ><Ch 37>

CHAPTER 37 = DENDROX AND WEENA

It was late afternoon when Weena arrived back at camp. She had gotten lost for several hours trying to retrace her steps. The others were roasting some sort of animal over the fire and it was the smell that had eventually helped her find the way. She was getting hungry. She normally didn't eat very much meat, but hunger ruled over preference.

"Weena!" Nodwel scolded, "You were told not to go far from the camp. Vordin, Dendrox, and Candra have been out looking for you for hours!"

"I got lost," she said sheepishly, "I didn't mean to."

"Didn't you hear us calling you?" Dendrox asked, "We all eventually gave up and came back here hoping you would show up on your own."

It was obvious that they all had been very worried for her. "Funny, they didn't make such a fuss over Asdella," Weena thought to herself, "She's been missing all day. Do they really see me as being so incredibly weak? I guess I am compared to them." "What's that cooking?" she asked.

Candra answered, "Squirrels, it was all we could find when we were out looking for you. Broke another arrow too. I'm usually more cautious than that. We better hope that the majority of our troubles are already over as I'm down to only two arrows now."

"There is no way I'm going to eat a squirrel," she said in disgust. She happened to be very fond of squirrels and the thought of devouring one made her sick to her stomach. Also, without their fur, they resembled large rats which didn't help her appetite much either.

"You have to eat," Candra told her, "It's a long trek to Vackiindmire, and we're probably leaving early in the morning tomorrow. You'll need your strength."

"There's plenty of vegetation. I'm sure I can find something," Weena said, but she was doubtful.

Dendrox asked, "Do you even know anything about plants? Which ones are edible? Which ones contain deadly poison?"

"Well no," she admitted, feeling foolish.

"I'll come with you then," he offered.

Weena smiled as Dendrox led her away from the camp and into the trees. He was nervous about being alone with her, and he could tell that she was too, but she seemed pleased.

Squatting down, he said nervously, "Oh look here. Now this won't taste very good, but it is edible. Come on, help me pull up the roots."

She knelt beside him and begun pulling at the little plant. Weena raised her hand up to brush her hair away from her face, and in doing so, smudged a little bit of dirt onto her cheek. Dendrox looked at her with a warm smile. "You have a smudge," he said.

"Where?" she asked.

"Right here," he told her and gently wiped the dirt from her cheek with his thumb. Her skin was so soft and smooth, and he let his hand linger there. She wore a pleasant expression, and her eyes were wide with an excited spark which seemed to invite him in. "Would she let me kiss those rosy lips I wonder," he thought with a smile.

<Zaylyn ><Quest For The Sword Of Anthrowst ><By Katrina Mandrake-Johnston >   <Ch 37> < 117 >

Weena's mind warned, *"The way he's looking at me gives me shivers, but in a good way. If I try to kiss him and he pulls away, I'll look like such a fool. I wouldn't be able to look at him ever again without feeling like he's laughing at me."*

"Will she slap me if I just go for it? Oh come on, do it or you'll never know," he told himself, *"Any humiliation would be worth it. Just look at her; how can you resist?"*

"I think he's going to kiss me! Oh please! I can't believe this is going to happen! He really does like me," Weena thought excitedly.

Dendrox scolded himself, *"This 'just do it' stuff isn't supposed to take so long, now is it? If you wait too long, the moment will pass and who knows if you'll get a second chance."* And then he kissed her, pulling her close against him.

"Oh wow, I can't believe this is happening. I have tingles all over my body," Weena said to herself enjoying the moment and eagerly pushing herself closer.

"Oh, I want her so bad! I never imagined that she had such passion," he thought kissing her again and again, *"Damn these clothes, why can't they just melt away or something. I wonder if she has anything on under that robe?"* He turned away from her lips, kissing his way down the curve of her neck relishing the little excited breaths she made. He let his hand roam over the curves of her leg, over her hip and waist, up to her soft breast. Weena let her fingertips run along his side and down his back.

"Things are moving too fast," her mind warned, *"But I think I kind of want them to. What happens if I give in to him? What then? Sure, every inch of my body is aching to be invaded by him, but then what? Does it continue, or is it over? Will he stop pursuing me once he has taken all of me? Am I just a prize? Another number on his list of women he's gotten? Does he realize that I wouldn't act this way with just anyone? Or does he even care? If he gets what he wants, where will that leave me? How can I please him enough to make him want to stay? I'm inadequate. I don't know what I'm doing. What if I'm just a big joke to him? He'll brag about what happened and laugh at how horrible I was. Even if his intentions are good, what then? If I give myself to him fully so fast, I'll feel dirty, not being able to control my instincts. I'm supposed to be a lady. This is supposed to be a wonderful romantic and passionate experience. I'm scared. We've kissed. We've touched. I need to save the rest for later, draw it out, feel out the situation now that we know there's something here. I need to find out if it's purely a physical thing that he feels or not, and if that's what I feel for him. I don't want to be used like that and have my feelings tossed aside after he's done. I have to stop this, even though my body is crying out for more. My mind says no."* Then she began to get scared, *"What if he doesn't stop when I ask him to? It's obvious he's not intending to. If I stop things, will he take it the wrong way and think I'm not interested in him anymore? I don't want him to lose interest in me, but I want him to like me for who I am. Unless I try to stop this, I'll never know for sure if it's me he truly likes, or if it's just a passing physical attraction."* Dendrox inched up her robes to touch the skin of her calf and began slowly caressing his way up along her leg. *"Oh it's going to be very hard to stop. Very, very hard. I can most likely stop myself, but what if he doesn't stop?"* she thought getting extremely frightened now, *"What if he doesn't care whether or not I want to experience everything right away with him? He could take me, and I wouldn't be able to do anything to stop him, except say no and hope he listens and obeys. He's so strong. What if I make him angry? I don't know what he's capable of. We're all alone here. No one could hear me call for help. And like an idiot, I was actually excited about getting so far away from the others, hoping something like this would happen."* "Please don't," she whispered, as he began to caress her bare thigh under her robes.

"What do you mean? I thought you wanted this. Did I do something wrong?" he asked, a worried and disappointed look in his eyes.

"I do want this, and you did nothing wrong, it's just too soon," she told him gently pushing him away.

"Oh…" he said. She could see the frustration in his eyes. He continued, "Well we don't have to go as far as that. We could do other things. It's not as if I was expecting anything, if that's what you're getting at. I don't want you to feel you need to do anything you don't want to."

Weena was still afraid of what he might do, and what 'other things' might lead into. Also, whether

<Zaylyn ><Quest For The Sword Of Anthrowst ><By Katrina Mandrake-Johnston >   <Ch 37> < 118 >
or not resistance was a possibility for both of them, if things went further. Besides, to Weena, his little speech sounded a little bit too rehearsed for her liking. She said, "No, I think we should get back to the others. We've been gone for quite awhile. They might start to worry."

They got up and walked back to camp in silence, with both of them feeling very awkward.

"Back so soon?" Candra said with a glint in her eye.

Vordin stated, "Asdella's been gone so long. Do you think she's okay?"

Nodwel told him, "Just leave her alone. She'll come to us when she's ready. It'll be dark in a few hours. I'm sure she'll be back before then."

"Maybe she's in trouble," Vordin added, "I'm going to go find her."

"Don't go far, and be careful," Nodwel told him.

"I'll be careful," Vordin assured him.

"You did realize, I was warning to be wary of Asdella, right?" Nodwel asked.

"Oh," he said, not realizing before that Asdella herself might prove to be a threat, "Well, I'm still going to go check on her."

Vordin went off in the direction he thought Asdella might have gone.

After fumbling about in the forest for quite some time, he eventually found her sitting quietly on a fallen log starring absentmindedly at the ground in front of her. He continued to approach her position and made quite a lot of noise doing so.

Startled, she jumped up and turned to him snarling with her sword raised menacingly and making such a grimace that it distorted her pretty face. "Oh, it's you," she said when she recognized him, "Come on and have a seat."

He did not sit, and instead said, "Are you wanting to head back to camp? I can show you the way." He was unsure of exactly how to get back to the camp and was hoping she would return with him and help him find his way back.

"Yeah, sure. You the only one brave enough to come find me, eh?" she said walking toward him.

"Ah, yeah," he said sheepishly.

She asked him, "So they scrounge up some food? I'm starved."

"Yeah, Nodwel's holding on to some nuts and berries for you, and when I left they were roasting some squirrels. You missed out on the rabbits," Vordin told her.

"Okay, great, which way to the campsite?" she asked him expectantly.

"This way, I think," he said apologetically.

"You have no clue, do you? Don't worry about it, I'll find it. Follow me," she said with a smile which put him at ease.

The two of them then made their way back to the others.

<World of Zaylyn ><Quest For The Sword Of Anthrowst ><By Katrina Mandrake-Johnston ><Ch 38>

CHAPTER 38 =   WEENA AND CANDRA

When Vordin had left to find Asdella, Candra announced shortly after, "I'm going to scout around the surrounding area before it gets dark. Anyone want to come with? Weena?"

"I will," said Weena. She still felt awkward around Dendrox and kept avoiding eye contact with him.

Candra said, "Alright," with a quirk to her smile. She was hoping Weena would go with her.

They walked in silence through the forest and Candra returned Weena's yellow sash. Weena re-tied and straightened it about her waist.

Weena was trying to decide on something to say, wanting to make a good impression and wanting to be accepted by Candra. Weena thought to herself, "*Candra's slender form, my chubbiness; even in personality we're opposites. Her with her courage and strong will, and me with my weak crybaby attitude. We have nothing in common. Actually, I have nothing in common with Dendrox either, except for a physical attraction that was made clear by both of us earlier. What am I doing? I can't fit in with*

<Zaylyn ><Quest For The Sword Of Anthrowst ><By Katrina Mandrake-Johnston >   <Ch 38> < 119 >

these people and I never will. Except for maybe Vordin and even he's braver than I am. Yarin's gone from our little vulnerable group, so there's just me and Vordin left in the expendable category. And Vordin's more useful than me by far, so that means I'll probably be next to perish. Maybe I should have done more with Dendrox. I could be dead by tonight. That could have been my one and only chance. Oh would you stop being so paranoid and just think of something to say to her, anything will do as long as you don't sound like a fool, which is going to be a definite. But what happens if you go this whole scouting trip without saying anything? This is obviously a test, her wanting to talk one on one to find out what kind of person I am, to see if I'm worthy of her company and probably Dendrox's too. Why else would she want such a useless person to come on a scouting mission? I'm sure she could persuade Dendrox away from me, if she really wanted to, without much problem."

"That's an interesting ring," Candra commented as she stopped to rest a moment.

"It was my mother's," she told her as she held it up so Candra could take a better look at it.

"Yes, that's very nice. It would fetch quite a fair price. It looks valuable," Candra added looking eagerly at the ring.

This immediately made Weena very nervous, and she moved her ringed hand back to her side where she was able to hide it from view within the folds of her robes. Weena hoped that Candra might have been just joking around, but by the elf's serious face, she realized the true nature of a thief.

She hoped that she was simply being overly paranoid and was reading too much into Candra's words and expression. Weena nervously said, "Oh I could never sell it. It means too much to me," then she added, "But that's not what you meant, is it? You wouldn't take it, would you? I know you and Dendrox are thieves, but we're friends, aren't we?"

Candra started walking again and wore a smirk at the corner of her mouth. Weena reluctantly followed her. "For one," the thief told her, "I can't tell you how to be a good judge of character. Whether you should trust someone is completely up to you. As for thieves, there are no boundaries. The sentimental value of an object, whether it be of a friend or not, has no sway with a thief. If it's worth a fair amount of gold, I suggest you keep it well hidden and not display it so clearly for all to see."

Weena quickly removed the ring and placed it in her pouch once more.

The two women walked side-by-side in silence for awhile until Candra asked Weena, "How do you like my ring?" and she held her hand up for the human to see.

"Isn't that…" Weena started, and then felt inside her pouch for her mother's ring. It was gone. "That's mine!" Weena blurted out.

"Says you," the thief said with a grin.

"How did you…" Weena began, but was interrupted by the elf.

"A thief never explains its secrets." Candra waited just long enough for Weena's face to fall with the realization that her ring, which meant so much to her, was gone and could do nothing about it. "I wasn't going to keep it. I was just trying to prove a point. Have we learnt something?" Candra asked handing Weena her ring back.

"Yes," Weena answered relieved.

"Now watch my eyes," Candra told her.

"What? Why?" she asked puzzled.

"Just do it, and hide the ring at the appropriate moment," said the thief.

"What, I'm supposed to hide it with you looking straight at me?" Weena asked astonished.

"That's why I told you to watch my eyes. If I look the other way for a second or two, that's your chance to hide it," she explained.

"What? I can't possibly do it that fast," the wizard told her.

"You have to, because next time I won't give it back," Candra said seriously.

Weena realized that she wasn't kidding. She clutched the ring tightly in her palm and watched Candra's eyes. Her eyes sparkled like the greenest of emeralds and they darted around their surroundings, always watchful. The eyes also fell very often to the ring held tightly in her hand. *"Too*

<Zaylyn ><Quest For The Sword Of Anthrowst ><By Katrina Mandrake-Johnston >   <Ch 38> < 120 >

bad I couldn't just do some sort of spell and fool Candra completely," Weena thought feeling hopeless. A bird chirped. The eyes darted to where the sound had come from. *"I guess that's why thieves have such luck in crowds, since everyone's attention is usually somewhere else. If I fail, I lose my mother's ring forever. I have to do this,"* she told herself. She watched the eyes. *"Where am I going to put it so she doesn't see?"* she asked herself desperately.

"Hey what's that!" Weena shouted pointing off into the trees hoping to fool Candra into looking. Candra's eyes didn't stray as Weena had expected, and the elf gave her a mocking smile. "Okay, of course that's not going to work," Weena admitted.

"Obviously," she chuckled, "You could push me and use the commotion to get a chance to hide it, but that would just make me angry. That would not be very safe for you to do that," Candra said with a sly smile.

A squirrel scampered down a tree and rustled the leaves of the bushes beneath. Candra's eyes darted toward the sound and Weena tucked the ring into her yellow sash.

When Weena looked up again to check Candra's eyes, they were looking straight at her again. *"Was I fast enough?"* Weena immediately thought, *"I guess I won't find out until later."*

Candra and Weena continued their walk through the forest, getting farther and farther away from the others and the campsite.

After awhile Candra said to her, "One thing you should keep in mind, is that objects just get moved, not lost. A good trick is to sell something, get some gold for it, and then take back what you've sold. That's for master thieves. I haven't been able to accomplish that one yet. If your ring is taken, you always have the chance of trying to steal it back. Won't that be an interesting task for you?"

"I guess so," was Weena's reply, a little confused about what exactly Candra expected from her.

They continued in silence. Weena knew that at any time Candra could snatch her ring with ease, and she probably would never feel it. Perhaps she already had. *"I'll get it back. If she wants me to try to steal it back, so be it. I can play her game. I'll just have to be patient and wait for the right time and place."* Weena felt the icy buildup of frustration in her gut. *"I have to be calm. I can't give in to my anger, or I'll never get my ring back if she ends up taking it again."*

They stopped to rest once more, and Weena sat down upon a large boulder while Candra leaned against the bark of a large cedar tree. "You ready?" Candra asked with a smirk.

"Sure, I guess so. Back to camp then?" Weena said standing up and turning to head back the way they came.

"Not exactly," Candra said as she took an arrow from her quiver and turned to Weena.

"What are you doing?" she asked her, the growing fear showing in her voice.

Candra pulled the arrow back in her bow and asked calmly, "You know a Shield spell and a Heal spell, don't you?

"Well yes, but what are you doing?" she asked very frightened.

Candra said plainly, "Use your Shield spell to block my arrow. If you don't, you'll have to use your Heal spell to heal yourself. Or don't, and bleed to death, in which case I go back alone."

"You're not really going to shoot an arrow at me, are you?" she repeated, backing slowly away from her.

"They'll believe anything I tell them regarding your fate. Death by one of the Killnarin, or perhaps by some other terrible misfortune. I'd think of something. You'd be forgotten," Candra said coldly, "So fight back."

Weena's voice trembled with emotion, "After all we've been through? You're just going to kill me?!" Her mind raced, *"It can't be because I kissed Dendrox, can it? She's crazy!"*

Candra told her, "I'm not trying to kill you, but I'd rather see you die here than ripped apart by some creature because you can't protect yourself. You said you needed practice. Here it is."

"Not like this!" she practically screamed at her.

"I'm losing patience, Weena," she warned.

"She's seriously going to kill me! What do I do? What can I do?!" Weena asked herself and then

<Zaylyn ><Quest For The Sword Of Anthrowst ><By Katrina Mandrake-Johnston >   <Ch 38> < 121 >
said, "Well at least give me some warning before you fire!"

"Real life doesn't work that way. Do you think an enemy would give you a warning before an attack? An enemy will seek out any and every weakness in your defense," and Candra loosed the arrow.

Everything seemed to move in slow motion, as Weena watched in utter fear as the arrow left the bow and came at her. Like a reflex, the words flashed through her mind, and a multi-colored film surrounded her as before. She watched the arrow stop in mid air and fall harmlessly to the ground. The shield, having absorbed the force of the arrow, vanished. Everything all happened in what seemed less than a second. Weena stared at Candra's face in disbelief.

"I knew you could do it," Candra said as she took out another arrow.

Weena thought about fleeing but knew she would be any easy target for the elf and to run would be completely useless. Her only hope was to spark some sort of compassion within her. "*Surely Candra could not seriously mean to kill me. Can she truly despise me so deeply?! I saved her life! Twice, if you count the wound and poisoning as two. No, it's three times! She was to be held responsible for the wounded spider. Can this actually be some insane idea of hers to get me to practice my spells?!*"

The corner of Candra's mouth turned up in a malicious and contemptuous sneer. With slender and nimble fingers, she pulled back the arrow in the bow.

"My spell! I can't use it twice in a row!" Weena yelled at her, trying desperately to reason with her somehow.

"I know," Candra said calmly, "An enemy won't care. In fact, they'll count on it."

"No don't!" Weena screamed at her.

The elf loosed the second arrow and hit Weena in the shoulder, throwing her back in shock and pain as it struck her. She was now on the ground. Blood began to flow heavily from her wound. Weena stared in horror and amazement at the thin shaft of wood protruding from her, and she could feel it within her body. Her shoulder felt like it was on fire.

Candra stood over her, staring down coldly.

Weena tried to use her Heal spell and it failed miserably. The pain and the shock of what Candra had done, was almost unbearable.

"*She can't just leave me here to die! The others will come to rescue me,*" her mind said to her. Then she realized that Candra was right. They would believe anything Candra told them. She would become yet another casualty added to the long list. There would be no questions asked. They would have to concentrate on their own survival. There would be no one coming to rescue her. If she were going to survive, she had to do it on her own. This was what Candra wanted her to realize in such a frightful way. This was her test to see if she were going to be a survivor or weigh the group down, endangering others. Weena realized that if she didn't fight back, she truly was going to be left alone to bleed to death. Candra wasn't going to have a second thought about doing it either.

Weena bit back the pain, and tried to ignore the fact that the loss of blood had already started to make her lightheaded. She mouthed the words of the spell, willing them to work with all of her body and soul, and felt the arrow slowly being pushed out of her shoulder as the flesh mended itself.

She felt the arrow drop to the ground and the pain subsided. When she looked up at Candra again, the elf had her hand outstretched toward her. "You need some help up?" she offered.

Weena felt like punching her right in the jaw with all her might, but she was far too weak and afraid to do so. Weena accepted Candra's hand and the thief helped the wizard to her feet.

"I knew you could do it," she said picking up the arrows and replacing them back into her quiver, "I really didn't want to have to leave you there. Plus, having to explain things to Dendrox. You do understand why I did it, right? No hard feelings?"

Weena glared at her, but did understand what Candra meant for her to learn from all of this. "*People you call friends can turn on you, so never let your guard down. Rely on yourself and not on others to save you. Don't give in to fear, use it to fuel the desire to survive. Turn anger and frustration into determination. But what I have truly learnt here most of all is, that jealousy can cloud someone's*

<Zaylyn ><Quest For The Sword Of Anthrowst ><By Katrina Mandrake-Johnston >   <Ch 38> < 122 >

mind to the point of insanity. I'm not trying to steal her friend away from her or somehow take her place. Surely she cannot believe this to be true. Maybe she is not even aware of it, but it would explain why she is so determined to teach me the ways of a thief, to hold me close for fear of losing Dendrox. She's willing to kill me, even after everything we've been through. Can I ever trust her again? Will she let me perish instead of coming to my rescue when she is able?" Weena hesitated but finally replied, "Yes, no hard feelings."

Candra suggested, "You better do something about that blood. You'll attract predators right to you. Rub some dirt on it. That should work well enough. It will look like you fell. The others wouldn't understand what I was trying to teach you," and then she warned, "You say anything stupid, no amount of luck or magic will save you. I'm very fast and a deadly shot. Are we clear on this?"

"Yes," she answered, her voice trembling slightly, "I fell. I won't say anything."

Weena began to rub handfuls of soil onto the blood soaked areas of her robes, and when she had finished to Candra's satisfaction, the elf smiled and said, "Let's get back to camp then."

Weena felt the sash for her mother's ring and discovered it to be missing. *"How dare she threaten me! I'm not going to say anything. I'm not a complete wimp. Besides, I've got to try to find a way of getting my mother's ring back. She thinks she's so clever. Wants me to try to steal it back? I'll find a way. I don't know how, but I'll figure something out. I just have to be patient about it,"* thought Weena.

They both started walking back to the camp.

<World of Zaylyn ><Quest For The Sword Of Anthrowst ><By Katrina Mandrake-Johnston ><Ch 39>

CHAPTER 39 =   DENDROX AND CANDRA'S WATCH

It was dark by the time Candra and Weena returned. The warm glow of the campfire was a comfort to all in the growing blackness of the forest. No one seemed to notice that Weena had apparently fell.

Candra and Dendrox offered to take first watch, and it didn't take the others very long to fall asleep with all of them being extremely exhausted.

Candra was seated on a rock while she absentmindedly poked at the fire with a stick, and Dendrox sat leaning up against a tree. He put his hands behind his head as he stretched out, decided to prop his feet up on a small nearby rock, and let out a sigh. "Hey, Candra?" Dendrox said looking very relaxed.

"Yeah," she replied still poking at the logs in the fire and watching the little sparks fly about.

"I thought I was the one that always fidgets with stuff. There something bothering you?" he asked her.

"No, not really. Just all that's been happening I guess," she answered.

They sat in silence for awhile, listening to the crackling fire as the others slept.

"Candra, you do know, that if you keep fiddling with the fire, you'll eventually make it go out," he warned.

"Yeah, I know. I've said the same thing to you a million times," she told him.

"That's why I said it," he said with a smile.

She stopped attacking the fire with the stick and turned to him. He could tell she had a lot on her mind and that she wanted to talk to him about something that was difficult for her to bring up. She finally said, "You know, I see more of your mother in you than of your father. I see a lot of your parents passed down into you."

"Why all of a sudden all about my parents?" he asked with a puzzled expression, "What's wrong?"

"I was just thinking, that's all. When was the last time we passed by Cranok anyway, to see how they were doing?" she asked.

"I don't know, a year maybe two. Or no, I think it might be three now, but why?" he asked. He had been expecting her to maybe say something about Weena. *"I highly doubt it, but maybe they had a long talk together on their walk and actually get along okay."*

"Well you know how my parents are gone, and I know I've sort of shut down since then. You know, a little standoffish now and then, sometimes a little too often. I was just thinking…" she trailed

<Zaylyn ><Quest For The Sword Of Anthrowst ><By Katrina Mandrake-Johnston >   <Ch 39> < 123 >
off.

"You miss them, don't you?" he said. "*She hasn't mentioned her own parents since we were kids, not since after retrieving her mother's necklace and visiting their graves that one time. It isn't something she talks about.*" He added, "You actually miss my parents, don't you?" "*She never really cared for my parents, or at least that's what we all thought. She would hardly talk to them or spend very much time around them. They did adopt her into the family, treated her and even loved her as a daughter. She has always been so cold around them though. She would show respect, of course, but was always so distant. I was the only one she would really open up to.*"

"Well, yeah, of course I miss them," she said finally and there was the beginnings of a tear in her eye.

"Wow, you've never admitted to that much feeling before," he said jokingly.

"Oh shut up," she said with a smile.

"So you actually care about them? But you always acted and treated them like they were more of an inconvenience, although a necessity," he said wanting to get everything said while she was willing to talk about it, "That you tolerated them because they happened to be my parents, and because they were providing for you. You would show them a small amount of respect and appreciation, but not much. 'Little Miss Independent' could do everything on her own, not needing anyone. Sometimes I even felt like you didn't want me around either." He knew that at any other time, she would forcefully change the subject, refusing to speak to him at all about anything to do with his parents. "*She wants to be completely free, living day to day, moment to moment, adventure to adventure. The thought of being tied down with thoughts of family, of being part of one, caring and worrying about others, having others worrying and caring about what might happen to her... Maybe that's the core of it. Knowing that they would disapprove of the thieving. That if she got in trouble or injured, they would be worried about her. Could it be that she has associated my parents along with the guilt of how we make our living, and has just pushed it all away? That would explain now maybe, but when we were kids? I guess she just felt strange being part of a family after losing hers. Feeling like she didn't belong, even though we made every effort to welcome her in. I mean, sure she's an elf and we're a family of humans, but the only real difference is the ears. We're all the same and she knows that. My parents didn't feel obligated to take her in. They didn't feel like she was invading their family and that she was an inconvenience they had to put up with. Although she sure acted as if this were so, despite all the effort they made to include her. Half the time I felt like she was getting all the attention. I used to feel so jealous of her sometimes and angry too, because all the attention was just being wasted on her when they could have been spending time with me, and I would have appreciated it. I don't know what her problem is. I mean, sure, I had my rebellious moments, but what she did was just not normal or fair. They didn't know what they were doing wrong, wanting to connect with her somehow but always getting an icy shoulder in return.*"

Candra told him, "Yes, I know, I know. What I'm trying to say is that I know that now. I'm admitting that, and that I was wrong to be so cold. I am sorry, and I really do miss them. We should go see them soon, even if it means going out of our way to see them. Maybe even bring them a gift or something. Something that we didn't steal. It would feel funny if it was."

Dendrox was a little shocked by her. "Wow, is all I can say. They would just love to hear all this coming out of you."

"Yeah, well just keep it to yourself. No one needs to know that I might be going a bit soft," she said with a smile.

"I guess looking at Asdella and the way she is, it gets you thinking, doesn't it?" Dendrox added.

"Yeah, I know. I don't want to turn out like that, shutting everyone out with such bitterness," she said, and then she got a fearful look in her eye saying, "Hey..."

"Yeah?" he asked.

She asked in a worried voice, "You don't think that these creatures have made it all the way to Cranok, do you? And that your parents... well... you know?"

The thought of the creatures attacking Cranok, their home village, and doing what they did to

<Zaylyn ><Quest For The Sword Of Anthrowst ><By Katrina Mandrake-Johnston >   <Ch 39> < 124 >

Nilnont and Dexcsin, made him shudder. Visions of his kind parents screaming, running for their lives, hiding and desperately hoping the horrid beasts would pass them by. He came to a new realization of what Vordin must have gone through. Finding his parents slain, knowing what happened, and knowing that the creatures enjoyed every moment of it... And poor Yarin, so scared, but brave, so very brave. The talk about his parents seemed frivolous after the thought that the creatures may have gotten to them and that they could be dead. He said, "Yeah, I've been thinking about that too. Let's not, okay? We'll just have to stop them before any of that happens."

"Okay," and then Candra changed the subject by saying, "So, you and Weena, huh?"

Dendrox tried to keep a straight face but ended up blushing, "What about us?"

"Come on, I see the way you look at her. Anything happen when you two went on that so-called walk?" she said with a sly smile.

"Hey, come on, that stuff is supposed to be private," he grinned. He knew she would try to weasel every bit of information out of him and it would be fun keeping it from her for as long as he could.

"You know there's no such thing as that around me. Since when have we ever kept secrets from each other? Including the personal private stuff. What, you're just going to let this little piece of information boil up inside you until you burst? You know you want to tell somebody," she said with her mischievous smile.

"Oh, come on, Candra," he whined, "What if they're awake? What if she's awake?"

"Everybody is asleep," she told him, knowing that he was playing around with her. She was having fun with it too.

"You sure?" he asked.

"Yes, of course. You know me, I can just tell. What kind of thief would I be, if I can't tell whether someone's really asleep or just pretending?" she said with a smile.

"Okay fine," he said.

"Oh and don't forget, I can tell if you're lying, so no exaggerations," she added.

"Yeah, well just remember, that I happen to be better at the whole lie detecting thing. Remember the time when..." he pretended to start.

She made a little frustrated growl and said, "Quit trying to sidetrack the topic, you. I'm all ears."

"Yeah I know, you're an elf, remember?" he said trying to stifle a laugh.

"Hey," she said with a smile, "Just spill it already."

"Okay, we kissed," he admitted blushing slightly.

"And?" she pried.

"That's it... Well... I touched her thigh briefly but that's it," he told her.

"Naked?" Candra said, her sly smile gleaming.

"No," he chuckled. He knew how much fun she was having with her interrogation and at how uncomfortable it was making him, especially where Weena was asleep only a few feet away. Dendrox continued, "Just over her clothes. Well, her thigh was bare."

"So that's all? Yeah right," Candra said.

"I swear," he said trying to look as innocent as possible.

"Really?" she asked, "That's not at all like you."

He said, partially hoping that Weena was awake to hear, "Well, I don't know, she's different somehow. She's special; I actually care about her."

Candra told him, "Oh I didn't mean anything like that. I can tell, you know, the difference between just a physical interest and the other type. I just thought more would happen, especially with the way you two have been eyeing each other."

"It can't be that obvious, and anyway, I don't think things are going to continue any further," he said.

"What do you mean?" she asked.

He answered, "It was as if one minute she wanted me and couldn't keep her hands off me, and then she just stopped cold. I don't understand. Did I do something wrong?"

"Couldn't keep her hands off, eh? You forgot to mention that part," Candra said with a sly smirk.

<Zaylyn ><Quest For The Sword Of Anthrowst ><By Katrina Mandrake-Johnston >   <Ch 39> < 125 >

"No, that was nothing. Come on, Candra, I'm being serious," he said hoping she could clarify things for him. "It was as if she was scared to touch me, or just didn't want to. I don't know what to think," he said honestly.

Candra felt very awkward talking about this and continued to joke around. "Hey, you know what?"

"What?" he said plainly.

"Maybe you're just a bad kisser," she laughed.

"Oh gee, thanks," he said sarcastically and smiled at her.

"Well, it is a turn off when someone is trying to swallow your whole face or drown you in slobber," she told him matter-of-factly.

"Hey, that can go both ways, you know," he laughed.

"She definitely has an interest in you. You probably can't see it, but it's clear to me. So you think it might be the kissing then?" she asked with a mischievous look.

He replied, "I don't know. I've never tried to kiss myself, now have I? Besides, it's not as if anybody's going to be honest enough to tell me any different."

"Well, okay, kiss me then," she said plainly.

"What?!" he said shocked that she had suggested this.

"Yeah, I'll give you the truth. I might even be a bit insulting," she said grinning.

"Really?" he said doubting her, "You're serious? So what, you like me too all of a sudden?" Dendrox thought to himself, "*Could that be why she's been acting so strangely? Could Candra have been interested in me all this time and not said anything? No, that's silly. Unless she just realized it, now that I like Weena. Candra jealous; …that's a scary thought. I wonder what went on during their walk?*"

"Well of course I like you, but just not in the romantic way. The kiss is not going to mean anything. Well, unless you secretly have an interest in me or something like that. You don't, do you? You would have said something, right?" she asked him. He couldn't tell for sure, but he thought there might have been a slight hint of hopefulness in her voice.

"*What should I say?*" he asked himself, "*I mean, sure, I've thought about it. We'd be perfect together, probably. I never thought that she might have had feelings that way. She always made it clear that she didn't, but now I don't know what to think. If I say the wrong thing, I could really screw things up here.*" "I don't know, I feel the same way you do, I guess," was his reply, "So you really want to do this?"

"I'll be honest. Now where else are you going to get that?" she said.

"Okay, so just do it, and then you'll tell me what you think?" he asked.

"Yes, exactly," she said moving over to where he was sitting.

She sat close beside him as she had done earlier when she had been preparing the rabbits. It was different now, however, and for the first time he felt uncomfortable around her. "Okay," he said and found himself hesitating.

"Well?" Candra said.

"Just give me a minute," he told her.

"Oh, somebody's shy," she teased with an overly large grin and a bit of a giggle.

"Hey, come on. Don't bother me about it," said Dendrox.

"Okay," she said, making it obvious that she was trying to hold back her smile and put on a serious face.

"You know, it's like you are two separate people," he commented, "One person around me and then someone totally different around everyone else."

"Yeah, I know. It's 'cause I can trust you. I can be myself around you," she said simply, "Quit trying to distract the situation. It's just me."

"Okay fine," he said, "You ready?"

"Am I ready?" she laughed, "I've been ready for awhile. I'm waiting for this shy little boy to get up enough nerve to do it. I'm surprised now that you were able to pull yourself together enough to kiss

Weena."

"Well it's not like I've gotten complaints before," he said stalling, "I've kissed a fair number of women."

"But you're afraid to kiss me?" she challenged.

"I'm not afraid," he said defensively, "All this has just gotten me a bit paranoid. I've never really cared before whether or not a woman had feelings in return."

"Okay, so Weena's special and you want to find out whether your kissing turned her off or not, so you've got to kiss me or you'll never know. Oh, and by the way, being afraid and being paranoid are basically the same thing. So, are you going to do it, or not?" she dared him getting impatient.

"Yes," he told her, but again hesitated.

"Well?" Candra said expectantly.

"I'm going to," he assured her.

"It has to be an actual kiss or it won't serve its purpose," Candra reminded him.

"Okay," he said, this time looking into her beautiful emerald green eyes. This was the first time he was able to bring himself to do so, since she came to sit next to him for the awaited kiss.

"Oh, this is ridiculous. Come here," and she pulled him close and gave him a quick kiss to his lips.

"There. Is the tension gone now?" she whispered, "Now show me how you kiss."

She was very close to him now, looking into his eyes in a way he had never seen before. Drawn to her as if it always had meant to be so, his lips met hers. She had the scent of pine needles and honeysuckle about her.

Her kisses were soft and moist. They were long passionate kisses. He couldn't describe the love he felt for her. Weena didn't mean anything to him at this moment; she was but a passing interest compared to Candra. Dendrox pulled her closer to him in a warm embrace. No other woman was worth his attention, not if he could have Candra.

He had thought about it, imagined what it would be like to kiss her, and now he knew. It felt good to hold her close. They were meant to be together, but somehow it just didn't feel right. He couldn't exactly tell what it was. *"I love her more than anything, but could the kiss be just a result of us thinking this to be the next logical step? Could it be that the kiss happened simply because we thought it to be the right thing to do and not led by our hearts to do so as we had first thought? Is our love for each other more like that one has for a family member... No, it is much more than that, but not exactly to the point of romance... Well, could it be? Perhaps..."*

"Well?" he finally asked her, pretending that the kiss was merely an experiment as they had suggested it was to be. He wondered if she really did have feelings for him. It felt like she did. He wondered if she too had imagined it and thought about it before. If by some chance it had started out as some jealous move against Weena, it hadn't ended as such.

"That... that was pretty good," she said, stumbling over her words.

Her face was flushed and she wore a smile that was almost bashful. As she was, there at that moment, her beauty accentuated by the firelight, that smile, that magical look in her eye... He would forever remember her at that moment; the moment at which their love was expressed. He could see the love and affection she felt for him reflected in her, but he knew that he would probably never see that passionate spark in her again. He knew his realization to be true.

"You're pretty good yourself too," he admitted, not knowing what else to say in such an awkward moment of silence.

"Ah, thanks," she said, trying to hide the fact that she was blushing.

"So no hidden feelings or anything, right?" he questioned, truly wanting to know.

"Okay, yes, it felt good, and yes, I care for you more than anyone I know, but it just felt strange somehow," she admitted, "At first it was what I thought I wanted, but then... I don't know."

"Okay, that's a relief. Same here," he told her.

"So the problem is definitely not the kissing," Candra said pretending that the kiss had been completely meaningless to them, "You know what? It's probably just her."

Dendrox asked, "What do you mean?"

<Zaylyn ><Quest For The Sword Of Anthrowst ><By Katrina Mandrake-Johnston >   <Ch 39> < 127 >

"She's probably just shy and insecure. She'll get over it," she explained, "Just give her time. She'll come around."

"You think?" he asked and was answered with a nod.

"Yeah, I like her," Candra commented, "I just hope I didn't scare her too badly. When we took that walk to scout the area, well, I wanted to see how well she could handle herself when it came to a life or death situation. She's not as terrible as she thinks she is. If she learns a couple more spells, she'll be fine. I just don't want her to end up defenseless and dead, you know?"

"So what exactly went on with you two?" he asked imagining the worst.

"Never mind," was her answer, knowing he would pry.

Dendrox instantly knew that Candra had done something awful. "What did you do?" he said in a scolding tone, "You did something, didn't you?"

She winced as she told him, "I kind of shot an arrow at her."

"What?!" he exclaimed in disbelief, looking to Weena and her mud-covered robes with worry.

"Hey, I was all mixed up. I didn't know what I wanted. I was sick of her being a wimp. I wanted to see what she was really capable of and I had to scare her to find out," Candra said, getting defensive.

"So you shot an arrow at her?! What if you missed and hit her? You could have killed her by accident," and then seeing the shameful look beginning on Candra's face, hinted with an underlying maliciousness, and by the way the corner of her mouth was turned up revealing to him that she had done something rather nasty, and knowing what she was capable of, he knew to ask, "Candra, you didn't hurt her, did you?" The tone of his words showed that he already knew the answer.

"Okay, I'll tell you everything," she said and now almost looked pleased with herself, "Okay, I stole her ring, but I was teaching her a lesson with that, still am. Then, I shot an arrow at her and she blocked it with that Shield spell she has. Then I shot another arrow at her, and she had to use her Heal spell to get it out of her shoulder. But she's fine now. I kind of told her I was going to leave her there to bleed to death too. But I'm okay with her now. I got out my frustration with her and I think she's better for it too. I know I am. I actually kind of like her now."

"You just had to almost kill her first," he said with a chuckle. He was finding it hard to believe that Candra had actually resorted to such extreme methods and was even willing to kill Weena just because she found her annoying at times and unable to defend herself as Candra thought she ought to.

"Yeah, I'm really sorry," she told him, but he knew that the apology wasn't really sincere. Candra added, "It's just that she's always whine, whine, whine. And then, 'I can't do this, I can't do that', all the time. It was driving me nuts! She has the skills. She's just acting like a spoiled little baby, too afraid to even try. I didn't want to have her blubbering all over us when there's danger, not when she's perfectly capable of defending herself. Okay there, I've said it to you. She's proven that she can handle herself in a crisis and hopefully she'll have learnt something by it. And if she doesn't go back to being completely spineless, I think I can actually get along with her. I like her; she has spirit."

"So if things escalate with her and me, you'd be fine with it? You wouldn't be mean to her or anything?" Dendrox asked Candra knowing that she could be vicious at times.

"No, I'm actually willing to let her into our little group. Teach her the skills of the trade," she told him.

"You're going to try to teach her some thieving skills? The kind of things that we do?" he asked in disbelief, "Don't you think maybe you're trying a little too hard to accept her now? All you have to do is be nice to her."

"What, you don't think I can do it? Imagine the possibilities when you add a bit of magic into the mix," she explained.

He thought to himself, *"Candra's talking about adding a third member into our little group? It's probably going to get us killed and all because I like some girl. She's talking as if this is going to last forever with Weena. Candra's trying way too hard to make this work for me. Weena's not a thief. It's not in her nature. She can't change to suit our life style and she shouldn't have to change just to fit in with us. Or the other way around. I can't see myself settling down, giving up the pursuit of riches and adventure, and saying good-bye to all the excitement. I don't know, if Weena wants to learn to be a*

<Zaylyn ><Quest For The Sword Of Anthrowst ><By Katrina Mandrake-Johnston >   <Ch 39> < 128 >

thief, fine. She can pretend and Candra can play out her little fantasy. The first sign of real danger though, reality must take over, no matter how cold it is." "All I'm saying is it's going to be difficult. In fact extremely difficult," Dendrox said to her, "What are you going to start out with first?"

"I already have. I've started with a little pickpocket trial. She has to try to get her mother's ring back from me," Candra grinned.

"We'll see," he chuckled, "You're going to have your hands full, you know?"

"Yeah, but it'll be fun. I can hardly wait to see what she does. You should have seen her. She was furious. She's going to be coming after me and that ring with all she's got."

He thought to himself, "*Kind of like whoever those damn scissors belong to.*"

"I'm going to catch some rest," Candra announced standing up and heading over to where she had put her belongings.

"Sure," he said, "I'm going to stay up for a bit longer."

Candra wrapped herself up tightly in her blanket and went to sleep. Dendrox watched the flames of the fire dance as they reached for the stars in the night sky.

<World of Zaylyn ><Quest For The Sword Of Anthrowst ><By Katrina Mandrake-Johnston ><Ch 40>

CHAPTER 40 = NODWEL AND ASDELLA'S WATCH

"Nodwel," Dendrox whispered. The dwarf stirred slightly, but did not wake. "Hey, Nodwel, wake up," he said shaking him gently, "Wake up, it's your watch. I've got to get some sleep too."

Nodwel opened his eyes and jolted into sitting position. "What is it? Is there danger?" he asked urgently.

"No, no, relax," Dendrox told him, "It's just time for your watch. Candra's already asleep, and I've been fighting to keep my eyes open for awhile now. All has been quiet, but you better wake up Asdella too, just to be safe. I'm a little nervous of waking her actually. I thought about it, but then visions of her stabbing that sword of hers through my gut keeps coming to mind. I really think it would be safer if you got her up for the watch."

"Oh, what? Ah, yeah, sure," Nodwel said still trying to fully wake up, despite the first jolt of adrenalin.

"You sure you're awake?" he asked, knowing of his own habit of falling back to sleep right away after being woken to take watch.

"Yeah, I'm fine," the dwarf said standing up and heading over to a rock by the fire, "Get some sleep. There's no telling what we may have to deal with tomorrow. Everyone will need their rest."

Dendrox found what looked to be a somewhat comfortable spot to sleep, stretching himself out with his head resting on his arm. "*This is supposed to be the most comfortable spot? We better get to an inn soon. I mean, sure, I'm pretty much used to it by now, but I'm really starting to get sick of sleeping outside with rocks and twigs digging into my side and creepy crawly bugs swarming all over me,*" he muttered to himself. He looked over with mixed emotions to where Weena was sleeping. Finally, he got up, draped his blanket over her, and then quickly returned to his chosen spot once more.

"You going to wake up Asdella?" he reminded Nodwel, as it was obvious the dwarf had forgotten or was also nervous of waking the warrior woman and trying to avoid it.

Nodwel said, "Yeah," and headed over to where she was sleeping. Dendrox was already sound asleep by the time Nodwel reached her.

"Asdella?" Nodwel called, trying not to wake the others. "Asdella?" he repeated when he saw she hadn't woken. He thought about nudging her slightly, but then decided against it, being wary of what her reaction might be as Dendrox had been. "Asdella?" he said a little louder, "Wake up, it's me Nodwel. You're supposed to take the watch with me."

Her eyes opened and she sat up, giving him a withering stare. Then she stood, staring out into the forest for several moments, her eyes heavy with sleep, before finally stumbling sleepily over to the boulders by the fire, dragging her sword along behind her.

"*Okay, she's awake. Whether that's a good thing or not, I'm not sure,*" he chuckled to himself. He joined her by the fire and they sat in silence for quite a long while.

<Zaylyn ><Quest For The Sword Of Anthrowst ><By Katrina Mandrake-Johnston >   <Ch 40> < 129 >

Nodwel was the one to finally say something. "You know, Asdella," he said, "I thought Borin was dead. I was trying to accept that he was gone, like the others. And then, there he was, alive and well. And now, I have to go through the pain of losing my friend all over again."

Asdella asked, "What are you trying to say? It's the same for me."

He let out a big sigh and told her, "I'm just glad that you're still here, that's all. Running, trying to make it to Vackiindmire in time, trying to find someone to help us, well, I thought it was hopeless, after seeing Dimwar and Nimdor taken down so easily. I thought I had lost you too."

"You did, or would have if that amulet hadn't been around and if Candra and Dendrox hadn't come across me when they did," she said, "The fact of it is, that I didn't really care whether I lived or died. Whatever fate was coming for me, I was prepared to accept it. And yet, I found myself fighting to live, and for what reason I don't know, as none came to mind, but I was fighting just the same. Whatever that means, I don't know, but maybe at that last moment, when my final fate had already been decided, I was fighting to live just so if you did return, there would be someone around to find. So you wouldn't feel as if you failed, and so you wouldn't have to suffer through all of it alone."

This was the most compassionate thing he had ever heard her say. He had no idea that she in fact held their friendship more dear than what he had imagined. Past the hard warrior exterior, there was more to her than he had realized. He was beginning to see a little of what Narr had seen in her. "*You get her to talk enough, her inner self starts to peek out here and there through the tough outer wall she puts up. She isn't really as harsh as she makes herself out to be and maybe not as insane as she gets everyone to believe.*"

He didn't really know what to say, so he ended up saying, "I can take the watch alone, if you want to get some rest."

"Thanks," she replied, and she lay down where she was on the hard rocky ground by the fire, stretched out on her back with a hand resting across her stomach, and she closed her eyes.

Nodwel chuckled to himself as she had the hilt of her sword clutched tightly in her right hand as always. "*Even in sleep, she's ready for battle...*" and then as a second realization thought, "*I guess, no matter what the situation, she never really feels safe. It must be hard for her, whatever the reason.*"

<World of Zaylyn ><Quest For The Sword Of Anthrowst ><By Katrina Mandrake-Johnston ><Ch 41>

CHAPTER 41 =   THE MIND LINK

Nodwel tossed the last piece of firewood into the fire. It sent sparks flying up into the sky. Above, he could see the stars through the treetops, and he was looking up at them when out of the corner of his eye he thought he saw something move. He quickly and silently took up his axe and scanned the darkness.

Finally, he decided that it must have been his imagination, being so tired and all. He looked back to his fellow companions and was surprised to see Lorenta leaning over Vordin.

"How did you... What are you doing?" he asked.

"Sorry Nodwel, being a spider I tend to move silently. I didn't mean to startle you. I just wanted to talk to Vordin," she answered and the dwarf nodded. "Vordin?" she whispered as she lay a hand gently on his cheek, "Vordin?"

He woke and exclaimed with surprise, "Lorenta?"

"I've finally learnt how to fully communicate with the other spiders. I can actually do it," she whispered with pride.

"Well, that's great," Vordin told her.

"They wanted me to ask you what is being planned. Is anything to be done about the creatures? And, what about this wizard behind them? They are accepting the loss of their home of course and that they will have to find a new one eventually. They are mourning their dead, but they refuse to sit idly by any longer. The spiders want to help in anyway they can. They have suggested that they monitor the activity of the Killnarin. They have this other ability where they can create a mind link with another, which allows them to communicate over long distances. The spider who has been decided as their new leader has created such a link with me and will relay any information they gather. I would like to try to

<Zaylyn ><Quest For The Sword Of Anthrowst ><By Katrina Mandrake-Johnston >   <Ch 41> < 130 >

create a link to you, Vordin, in case anything happens," she explained, "in case we get separated."

"Ah, yeah, sure, I guess. It won't hurt, will it?" he asked nervously.

"I don't know. It didn't hurt me when the leader made his link to me," Lorenta told him, "This will be my first time doing this of course, so I don't know what will happen. You do think that it's a good idea to do so, don't you?

"Sure. What do I do?" asked Vordin, "I'm nothing like a spider. Doesn't that matter?"

"No, I asked him. It will be all right," she said as she placed her hands to his forehead, "Just relax."

Green flames started to erupt from her body as she concentrated. Vordin looked up to the sky wondering if it were dawn, but it was not, and Lorenta did not change form.

Nodwel shot them a wary glance saying, "Everything all right over there?"

"Yes," Lorenta answered a little annoyed that he had broken her concentration.

"Vordin?" Nodwel asked.

"Yes, everything's fine," Vordin hoped, still nervous about Lorenta's ability.

"If I could just interrupt for a second," said Nodwel, "Lorenta, you didn't see anything out of the ordinary? Not any of the spiders are out there roaming about?"

"No, I didn't. I'm sorry, but I really need to concentrate," she explained.

A heavy weight began to push into Vordin's head from her hands, yet it was not her hands that were doing the pushing. It was a horrible feeling, and Vordin felt as if his mind were being squished into the bottom of his throat, as if another were trying to take its place.

He began to panic and almost cried out, but Lorenta whispered, "Shh, don't fight me. I'm not trying to hurt you. Relax and let me in."

Vordin got a horrible thought that maybe this was not Lorenta and that this was yet another trick by the Killnarin which he was so foolishly falling for. "Wait," he said, and the sound of his voice made him wince and it sounded so very far away.

"What's wrong?" she asked, stopping and taking her hands away from his forehead.

"I felt like I was slipping away. Like something was taking me over," he said looking at her suspiciously.

"Oh, perhaps I was doing it wrong then. It is possible to take over someone's mind for a short time, if the invading mind is strong enough. The others told me that occasionally they would do this with the villagers if they needed to listen for information or to gain food if they were short on supply," she explained.

Shocked, he asked, "You mean they would sometimes eat the villagers?"

"What? No, they would gain control over a villager and use him to deposit livestock and other food items down the well," she said giving him a disappointed look, "After all they've proven themselves to be, you still can think something like that?"

"I... Sorry," said Vordin.

"So, do you want me to try again?" she asked him, "I'll try to be less forceful this time, but for it to work, you have to accept me into your mind. Then I'm supposed to leave a bit of my mind in yours to maintain the connection. You will see this when you close your eyes as a little spot of red. If you want to contact me, concentrate on it, opening it up and enlarging it until it fills your mind, and I will answer. That is, if I do it right. Most importantly, if you resist me and try to reject my mind, it won't work. So, you really want me to do this?"

"I don't know. It doesn't sound very safe," he answered, but her eyes seemed to beg him with such a desperateness that he said, "but alright."

She replaced her hands to his forehead and the green flames once more began to whip about her. Vordin felt the push from her mind into his. It was slightly less forceful, but still felt invasive and made him start to panic. He fought the urge and let himself open up to her. He felt so vulnerable. He could feel her in his mind like a heavy stone inside his skull. Then he felt a sharp pain, as if a needle had been punched into his brain. She removed her hands and the weight subsided except for a spot about the size of a pebble.

<Zaylyn ><Quest For The Sword Of Anthrowst ><By Katrina Mandrake-Johnston >   <Ch 41> < 131 >

Lorenta announced, "It is done." Vordin rubbed at his forehead. "Are you okay?" she asked.

"I think so," Vordin told her.

"What are you two doing over there?" Nodwel asked with curiosity.

"Lorenta has learnt to communicate with the spiders, and she's trying to use the same method to communicate with me," Vordin answered.

"Oh, well that's good. We're out of firewood," he informed them, "Should I get some more?"

"Sure, I'll keep a look out," Vordin said.

"So is there a plan for what to do next?" Lorenta asked Vordin.

"We're planning to go to Vackiindmire to find out about that sword," he told her, "Am I supposed to have this horrible headache?"

"Oh, that's normal. I had one too when the leader made his link to me. It will go away in a few minutes," she assured him, "So you're going to find out about the sword at Vackiindmire? That's a good idea. Maybe the spiders will be able to find out something about the wizard. I doubt they'll be able to find out his location, but their efforts will help us out greatly. At least they'll be able to tell us where the Killnarin might be headed next. We could at least maybe warn some of the people before they strike. That is, if they even believe us."

"Do you really think we can make some sort of difference?" Vordin asked her.

"I've seen the way you've all been acting. You all think that coming to Dexcsin was a big failure. That since Yarin died, that no one was saved. We saved the lives of the remaining spiders. We helped save twenty-six lives! I hate how you all see them as unimportant," she said sadly. "Anyway," she continued, "they will try to monitor the Killnarin's activity. I shouldn't have to add, that this will be done at great risk to their lives. They will report anything they find to me. I'm coming with you all to Vackiindmire. They said that they will contact me every few days or so regardless, and sooner if there is anything of importance to report."

Nodwel, who had been listening in on their conversation, said, "That's great. Knowing where the main group of these creatures are will aid us more than anything. Also," he said deciding to wait until later to gather more wood, "if we do decide to look for the sword, we'll have less of a chance of running into them."

"What do you mean 'if '," Lorenta asked him, "We're useless against the wizard without the sword."

"It's good that you have faith in us, but we are but a few people. The truth is, if we do succeed in gaining the sword and finding out where this Dranngore is, there may not be anyone left to save. The Killnarin can destroy entire villages in but a single night," Nodwel explained.

"But we have to try," said Vordin.

"Yes, I agree. We will try," said the dwarf.

"It's not quite sunrise," Lorenta told them, "Perhaps we should start for Vackiindmire now. They only seem to come out at night anyway. This way we'll hopefully make it to town before sunset the next day. I really don't want to stay here any longer. I don't feel safe."

"You think we should leave now? It's still dark," Nodwel told her.

"Please, wake everyone up," Lorenta pleaded.

Nodwel finally gave in to her and bellowed, "Everyone up! Wake up! We're leaving."

<World of Zaylyn ><Quest For The Sword Of Anthrowst ><By Katrina Mandrake-Johnston ><Ch 42>

CHAPTER 42 =   EARLY DEPARTURE

Everyone awoke.

"What did you say?" Dendrox asked, "We're leaving now? While it's still dark? What's the matter?"

"It doesn't feel safe here," Nodwel replied.

"Yes, please, let's leave right away," Lorenta said.

Asdella said angrily, "So there's no danger? You just decided to wake everyone up for no reason?"

<Zaylyn ><Quest For The Sword Of Anthrowst ><By Katrina Mandrake-Johnston >   <Ch 42> < 132 >

Nodwel stated, "Lorenta can communicate with the spiders now. She will be coming with us and the spiders will remain in the forest to observe the Killnarin's activity as best they can. She's been having a bad feeling, and it's probably right. We should leave, and this way we'll make it to Vackiindmire before sunset tomorrow."

"Fine," Asdella snapped, clearly annoyed.

"It just doesn't make any sense," Dendrox said starting to pack up their blankets, "We'll have to travel back toward Dexcsin to reach Vackiindmire. I don't know exactly how long it will take us to reach town, but I don't want to be passing by the village in the dark."

Candra asked, "So what about breakfast? It's still too dark to see. Why don't we wait a bit longer until first light? Don't you think it would be dangerous to go through the forest by just the light of the lanterns? We could end up going around in circles, and if those creatures are out there…"

"Yeah, I agree with Candra," Dendrox said.

"I could use more sleep," Asdella grumbled.

"I'd like to wait until there's enough light to see by too. If you think it's safe enough," Weena added.

Vordin suggested, "Why don't we get everything ready to go first, and then see how things are."

"There's not much to get ready," Candra explained to him, "We basically are right now. Just our weapons, backpacks, lanterns, and pouches. Everything's ready for travel as soon as we are. All we have left to do is put out the fire. A couple full bladders from the guys should do the trick."

Weena commented, "Oh, that's disgusting!"

Candra told her, "Hey, it's the fastest way and it's not like there's a stream or anything to collect water from. And, that would be foolish carting water back and forth in the dark!"

"Can't we just let it burn out on its own? It doesn't look like it will last for much longer anyway," Weena suggested.

Candra laughed cruelly, "Yeah, if you want the whole forest to go up in flames. It only takes one little spark in the right place. I don't want to get roasted alive in a forest fire thanks."

"No, don't say that!" Weena shouted at her, "I'll put the fire out myself if I have to then, alright?" She was so upset, she was practically in tears.

Dendrox spoke up, "We just need to smother it. Just kick a bit of dirt onto it until it's out. Weena, there's no need to worry about it. We know what to do."

Asdella sneered, "What's her problem? So she didn't know how to put out a fire properly. What's the big deal? She has to cry about it?"

Nodwel thought he saw something move within the trees again. *Maybe it wasn't Lorenta I saw earlier, like I thought. Could it be one of the spiders, I wonder? Lorenta may be right about it not being safe here anymore,* he said to himself nervously, *It's best not to panic. We should remain calm. If it is one of the beasts, our heightened emotions will give it the perfect opportunity to use one of its damn spells. I'm probably the one with the best night vision. I can't allow myself to get distracted; not like I did with Yarin. I want to see it and kill the damn thing before anyone gets hurt.*

Weena heard Dendrox say to her, *"What? You think that I like you? You're disgustingly pathetic! Get away from me! I don't want you anywhere near me! You were an awful mistake! If I knew you'd be begging and groveling after me, I never would have kissed you. Go away! I don't want to even look at you! Stop bothering me! Go away!"*

"How could you say such things, Dendrox!" Weena wailed, and then sobbing miserably, ran off into the woods.

"I didn't say anything; not a single word to her," Dendrox exclaimed, "Where's she going? She could get hurt."

"What's wrong with her?" Candra asked in confusion.

Nodwel alerted them all, keeping a watchful eye to the trees, "This doesn't feel at all right. I feel as if we're being watched."

Vordin said with worry, "We should go after Weena."

"No one's leaving!" Asdella yelled at them, "You think it's funny?! I know you talk behind my back!"

Dendrox said wearing a confused expression, "What?!"

"Stop it! Stop it, all of you! Stop laughing at me!" she screamed.

"No one's laughing at you! What the hell are you talking about?!" Candra blurted out.

"Something's not right here," Nodwel said lifting his axe, as his eyes searched the trees with his heightened night vision. "*It must be one of them. I have to find it while it's off guard, while it fools with our minds. It's our only chance! I have to find it!*"

"Oh yeah?" Asdella said through clenched teeth, "You feel like dying a little? Just keep it up then!"

"What's wrong with her?" Vordin asked anxiously.

"That's done it!" Asdella said taking up her sword into a threatening position, "Who's going to be the first to die? Stop laughing! Stop it! I'm serious! I'll do it! I'll kill you all!"

"She really means to attack us?!" Vordin exclaimed in fear, "Someone do something!"

"It must be the Killnarin," Nodwel told them all, "I doubt she can hear us. She must be trapped in whatever illusion they're creating. Same with Weena. I can't see where the beast is! I thought I saw something moving around in the trees earlier, but now I can't see a damn thing!"

Asdella screamed at them in rage and yelled, "Stop it now!" She swung her sword at Dendrox, but missed him. Dendrox backed away from her as quickly as he could. She snarled at them all and after several threatening gestures finally decided, "None of you are worth the effort."

She then stormed off to the far edge of the campsite, crossed her arms in front of her chest, and sitting on a boulder there, stared off into the forest.

"Asdella?" Vordin asked timidly. She turned and glared at him, but said nothing in return.

Weena was stumbling blindly through the woods with tears streaming down her face.

Suddenly, a dark figure stepped out right in front of her from the shadows to block her path. He was dressed all in black. A hooded cloak hung about his shoulders, the features of his face hidden in shadow. A short sword in a black scabbard hung from his belt.

Weena, extremely startled, gasped and said hurriedly, "Who... Who are you?!" Something about him sent chills down her spine.

"I am The Black Shadow," he answered, speaking in a calm, soothing voice, "but that's not important now."

"The... The Black Shadow..." she managed to utter as she slowly started to back away from him.

"I'm not going to hurt you," he told her, "The creatures, the Killnarin, they are using hallucinogenic spells to frighten you. By nature, they will try to divide your group, make you panic, make you doubt yourselves and your abilities. You are running into a trap. There is only one Killnarin threatening your group at this time. It made its way up the well and has discovered the campsite. It has led you astray, distracted the others, and is now coming to claim its victim... you. Do you understand how they like to attack? They aren't following orders now. Now they are playing with their prey simply for pleasure. The attack on the spider lair, that was organized. That was Dranngore's doing. Same with Dexcsin and Vordin's village, Nilnont. Listen to me carefully, all of you have to learn how to detect when you are under the influence of their spells. It's only an extremely slight variance from reality, but it can be detected. Heightened uncontrollable bursts of anger and unnatural conversations and expressions can be signs. Their hallucinogenic spells are not strong enough to make you see or hear anything more than this, and only the ones with stronger magic ability can make you hear conversations that aren't real. A Killnarin is very difficult to kill and when there are more than one of them, they are stronger and even harder to kill, almost impossible. They draw strength from each other. Do you see what I am telling you? Do things make better sense to you now? You have to help hold the group together and make it to Vackiindmire. It will be safer there. They need the dark to regenerate and to draw their strength. That's why they only came out at night before, now that they have captured the home of the giant spiders, they will be able to draw strength from the darkness there. This means they will be able to venture out during the day and be stronger for longer when they do so. They are

<Zaylyn ><Quest For The Sword Of Anthrowst ><By Katrina Mandrake-Johnston >   <Ch 42> < 134 >

weaker during the day, but in numbers that won't matter and they are driven by a mad man who doesn't care whether a few of his creatures are sacrificed in his plans. Even though you have tried to cover it up, it is not wise to be covered in blood as you are…" Weena noted the unnerving pause he had made here. "The scent will draw predators straight to you."

Weena felt a strange tingling sensation all over her body, and then she noticed the ball of grime forming before her being drawn from her body and clothing. She stared in amazement at her robes which were incredibly clean now, and where Candra's arrow had torn into the cloth, it was completely mended as if it had never happened. She caught the scent of wild flowers, as if she had been cleansed by a fragrant soap.

"The scent of blood will no longer give away your location," he told her, "but it will not stop the beast for long. I have removed the blood from the elf's blanket just now in the same manner."

"How could you possibly do…" Weena began and then instead started to ask, "How did you know about…"

"Remember what I've told you. Have you understood?" he asked her quickly, and there was a hint of desperateness to his voice, "The Killnarin is drawing near." She stared blankly at him, not knowing what to do or if she should say anything further. "Go!" he commanded, "or I shall take your life before the creature does! It will, if you remain here. This is not an idle threat!"

Weena turned and started to stumble through the woods in what she hoped was the direction of the camp as quickly as she could, fear pushing her forward. She searched frantically into the darkness of the forest as she ran for any sign of the Killnarin.

She finally reached the others, gasping for air and with a horrified expression on her face. She told the others what had happened and of what The Black Shadow had said to her.

Asdella blurted out, "This Black Shadow doesn't scare me. I've heard the rumors. If it came down to it, I could beat him."

Nodwel scolded her, "Don't be so damn arrogant. You still have that death wish? The all or nothing attitude? If even a few of the things I've heard are even remotely true, you wouldn't last a single second. In fact, he'd most likely just laugh and walk away. There's a Killnarin out here somewhere. Focus on what's important!"

Asdella just said to him, "You forget, old man, that I see things as a threat only if they present themselves as one. It's either react or don't. It's as plain as that for everything. I don't waste my time worrying about problems that haven't arrived yet." The dwarf just nodded at the warrior woman not wanting to get into an argument with her about anything. "Okay," Asdella said to him, "I take that back. About The Black Shadow, I shouldn't have said that. I know damn well what that horrible being is capable of. Whatever he is, I know well to stay clear of him at all costs. You know me, it's a rare day that I back away from a fight. So believe me when I say this."

Nodwel apologized, "Hey, I'm sorry. It's just, some of the things I've heard, well, it's like something out of a nightmare. I didn't want you just running off and…"

Asdella interrupted, "So are we heading to Vackiindmire or not? I don't want to stick around here. I've been pestered enough by those damn Killnarin creatures. I don't feel like running into any more of them."

<World of Zaylyn ><Quest For The Sword Of Anthrowst ><By Katrina Mandrake-Johnston ><Ch 43>

CHAPTER 43 =   LEAVING FOR VACKIINDMIRE

"Please, let's leave," Lorenta pleaded.

"The Black Shadow, he said there was a Killnarin out here! He said it was hunting us down, that it came through the well, that it tried to divide us, that it was coming for me because I was separated and alone! It must be on its way back to us! It's going to kill us all! We couldn't stop that one when it killed Yarin! What makes you think we can survive this one?" Weena said to them all in a panic.

"The other spiders, do you think they could be in danger? What should I say to them? What should I do?" Lorenta asked anxiously.

Dendrox told them, "We should head out toward Vackiindmire as quickly as we can."

<Zaylyn ><Quest For The Sword Of Anthrowst ><By Katrina Mandrake-Johnston >   <Ch 43> < 135 >

"What about the spiders?! They can't escape to the town! The people there will kill them! You saw what happened to the ones back at Dexcsin! They were just trying to save the villagers and were killed for it. They won't believe us if we tell them they mean no harm," Lorenta explained.

"The Killnarin could be anywhere. The Black Shadow said that it would be safer in Vackiindmire," said Weena nervously looking about her into the darkness of the forest.

"For us maybe," Lorenta said, her anger rising, "and only for me because I look human. I'll have to hide there during the day as it is. I shouldn't have to hide! If they weren't so quick to judge, everything would be fine! I shouldn't have to hide within my human form, hiding my true self as if I am some sort of monster! I'm not an evil being and neither are these spiders. It's not fair! They can't hide themselves as I can! What are they to do? We can't just abandon them! We just finished saving them!"

A terrifying howl filled the forest.

"It's drawing closer!" Vordin exclaimed, his words showing the terror he felt.

"Was anyone able to tell which direction it was coming from?" Candra asked, her voice taking on a commanding tone as she scanned the darkness around them with a stern face.

"No," Nodwel answered with a worried expression, "I really think we should leave though. We'll have to take our chances and hope we don't end up running toward the thing."

"What about the spiders? Could it be that it was never about saving them? That they just happened to escape with us and that it didn't matter one way or another whether they got out alive or not?" Lorenta said with tears starting in her eyes.

Vordin said, "I'm sure no one thinks that," although he wasn't sure if this were entirely true, but he hated to see her upset.

"So what makes all of you so eager to trust The Black Shadow?" Asdella asked them flatly, "Do you even realize that he is ten times worse than any Killnarin? I'm not about to believe that the creatures are weaker when alone. Even if it is true, it's well into the night which means the creature's strength has increased within the darkness. But that is according to The Black Shadow. And another thing, about this wizard Dranngore who is supposed to be behind these creatures, how do we know any of that is true? It was The Black Shadow that gave Vordin the information, wasn't it? Oh and a fairy, but I doubt that matters. Besides, I'm sure he is able to manipulate our minds far easier than any Killnarin. The images of the fairy queen could have just been planted in Vordin's mind. This could all be some twisted game. Directing us down some pre-chosen path, watching us suffer and die. I'm sure he was thinking about killing Weena out there, whether all that is true or not. Why a creature like that would want to help us, I don't know. He's certainly powerful enough just to kill Dranngore with a single thought from across an entire ocean if he wanted to, or so I've heard. Why bother with us? So Weena, what was he like? I bet he was thinking about ripping your throat out, wondering if anyone would notice or care if you were missing. Thinking about letting the Killnarin take the blame. How sure are we that it was even the Killnarin that did the bulk of the damage at the two villages? They may have just interfered with The Black Shadow's enjoyment. You have no idea what he's capable of, do you? You think just because The Black Shadow hasn't killed any of us yet, that we should just blindly do what he says and believe what he tells us?"

Everyone was silent. Not any of them had heard Asdella make such a large meaningful speech before and were a little shocked by it.

After several moments of silence, Nodwel asked them all, "So what do we do?"

The Killnarin made another shrieking howl. It was very close now.

"I don't want to die," Vordin whispered, trembling with fear. His eyes darted frantically around him, expecting the creature to leap at him from out of the darkness.

"Get your weapons ready," Nodwel commanded, trying to be strong and give the others courage, "It shouldn't be long now."

The beast began to howl again, and to the group's amazement, its howl turned into a frightened squealing. Then they heard a tremendous thud and felt the vibration through the ground, as something large and heavy fell to the forest floor with an incredible force. The terrified squealing had stopped and

<Zaylyn ><Quest For The Sword Of Anthrowst ><By Katrina Mandrake-Johnston >   <Ch 43> < 136 >
all was silent.

No one spoke. They just stared blankly into the darkness around them and then at each other.

"We don't have to worry about the Killnarin anymore," Vordin whispered finally.

Trying to accept what had just happened, Weena whispered, "The Black Shadow; it must have been. The Killnarin was actually frightened of him and was killed in a matter of seconds. It must be true."

Asdella said forcefully, "It was frightened for good reason. I say we get the hell out of here now. Just because he took out the threat of the Killnarin, doesn't mean we're safe."

"Which way do we go?" Candra asked, "Which way is Vackiindmire?"

"Let's head south, get out of the trees, and then head east across the plains until we see signs of the town," Dendrox suggested, "That way we'll be out in the open, but at least we'll be able to see what's coming."

"And the spiders, they will be safe? Now that the Killnarin is dead?" Lorenta asked them.

Asdella said getting frustrated, "Looks that way, let's go."

"We have to put out the fire," Weena said urgently. The fire she was responsible for starting at her school as a child constantly haunted her. The thought of causing yet another devastating fire was unbearable.

"We'll have to do all this in a hurry," Candra said, "Weena, grab your lantern and light it. You still have your flame box, right?"

Weena nodded and thought, "*You don't have to ask, Candra. You were in my pouch and know exactly what I have. Thanks to you, the flame box is the only thing I have left now. Well, and the few coins I had managed to save. I thought for sure she would have taken them as well.*"

"Alright then, the girls will head out first, while you three put out the fire," Candra decided.

"We're splitting up?" Weena asked the elf as she lit her lantern and shone it into her face, "Do you really think that's wise?"

She told her, trying to block the light with her hand, "They'll just have to catch up to us when they're done. Hopefully we won't run into trouble before then. And stop shining that light into my eyes!"

"Oh, sorry Candra," Weena apologized lowering the lantern, but found that she did not at all feel sorry she had done it after all Candra had put her through. In fact, it was probably Candra's fault the Killnarin chose her as its victim. She was made vulnerable through her weak emotional state which Candra was mostly responsible for, not to mention the smell of blood that had been on her clothing because of her.

"It is best to split up. Two targets means for a better chance of survival for at least one group," Asdella stated as she headed into the trees.

The women hurried through the forest by lantern light, and Weena had enough courage to ask Asdella, "How is it that you know so much about The Black Shadow?"

"I've heard enough about him to know he's one to be feared," she answered.

"So you don't know for certain if anything you've heard is actually true then," said Weena.

Asdella shot her an angry glare but said nothing.

The others arrived soon after and all seven of them met up on the southwestern edge of the forest. The mountain range could be seen to the west, and to the south beyond the grassy plains, were enormous cliffs rising up into the sky. Beyond these cliffs was the sea.

"Vackiindmire should be situated just south of the forest. If we travel far enough east, we should come across it," Dendrox told them, trusting his memory of the map he had seen of Dee'ellkka Valley.

"Do you think we'll be safe enough here? I've had pine needles wedged inside my sandals for such a long time and I'd really like to get them out," Weena said trying to shake out the debris, "You made sure that the fire was completely out?"

"Yes," Nodwel told her and then looking nervously to the nearby trees said, "Sure, we can take a minute, I guess."

"Looks like it's almost dawn, Lorenta. Did you want to get yourself into the safety of the

<Zaylyn ><Quest For The Sword Of Anthrowst ><By Katrina Mandrake-Johnston >   <Ch 43> < 137 >
backpack?" Vordin asked her.

"Sure, it will be easier for me to travel that way," she agreed, "I remember, Rasindell, he sometimes would take me along with him to gather food and herbs from the forest, and when I was a small child, on rare occasions to a town or village for supplies. I would ride along in that same backpack, with its magically created compartment to keep me safe from harm during the journey. To think that I actually wanted to go on an adventure of my own... Perhaps I should have just stayed at the hut and lived out the rest of my days alone and unaware of all the cruelty in this world," she said sadly, beginning to lose hope.

Vordin couldn't think of any comforting words for her. He opened up the backpack for her and watched the green flames arise. In a matter of seconds, her human body had melted down into a small pool of black shimmering liquid and then had reformed into her true spider form. Once Lorenta had climbed inside the compartment, Vordin swung it carefully onto his back.

"Is everyone ready?" Nodwel questioned, still keeping a watchful eye toward the tree line.

The group then embarked on their trek toward Vackiindmire once more, as the early morning light began to take over the night sky.

***

The Black Shadow looked over at the broken heap of flesh that had once been the fearsome Killnarin threatening the group. "*So easily, I bring death,*" he thought to himself, "*I don't want to be seen as an evil thing. They are safe for now, now that I have killed this beast. The fact that I seem to care what happens to this group of people, shows that I am not all evil, doesn't it? Perhaps I can fight my evil urges. Perhaps I can fight back the hunger and restrain myself from killing my victims. I've failed so often in the past when I have tried this, however, resulting in mass uncontrolled slaughter when the hunger took me over completely. Maybe now it will be different. I feel some sort of connection to these people. Maybe I can learn from them somehow. Perhaps what I lack is a better understanding. Sure, everyone seems to fear and hate me, and it's for good reason, but does it always have to be so? If I can suppress my powers enough, perhaps I can learn to understand things from their point of view better. Reading their minds isn't the same. I need to live as they do and try to hide the monster that is at my core. Am I fool to think it possible? Do I dare put lives at risk trying to interact with others?*"

A searing pain began to grow in his gut, causing him to double over and almost collapse to the ground. "*My hunger grows... I must feed. I must get far away from them, for fear of attacking them despite my efforts.*"

The pain subsided. He was losing control over himself. The next time the pain came it would be much stronger and he would not be able to hold himself back. Many would die horrible and very violent deaths. The pain that often came, it was as if his evil nature would physically fight against him every time he resisted, trying to force him to lose control, trying to make him give in, trying to free itself and unleash tremendous pain and suffering onto the world.

With his heightened senses he could feel the warmth of their bodies. He could hear them. They were close by and their fear had excited him. "*No, I must not! I have to get away from them before it's too late!*" he screamed at himself, but felt the evil part of himself argue. That part of him wanted to sink his fangs into their soft flesh and drain their blood and their warmth away. That part of him wanted to hear them scream and attempt to flee in terror. That part of him wanted to kill.

"*No, I have to fight it!*" he told himself, but the hunger only intensified and his eyes flashed red beneath his black hooded cloak. "No!" he screamed aloud, "No!" and finally he was able to push himself away from the others and soar into the night sky.

Dawn was approaching, but that didn't matter to him. He simply preferred the night over the day. He felt a serenity within the cool darkness of night, feeling hidden away from everything else in some way.

As he flew over the forest, he discovered the camp of three men. The camp was in the middle of the forest, a slight distance from the main road leading from Vackiindmire to the town of Shirkint.

<Zaylyn ><Quest For The Sword Of Anthrowst ><By Katrina Mandrake-Johnston >   <Ch 43> < 138 >

The Black Shadow fell silently from the sky upon the three unsuspecting bandits and fed eagerly. There would be three more corpses for their leader to puzzle over in the morning.

<World of Zaylyn ><Quest For The Sword Of Anthrowst ><By Katrina Mandrake-Johnston ><Ch 44>

CHAPTER 44 =   TO VACKIINDMIRE

They all walked at a steady pace toward where they thought Vackiindmire would be, keeping the forest line in sight. Occasionally, a small animal would scamper through the grass startling them slightly, but all was peaceful. There were no signs of the Killnarin or of any other danger. For most of the day, they had been walking through knee high vegetation and a couple of times they found themselves wading through waist high grasses.

"Looks like we're closer to Dexcsin. Look here, how the grass and plants are shorter and the ground looks well trampled in places," Dendrox pointed out, "They probably used to bring their livestock out here to graze. I saw several different kinds of grain ready to be harvested back there as well. If I'm right, we might find some vegetables or perhaps a couple of fruit trees near here. I wouldn't want to get too close to the village of course, but if we stick to the outskirts like this, we might be able to find some food. If there is anything left, it would be a shame for it to go to waste."

Nodwel told them, "If we come across any, fine, but I don't want to stop. We're too close to the village and the Killnarin. More may come up out of the well. I want to keep moving and make it to Vackiindmire before nightfall."

Candra complained, "This is ridiculous. Do you even realize how much effort it's taking us to get to Vackiindmire?"

Dendrox said to her, "Well, of course, look at all that's happened."

"That's not what I mean," she explained, "We came down through the mountains and traveled all that way just to almost reach Vackiindmire. The town was just a little farther south from where we were at the crossroads, and then we traveled all the way to Dexcsin taking us almost all the way back to the mountains. Then, traveling through the spider lair tunnels, took us even closer to the mountains and even farther away from Vackiindmire. Now we happen to be a little farther south, but we still have to travel all the way back east to Vackiindmire again. We've been zigzagging our way back and forth ever since we entered this damn valley. Do you think we'll actually get there this time, or are we going to almost get there and then end up going all the way back to the mountains again? Because, I'm getting really frustrated with all of this."

Dendrox exclaimed, "Hey, calm down. I don't see any reason why we shouldn't get there. We're out of the forest now. We just have to travel across the plains until we reach Vackiindmire. We're so far south now, that we'll travel right past Dexcsin and probably not even know it."

"I don't want to go anywhere near that village," Vordin added.

Weena reminded them, "The Black Shadow had said that the Killnarin near our camp had climbed up out of the well there."

Asdella muttered, "Yeah, so what?" and then she said to them all, "I think we should get all the information out in the open. Every one of us should explain everything that has happened to him or her and see if we have something that will help us that we didn't realize. Besides, it will pass the time as we walk."

Nodwel thought to himself, "*That sure sounds like something Narr would say. A good idea though*." He suggested, "Okay, I guess Vordin should start."

Vordin told how the beasts destroyed Nilnont and burned everything to the ground. He told how he had hidden and then made his way to Rasindell's hut.

Nodwel commented, "Rasindell, remember how I said before that name sounded familiar? I'm sure I've heard it before, but I just can't remember where."

Vordin told how he encountered the fairy queen and what she had said to him. He then told how he met Lorenta and how The Black Shadow rescued him from the scouting Killnarin. Vordin spoke of how he was kept in a mountainous prison, then taken into Dee'ellkka Valley, shown the slain Killnarin, and taken to the crossroads where they encountered the man with the medallion. Vordin also mentioned

<Zaylyn ><Quest For The Sword Of Anthrowst ><By Katrina Mandrake-Johnston >   <Ch 44> < 139 >

how The Black Shadow had told him of the potion given to Rasindell which enabled Lorenta's creation. He explained that Lorenta had hidden herself inside the magic compartment of the backpack when he had been at Rasindell's hut and remained hidden until emerging at the crossroads and encountered the man with the medallion. Vordin spoke of how the man had attacked her and that she had defended herself not realizing just how deadly she could be. He told how she hid again in the backpack, afraid of what the others might think of her, and that she had traveled with them to Dexcsin hidden in the backpack. He said that she must have emerged from the backpack when they were in the building beside the well and discovered the spider that had come up from it and then met the rest of them face to face for the first time.

Candra and Dendrox both told how they had discovered Nilnont destroyed, traveled through the mountains, and encountered the invisible wizard, later finding him dead. They spoke of how the Killnarin had played its mind games with them and how they finally defeated it. They told how Weena had come to save Candra and had traveled with them to meet Vordin.

Weena told how she had wanted to travel to the larger towns in Dee'ellkka Valley in hope of learning more magic, as she had heard Dee'ellkka Valley was the best place to go. She had traveled alone and had hoped to find an escort over the mountains at Nilnont, even though she hardly had any money at all. She told how she had seen that Nilnont had been destroyed, and being frightened, avoided the village and went directly up the mountain trail. She spoke of how she had been traveling through the forest and discovered the man slain at the side of the road and that she had therefore decided to continue traveling by the light of her lantern in the dark. Then she told that she had healed Candra's wound and then later found her to be poisoned. Weena explained that she had cured her and then they all traveled to the road junction where they met Vordin. She also retold what she had suspected about the man with the medallion and about the wizard's guild and their evil deeds. She then explained that they had to bury the man and his medallion to ensure that no one else would suffer from it, and that shortly after this, they had met Nodwel at the second junction where the road to Dexcsin met the main road.

Nodwel told them how he and his group had passed by Nilnont on their journey into Dee'ellkka Valley and it had been intact and full of life. He explained that they did not stop at Nilnont, but instead had headed up the mountain trail and had camped in the mountains that night. Then he told how they had made their way down into the valley and partially into the forest before making their camp there the next night. He explained that the following morning, the wizard who had recently joined their group, went off into the forest and didn't return. Nodwel told how his group eventually went looking for him and had traveled into the forest.

Asdella commented, "As you remember, dwarf, I was completely against looking for the fool."

Nodwel continued, telling that there had been no sign of the wizard and that they had finally ended up at Dexcsin. He told that the village leader had invited them for dinner and how the Killnarin first attacked the village. He told how Dimwar had been the first to rush out to defend the villagers and had been decapitated. He spoke of how they had to pull Asdella back from running into battle, as she was going berserk with such a furious rage that it would have gotten her killed. Asdella sneered at him. Nodwel explained that they had tried to get all the villagers into one location where they would be easier to defend and how Nimdor had been slain. He also told how the decision to send him for help was made, and that he had managed to escape Dexcsin, but his leg was injured by a Killnarin in the attempt. He spoke of how he had tried to run despite his injury and had hurried all night and half the day, as best as he could, to finally end up meeting the others at the road junction.

Asdella was the last to speak, and she retold how Nodwel had left to find help. She explained that come morning one of the villagers had tried to flee and that's when they discovered that the Killnarin were merely lying in wait and would not allow anyone to escape the village. She told how they had all remained in the building being cautious about leaving and giving away their location after Nimdor had gone to so much effort to keep their location somewhat hidden from them. They had spent the day tending to the wounded and trying to give them hope as best as they could. Asdella went on to say that come nightfall, the Killnarin eventually were able to discover their location and began to tear down the

<Zaylyn ><Quest For The Sword Of Anthrowst ><By Katrina Mandrake-Johnston >   <Ch 44> < 140 >

walls of the building. She explained that they had separated, running in different directions and each taking as many villagers with them as they could. She mentioned again that she had taken Nimdor's amulet and that Borin had obviously snatched up the Camouflage amulet and Blast potion off of him. She told how the villagers in her care were all eventually killed despite her efforts except for a young girl and that she had given the amulet to this girl in hope that it would help her to survive. Asdella then told how the Killnarin was intent on slaying her and the girl as well as it had done with the others and how she then had engaged in a fierce battle with it. She explained that she defeated the Killnarin but at great cost. Asdella said that she would have died if Candra and Dendrox had not discovered her and found and used the amulet to revive her.

Nodwel asked, "Why didn't Nimdor use the amulet? There was time, we could have saved him."

Asdella shook her head sadly and said, "I guess he never told you. You never were very interested in the workings of magic, eh? I remember how excited he was when he first got it. The amulet he had wouldn't have worked. His ribs were crushed. The amulet would have only healed his flesh, not his bone. He would have died either way."

"Oh," the dwarf said sadly, and then he went on to tell them how he had discovered Narr's body and Yarin hidden in the cabinet. Nodwel also mentioned how he had been slightly wary of Yarin, as he had been a twin and how he thought perhaps a creature had somehow copied the dead boy's appearance to fool and spy on them. "I, of course, had dismissed the suspicion shortly after," he told them, "I just thought that I better mention that. The Killnarin create distrust and paranoia in us even when they are not around. They like to divide us, to pick us off one by one, to turn us against each other, to create fear and hatred in us where there shouldn't be," and then, after a deep sigh, suggested, "Why don't we take a much needed rest?"

Everyone stopped walking and started looking around for somewhere to sit and rest their legs.

Weena mentioned, "The Black Shadow said basically the same thing. That they would try to divide us and that we should stand together against them. That way we would have a better chance of surviving."

Before anyone could seat themselves, Asdella snarled at them, "Black Shadow this! Black Shadow that! You don't get it, do you?! He's evil! We have no idea of what his true intentions are, and you still blindly trust him?!"

"So what happened when you left us back at Dexcsin? You know, before we went into the well?" Weena asked her coldly. She was getting annoyed with Asdella's attitude and her constant insensitivity toward everyone.

Nodwel was curious as well, as she had been acting out of character now and then ever since she had gone to see Narr, but he was still wary about saying anything.

Asdella shot her an icy glare and wore a bitter look on her face. "What do you think I did?" she snapped cruelly, "I heard that Narr was dead, and I went to see for myself."

"So you thought Nodwel lied to you? Why would he lie about something like that?" Weena interrogated.

Asdella glared at her again and snarled, "No, that's just what I did, alright? Now drop it."

"No," Weena said sternly, "Why did you go? You knew that the Killnarin were coming. What were you doing? Going to tell them of our location? I think it's very suspicious that they would just leave you out in the open still alive for Candra and Dendrox to find, when they were so intent on making sure that everyone was dead. It seems like a perfect opportunity to plant a spy. Yarin would have been too obvious, maybe so obvious that we would dismiss the idea all together and overlook the possibility that you in fact are the spy. They make it look like we saved you, so we let our guard down even further. Nodwel even thinks that you've been acting strangely, don't you Nodwel?" She didn't give him time to say anything in his defense. She accused, "That's how they were able to find us so easily every time, isn't it? Is that why you went off into the forest after we escaped the spiders' lair? To report to them?"

"I," Asdella said through clenched teeth, "am not a spy!"

Vordin suggested, "There must be a Killnarin around, trying to manipulate us again."

<Zaylyn ><Quest For The Sword Of Anthrowst ><By Katrina Mandrake-Johnston >   <Ch 44> < 141 >

"No!" Weena said angrily, "I'm just really fed up with all her insanity! I want answers! I'm tired of all this! I don't care if she's so insane that she might attack us if we say the wrong thing or ask the wrong questions."

"I am not insane!!" Asdella screamed raising her sword to Weena. Weena jumped back defensively, a little shocked at Asdella's outburst, even though she had provoked it.

"So why are you so defensive about telling us why you had to leave like that?" Weena dared to ask.

"*Just admit it,*" Narr's voice said in Asdella's head, "*You're in love with me, or were. It's true isn't it? It was that important to you that you say your final farewells to me, that you would risk encountering a whole swarm of Killnarin to do so. Admit it. It will end all these suspicions. Just tell them.*"

"Shut up!" Asdella screamed. Weena thought this was directed at her, even though it was meant for Narr's ghost.

Asdella would never tell them about his voice inside her head. This would confirm to them that she was truly insane. Asdella gave Weena a fierce look and her words were full of malice, each word spoken slowly for emphasis. "I'll gut you," Asdella threatened Weena with her sword, "If you ever say anything like that again or ask me again about wanting to pay my respects to a fallen comrade, I will kill you. Do you understand? I will slice you open and mash your insides into the dirt. Do you understand?"

Weena frightened and shocked, looked at her with a pale face and nodded.

"Maybe we should all just continue on our way," Nodwel told them.

The group began walking again with Asdella leading the way in a fierce stride.

Nodwel whispered to Weena, "She's serious about that. I wouldn't push her too far, if I were you. If she were a spy in disguise, I think she would have disposed of us long ago."

"Yeah, I think you're right," Weena admitted.

<World of Zaylyn ><Quest For The Sword Of Anthrowst ><By Katrina Mandrake-Johnston ><Ch 45>

CHAPTER 45 =   THE APPLE TREE

They continued to walk, even though everyone was greatly in need of a rest and most of all water.

"I'm so thirsty. My mouth feels like a desert," Weena complained, lagging behind.

"Hey, isn't that an apple tree?" Vordin said, being the first one to spot it, "That big one over there?"

Dendrox squinted and, with his hand shielding his eyes from the noonday sun, exclaimed, "Yeah, I think it is."

Everyone headed over to the great tree. Plump red apples hung from its branches.

"I can climb up easily enough," Vordin told them, "I could throw them down to you." Everyone eyed the delicious looking apples as Vordin removed the backpack and climbed up the trunk into the sturdy branches of the apple tree.

"Hey, Vordin," Candra called, "See if you can get me that really big one over there."

"Which one?" he asked, "This one?"

"No, the one just next to that one and over a bit," she told him.

"Candra," Dendrox scolded, "It doesn't matter. You're going to make him fall." She just ignored him. "Vordin," Dendrox called, "Just throw down as many as you can, okay?"

Vordin nodded and began to pass down several apples at a time. Weena immediately bit into a large juicy one and ate greedily. Vordin soon joined them after collecting as many apples as he could.

"We should probably take some of these with us," Nodwel commented sitting on the shaded grass and taking a large bite from an apple.

Soon all of their hunger and thirst were satisfied, but none of the apples remained.

"I should probably get some more," Vordin suggested, "to take with us, like Nodwel said."

"I think we've been here long enough," Asdella told them, "Dexcsin is not far, which means the Killnarin are not far, and I want to get to the damn town as quickly as possible."

<Zaylyn ><Quest For The Sword Of Anthrowst ><By Katrina Mandrake-Johnston >   <Ch 45> < 142 >

"It won't take long," Vordin told her.

"No, we leave now," she ordered holding up a small cloth doll not much larger than her hand. She had found and retrieved it from around the base of the tree. Its yellow stringy hair made of wool was frayed at the ends, and the hair had been collected and a small white ribbon had been carefully tied around it. The once deep blue color of the tiny dress it wore had faded with age. The doll was well used with a few stains and it had obviously been mended numerous times. "Look!" Asdella said wearing a foul expression as she shook the doll at them, "We are too damn close to the damn village! We are leaving, right now!" she commanded. Her eyes seemed exceptionally cold and bitter as she tossed the doll aside and started walking toward Vackiindmire again.

"We better catch up to her," Nodwel told them and stood.

Asdella was already a fair distance ahead of them by the time the others ran after her.

Weena, however, hesitated and picked up the doll from where it lay. Weena, remembering all the small children she had seen brutally slain at Dexcsin, wondered if this doll belonged to one of them. She imagined the owner of the doll laughing and playing happily here in her favorite spot under the large apple tree and feeling safe in its shadow.

How Asdella could just throw the object of a child's love away like that, was almost incomprehensible to her. *"This doll is probably all that remains of this child,"* Weena thought to herself, *"and Asdella just tosses it away, as if it were totally meaningless!"*

Weena propped the doll up against the base of the tree in sitting position. Its black button eyes stared up at her. Weena stared back imagining how the child must have cared so much for this little doll.

"Weena?" Vordin called, "You coming? The others are getting pretty far ahead trying to keep up with Asdella."

"Yes, I'm coming," she called back.

She looked back to the doll. It seemed to look sadly up at her, wanting to be remembered and being all alone now that its child was gone. Weena was about to leave, but she knew that if she did, the doll would just be a bit of cloth and string to the next person who came across it.

This was a child's love, not just a doll. Weena quickly picked it up and put it into her cloth pouch. She then hurried after the others.

"So what's with Asdella?" Weena whispered to Vordin.

"I don't know. She started to act strangely after she found out The Black Shadow was around. Could it be that she's truly afraid of him? I didn't think she was even capable of fear," he whispered back to her as they walked.

"We both encountered him. He made it clear that he wanted to help us. I don't think we have anything to fear from him. He saved us from the Killnarin, didn't he?" she said quietly.

"And me before, as well," he whispered, "He protected me from one of the beasts before taking me over the mountains to meet all of you. Remember?"

"I don't know. It's like she'd rather be surrounded by hundreds of Killnarin than be anywhere near The Black Shadow. You heard how she was talking back there," Weena whispered.

Asdella slowed her pace and let the others get ahead of her until she was walking beside Weena and Vordin. "You know, I can hear you. Sound travels in the open like this," Asdella explained to them. She was calmer now and there was a hint of sadness in her eyes. She sighed and said to them, "I have to tell you that, yes, I am afraid of The Black Shadow. I am utterly terrified of him. I pretend not to be, but I am, and it's because I've seen what he's capable of. Don't be so swift to call him friend."

"Why? What did you see?" Weena asked her.

"Just get to Vackiindmire," was her answer, and she sped ahead of them.

"But…" Weena began.

Vordin told her, "I don't think she's going to talk about it. This is Asdella, remember? Plus, did you see the look in her eye when you asked her? It must have been something terrible."

<Zaylyn ><Quest For The Sword Of Anthrowst ><By Katrina Mandrake-Johnston >   <Ch 46> < 143 >

CHAPTER 46 = VACKIINDMIRE

The vision of the walled town of Vackiindmire was a welcome sight. It was just about sunset and wouldn't take them very long to reach the safety within its walls. As they neared, they could see that the large gates were wide open and seemed to be inviting the weary travelers in. The great rocky cliffs towered over the town to the south and the group could see the road leading from the forest as it sloped downward to eventually end at the town's gates.

"This valley must have some sort of magic on it," Dendrox commented as they walked, "It's enclosed on three sides by enormous rock formations and yet there is no shadow cast from them on the valley below."

"That's what you're thinking about?" said Candra, "All my brain is saying is 'warm bed', 'hot meal', 'hot bath', and 'hurry up because we're almost there'. I'm not thinking about anything else but that."

"So do you think there will be anything there about this sword we're supposed to find?" Vordin asked them all.

"You really are planning to go on that insane quest?" Candra scoffed, "What, if by some miracle, you actually find this sword? You're then planning to find an illusive wizard and then kill him with this magic sword, eh? Are you forgetting that this wizard also commands a huge army of Killnarin? It's a fool's errand. If anything, if we manage to obtain the sword, the wizard will just have to take it off our mangled corpses and then possess the one thing that could have stopped him and his army."

"Then I guess we're not allowed to fail in our quest then. We have to succeed in destroying the wizard," he told her.

"Yeah, okay. Count me out," she said with an insulting look.

Vordin was becoming frustrated, "If not us, then who?"

"I don't know, an enormous army?" she said with contempt, "Even then, they probably wouldn't stand a chance. All the wizard has to do is conjure up more of the beasts to replenish his numbers, right?"

"That's why we have to defeat him. Defeat him, and the Killnarin go back to wherever they came from," he explained.

"Wake up to the reality of it! If you think I'm just going to throw my life away…" Candra barked angrily at him, "There's nothing we can do!" Then she added, "Besides, you're not even sure if that will happen. Also, what's to prove that the Killnarin will go away once the wizard is dead? They've made it clear that they are enjoying the slaughter far too much to just simply go back where they came from."

"Well, why else would we be sent on such a quest?" Vordin asked the elf.

"I don't know, for sport? A bit of fun? To have a good and hearty laugh at what fools we are and how easily we get killed?" she laughed coldly, "Look at the source! A tiny fairy queen whose people are legendary for their pranks and mischief? Very few have ever seen this race of fairy and all who claim to have encountered them always have a story of disaster to go along with it. And don't forget about The Black Shadow! I'm nervous even to say his name! He is possibly the most feared and powerful creature or being or whatever he is, ever! They say he hears and knows everything, and can sneak up on you before you even know he's there, I don't know, like an evil shadow or something. One thing I do know, is that when there's an unusual death in a town or village, everyone is smart enough not to say anything about it, and those that do are usually next."

"So what's his concern then with all this?" Vordin asked her.

"I don't know!" she said giving him an annoyed look, "Maybe he's mad that all his potential victims are getting killed off by the Killnarin before he has a chance to get to them."

"Maybe you shouldn't be talking about all this," Nodwel warned them, "He could be anywhere, right?"

It was just after sunset by the time they finally arrived at Vackiindmire and stepped through its gates.

<Zaylyn ><Quest For The Sword Of Anthrowst ><By Katrina Mandrake-Johnston >   <Ch 46> < 144 >

"I can't believe we're actually here, Dendrox!" Candra exclaimed, "There's the inn. That building to the right there."

"The Twisted Eye," Dendrox read on the wooden sign hung over the door. It squeaked every time the breeze hit it, making the quiet eeriness of the empty street even more unnerving.

"Let's go in," Candra said eagerly.

"That's a weird name, not very appealing," Weena commented.

"Does it really matter?" Asdella said to her.

Nodwel asked, "Do we even have enough money between all of us?"

"Who cares, we can worry about that later. Right now, I just want to see another person alive," Candra told them with an excited tone to her voice, "Come on, Dendrox, let's go in."

"It's so quiet. Should it be?" Vordin questioned nervously, "You don't suppose the creatures have attacked here as well, do you? Could it be that not anywhere is safe anymore? It's so very quiet. I don't see anyone about. It's eerie, don't you think?"

Just then, the door to 'The Twisted Eye' burst open and two men staggered out. They were clearly drunk and as happy as could be. They were laughing and stumbling about. The glow of the room inside could be seen through the door. As the entrance had been built on a slight slant, the weight of the heavy oak door slowly began to pull itself closed behind them.

The entire group breathed a sigh of relief as they were all fearing the worst. After seeing such horrible sights, these two men were a welcome sight. One of the men noticed the travelers and cheered for no apparent reason. He was a portly man with shaggy blonde hair and a large bushy mustache. He had a round face, rosy cheeks, and small bright blue eyes that had heavy laugh lines at the corners. The man wore a beige shirt with a navy waistcoat, the buttons of which strained over his belly to remain fastened. The front of his matching navy jacket hung at his sides and was far too small for his size. The wide leather belt he wore, which had a large metal buckle, he had tightened over the waistline of his dark brown pants, and as was common among most town and village folk, he wore a pair of brown leather shoes.

The other man, with the narrow face and black hair, slurred in an overly happy tone, "Oh would ya look... dare be sem real purdy ladies!" This man appeared to be just the opposite of his friend. He wore a grey long-sleeved shirt, a dark green vest, and dark brown pants, but was slender with brown eyes, a thin black mustache, and had a short beard at his chin.

The portly man, who had first noticed them, nudged his friend saying, "Watch, dis be how a gentlemen do it." Then he slurred, "Welcome to Vackiindmire, ladies!" and took an overzealous bow that almost landed himself on the ground.

"Okay, okay," said the black haired man, clasping the other's shoulder in an effort to balance himself, "Quit yer showin' off. Let's go."

They both turned and headed down the empty street, leaning on each other as they stumbled. They began to sing some sort of drinking song for which they had forgotten the words and had obviously made up themselves. The group all chuckled as they listened to the two men singing their song.

"He drinks up all the ale, and..." then they fumbled over several undeterminable words before continuing loudly, "his brother's girl! Then he takes me bottle and..." they trailed off again before breaking into a bout of laughter and singing loudly, "and it be so old it made his hair curl!"

"At least they're happy," Weena commented with a pleasant smile.

"Come on," Candra called to them impatiently, already at the door.

<World of Zaylyn ><Quest For The Sword Of Anthrowst ><By Katrina Mandrake-Johnston ><Ch 47>

CHAPTER 47 =   THE TWISTED EYE TAVERN

Inside, the atmosphere was cheerful and inviting. A warm fire burned brightly in the hearth situated in the right wall. Three large tables were along this wall: one close to the entrance, one on the other side of the fireplace, and one next to that and closest to the doorway leading to the guest rooms beyond. Numerous lanterns were hung on the walls lighting the room in a comforting glow.

At the table closest to the entrance, was seated a man in a dark blue hooded cloak. He had the

<Zaylyn ><Quest For The Sword Of Anthrowst ><By Katrina Mandrake-Johnston >   <Ch 47> < 145 >

hood drawn up about his face and cupped his mug of ale with both his hands. He paid them no notice upon their entry. The other two large tables were empty.

To the left of the entrance, a long bench ran the length of the wall under a large mottled window. Four smaller tables were situated in front of the bench with accompanying wooden chairs.

This large room of the tavern was quite beautiful with both dark and light colored wood used in appealing ways. The tables and chairs, although they looked well used, still maintained some of their former beauty and were clearly very well made.

The room was designed in the shape of an 'L', with the length of the room running along the front window and ending at the large double door leading to the kitchen. Next to the kitchen door and opposite the last smaller table was a large wooden desk with beautifully carved markings. Behind the desk were a few shelves with various bottles and mugs with two large kegs beneath on the floor. At the other end of the room, beside the doorway leading to the guest rooms, there was a small square stage.

Behind the desk stood a cheerful man with a round face and black curly hair. He was an average-sized man wearing a grey long-sleeved woolen shirt with a dark green vest over it and a pair of dark brown pants. He was checking over a supply list when he noticed the group enter. He put the list down, smiled, and waved a greeting to them.

At one of the smaller tables, the one closest to the kitchen, a woman and an older man were seated, engaged in a pleasant conversation and enjoying a dish of small seasoned potatoes. The man was obviously her father by the resemblance.

"We should speak with the innkeeper, maybe we can get some drinks or a bit of food with our combined money," Nodwel suggested.

"Maybe I can get something for my glowing rock," added in Vordin hopefully.

They all headed over to the desk to greet the innkeeper.

"Gee, looks like you lot have been through quite an ordeal. We have rooms available, our cook does wonders with roast lamb, and if you'd like hot baths, that can be arranged as well," the innkeeper said with a wide smile.

"How much would this cost?" Nodwel asked, a concerned expression growing on his face.

"Well, about five gold pieces for a room, two for a bath, and three for both food and drink. We like to keep our prices cheap. We get enough business to not have to be greedy," he laughed.

"First time I've heard of that," Nodwel chuckled.

"Yeah, that is pretty cheap," Candra commented.

"It keeps our patrons happy. We're the only town for quite a ways in both directions. Plus, we don't have all the extras that the town of Shirkint does, but we do a fine job. Oh, we have a special show planned for tonight: an excellent juggler. I'm sure you'll enjoy it, if you decide to stay for it."

"What kind of extras does Shirkint have?" Weena asked him, hoping her curiosity would not result in him taking offense.

The innkeeper beckoned them all closer and he lowered his voice to a whisper, "It's on account of The Black Shadow, I reckon. Ain't no one powerful enough to do the sort of things they have, but him. Instead of an outhouse, they have pots that when you do your business into them, it flames it up or disintegrates it or something. Anyways, the pot is empty when you're done. We acquired one from Shirkint for the inn here. It's convenient, yes, but I'm not entirely sure if it was very wise to do so. You know, on account of The Black Shadow and all. Oh and in Shirkint, you pull a lever on a wall or perhaps it's on the side of the bathing basin, anyway, it magically fills with water. Warm, hot, cold, whatever to your liking. Then when you're done bathing, you pull another lever, I suppose, and the water will just magically disappear. Then the town's shops all have a special protection against thieves. When you enter the shop, you are unable to discern what any of the objects are. So it's impossible to steal anything because the spell is only broken when the item is paid for. So you just ask the shopkeeper for what you want. They have everything you can think of too, or at least it seems that way. Oh and if you're the sort that takes a liking to whores, they have them there too. And with them, no matter what you do, you can't get 'em pregnant or receive any sort of nasty sickness in return, not even a common cold. Sorry, if that information offended any of you ladies. I didn't mean to be insulting or

<Zaylyn ><Quest For The Sword Of Anthrowst ><By Katrina Mandrake-Johnston >   <Ch 47> < 146 >

to suggest that any of you explore that matter further or anything. Now, I may seem like I'm talking highly of this town, and true, it is great in some aspects. They hold competitions, have a visiting storyteller, and I believe they have a thieves guild there although they are very secretive about that and I've only heard vague rumors about the guild's existence. Oh and speaking of thieves, it's supposed to be a thief's greatest challenge, that town, and not because of those spells and all. No one can get past that. I'm speaking of their law, that if a home is robbed of valuables, it's their own fault for not protecting it well enough. So all the homes are trapped with horrible deadly traps and mind-bending puzzles and such. Here, I'm getting off topic. You see this is the town that The Black Shadow frequents, and he is said to be seen now and then at The Old Scabbard Inn there." The innkeeper paused and then said in a sorrowful tone, "So many people have gone missing from that town, some even wound up dead clear in plain view and everyone just looks the other way. It makes me sick. Sure they grieve for their lost ones, but no one tries to do anything for fear of losing their own life or worse. And believe me, there's always worse things than death. They just accept their luxuries and watch helplessly as friends and acquaintances slowly disappear, always living in fear that they will be next, that they may say the wrong thing and anger him, as he is always listening, said to even knowing your very thoughts. I've probably said too much already." He looked nervously around and then continued, "It's just that my good friend Yorif went to Shirkint three days ago and still hasn't returned. I know that there are bandits within the forest as of late, who have been ambushing people along the road between here and there, but I doubt they would have bothered with him. I wouldn't be surprised if he had crossed paths with that monster The Black Shadow. There is a carriage that travels between the two towns. It may be faster and safer to travel that way if you are planning to head up to Shirkint, but if you can conduct your business here in Vackiindmire, I suggest you do so and stay clear of that town, especially when the bandits have become so bold in their attacks. Listen to me, I've been rambling on and on, when you clearly want to rest."

"Sounds like somebody else I know," Candra whispered and gave Weena a slight nudge as she teased.

The wizard returned a glare, but was glad Candra was in such a joyful mood. "What's his interest then with the other town?" Weena inquired.

"Don't know. Don't think anyone does," and then the innkeeper asked, "So what can I get for you? A drink perhaps? Oh, and it's getting pretty late, you may want to get your rooms now before they get snatched up. Perhaps a hot bath for each of you first? You still have time before the show starts, I think. So what'll it be?"

"He must think we stink pretty bad, and I wouldn't doubt it," Candra whispered to Dendrox with a bit of a giggle. She was thrilled at finally being in a town and among familiar things. Here, being a thief, she knew how to survive.

Nodwel told him, "Drinks, food, baths, and beds for all of us would be great as we've been through more than you could believe, but unfortunately all we have is this." He placed the few coins that the group had pooled together on the desk.

The innkeeper looked down at the coins with a frown and said, "Oh, I see."

Nodwel turned to his companions and said, "Well food is the most important thing, I suppose we'll get as much food as that will give us and then everyone can have a share."

Dendrox rolled his eyes and said to the dwarf, "I think I may have dropped my money pouch, I'll just go and have a look for it."

Nodwel gave him a stern look. "It would be too much trouble," he said emphasizing the word 'trouble' to get his point across, as he knew well that Dendrox meant to pick a few pockets. Sure it was for the good of the group, but it was still wrong and if he got caught, they would have an encounter they really could do without.

"I have this. Will this help at all?" Vordin asked offering the glowing rock he had made, placing it on the desk beside the coins.

The innkeeper looked all of them over for several moments before saying, "Okay, I'll tell you what I'll do. I'm taking a loss here, but I hate to turn you away. Because of the increased attacks by the

<Zaylyn ><Quest For The Sword Of Anthrowst ><By Katrina Mandrake-Johnston >   <Ch 47> < 147 >

bandits, I'm going to need extra protection for the horses of my customers out in the stable. A few of you stand guard for me during the night and I'll provide you with four rooms, a bath for each of you if you'd like, a hearty meal and one drink for each. If you manage to find out what happened to my good friend Yorif in your future travels and are able to send me a message, please do. As you can see, I'm taking a huge loss here, but I'd like to help you." The innkeeper pocketed the few coins and handed the glowing rock back to Vordin. "You keep this, it must be pretty special," he said with a smile.

Nodwel told the innkeeper, "Thank-you. You are a very kind soul, and we shall not forget this."

Asdella said to the innkeeper, "We are eternally grateful. I'll take first guard for the horses. I won't need any help so I'll take the little one with me, okay Vordin?"

"I guess so," he replied, not knowing what to think. Vordin thought that she would think of him as merely getting in her way. Why she would pick him to come along with her, he had no clue. Perhaps she thought he knew something about caring for horses, which he didn't really. Maybe it was because he had been the only one that had shown concern and gone to find her back when they had been in the forest.

"I'll take that bath right away and make it hot, my muscles are getting stiff. Tell someone to get me out when the food is ready," she forcefully told the man at the desk.

"Sure thing, miss," he replied.

"I guess I'll get washed up too then, if it's not too much trouble to have a bath poured right away," Vordin said timidly.

"Sure, it's no trouble," he told him, "So drinks then while you wait for your meals?"

"Yes, please, thank-you," said Weena.

The innkeeper rang a small bell, which made a soft tinkle. A boy in his late teens entered from the kitchen. He wore a pair of brown pants, a plain white shirt with short sleeves, and a white apron tied around his waist. His brownish-blonde hair hung just long enough to obscure his ears. His eyes were bright blue, and he kept a lowered gaze as he said, "Yes, sir?"

"Six lamb dinners are needed, and could you prepare two hot baths for these two and show them to the bathing rooms?" the innkeeper asked him.

"Yes sir," the boy answered and returned to the kitchen.

Nodwel spoke up saying, "We would be happy with a simple stew. There's no need for such an elaborate meal." Candra gave him a nasty jab with her elbow trying to shut the dwarf up that he simply ignored.

"Oh nonsense. Your stay here will be one to remember," and then the innkeeper told Asdella and Vordin, "It should only take him a short while to prepare the baths once the meals are prepared." He clasped his hands together and with a friendly smile asked, "Alright, so for drinks, what can I get you while you wait? Ale for everyone?"

"Just water," Asdella told him. Nodwel was surprised, as she normally was a heavy drinker.

"Me too," said Vordin, "I don't think ale would sit too well with me."

The group sat at the middle large table beside the hearth. The innkeeper quickly brought them their drinks and everyone gave their thanks as they accepted them.

"I have to thank you again for all that you've done for us," Nodwel told him.

"Don't worry about it. Just don't spread it around; I'm not planning to make a habit of it," he said with a smile before returning to his desk.

"I can't believe we're actually here, in Vackiindmire, in an inn, about to eat a delicious meal," Candra said draining her mug, "and a hot relaxing bath, and a soft comfortable bed to sleep in finally. I've been dreaming about this for days."

"I feel bad for the innkeeper though. He's being so kind and we have no way to repay him really," Weena commented.

"Hey, don't worry so much and just enjoy it," Candra told her.

A skinny man in a colorful costume of red, blue, and green stripes with a matching cap entered the room through the doorway, obviously coming from one of the guest rooms. He carried a medium-sized leather bag and was clearly the juggler the innkeeper had spoken of. The man had bright green eyes, a

<Zaylyn ><Quest For The Sword Of Anthrowst ><By Katrina Mandrake-Johnston >   <Ch 47> < 148 >
long nose, and a great smile of pearly white teeth.

The man stepped up onto the small stage and announced, "I am Beebarr The Juggling Wonder, and I have an incredible show set out for you this evening. I hope you enjoy."

The man took from the bag five different colored balls, which he juggled several different ways to the audience's delight, followed by a dangerous feat done with a collection of throwing knives. Finally, he lit three torches from out of his bag and juggled them as the climax and end of his show. Beebarr the juggler then took a low bow, packed up his bag, and left the tavern.

Their meals soon came, and they all ate hungrily, not leaving a single morsel behind.

The boy eventually came back from preparing the baths. Asdella and Vordin were led toward the back rooms and then down the hallway to the right. The room they entered, at the end of the hall, was a fair sized room with two tubs. A curtain hung from the ceiling on a rod and could be drawn across the room to give privacy between the two baths.

<World of Zaylyn ><Quest For The Sword Of Anthrowst ><By Katrina Mandrake-Johnston ><Ch 48>

CHAPTER 48 =   NARTEN

The boy said to both Asdella and Vordin, "Well, this is the bathing room. It's not very glamorous, but I've made sure the water is hot enough and that you have clean towels and washcloths. The soap doesn't have a fancy fragrance, but it gets the job done. Is there anything else I can get for you at all?"

"Thank-you," Vordin said to him, "I'll take the bath at the far end, I guess, unless you'd like that one, Asdella?"

"No, go ahead. Doesn't matter to me," she said inspecting the room.

There were two small tables, one on either size of the curtain and against the wall. On each table, three large candles were situated as well as a bar of soap and a neatly folded towel and washcloth. A small wooden stool was placed below each table. The room was without windows, and the walls, which were made of a dark richly-colored wood, had been affected by the constant moisture here. Beside the door was a wooden bucket with steaming hot water in it.

Vordin went over to his chosen bath and placed his backpack, with Lorenta within, safely in the corner and then pulled the curtain across to divide the room.

"Okay then, enjoy," the boy said clearly without enthusiasm and was about to leave to resume his choirs once more when Asdella asked him a question.

"So what's your name?" she asked with a slight smile.

"Narten," he answered plainly.

Asdella, who was looking into the inviting bath water, started undoing her halter-top. Knowing that it was inappropriate to linger any further, Narten started toward the door trying to avert his eyes.

She said to him, "Hold on a minute."

"I'm not really supposed to stay in the room," he explained as he nervously rubbed a hand through his short hair and kept his gaze fixated on the door.

"That's okay, I don't mind," she told him tossing her halter-top into the corner followed by her shorts. She slipped into the tub and by this time Narten's face was visibly flushed.

"Maybe I should…" he stammered.

He knew he shouldn't look at the shapely naked woman behind him, as it would be inappropriate, but he desperately wanted to. Narten nervously fidgeted with the side of his apron, and he felt uncomfortably hot under his thin white shirt.

"I just want you to run hot water over my shoulder," she explained with almost a giggle.

He didn't really know what to say or do. He was in disbelief that such a beautiful woman would ask him, of all people, to do such a thing. "Are you sure you really want me to? I could get in trouble," he told her.

"I'm injured. I don't know if it was during battle or from the fall I took, but it really hurts," she explained, "If you could just put the hot water on it and maybe tell me if it looks bad or not?"

"Well, okay," Narten decided despite his nervousness. "Did you want to cover up or something?" he asked not wanting to offend her by catching a much desired glimpse of her exposed form beneath the

<Zaylyn ><Quest For The Sword Of Anthrowst ><By Katrina Mandrake-Johnston >   <Ch 48> < 149 >
clear water.

"It doesn't really matter to me. Am I really so repulsive?" she asked with a mischievous smile.

"Oh, no, no," he assured her, "I didn't mean anything like that," and then hesitating he asked tentatively, "So you don't mind if I happen to see…"

"Please just take a look at my shoulder for me. It's the left one," Asdella said getting impatient.

"Alright," said Narten picking up the bucket of hot water, taking a washcloth from the table, and pulling the little stool up behind her at the edge of the tub. The whole time he had been too shy to steal a glance in Asdella's direction.

He placed the cloth in the bucket and squeezed the hot water over her neck and shoulder. "That's ah, not too hot or anything?" he said nervously as he gazed longingly at her form before him.

She sighed, "No, it feels great. But my shoulder still hurts like hell."

He leaned over and grabbed the soap from the table, as she definitely needed it. Narten dipped the cloth once again into the bucket, created a lather with the soap, and gently began to wash the grime from her neck.

"Thanks. Does it look like there's bruising?" she asked in a pleasant whisper.

"Ah, I don't know. Does this hurt?" he questioned and placed his hand on the side of her neck and let his fingers slide down and over the skin of her shoulder. He wasn't really interested in what her answer was; he was relishing the feel of her skin.

Vordin, already soaking in his own bath, tried not to pay attention to the conversation and to what was going on, but it was hard not to.

She winced saying, "Oh, right there. Can you feel anything?"

"It doesn't feel too bad, but then I really don't know anything about all this. Maybe I should get someone else to take a look at it later," he suggested realizing that she probably really needed proper care and sitting here selfishly enjoying himself wasn't the right thing to do.

"No, it's fine. I'd like you to do it," she told him, "Just does anything feel out of place?"

"Wouldn't you be in a lot more pain if something was?" Narten asked with concern.

"I am in a lot of pain," she said through gritted teeth and then said in a gentler tone almost as an apology, "Put more heat on it please?"

He dipped the cloth in the bucket and squeezed hot water over her neck and shoulder again.

"You know, I think I might have something that will help," he told her, "It'll just take me a little while to get it."

"Is it lots and lots of whiskey?" she chuckled.

"Ah, no," he smiled. "A healing ointment made from both magical and herbal plants. My grandmother was a bit of a healer," he explained, "Unfortunately, I never took the time to learn much myself about it. But if you'd like to try the ointment, it's no trouble."

"Alright," she accepted.

He went quickly out of the room but not before taking a lingering glance at her naked form beneath the water. After he had closed the door behind him, Asdella sunk down into the water trying to immerse her neck and shoulder in the warm bath. As the tub was deep, she was able to submerge her head without too much pain to her injury, and then using her right arm, she scrubbed at her short reddish-blonde hair in an awkward attempt to wash it. She finally gave up and relaxed down into the bath again, keeping the injured area in the warmth. Her dark brown eyes grew heavy and she allowed them to close as she enjoyed the heat.

She heard Narten say, "Hello, I'm back." It seemed as if only seconds had passed since he had departed, but she then realized that she must have dozed off. She didn't know if it had been from the pain or a combination of exhaustion and warmth from the water.

"Hi," she said meekly.

"Okay, now I'm supposed to rub this in," he explained as he scooped a creamy white paste out of a jar and smeared it over her neck and shoulder.

"It's icy cold," she commented as his fingers slid back and forth over her skin.

<Zaylyn ><Quest For The Sword Of Anthrowst ><By Katrina Mandrake-Johnston >   <Ch 48> < 150 >

"Yeah, sorry. Does it feel any better?" asked Narten.

She thought a moment and then said, "I can't tell."

"It probably takes a while before it starts to work," he suggested.

"Okay, thanks. If there's any way I can repay you for your kindness…" she began.

"Maybe…" Narten began and let his hand slowly slip from her shoulder down to touch her bare breast, "Maybe I…" he began again.

"Just make it quick," she snapped viciously at him.

He was a little taken aback, but continued, "Maybe I could get a kiss?" he asked softly.

"No," she said sharply again, "I want you to leave, now."

"But I thought…" he said removing his hand immediately.

"Leave now," she ordered.

"I didn't mean anything by it, I just thought that…" he stammered, horribly upset and feeling incredibly guilty. He got up, walked over to the door, and looked at her with his kind blue eyes searching her face for some kind of explanation.

"I said," she said angrily, "I want you to leave now!!"

Just before he exited the room, he turned to her and said, "If you think that's why I wanted to help you, you're wrong. I'm sorry, I didn't mean to offend you." He looked away and took hold of the door handle saying, "Please don't say anything to the innkeeper. I really need this job."

The door closed behind him with a gentle click.

Narr's voice inside her head began, *What the hell was that all about?!*

"Don't. Just please don't," she whispered, and the ghost left her alone.

She closed her eyes again and sat there in silence beneath the water.

<World of Zaylyn ><Quest For The Sword Of Anthrowst ><By Katrina Mandrake-Johnston ><Ch 49>

CHAPTER 49 =   THE STABLE

Vordin had finished his bath and dressed quite some time ago, but found himself now awkwardly waiting for Asdella to finish hers and call out for him.

"Vordin? We should be out to watch those horses. You ready?" she asked coldly.

"Yes," he replied carefully cradling the backpack in his arms.

Asdella yanked back the curtain and ushered him out of the room, down the hall, and into the main room.

Narten was nowhere in sight. The innkeeper waved a greeting and told them, "Horses are located at the side of the building. You'll have to go out the front door here. Oh and thank-you by the way. Shouldn't be too much trouble. There's plenty of hay and water. The horses we get around here are pretty much used to the routine, shouldn't be a problem for ya."

"Thanks," the warrior woman grumbled and ushered Vordin out of the inn.

"Here we go," Vordin told her, "It's just around the corner here."

The tiny and narrow stable appeared to have been built as an after thought, with the side wall being shared with the tavern and the other being the thick outer wall of the town. The stalls were lined up along the shared wall of the tavern and there was a small area near the entrance in which hay had been heaped into several disarrayed piles against the wall. Also in this area were a couple of large rain barrels filled with water, a couple of wooden crates, a medium-sized pitch fork, a well-used shovel, and various pieces of equipment that Vordin was unfamiliar with.

Only two of the stalls were occupied. There was a tired looking grey mare and a younger horse with a chestnut brown coat. Vordin went over to the younger horse and gave him a friendly pat on the nose.

Asdella looked at the stalls and horses with a scowl. She then sat down on a pile of hay with her back against the wall of the tavern.

"Hey, I think this one likes me," Vordin smiled.

"Yeah, lucky you," she said bitterly.

Vordin reluctantly came and sat opposite Asdella on a small wooden crate.

<Zaylyn ><Quest For The Sword Of Anthrowst ><By Katrina Mandrake-Johnston >   <Ch 49> < 151 >

Asdella stabbed her sword into the hay beside her and then tried to get herself into a comfortable position.

"Why didn't you tell anyone you had been hurt?" he finally had the courage to ask.

"It wouldn't have mattered. If I need to, I will fight again. It's nothing," she told him.

"That's not the point," he tried to explain.

Asdella jumped for her sword yelling, "What the hell is that?!"

Vordin was almost scared out of his wits by this, but then noticed the green glow coming from inside his backpack beside him.

"Oh, hey, Asdella, calm down, relax, it's just Lorenta. Remember? I guess she's decided to transform tonight after all. You'll spook the horses yelling like that. Put your sword down," Vordin coaxed.

"Sorry," she said returning the sword to the hay beside her and wincing at the pain the effort had caused her.

"Is it me or is your injury getting worse?" Vordin asked with a concerned look on his face.

Lorenta now stood before them in her human form. "Asdella, maybe you should try not to force use of the area," Lorenta suggested, "It needs time to heal, even for magical ointments to do their task. I am going to explore this town. I've often wondered what Vackiindmire would be like. Rasindell brought me here once when I was little, but I wasn't allowed to leave the backpack." Lorenta then ran off down the street in excitement before either of them could say anything.

"Do you think she'll be okay?" Vordin asked, "She took this long even to show herself. She's clearly nervous here, perhaps even afraid. You heard what she said back in the forest and how she feared for the other spiders. Do you think she'll be safe all alone out there and at night?"

"Don't know, don't care," she said rubbing at her shoulder and moving it around.

"I guess she'll be all right," Vordin told himself. He shook his head and said, "She's right you know, just give it time to heal."

"Fine," Asdella submitted and then rolled her eyes.

"Why don't you get some sleep," he suggested to her, "I'm sure that will help, and you definitely need it."

With a glowering look, she snapped, "And what is that supposed to mean? I'm every bit as capable…"

Vordin interrupted her quickly, "We all need sleep. Don't you agree?"

"Then you sleep. I'll keep watch," she told him sharply.

Vordin decided it was useless to say anything more about her wound. "When I sleep, it's usually only nightmares that fill my dreams, so you go ahead," he told her.

"It's that way for all of us, but sure, okay," Asdella finally said, and closing her eyes, fell fast asleep.

<World of Zaylyn ><Quest For The Sword Of Anthrowst ><By Katrina Mandrake-Johnston ><Ch 50>

CHAPTER 50 = THE SCISSORS

The others had finally decided it was time to retire to the four rooms the innkeeper had provided for them.

There were two rooms opposite each other at the very end of the hall. Weena took the only room on the left, and Dendrox chose the end room on the right opposite Weena's. The rest of the guest rooms were along the right wall. Next to Dendrox's room, was the room Candra had taken for herself and beside hers was Nodwel's.

Before entering her room, Candra announced to Dendrox, "I'll be taking my bath in the morning," and then asked, "You doing the same?"

Dendrox, standing with his door ajar and about to enter, answered, "Yeah, I'll see you in the morning. I'll be sleeping in late though. At least I'm hoping to. Nightmares… might keep me up. I'm sure everyone will have plenty after all we've seen. I sure did past couple nights."

"I know what you mean," she said with a weak smile, "Good-night."

<Zaylyn ><Quest For The Sword Of Anthrowst ><By Katrina Mandrake-Johnston >   <Ch 50> < 152 >

"Sleep well everyone," said Nodwel rubbing his stubby fingers through his matted and tangled hair as he entered his room next to Candra's.

"Good-night," Weena called, already in her room and half way closing the door behind her.

Dendrox entered, closed his door, and looked around the room. Against the far wall in the right hand corner of the room, there was a wardrobe, and on the right wall, an oil lamp hung from a hook, its light illuminating the room with a flickering light.

Close to the door, against the left wall, was the bed. It was a simple mattress stuffed with straw with a couple of linen sheets and a thick grey blanket draped over it. A single large goose down pillow lay propped at the head of the bed.

Near the foot of the bed was a window made of thick glass. The bottom half slid up to open and was locked by a simple latch. Dendrox made a mental note of this as he usually did. He always liked to keep in mind possible escape routes, no matter what the situation, and also liked to be aware of accessible entry points for the future if the need came.

The room was adequate enough and would be a welcome comfort. Dendrox sat on the bed and for the first time truly realized how exhausted he really was. Ever since the wizard had stolen his pouch, Dendrox had been wanting to take a look inside it, suspecting that the scissors were still in his possession. He removed his pouch, opened it, and searched around in the lining until he found them.

As Dendrox held the scissors, the gold and silver on the ivory shimmered in the light. *"What is so special about this damn thing?"* he asked himself, *"I mean, sure, it should be worth a fair price, but to go to all that trouble and the extreme expense of hiring mercenaries to retrieve it? They even went as far as to send a wizard after us. To think what kind of spells he could have used on us… I'm glad he only chose to use the Invisible ones. I don't know what we would have done if he sent out a ball of fire at us or a lightening bolt or something like that. Perhaps the Invisible spells were all he knew or maybe he had a magic item of some sort that allowed him to become invisible for a short time. We should have searched the body more thoroughly. Something that could turn us invisible could be very valuable. Not against the Killnarin as that wizard had made obvious with his death, but as for doing a little thieving now and then, it could be very handy. Candra would have found anything like that though, I guess. So I guess he must have had several Invisible spells all jumbled up inside his head to be able to cast consecutive spells like that. Weena said that the spells need time to recharge themselves, so it has to be something like that. It's not very important, but I should ask her about it. It doesn't make any sense, even if the scissors were of some sentimental value, it still wouldn't be worth all the effort they've gone to. Hey, maybe the scissors are magical or something. I wonder what they do? They certainly can't really cut anything very well, being made of ivory, can they? Weena might know, being a wizard and all. I'll ask her. Plus, it'll give me something to talk with her about. Hopefully, it will give me a chance to smooth over some of the awkwardness that occurred after that kiss."*

Dendrox quietly left his room and knocked softly on the door opposite his. Weena answered the door and gave him a shy smile.

"Hi, um, I have something to ask you about," he whispered.

She asked, "What is it?"

He replied, "It's about a pair of scissors. I think they might be magical. I'd like it if you came to take a look."

A little surprised, Weena said, "Sure, I guess. A pair of scissors? That's unusual."

He whispered, "Hey, shh, keep it down. I don't want Candra to hear. She thinks I got rid of them, and I thought I did… It's a long story. Why don't you just come to my room and I'll explain things a little better."

"What is he really up to?" Weena thought, *"Does he think I'm fool enough to fall for such a silly plan? I'm not sure I like where this is going. I mean, people do tend to form a special kind of bond when they go through a traumatic experience together. Is that what this is? Am I even really attracted to him or is it just some kind of false attachment? He can't be good for me, that's for sure. I mean, he's a thief. He robs people. I guess I'll never know, if I don't go. Now that the danger is over, I'll be*

<Zaylyn ><Quest For The Sword Of Anthrowst ><By Katrina Mandrake-Johnston >   <Ch 50> < 153 >

able to tell. I'll be able to make the right choices, won't I? I'll look like such an idiot, going into his room to see about a pair of magic scissors. He could have come up with a better excuse to persuade me over there than that."

Weena closed her door behind her.

"I didn't wake you, did I?" Dendrox asked her, realizing that he may have woken her.

"Oh no," she said following him across the hall and into his room, "Every time I close my eyes, all I see are images of the villagers we found at Dexcsin, and of Yarin, and that man Borin and what he did to save us."

"With me," he said closing the door and sitting down on the bed beside his open pouch, "I see the shiny black skin of the creatures, their huge teeth oozing that foul yellow slime, their black staring eyes, their claws… And Yarin, I liked the little guy. I think he liked me too. Remember how I stayed with him back at the village? When we were in the building by the well? Remember? With all the commotion when the first spider came out of the well, and with Lorenta?"

"Yes, I remember," Weena told him, feeling his sorrow.

"I really thought we would all get out of it together," he told her, "That we would all survive together. I made myself believe it then, for him. And then he was gone."

"Do you think the others are able to get any sleep?" asked Weena, not wanting to talk about what had happened.

"I hope so. Everyone needs a good night's rest," he commented.

He retrieved the scissors from his pouch and handed them to Weena. "These are them," Dendrox told her.

"Oh, I don't believe it! There really is a pair of scissors. What are the odds of that? So it wasn't just a ploy to get me into bed?" she thought a little shocked and confused, *"I hope that doesn't mean he's given up on me though. Maybe he's not so bad after all. I mean, he doesn't really act like a thief should. Well, or how I imagine a thief to act. I mean, he hasn't stolen anything since I've known him. He's had plenty of opportunity, hasn't he? Maybe he has and I haven't realized it. Candra still has my mother's ring, damn it."* "So what's the story on this then?" she asked him.

"Yeah, well as long as you don't tell Candra. I just had to tell someone that I still had them. I don't really know what to do," said Dendrox, "I told Candra I got rid of them and I really thought I did. Perhaps I was under a spell to make me forget. I only realized that I still had them when I found out that wizard was looking for them, the one the beast got."

"You mean the one I saw along the side of the road? The one that had been with Nodwel and Asdella's group?" she questioned.

"Yes, he had turned himself invisible and found our camp. He snatched my pouch right from under our noses and took off with it only to run into a Killnarin. He was after the scissors. Is it possible to have more than one of the same spell? Would that account for there not being a wait for the spell to recharge?"

"Yes, it would, or a magic item with several magic charges in it," she explained.

"Yeah, I had hidden the scissors in the lining of my pouch and forgotten about them. Candra and I have had bounty hunters after us, now and then, ever since we stole that horrible thing. It's been pretty quiet for awhile and maybe that's why I had forgotten about them."

Weena said, "There's a bounty on you two? I can't even imagine… People hired to kill the two of you? I would go insane with paranoia. I mean, it could be anyone really, couldn't it? I think I remember Nodwel saying that the wizard had muttered something about a pair of scissors. So the guy wasn't sputtering nonsense. There really is a pair of scissors. Who would go to all that trouble over a pair of scissors? It's elegant and pretty, but it's strictly just ornamental, right?"

"That's what makes me think that maybe it's magical or something. It must be something really important and special to go to all this trouble to get them back," he told her.

"Or they just have a lot of money and time on their hands. The scissors probably have sentimental value; a family heirloom perhaps?" she commented, "I can't tell if this is a magical item or not, if that's what you're asking. I have no clue whatsoever. Sorry."

<Zaylyn ><Quest For The Sword Of Anthrowst ><By Katrina Mandrake-Johnston >   <Ch 50> < 154 >

"I really don't know what to do," he said honestly, "I feel like throwing the retched thing away, but I doubt it will stop me and Candra from being hunted down. I don't know if these bounty hunters somehow have a locater spell or something on the scissors or somehow on us. If there is such a thing, I don't know. How do you tell? I thought maybe you would know."

Weena was pleased that he had come to her with his problem and that he and confided in her. *"This is something that Candra doesn't know. This is a secret shared by just the two of us. Oh you silly girl!"* she scolded herself, *"This is serious! Look at the poor guy, he's frightened out of his wits about this!"*

Then a solution to his problem came to her. It was so simple it almost made her laugh out loud. But then she realized that of course this solution obviously must have occurred to him and there was probably some reason why it wouldn't work and that she would sound like a complete fool to suggest such a thing. She said it anyway, as he was staring at her intensely, expecting some sort of answer. "Why don't you just return the scissors to the owner? Then the bounty will be called off and everyone would be happy," she told him.

Dendrox got a puzzled and astonished look on his face, as he pondered this. "Okay, I feel like an idiot now. Why didn't I think of that?" He paused a moment considering how to go about this and then said, "Wouldn't it be kind of suspicious, just one day the scissors showing up on their doorstep? It's obvious they want us dead, as well as the return of the damn thing. I don't think it would be enough. And besides, they moved from their place. I have no idea where they might be. We happened to pass by there once, and they definitely don't live there anymore. Don't know what they look like either. Asking around trying to find their new location would leave a trail right to us."

Weena suggested, "Okay, well, what if I returned the scissors and said something like, 'I discovered a couple of thieves slain by the road side. I checked their belongings to find out who they were and found the scissors and am returning them to the rightful owner'. Of course, there's the matter of finding out where they live, but that way they'll think that the two of you are dead."

Dendrox shook his head, "I know you're trying to help, but no one would believe that."

"Why not? If we just find out where their new house is…" she began.

He explained, "For one thing, anyone dead along a road side would have pretty much all their belongings picked clean, especially something this valuable."

She offered, "Well, I could say one of the beasts got you."

He chuckled, "Yeah right, would you believe me if I told you about these creatures, not knowing what you do now?"

"Okay, that's true," she admitted.

"And as for some other wild creature," Dendrox continued to explain, "you don't live very long as a thief, if you don't know how to handle yourself. They'd see right through your story anyway, if they had any experience. They would detect your lies through the way you handle yourself, and wonder how you came to know the scissors were stolen in the first place. You definitely don't look the part of a bounty hunter looking for a hire. I just thought maybe you could help me to understand the magical aspect of this all, like how they are tracking us or what exactly these scissors do."

"No, I'm sorry," she apologized, "I wish I could help, I really do. But it looks like I might end up making things worse for you if I try to get involved."

"As far as I know, they don't know who we are or what we look like," Dendrox told her, "so it must mean that the location of the scissors is being tracked, right? That makes sense, doesn't it?"

Weena didn't want to add to his anxiety, but she wanted to help him in any way she could. She said, "Actually, I think it might be possible to locate you as well, like the last person to possess them, or the last person to touch them. Or no, because they wouldn't know if you kept them, you could have sold them to someone. The person holding them? No, because that would be the same as just locating the scissors."

"What are you doing?" he asked her, slightly puzzled.

"Just give me a minute. I'm trying to figure out if it's possible to track you with magic and not just the scissors," Weena explained to him, "Okay, if they try to track the one who stole them, it would be

<Zaylyn ><Quest For The Sword Of Anthrowst ><By Katrina Mandrake-Johnston >   <Ch 50> < 155 >
too broad of a thing, so no. It would need to be more specific, more precise… Oh, oh, I know, I know!" With these last words, she almost did a little excited dance as if she had the winning answer to a contest question. Dendrox just smiled affectionately at this. She announced her answer, "Okay, the first person to touch the scissors after the owners."

She had a triumphant grin on her face. He smiled back at her. She was so intent on helping him. He wondered if she realized the gravity of his situation and that helping him or even to try would mean she would be putting her life at risk as well. They already had the threat of the Killnarin to deal with.

He suddenly felt like the biggest fool of all. "*Why did I even mention all this to her?*" he asked himself, "*Even to know puts her in grave danger. I should have just talked to Candra about it. So what if she gets mad? I've dealt with her temper before. I was so determined to find something in common with Weena and to have something to talk about. How is she supposed to understand the life of a thief? She'd probably end up getting us all killed trying to fit in. She even said something like that herself. Besides, a thief is always on the run, having to leave town on a moment's notice. It's thrills and adventure and plenty of danger. It's no place for someone like her. She'd want to study her magic, walk in the open, and all that… not sneaking about through back alleys. Oh and she would protest profusely every time something slips into our possession out of someone else's pocket, getting us caught for sure. And then as Candra always says, 'end up squirming on the wrong end of someone's sword'. Maybe it's best if Candra and I just take off. It'll be best for all of us that way. With the Killnarin to worry about, they don't need this added to their plate.*" "Weena, I…" he began to say to her. "*Oh yeah, break her heart in two,*" he scolded himself, "*You told yourself this one was special… and she is. Don't be an idiot. You have to take off, fine, but that doesn't mean you should have to watch the innocence in her eyes turn to pain. She thinks the world of you and you know it, and this is knowing that you're a thief and an outlaw. Maybe she finds that exciting, but the more time she spends with us, she'll soon realize the reality of it.*" "I just…" he started to tell her. "*You're just going to make things harder for yourself,*" his mind warned him, "*Remember, this is for her own safety more so than yours. So there, the decision's final. Early tomorrow morning, before the rest are up, Candra and I will take our leave and the others will be better for it. This means this is the last time you'll see Weena. Hell, who knows, I could be dead in the next couple of days. It looks like the bounty hunters are getting more and more efficient at finding us. We've had one too many close calls already. Not to mention those damn Killnarin. Hell, I'm surprised any of us survived this far dealing with those beasts. So this is definitely your last chance to be with her.*"

He pulled her close and kissed her passionately and felt her arms wrap around him in a warm embrace. He did not want to think of leaving, he did not want to think of the scissors and the bounty hunters, and he did not want to think of the Killnarin and the insane wizard behind them. He did not want to think of all the death and companions lost.

Weena was warm and soft, and her skin and hair had the faint and inviting scent of wild flowers. There was desire in her kisses and it was desire for him. No fake names or titles were needed, no pretend personalities and backgrounds. It didn't matter how much gold was in his pouch. She wanted him; Dendrox. It was him; Dendrox, the thief. Why? He didn't care. He was lost in the moment and willingly let all his worries melt away wanting the moment to last forever as he held her close.

<World of Zaylyn ><Quest For The Sword Of Anthrowst ><By Katrina Mandrake-Johnston ><Ch 51>

CHAPTER 51 = THE BOUNTY HUNTERS

There was a commotion out in the front room of the inn. They thought nothing of it at first, lost in each other's eyes and soft kisses, until they heard someone announce in a deep bellowing voice that he and his heavily armed friends were looking for a couple of thieves that had long overstayed their welcome among the living.

"Could he mean you and Candra?" Weena asked with a worried look.

"*Not now, why right now!*" his mind complained. "Sounds like it. I have to get to Candra," he said urgently.

"Search the rooms!" the deep voice loudly commanded.

<Zaylyn ><Quest For The Sword Of Anthrowst ><By Katrina Mandrake-Johnston >   <Ch 51> < 156 >

"*Damn it, no time! I've got to get out of here,*" he told himself, "*I'll have to meet up with her later.*" He ran over to the window and tried to open it. "It's jammed! If I break it, they'll hear, and if they have horses, I'm dead meat on foot. What do I do?" he said frantically, his eyes darting madly around the room, "I can't hide, they have that locater thing they do."

Weena stood there looking as if she were about to say something but her mind was coming up blank. He could see she was starting to panic as well. He wondered what might happen to her, if she would be named as his partner in crime or that they might not even care if she was one of the accused or not. "*It would be less hassle just to slaughter anyone in the way. No one would have the nerve or be foolish enough to protest their actions either, lest they meet the same fate,*" thought Dendrox.

Nodwel's voice could be heard bellowing in a heated argument with the men.

Dendrox thought, "*At least I have a few minutes before they reach my room. Would I be able to fight my way out? Against trained assassins? Yeah right, play the dying hero protecting his lady to his last breath. Sounds like a nice way to die, but I'd rather not. There has to be some way. Damn it, and what about Candra? Did she make it to safety? Should I break the window? At least I might have a slim chance of escape. Of course, if they have half a brain, they'll be expecting this and have men positioned outside waiting for the two thieves to attempt their escape. If that locater is on the scissors, I could plant them on some drunk and maybe escape that way, but there's no time, and I do have a conscience to deal with. There has to be somewhere for me to hide. The floorboards maybe? No time, and they'd notice, and probably no room. Bed's out too. Maybe the walls? The ceiling? No, no, no! Damn it, I'm trapped! What's Candra doing?*"

He grabbed Weena by the shoulders and whispered frantically, "Weena, what can I do? I'm trapped! They'll most likely kill you as well! Do you realize this?! Think, damn it! I'm all out of ideas! What about magic?! Is there anything you can do?!"

Her face was pale and fear-stricken. Panic filled her eyes. "Magic… magic," she mumbled, "They're using some sort of magic to find you, right? So maybe we can block it somehow, so they can't detect you."

"But what about Candra? And if they search the room and find the scissors, we're dead!" he emphasized.

"My Shield spell might be able to block the locater magic, if the spell they are using is a weak one, which I doubt, but I will try. And this is all provided that my spell works for me, it might not," Weena told him.

"Okay, fine, get started," he said, quickly taking a dagger from his belt and prying up a section of the floor.

"What are you doing?" she asked puzzled.

"Just start the spell, there's no time to try anything else. They're on their way to this room now," he whispered, slipping the scissors out of his pouch and down into the alcove in the floor. He jammed the floorboard back into place with the heel of his boot just as Weena finished casting her Shield spell around him. Weena breathed a sigh of relief when she saw that the bubble-like film was not present when cast on another. The spell had worked. She was sure of it. As long as the shield was not being used to absorb a physical attack or that of another spell, it would hold for a short while at least.

Seconds after the spell was in place, the door to the room was kicked in and four large burly men entered.

One wore an eye patch over his right eye and had a scimitar at his belt. A brown leather jerkin was over this man's chest. His muscular arms displayed a great number of colorful serpent-like tattoos. He had black greasy hair and had a satisfied grin on his face.

Another was bald and wore a brown bushy mustache under his bulbous nose. As he grinned a wicked smile, Weena could see that one of his front teeth had been replaced by a gold one. This man had a heavy looking spiked mace in his right hand.

The third had a whip strapped to his belt and five large daggers at his waist. The daggers were easily double the size of Dendrox's largest one. He had short dirty-blonde hair, and to Weena, appeared to have his eyes set a little too far apart reminding her of a funny looking lizard she had once seen.

<Zaylyn ><Quest For The Sword Of Anthrowst ><By Katrina Mandrake-Johnston >   <Ch 51> < 157 >

The men stood aside, as a fourth stepped forward. He seemed to be their leader. He was taller than the other men and almost twice as wide. A huge war hammer, which he held in his right hand, was balanced on his shoulder by a large, visibly muscular arm. He wore a small black vest over his wide bare chest on which many tiny scars could be seen. It made Weena think that perhaps he had been a blacksmith at one time. She also decided that he must have gotten in a lot of battles to receive such a display as well. He was bald, and had dark green eyes which gazed over the two of them suspiciously.

"Well, what do we have here?" the leader bellowed through a mouthful of misshapen and rotting teeth.

Dendrox was about to make some sly remark, but Weena spoke up surprisingly. "Thank goodness you're here! We heard a commotion out there but thought nothing of it until this filthy little man burst out of that wardrobe there and leapt out the window. I think he was planning to rob us, slit our throats in the night! Good thing you came looking for him and scared him off, or we would have been goners for sure."

Weena's face became flushed as the men looked her over. *"Oh no, Weena, they're going to see right through you. You should have let me handle this,"* Dendrox thought nervously to her, wishing she could hear him.

"Please excuse me, I just realized that he must have been here the whole time, and when I was getting undressed, he must have been watching me. The dirty little pervert! Who knows what he might have done to me, if you hadn't shown up to rescue us," Weena explained, realizing that her body language must be giving her away and trying to justify it.

"Good save, Weena, I guess," Dendrox thought nervously, *"Maybe I underestimated you a little. You're a terrible liar, but you probably saved it there, I hope."*

The man with the eye patch and the serpent tattoos took a couple of steps toward the window and viciously criticized, "So this thief, he just jumps out and takes a leap out da window, eh? This window that's shut?"

"Oh no, I have to say something! But what?" Dendrox's mind panicked.

"Well obviously it was open when he jumped out," she said, trying to sound offended, but her fear was starting to show.

"I could say that we closed it after him, thinking he might come back to take us hostage," he suggested to himself, *"Yeah, right, and me with my daggers all along my belt here."*

But Weena continued, "I was so frightened," she said trying to justify her body language to her story, hoping to keep from giving herself away, "I'll never forget his words. He said that if we told anyone that he had been here, that he would come back and kill us, and he pointed a huge dagger at us, and looked at us with an insane look in his eyes, and then he shut the window behind him. I guess to make it look like he didn't escape that way."

Dendrox's mind said, *"Weena slow down, don't panic. Not so much information, it makes it more like a story, fabricated, definitely not natural, which means dead, dead, dead. There's no way we can make it out alive."*

"Oh and the dagger he had, it was at least the length of my forearm, easy," she added.

"Weena, please stop, no more," he pleaded.

The man with the bushy mustache and spiked mace went to the window and tried to open it, finding it stuck. The others were eyeing Dendrox suspiciously.

"Window's stuck, how he manage that?" the man said with a smug look on his face, the flickering light glinting off his gold tooth. The man with the tattoos gave his companion a nod at this and let out a faint snort.

"We're dead, so dead," Dendrox told himself, *"They're mocking her. Doesn't she realize this?"*

"That's simple. I thought you would have been intelligent enough to realize," she answered.

"Oh yeah, make them angry, insult them, that will convince them to let us live," he thought hopelessly with great sarcasm. He let out a sheepish smile trying to appear as apologetic as possible for Weena's curtness.

"Oh? Please, enlighten us," the leader growled, displaying that his temper was shorter than the

<Zaylyn ><Quest For The Sword Of Anthrowst ><By Katrina Mandrake-Johnston >   <Ch 51> < 158 >
hair on a rat's tail.

"Magic of course," Weena said plainly, "He sealed the window with some sort of magic so you couldn't follow him as quickly. I'm a magic user myself, that's how I recognized the spell."

Dendrox let out a frustrated mental sigh, *"Oh great, if this Shield spell is working, they know now to check for one."*

"The spells don't last very long, so I'm assuming he had planned to delay you for just a few moments," she said as she gave Dendrox a nervous glance.

"I guess this means the Shield spell isn't going to last very much longer," he thought to himself.

"So, your man here. He's armed. He didn't try to stop the thief?" the leader questioned displaying his grotesquely misshapen teeth once again.

Weena quickly fabricated, "He's so brave. He was going to try to stop him, but I was so frightened and when I saw that huge knife the thief had, I grabbed on to my sweetheart and held him back. But now that you're here, you can catch him, right? He did say he was going to come back if we told anyone."

"Oh, we'll catch him," he said with a chuckle, readjusting his grip on his massive hammer, "Don't worry about that." He gave Dendrox a knowing look and then said, "Let's go boys."

The blonde man with the wide-set eyes was the last to depart, running his fingers along the leather of his whip as he looked them both up and down as an unspoken threat. "Pleasant evening then," he grinned at them and then headed down the hall after the others.

Weena quickly closed the door behind them, having to adjust it several times to get it into place as it had been damaged by the entrance of the men. Dendrox was about to say something, but Weena quickly put her finger to her lips motioning him not to say a word.

She came over and hugged him tightly whispering in his ear, "They are listening."

"We have to escape now," he replied.

She told him. "No, that's what they're waiting for."

"They saw through you," Dendrox explained to her.

"I know, but we're not dead. They're not completely sure. That's why we can't leave. If we leave, they'll know for sure," she whispered.

"I have to check on Candra. What if they did something horrible to her?!" he whispered with a worried look.

"No, that's too suspicious," Weena decided, "You're not thinking clearly. They'll be watching our every move. You contact her, they'll know you two are the ones they're looking for. I don't seem like a thief to them, you're safer with me right now."

"So you're staying here tonight? You're not going back to your own room?" he asked, thinking about the possibilities.

"I can't, it would be suspicious," she said with a cunning smile, "You don't mind do you?"

Dendrox answered her with a kiss. "Do you think they know where 'the item' is?" he whispered.

"Probably, but not exactly where. We're safe for now. If the locater is on it, I say we leave it here and then try to leave tomorrow. They don't seem the sort to give up easily," Weena commented.

He asked, "And if it's on me?"

"Let's worry about that in the morning," she said with a passionate kiss.

Dendrox quietly said, "Shh, listen."

"I don't hear anything…" Weena began and then she heard it too, "No, wait, a faint tapping sound, right?"

They rushed over to the wall, and Dendrox put his ear against it.

"Is it Candra?" Weena whispered.

"Shh, it's a special code we made up for emergencies. Let me concentrate, we haven't used it in years. I don't really remember too well how to decipher it. I need to concentrate."

Weena remained silent, as Dendrox listened for several minutes, and then watched as Dendrox returned a set of taps, scratches, and knocks. This continued back and forth for quite awhile.

"Okay," he whispered, "So basically what she said was, that she's okay. We're going to pretend

<Zaylyn ><Quest For The Sword Of Anthrowst ><By Katrina Mandrake-Johnston >   <Ch 51> < 159 >
we don't know each other, as you suggested, and wait to see how things are in the morning. And I'm in big trouble from her about 'the item'. And she heard everything and says that you did a pretty good job dealing with the bounty hunters, all you need is practice. Not in so many words, but that's basically what she meant."

Weena smiled at him, staring intensely into his eyes for a few moments before taking him by the hand and leading him over to the bed.

"We should get some sleep," she whispered pulling back the sheets and sitting down on the bed.

Dendrox also seated himself and removed his boots, as well as his belt of daggers. Weena, who was blushing, slipped her feet out of her sandals and tucked herself under the blanket. Dendrox followed.

He gazed longingly into her eyes and then his lips met hers. Each kiss led to another and another. Each touch led to yet another and another, and soon they were in a romantic embrace, despite all that had happened.

<World of Zaylyn ><Quest For The Sword Of Anthrowst ><By Katrina Mandrake-Johnston ><Ch 52>

CHAPTER 52 = DENDROX'S SCAR

Weena and Dendrox lay awake in the room unable to fall asleep. They lay beside each other in the small bed staring into each other's eyes, listening to the creaks of nearby floorboards and the muffled conversation of people enjoying themselves in the main room of the inn. There was no further indication that they were in any immediate danger from the bounty hunters and the rest of the night would probably be uneventful. Still, they both were wary of falling asleep.

Dendrox shook his head in disapproval and at the same time the corner of his mouth turned up in slight amusement. He said to her, "I can't believe she stole your mother's ring. She's gone, I take it?"

"Yes, she died when I was very young, but I still remember her very well," she replied.

Dendrox explained, "You see, when Candra was a girl, her father was murdered right in their very home by a couple of thugs and they stole her mother's necklace. It was the only thing they had left of hers and it was also their only item of value. She came to live with my family. We practiced our weapons until we were old enough to leave home and go after the thugs, as Candra desperately wanted revenge. Ironically, that's how we became thieves ourselves. We had to adopt the trade, mingle with the right people, and show our worth in order to eventually find them. They actually still had the necklace too. I guess they felt guilty or something, or more likely they had kept it as some gruesome trophy of what they had done."

Even though Weena suspected what the answer might be, she still asked, "Did she kill them?"

"Yes," he told her, "I don't really want to talk about that. It's a part of Candra I'd rather forget is there."

"I see," Weena said knowingly.

There was an awkward moment of silence between them; Dendrox lost in thought.

"I guess she's trying to create a thief out of you in sort of the same way she was made one, by stealing your mother's ring," he finally said, "To see if you have what it takes."

Weena displayed a cunning smile as she told him, "Oh, I'll get my ring back. I just don't know how yet."

"Candra's pretty sneaky and it sounds like she's taking these little trials of hers pretty seriously," he commented with a smirk.

"I don't know," Weena said, still trying to absorb the fact that Candra had killed two people and maybe more that she didn't know about. It made their little walk back in the forest even more frightening, as she knew for certain that Candra would have gone through with her threat to kill her. "One thing I know is, I'll never kill anyone," Weena decided about herself, "I just couldn't do it, even if it was in self-defense." The back of her mind whispered to her, "*Yeah, I didn't murder my classmates and brother. It was more of an accident, right? It's not as if I stared down at them with hatred in my eyes and painfully ended their lives as they begged for mercy.*" She ignored this little voice that kept trying to remind her of that horrible incident. That guilty little voice that would never leave her alone,

<Zaylyn ><Quest For The Sword Of Anthrowst ><By Katrina Mandrake-Johnston >   <Ch 52> < 160 >
that was always trying to destroy her illusion of innocence.

"Candra and I are thieves," he admitted, "but we never want to end up like those thugs that attacked her and her father. Being a thief means a lot of running, fast-talking, and…" he hesitated slightly, "sometimes you may have to kill in self-defense."

A chill ran down Weena's back as she asked, "Have you ever?" It was hard enough for her to imagine Candra taking her revenge. To imagine Dendrox in such a manner, frightened her.

Dendrox pulled back the blanket slightly to show the large scar across his torso and explained, "This is what made me realize that I had better learn." He tucked the blanket around Weena's exposed shoulder affectionately and continued, "Candra might not have been taken, I might not have been almost killed, and I might have been able to save her."

Weena, who was always very curious about everything, asked eagerly, "What happened?"

"Hey, you better not say anything to Candra about all this," he said, getting defensive, "If she found out that I told you about her past or of what I'm about to tell you, she'd kill me." Weena's eyes widened. He chuckled, "Not for real. It was merely a figure of speech."

"Oh," she said a little embarrassed and then assured him, "I won't say anything, I promise."

Dendrox continued, "Anyway, there was a fight in this tavern. I think it was called The Wyvern's Tail. These guys grabbed Candra to sell her to one of those whore caravans. It's slavery in the worst way. Two had their hands full holding Candra. I could have killed the third, the one with the sword. I would have been quick enough to do it too, and maybe even had a chance to kill or at least wound the two holding Candra. I could have at least distracted them long enough for her to maybe get free. Because I was unwilling to kill that bastard with the sword, I was almost killed myself. I was lucky to have survived it. Candra was taken, and I was helpless to save her. The one with the sword decided to give me this scar before following after the others with Candra. It was just by chance that she was freed by one of the whores who had escaped them on her own. To think that Candra could have been violated like that, makes my blood boil."

Weena decided it was wise not to bring up anymore unpleasant memories. Killing Killnarin was one thing, but to talk about killing people in such a way, even in self-defense, made her feel extremely uncomfortable around him. She hoped he did not seriously feel this way and that it was just the anger and frustration from the memory speaking. She told him, "We should really try to get some sleep. We'll need our wits about us tomorrow."

"Yeah," he agreed, although it was obvious that his thoughts were elsewhere. He caressed her shoulder and kissed her softly before turning over onto his back to try to sleep.

When Dendrox finally drifted off into a much-needed sleep that night, in his dream, he began to relive that awful event. His thoughts still lingered on the memory after the conversation with Weena.

It was quite a few years ago, back when he and Candra were still learning their skills as thieves, and just before he had acquired his scar. He and Candra were sitting around a small wooden table in a dark smoky tavern. They had just acquired a pouch with a fair amount of money in it from the belt of an unsuspecting traveler. Candra had distracted him, while Dendrox had skillfully removed the pouch by slicing through the cord with one of his daggers.

They were about to celebrate by ordering a large mug of ale each, when three men entered the tavern and their eyes scanned across the faces of the patrons. Dendrox and Candra had tried to avoid being identified, as they recognized one of the men as the one they had robbed. The thieves both knew that they were about to get into a very bad situation when they heard the man say to his companions, "That's them."

The men headed over to the table, as Candra and Dendrox desperately tried to come up with a plan.

The one man, the one they had robbed, laughed coldly and said to them, "I believe you have something that belongs to me."

"What do you mean?" Candra asked a little too innocently.

"Do you take me for a fool?" he chuckled.

<Zaylyn ><Quest For The Sword Of Anthrowst ><By Katrina Mandrake-Johnston >   <Ch 52> < 161 >

One of the man's companions had been eyeing Candra from the moment they had entered. He suggested, "We could sell her. She's pretty enough."

"Alright, grab her," said the man.

His two companions grabbed Candra by the arms, one on either side, and dragged her away from the table. Candra looked nervously to Dendrox, as she tried to force her way free of the strong grip each of them had on her. The other patrons looked on, but made no move to help the two of them.

Dendrox got up from his chair, trying his best to look somewhat threatening.

The man looked him up and down with contempt and chuckled. "Sit back down little man. What are you going to do?" he dared.

"Take your stupid pouch back. All the money's still there," Dendrox hissed, retrieving the pouch from the inside fold of his vest.

To Dendrox's dismay, the man simply laughed at him and his two companions joined him in his mirth to the point where Dendrox and Candra both began to think that maybe they had missed something. The man finally said, "Nice try, but this way we make a profit. You forced us to come after you, so we's gonna need a little something extra for all that trouble, now don't we?"

The other man holding Candra, who had remained silent until now, said, "Let's go, she's squirming about."

With a malicious grin the man quickly unsheathed his long sword. Dendrox looked nervously about, not knowing what to do, hoping someone would come to their aid. The man suddenly and viciously slashed his sword across Dendrox's stomach. Luckily, he had managed to move back slightly and save himself from being disemboweled, but the tip of the man's sword cut deeply into his flesh.

Dendrox doubled over in pain and shock, his eyes showing his fear and desperation as he looked into Candra's horrified face. Her green eyes welled with emotion and her thin-lipped mouth twisted in a hateful grimace toward their assailants.

The blood from his wound seeped through his fingers as he instinctively tried to hold the wound closed. The man sneered at him as Dendrox looked in disbelief at his blood-covered hands and the thick sticky pool forming below him. The man wiped his sword clean on the sleeve of Dendrox's shirt as a final insult, while the thief stood there dumbfounded and in complete shock.

"Dendrox! No!" Candra wailed and she desperately tried to wrestle herself free.

"Help me hold the bitch," one of the men holding her told the other.

His vision started to blur and his legs felt weak beneath him. He grabbed onto the back of his chair with one hand, the other still clutching at his wound. The sounds around him seemed to fade far away as if he were underwater, and he felt as if he were sinking into the floor.

He was vaguely aware of the men walking away from him and of Candra screaming.

"Dendrox!" she screamed and her voice echoed in his mind until there was only blackness…

<World of Zaylyn ><Quest For The Sword Of Anthrowst ><By Katrina Mandrake-Johnston ><Ch 53>

CHAPTER 53 =   DANGER IN THE WOODS

His heart was pounding hard in his chest. The Black Shadow had been running for quite a long while, somehow trying to escape himself. The blackness of the night enveloped him now as he sat in the forest clearing, his black cloak draped around him as he rested, his legs crossed beneath him. The hood of his cloak was drawn up about his face as always.

He had thought to himself once that it was almost funny how the village and town folk had become wary of anyone wearing a hooded cloak with the hood drawn up. It had become unspoken knowledge that if someone had their hood drawn up, that this meant they wanted to be left completely alone. He knew that this had arisen out of the incredible fear they have for him. Not many had the courage to wear a black cloak, and if they did, they definitely did not raise the hood. He thought surely a few would use this to their advantage, perhaps scare some folks out of their loot. No one ever dared. Could they think that he would take offense and inflict horrible death upon anyone who dared to resemble his likeness? He did not care. In fact he wished others would, making it easier for him to move about

<Zaylyn ><Quest For The Sword Of Anthrowst ><By Katrina Mandrake-Johnston >   <Ch 53> < 162 >
undetected. Maybe that was the whole point of it all.

Surrounded by dark looming cedar trees, the cool air chilled and numbed his body. He was alone and it was silent except for an occasional breeze now and then rustling the treetops.

Still sitting, he put his head back and looked up to the black sky. He watched the stars and the treetops dancing in the wind beneath them. He took a deep breath and relaxed slightly. The ground under him was cold and wet. The smells of earth and trees filled the air. The taste of blood still lingered on his lips and tongue. He felt somewhat safe now that he was here alone in the silence. Being alone meant that there wasn't anyone around for him to worry about harming.

"And what will happen if I succeed at sparing lives? What if they remember? What if they know who I am and what a horrible monster I truly am?" his mind asked, *"I will be greatly feared even more so than I already am. No, it's best forgotten. There's no use in worrying about it, because I'll just end up worrying about the same thing again tomorrow night. I don't want to think about it. All is best forgotten."*

Indescribable sensations flowed through him, numbing his body and mind. He licked the precious remaining droplets of the thick, dark crimson liquid, savoring its taste… and at the same time was disgusted with the savage beast within him. He knew the hunger would slowly begin to rise within him yet again to tear at his soul. He tried to enjoy the short amount of time and peace he had while the hunger was so briefly satisfied. He closed his eyes and let his mind wander.

"I have to admit that the hunt for victims is sometimes thrilling," he said to himself, his evil nature showing through, a wicked grin starting at the corner of his mouth exposing the tip of a fang.

Opening his eyes once more, he inhaled another deep breath, this time letting out a deep melancholy sigh which broke the silence for a moment. The wind then whistled through the trees making an eerie sound. He closed his eyes again.

The Black Shadow finally rose from the ground where he had been sitting and decided to walk. Folding his arms over his chest to keep warm, he walked briskly through the dark forest. He climbed over logs and pushed branches aside. Unseen animals scurried around in the bushes as he continued.

***

"I'm dead serious. That be exactly what I saw," one of the bandits on watch duty said to the other.

"Yeah, alright," the other laughed.

"I'm tellin' ya the truth," the bandit said to the other who clearly wasn't believing a word he had said.

"I admit, it was odd to be seeing a set of clothes neatly folded with a pair of shoes placed beside 'em and just there in the middle of the forest beside a tree. But that's all I be saying, it was a little odd and that's all," said the second bandit warming his hands over the tiny campfire.

The first continued, "But you never saw!"

"See what? What'd you see in your drunken haze, eh?" he asked with a laugh and then pulled a small bottle from out of his vest pocket.

"Hey, you remember what he said 'bout drinking on watch duty! If he catches us again…" the first warned.

"Oh relax," said the second bandit, "Besides, you sound like you be needin' a good shot of whiskey, maybe two."

"Alright, fine," he said taking the bottle, uncorking it, and taking two large gulps of the strong liquid.

"Hey, slow down there, pal, save some for me," the other chuckled taking back the small bottle and taking a swig.

"Listen, so you just need to believe me on this. I tell ya, so I go back towards where we saw them clothes. I was just heading in that direction and I thought I sees somethin'. Somethin' like a wolf, I think, out of the corner of my eye. So I gets nervous and I sort of stay a little bit out of sight," the first bandit explained.

"Wow, this is pretty exciting," the second said mockingly and took another swig from the bottle.

He was ignored and the first bandit continued, "Anyways, I still can't believe what I saw myself,

<Zaylyn ><Quest For The Sword Of Anthrowst ><By Katrina Mandrake-Johnston >   <Ch 53> < 163 >

but I swear it be real. This wolf, he comes into the clearing where the clothes be laid. He has an unusual intelligence behind the eyes, ya know, as if he wasn't really a wolf at all. He be lookin' all around, almost a bit nervous I think. I thought he was goin' ta find me, but I sat very still. Then right before my eyes, the wolf's body, it starts twistin' and flopping about. And as the beast was all thrashin' about, it be slowly changing from wolf into a man."

"Yeah, really? How much of a fool do ya take me for?" the other snorted.

"No, I swear, honest! He changed right before my eyes! The man, he then puts on the clothing as if nothin' happened. He looked like a common merchant! Then he just walks off into the woods," the first bandit told the other, his eyes wide.

"So, I take it this be why you were holdin' back then at the last raid? You were frightened the merchant was going to turn into some sort of ferocious monster wolf and be protectin' his goods? What a load of crap," he laughed and then said handing him the bottle once more, "Here, ya want some more of this?"

***

The Black Shadow thought he detected footsteps and movement behind him, but when he turned around, no one was there. If he wanted to, he could have used a little more of his power to become completely aware of his surroundings, but he had put a damper on his abilities in hope that with a less heightened awareness he would be unable to detect any people within the area. The awareness of unsuspecting prey would just fuel his hunger, and he was trying to suppress it and keep it under control.

"*I feel like I am being stalked by someone or something. It is almost the same techniques I sometimes use to hunt down my own victims, having fun with their fears. Could it be a Killnarin? No, they seem to know to be wary of me. Could it be that someone is so foolishly and willingly walking into the arms of death? Perhaps it is nothing. I am not used to relying on just my outer senses and having them diminished so. I must maintain this state for my own good though and for that of others, no matter how much the curiosity nags at me,*" he told himself.

He continued a short way through the trees where a majority of pine trees grew and visibility became a little more difficult. Then he stopped suddenly. He heard the distinct snap of a twig. "*Someone is following me,*" he exclaimed in disbelief.

The Black Shadow continued to walk, not wanting whomever was following him to know that he had been discovered. He was actually beginning to enjoy this. He walked quickly ahead and then hid himself in the bushes and the darkness. Then he waited, listened, and watched.

He heard the person approaching, the leaves rustling and twigs snapping. The person was moving more slowly and carefully, but it was too late as The Black Shadow was already aware of him.

"*Soon I will be able to see whoever this is, and then perhaps be able to enter his mind to discover who he is and his intentions,*" he thought to himself and then scolded, "*No, what's the point of learning to rely on the simple senses and abilities as do ordinary people, if you're just going to revert back to using them whenever it's convenient? No mind powers.*"

The man stopped and The Black Shadow could see him now from within the shadows of the forest. His pants were torn almost to shreds. The man's body was splattered with mud, and his short blonde hair was tangled. He looked nervously around.

The Black Shadow looked into the man's eyes trying to detect what he might be thinking without just quickly taking a look inside his mind.

"*Perhaps the curiosity will overpower the evil urges inside me,*" he thought hopefully, although horribly frightening scenarios were already forming in the back of his evil mind. This man would not be safe for long. A little bit of curiosity would not stop his evil self and The Black Shadow knew this too well. "*He is clearly lost and confused. I can see that now in his eyes. But why?*" he asked himself, "*Could it be that he was not following me at all, but had taken an unlucky turn which led him along my path? If so, what caused him to be in this state? What was he running from? Perhaps he is not the only one out here.*"

The Black Shadow watched his every move. He watched the man breathe and the blood pulse through his body, exciting his hunger. The sound of The Black Shadow's heartbeat and breathing got

<Zaylyn ><Quest For The Sword Of Anthrowst ><By Katrina Mandrake-Johnston >   <Ch 53> < 164 >

gradually louder and soon started to almost pound in his ears as the craving for blood grew and grew. The Black Shadow started to breathe in low rasping breaths, sucking the air in through his teeth as he desperately tried to maintain control over himself.

***

"The night before last, the three on watch duty," the first bandit said taking a swig from the bottle, "they were all found dead."

"Yeah, what of it? That's what happens when you go against the leader's orders. They probably tried to make some quick coin off someone traveling through the night, underestimated his abilities and got themselves killed," the other suggested with an uncaring chuckle and accepted the bottle back from him.

"What if it isn't that simple?" he said.

"Oh, gee, you think this wolf beast you imagined is responsible for that too, don't you?" the other laughed.

"No, actually I don't," the first said very seriously and tried to convince the other, "I think there is somethin' far worse out there. I think you know of who and what I mean."

"So what are you sayin'?" he asked with a mocking smile.

"I'm sayin'," the first told him snatching the bottle out of his hand, "Maybe we shouldn't be drinkin' anymore of this t'night. Who knows what could be lurkin' about in the night? And most frightening, in the blackest of shadows, if ya get what I mean."

"Well, the bottle's empty, and so's yer brain. You paranoid fool. Just relax, would ya?" chuckled the other.

***

Unable to resist any longer, with a great agility, he crept silently through the bushes, watching and listening like an animal stalking its prey. The Black Shadow had made his way silently around his intended victim until he was standing behind him.

In one swift movement he grabbed the man with one arm around his torso and sunk his fanged teeth deeply into the soft exposed flesh of his neck. The warm, thick liquid started to flow slowly over his lips.

"*Turning the natural pain of my bite into pleasure in the mind is the least I can do for my victims,*" he commented to himself and then as an after thought said, "*Of course it can work the other way as well, intensifying the pain to incredible levels for a deserving individual.*"

The man struggled a moment, as he bit deeper into him. Then the man surrendered himself to the pleasure and to The Black Shadow, as his blood began to gush from his neck.

"*Shut up,*" he yelled at himself, "*Just do what you must. Just try not to kill him.*"

The man, weakening, sunk slowly in his arms to the ground as The Black Shadow bent over him and drank heavily.

He withdrew, the hunger still burning fiercely within him, and desperately hoped that it wasn't too late to save the man. The Black Shadow willed the wound to heal and it quickly did until it was completely flawless.

The Black Shadow's fangs ached to be embedded once more in the soft flesh. He wiped his darkened, wet lips against the back of his gloved hand.

The man looked up at The Black Shadow, his eyes showing his fear and helplessness, his breathing shallow, as he lay there weak and afraid.

The hunger burned, pulsating within him. He bent down toward his exposed neck once more, almost without realizing what he was doing, but then he saw the look of horror on the man's face and he was able to stop himself again.

"*He looks so innocent, and he knows that his life is in my hands,*" he thought to himself.

The man stared at The Black Shadow's face beneath the hood. It was shrouded in shadow to the point where his features couldn't quite be seen clearly no matter which way he turned. Even if he allowed someone to see his face, which wasn't very often, he would make sure their mind could not remember it.

<Zaylyn ><Quest For The Sword Of Anthrowst ><By Katrina Mandrake-Johnston >   <Ch 53> < 165 >

After a few moments, the man was able to muster enough strength and courage to say in a weak and trembling voice full of confusion and fear, "What's going to happen to me?"

"Nothing," whispered The Black Shadow, "Go back to your life and enjoy it while you still can."

The man staggered up to his feet, still very weak, and started to make his way through the forest as fast as he could, having to hold onto trees for support every couple of steps.

The Black Shadow remained kneeling on the ground, fighting desperately with the urge to follow… to leap upon the helpless man and drain the last bit of life out of him.

Before the man was completely out of sight, he stopped and turned to look at the dark figure in the small forest clearing.

"Go, it will cost you your life if you linger here!" The Black Shadow growled at him.

The Black Shadow watched as the man continued until he was out of sight. He could smell his scent, hear him moving across the ground, and sense the warmth of his body. The man was still in danger from his hunger. He tried desperately to diminish his senses to that of an ordinary person in hope that in this way he may not be able to detect the man he had freed from death.

It was quiet now. Darkness surrounded The Black Shadow in complete silence. The man was safe now, at least from him. Something had been watching, lurking just out of sight. Whatever it was, it was furious that The Black Shadow had interfered with its prey.

<World of Zaylyn ><Quest For The Sword Of Anthrowst ><By Katrina Mandrake-Johnston ><Ch 54>

CHAPTER 54 = ASDELLA'S PAST

Asdella was now in a deep sleep upon the pile of hay. Vordin rested silently taking great care not to wake her. A dream filled her mind…

Asdella was in a forest glade. The sunlight filtered down through the treetops. The occasional bird chirped its song. It was a peaceful atmosphere; no sign of danger.

She of course was on guard, suspicious of every sound she heard, expecting the worst no matter how appealing this place was. Although after a few moments, she did allow herself to relax slightly.

She was uncertain of where she was. Asdella suspected that she must be experiencing a dream. It felt somehow different though, as if it weren't entirely coming from her own subconscious, but that of another. She did not want to move from the glade. She did not want to move from where she stood. She wanted this strange dream to end. It made her feel uneasy.

She heard a noise. It was footsteps coming toward her through the forest. She could hear the rustle of leaves as whomever it was approaching brushed past them. She instinctively raised her sword and then it slowly faded away until she was grasping at nothing but air.

Narr emerged from the forest, pushing away a leafy tree branch as he ducked his head under it. He was as she had remembered him. He gave her one of his sly smiles.

Narr's blue eyes met Asdella's, but she returned no emotion at seeing him there before her. He stepped into the sunlight, making his wavy blonde hair shimmer for a moment, before he decided to lean up against the trunk of a large oak tree. He crossed his arms in front of his chest in a relaxed position and looked at her expectantly.

As usual, he wore plain dark brown pants and his leather jerkin with a white long-sleeved shirt under it. At his waist hung his short sword in its scabbard. It was what he usually wore, and he looked the same as when she had last seen him alive, only he was exceptionally clean, especially his clothing. It was this that struck her as being especially odd. His shirt was extremely white and his pants were a deep rich brown, as if they had been worn for the first time. The leather of his jerkin looked comfortably broken in, but was very clean which also seemed unusual. As an adventurer who often got into trouble, his clothing was always well-worn and clearly showed it, especially the leather jerkin he wore almost every day.

Narr, however, still had that unique exuberance about him that she remembered. Narr rubbed at the stubble that was beginning to show at his chin and then said, "You're not even going to say 'hello', are you?"

<Zaylyn ><Quest For The Sword Of Anthrowst ><By Katrina Mandrake-Johnston >   <Ch 54> < 166 >

"Was I supposed to?" she replied rudely.

"Ah, come on," he grinned, "I find out this great trick and you don't even say hello? You're mad at me, aren't you?"

"Annoyed is more the word. What is the meaning of all this?" she said curtly, "You nag me all day, and now you've decided to invade my dreams as well?"

Narr let out a frustrated sigh. "I already apologized for that. And I also left you alone just like you wanted, for quite a long time," he told her and then announced, "Anyway, I've solved that problem. My thoughts won't be tumbling into your head all at once anymore."

"How so?" she asked impatiently.

"Wow, just relax," he said to her, "You're so tense and uptight. We have plenty of time and there's nothing to worry about here. Come on, why don't we sit down and talk? There's no harm in that, is there?"

He motioned with his hand to a wooden bench at the side of the clearing. Asdella was sure that it hadn't been there a second ago. Reluctantly, she finally submitted and sat down. The bench was surprisingly comfortable. Narr sat beside her, stretching his legs out in front of him and slouching down into the seat with his arm resting on the back of the bench and the other on the armrest. "So, pretty nice here, isn't it?" he commented.

Asdella, who sat rigidly upon the bench, said, "Just tell me what you want and then leave me alone."

"Cold as ever I see. It's not like you have anywhere to go. You might as well enjoy yourself," he explained.

"Is this my dream or yours? Things don't feel right here," she said looking about the forest.

"It's sort of a shared dream I think. A place created by both our minds," Narr told her, "Oh, and about our little problem? Well, you see, here, where our two minds meet, I can be more of the old me."

"And that's good how?" Asdella asked with the beginnings of a smile.

"Hey, that wasn't very nice," he gave her a mischievous look, "It means that all my thoughts won't get dumped on you anymore. I can center myself here and speak to you as if I were here in person. You know what I mean, don't you?"

"I guess," she answered.

"What I'm trying to say is, that I'm slowly gaining more control over myself, learning my abilities and boundaries," said Narr.

"So now what?" she asked looking him in the eyes, "What happens now?"

He was lost for words for a few seconds, as he stared longingly back into her dark brown eyes. Then he said, "Well, I don't know. Are you still mad at me? Because I can't really tell."

"I'm not angry with you," Asdella told him.

"Will you talk to me then?" he coaxed, "I feel as if I know nothing about you, and I want to know everything. You must know how I feel about you."

Asdella decided, "You know, I am angry after all at you, and it's not because you annoyed me."

"What did I do then? What else could there possibly be?" Narr questioned with surprise.

Asdella stared deeply into his eyes and for several moments couldn't bring herself to say anything. She was breaking down. She wanted to tell him many things, to finally be able to confide in someone, to let someone in past her hard outer shell she had hidden herself beneath.

"You died," she said, her words cracking with emotion.

"Oh," was all Narr could say. It looked as if Asdella was finally on the verge of opening up to him, which was something he never thought possible. He could see that tears were welling up in her eyes. He said, "So you're angry with me because I died? You do know that I didn't do it on purpose, right? It sort of just happened. It wasn't something I had planned on doing, you know? Will it help if I say I'm sorry?" He hoped that his words might cheer her up and take the weight off the subject, but she remained looking into his eyes with a hurt behind them that he wished he could just wipe away for her. "I did die trying to save some of the villagers. That was pretty heroic of me, wasn't it? To tell the truth, I always kind of imagined myself dying like a coward in some drunken brawl," he chuckled.

<Zaylyn ><Quest For The Sword Of Anthrowst ><By Katrina Mandrake-Johnston >   <Ch 54> < 167 >

"You did save someone, a boy named Yarin. As long as he lived, your death had meaning. Now that Yarin's dead, you died in vain," said Asdella.

"That's not true," said Narr, "I tried, and that's what matters."

"Fine," she said looking away, "So you wanted to talk. Let's talk. What do you want to know?"

"How did you come to be the Asdella I know today? You know what I mean. The warrior, the furious rage, where does it all come from? You've obviously had schooling like the rest of us. Most that call themselves barbarians can hardly string a sentence together. Although mostly the ones I'm thinking of happened to be half Garc, but you know what I'm asking. Something must have happened. I'm just curious as to what. If you don't want to talk about it, fine, I'll understand. I mean, I'm not going to ask about that bath boy incident. I mean, Narten, Narr, maybe you just got confused for a minute," he said trying to make a joke out of it and then fell silent at the fierce look he received.

She stared at the ground as she started to tell her story. "Asdella the warrior, the cold and bitter monster you joke about, the insane rage and pain, wasn't always so. You know how a circus travels from place to place with exotic animals in cages for people to see and poke at? Well imagine the same thing, only the animals are young girls taken against their will. I was part of that injustice. I was different then, innocent and vulnerable. Many of the girls who resisted or couldn't take the severe beatings that occurred regularly, didn't survive long."

"I'm so sorry. Why didn't you say something before?" asked Narr.

She snapped at him defensively, "What good would that do? Go around telling everyone that I had been a victim once? To have people dump heaps of their pity on me? To have them utter dry meaningless words of comfort over and over, again and again? So I can blame every little thing on that abuse? So that can be my reason for all I do wrong, instead of taking responsibility for my own actions? It's part of me unfortunately now, and I have to deal with it and live with it and work hard to eventually overcome it. That's all Narten was, to see if I am able to feel any sort of emotion other than hatred." She paused and then said, "Even you. I feel anger, instead of sorrow, because you died."

"I think you're feeling more than just anger," he told her, "You just don't know how to describe it or how to express it, but that's alright. We can work through all of it together, and like you said, eventually overcome it, even if it takes us years. Don't be afraid to talk to me. I mean, it's not even as if you are telling someone, you're actually only talking within your own mind."

Asdella continued, "Like I said, many of the girls that resisted didn't survive very long. I always fought back no matter what, and my hatred grew and grew. I survived every beating and every rape. I had to be chained up constantly, and since I was a 'resister', I got all the ones that liked it. All the ones that enjoyed the fact that they were able to cause such suffering in me. My one reason for surviving was my hatred of that bastard who ran the whole thing. I dreamed of revenge every second, and every bruise and every lashing just fueled that rage and frustration. If I ever got free of those chains, I would have brought death upon him five thousand times over. He knew this, and it amused him to see me suffer so. Most of the other women decided just to accept their fate and be submissive. The ones that did resist usually gave in after a fair amount of beating. Or, they ended up dead, their broken bodies tossed away at the side of the road or dragged into the trees for the wild animals to feast upon. They were treated like they were nothing, just untrainable pieces of meat to be thrown out with the rest of the trash. He would save me for the most brutal of men and laugh at my agony. He would never 'sample the merchandise', as he called it, with me, which I was thankful for. After about a year of constant torture, I trained myself to focus my pain and rage into my plot for revenge, one that in the end worked. I slowly and carefully executed my plan of seduction, learning to say the right things, and all that. Anyway, after several months of convincing him that I was only fighting back because I wanted him, and that I was jealous of the other girls he 'sampled', and that I wanted him all to myself, and that I could please him better than any of the others, and that I had proven that I had the stamina, and so on…" A tear rolled down her cheek. She wiped it away and continued, "Anyway, I got him to start entertaining himself with me, but with chains still restraining me of course, he knew that I despised him still. I think he enjoyed that fact more than anything. I tried very hard every time, saying the right things and all that. Eventually, after several months of this disgusting torture and further degrading with

<Zaylyn ><Quest For The Sword Of Anthrowst ><By Katrina Mandrake-Johnston >   <Ch 54> < 168 >
this creature of a man that I loathed most in the entire world, he began to be less cautious of me and the chains started to be taken off occasionally. I did not spring at that first moment the chains were off. He would have expected that. Instead, I continued my falsehood, hoping he would begin to let his guard down even more, and I waited patiently for the perfect moment to strike. I continued with the deception for several more months, all the time making sure that he never got bored of me, which was far harder than simply stomaching the nausea every time that revolting monster of a man touched me. But eventually, over time, he began to let his guard down. Finally, I got my chance and there was no one to come to his rescue. As strong as he was, he wasn't able to pry my hands and fingers away from his throat as I choked the life from his putrid mass of a body. He couldn't die enough for me, and when it was over, I didn't really feel avenged. He had ruined me and everything I was, and I could never get that back. I freed the others and went on my way. I naturally became a fighter, as it was the new me and what I had become."

"I don't really know what to say," Narr admitted.

"Asdella?" Nodwel's voice echoed throughout the forest clearing.

"What was that? It sounded like Nodwel. I think you better wake up, Asdella. I'll be here if you need me…" Narr's voice trailed off as Asdella slowly opened her eyes.

<World of Zaylyn ><Quest For The Sword Of Anthrowst ><By Katrina Mandrake-Johnston ><Ch 55>

CHAPTER 55 =   AWKWARD BREAKFAST

Asdella awoke. She saw that she was still in the stable next to The Twisted Eye Tavern. Vordin had fallen asleep while sitting awkwardly on the wooden box.

"Asdella, Vordin, wake up, the both of you," Nodwel said hurriedly.

"It's morning already? I thought someone was going to relieve us," Vordin said rubbing his eyes.

Asdella asked, "Is there something wrong, or you just fall asleep for too long?"

Vordin asked as he stood up and started to stretch, "What is it? There is something wrong, isn't there? Oh no, did someone steal the horses? I didn't mean to fall asleep…"

"No, no," Nodwel told him, "We have a bit of trouble. I don't know for sure, but I suspect our two friends are in a bit more trouble than we know. A group of bounty hunters entered the tavern last night looking for two thieves. I have a feeling that Dendrox and Candra were the ones they were looking for. Did you see anything last night?"

"No, we must have fallen asleep by then," Vordin told him and then commented meekly, "Some guard duty, eh?"

Nodwel said, "I'm sure the innkeeper has to deal with this sort of stuff a lot. He didn't look too upset by the whole ordeal and neither did anyone else in the tavern. Anyway, I was able to get a message from Candra."

"So it really does look like Candra and Dendrox are the ones they were looking for," commented Asdella.

Nodwel said to them, "Candra suggested, and I agree, that in case the bounty hunters are watching, which they probably are, it's best not to associate with them or Weena. She was caught in the middle of all this too. Gain all the information you can about the sword, the hunters, and anything else you might think useful. Then we'll spend another night at the tavern. I'm hoping I can get enough money for us all. I've already talked to several merchants about moving boxes of merchandise from their wagons to their market stalls for today. A few said they were willing to part with a bit of coin for the help. So we'll all meet back at the inn at sundown, feel out the situation, and decide what to do then."

Asdella questioned, "So where did Lorenta run off to?"

Vordin quickly checked the secret magical compartment in the backpack and found it to be empty. He said a little worried, "Don't know, she's not in the backpack. I thought she would have returned before dawn."

"You think someone squashed her?" Asdella asked calmly.

"Don't say that!" Vordin pleaded, imagining that it easily could be true.

<Zaylyn ><Quest For The Sword Of Anthrowst ><By Katrina Mandrake-Johnston >   <Ch 55> < 169 >

"Hey, I'm just being rational," she explained, "She'll probably turn up."

"Nodwel, do you know if anyone has seen Lorenta?" Vordin asked.

"No, sorry, I thought she was with you. I'm sure she's all right though," Nodwel told him.

"What about money?" Asdella asked him, "I doubt you'll be able to raise enough for all of us for tonight. You going to have the thieves get us some?"

"Hell no," Nodwel exclaimed, "They can't risk getting exposed. They're lucky to still be alive after last night. They have to be extremely careful. I'm hoping there may be a few odd jobs I can do around town to raise more. We'll at least have enough for rooms for tonight with the money I'll get for helping out those merchants I told you about. As for food and supplies, we'll have to see. It's probably a good idea for you two to stick around the tavern. Maybe you'll learn something about the hunters. If anything, you'll be there to overhear any messages our friends try to get to us. I'll see you two back at the tavern at sundown then, okay? Remember to stay clear of the others for all our safety." Nodwel left the two of them and quickly headed off down the street.

Asdella got up, retrieved her sword, and said, "Hey Vordin, how about getting a bit of breakfast? The innkeeper did say he was providing it, didn't he?"

Vordin, collecting his backpack and checking that his lantern and dagger were safely tucked inside, said, "I don't know. I don't think so, but we can go check."

The two of them entered the tavern. It was empty of customers at the moment and the innkeeper was behind the desk flipping idly through a book.

When they asked about maybe getting some breakfast and hinted that they hoped he could give it to them free of charge as he had done with the meals the night before, the innkeeper replied, "Greed never gets a person anywhere they really want to be. Listen, I'd like to, but I just can't do it. I can't give you free food again, you understand, don't you? I'm still trying to figure out how I'm going to make up the cost of what I've given you already."

"We understand. Thank-you, you've been very kind and very generous already," Vordin told him apologetically.

Narten, who had been listening from the kitchen doors, said, "I'll pay for their meals."

"What was that Narten?" the innkeeper asked a little shocked at his sudden offer.

He repeated, "I'll pay for their meals."

"Oh no, please, you shouldn't," said Vordin feeling even more ashamed for asking about breakfast.

Asdella grumbled, "I don't need your pity, Narten."

"No, I want to," Narten explained to them, "Please, let me do this for you."

The innkeeper shook his head slightly and asked, "I am to deduct the meals from your wage then? For these strangers? This is truly what you want to do?" The innkeeper was clearly trying to persuade the boy out of his decision and at least make sure that he had thought his decision completely through.

"Yes sir," Narten replied with pride, "I will go to prepare the meals now."

As soon as Narten had entered the kitchen and the innkeeper was sure that he was unable to overhear the conversation, he said to the two adventurers, "I am sad to say that he does not make a lot of money working here for me. If I could afford to pay him more, I would. What I am saying is, that for him to pay for your meals will mean he'll be tightening his own belt to do so. I just hope you two truly appreciate what he's doing for you."

Vordin felt even worse than he did before. "Yes, of course, but if he is making such a sacrifice to do so, he really shouldn't. We'll be fine, really."

The innkeeper shook his head and explained, "He's made up his mind. He's determined to do this, although I can't imagine why."

Asdella grabbed Vordin by the arm and dragged him away from the desk. Then she firmly said, "Let's go, Vordin."

"The food is being made for us already by now, we can't just leave," he told her in a hushed voice.

She whispered angrily at him through gritted teeth, "I don't need his pity. I don't want his kindness. I don't deserve it. I don't deserve any of it! Why does he insist so?"

Vordin awkwardly coaxed her over to a table and got her to sit down with him. He smiled at her

<Zaylyn ><Quest For The Sword Of Anthrowst ><By Katrina Mandrake-Johnston >   <Ch 55> < 170 >

and said, "I guess he's interested in you. It's not as if you're ugly to look at, you know. You're actually quite pretty."

"He's wasting his time. There can never be anything between us," she told Vordin.

"Well," Vordin said trying to think of something to say, "There is the age difference. He can't be very much older than I am. He looks about seventeen or so. It's probably just a silly crush."

"None of that matters," she said, her voice showing that there was a great hurt within her and that he did not understand at all what she was meaning. She looked into Vordin's eyes and he caught a glimpse of a well-hidden sorrow there. "I…" she started. Her voice had a weakness to it, and then she corrected herself forcing her words to be strong again, but Vordin could tell that she was pondering whether she were going to say anything at all. "I tested myself…" she continued, and now her words were angry, showing a great hatred toward herself, "to see if there was anything left inside this husk of a body. There is nothing. There is no feeling left inside me. There is no desire. To be adored by another, means nothing now. Everything has been stomped out and crushed into dust. There is no excitement at another's touch. I couldn't care less about another's kindness toward me. A smile from a handsome face does not bring me joy. I am full of hate and rage and that is all. I tried to feel something else. I should have at least felt something. Narten's innocence and his unconditional kindness to me, the way he looks at me… I'm incapable of any gentle emotion, and I feel guilty that I can't return any sort of kind feeling toward him. No, you know, I don't think I even feel guilty about it. I don't think I even care. I should care, shouldn't I? I want to care. I want to care so badly, about anything. I'm like an empty shell, and all that has been left inside is a hollow aching pain that makes my fury burn like the hottest fire to the point where I just want to choke and smash the life out of everything around me. That can't really be healthy, can it? Do you think I'm crazy, Vordin?"

"Ah, only sometimes," he said truthfully, "Maybe you just haven't found the right person yet. Feelings for others usually have to develop, don't they? Just because you think you should have feelings in a particular situation, doesn't necessarily mean that they're going to appear. Even if you deceive yourself into thinking so. Do you see what I'm trying to say?"

"Well," Asdella admitted, "I think maybe I could have felt something for this one man."

"Well, there, that's who you should pursue then. There's no sense in being alone, if there's someone who makes you happy in your life," he told her.

"Yeah," she said despondently, "He's dead now."

"Oh," Vordin said, "I'm sorry. I didn't know."

"It was Narr," she said plainly, "I never had the chance to tell him how I felt. Well, I had plenty of chances. I just never took any of them. I don't think I even realized it myself until it was too late."

"I'm so sorry," Vordin said knowing how she must feel, as there were many things he would have said to his parents if he had one more chance to do so.

"I'm… ah… haunted by his ghost now," she told him, and seeing the odd look forming on Vordin's face, quickly said, "I wasn't going to say anything at all because all of you think I'm crazy, but I feel more comfortable talking to you for some reason." She paused in thought and then said simply, "Perhaps it's because you are the easiest to kill." Vordin was more nervous and wary of her than usual now, his earlier thoughts that she perhaps wasn't as crazy as he had first thought quickly disappeared. "So, I hear his voice inside my head all the time. Most of the time, I can't get him to shut up. At times, I think he takes over my personality, makes me do things I normally wouldn't do," Asdella explained to Vordin.

"Really?" he commented nervously.

"I think I've gotten him to leave me alone for awhile though," she said and then narrowing her eyes questioned suspiciously, "Why are you looking at me like that? You look frightened."

"I… ah… Oh look," Vordin breathed with relief, "Here comes Narten with our meals."

<World of Zaylyn ><Quest For The Sword Of Anthrowst ><By Katrina Mandrake-Johnston ><Ch 56>

CHAPTER 56 = EXPLORING VACKIINDMIRE

Dendrox and Weena, who both had intended to wake with the early morning light, instead woke

<Zaylyn ><Quest For The Sword Of Anthrowst ><By Katrina Mandrake-Johnston >   <Ch 56> < 171 >
up late the next morning.

"I didn't mean to fall asleep for so long. Candra may have already tried to contact us," Dendrox said quickly dressing and adjusting his belt of daggers into a comfortable position.

"I thought," Weena said still half asleep, "I thought we weren't supposed to contact any of the group. You know, in case they're still looking for you two."

"Yes, I know. It puts us all in danger if we appear to be more than just a couple of tourists visiting the inn," he said, "But it's driving me insane not knowing what is happening. If only I could get a message to her, maybe find out something."

"Dendrox, this is silly," Weena said now fully dressed and tying her yellow sash about her waist. *"Why is my little pouch so full?"* she asked herself as it had distracted her attention, *"Oh, I picked up that doll. Why? I don't know. It just felt right at the time, I guess."*

"What's silly?" he asked her impatiently.

"You don't need to contact Candra," she explained, "and besides, you did that secret code tapping you two did to get a message through. You and I can go about getting the information and supplies we need just fine." *"Gee, you'd think he's never gone or done anything on his own,"* Weena commented to herself, *"Maybe he's so used to Candra bossing him around that he doesn't know anything else, not trusting himself to make his own decisions."*

"Maybe…" he began.

"Now he's going to make some excuse like 'maybe we should wait here until we hear something from Candra'. Candra, Candra, Candra! This is ridiculous!" she told herself, very annoyed. "Come on," she said taking him firmly by the hand and thinking to herself, *"If I have to act like Candra to get anything done around here, then so be it. I guess it helps that I'm not much of a morning person too, otherwise, I'd have a hard time being so stern."* Weena told him, "I think a magic shop or a library or something like that would be our best bet for finding some sort of reference to this sword we're looking for. Sound like a good place to start?"

"Yes, but Candra may have already checked…" he began to say.

"Well then we'll have double the information, maybe we'll find out something she didn't or vice versa," she explained. Seeing that he was still very reluctant, she added, "Maybe she has left a message with one of the clerks, or at least we can ask if anyone fitting her description passed by there. Oh, and most importantly, if anyone has been asking around about you two, maybe learn something about these bounty hunters and gain a bit of an advantage."

This surprised him a little and he submitted saying, "Sure, that sounds good to me. Remember, if you see her or anyone else, it would be wise not to acknowledge them just to be on the safe side. We don't know how much these bounty hunters know already. Best to let the others come to us."

"Agreed. What about the scissors?" Weena questioned.

"Best to leave them here. If they find them, they're welcome to them. Maybe they'll leave us alone then," he grumbled.

Weena suggested, "We should retrieve them before we leave Vackiindmire though. If another thief takes them, you'll still be to blame. Like you said before, it's better to have them."

He let out an unenthusiastic sigh and said, "Sure, let's be on our way then. We can probably save some time by asking the innkeeper about what shops would be the best to check. But I have to say, that I don't really want to be roaming the streets, especially by myself."

"I'll be with you," Weena said.

He gave her a halfhearted and seemingly forced smile. She then realized what his words had meant. *"Being with me is just the same as being alone, is it?"* thought Weena, her feelings deeply hurt, *"How can he be so rude after… Well, yes, I guess it is true. I'm no match for Candra's abilities in battle or in knowledge of how thieves behave. I'd walk right into a trap and not even know it. But damn it, how else am I supposed to learn? I'm trying my best and I do have my magic, don't I? Well, that's not very useful, not to the extent that we need. I could be the most powerful member of the group, if I had the right spells and supplies. I have to learn some offensive spells and quickly, provided we have enough time. It could mean the difference between life and death."*

<Zaylyn ><Quest For The Sword Of Anthrowst ><By Katrina Mandrake-Johnston >   <Ch 56> < 172 >

"What are you thinking about? Are we going or not? I thought you were so eager to leave," he said curtly.

They headed out the door, down the hall, and into the main room of the tavern.

Dendrox scanned the faces of the patrons, noting that Asdella and Vordin were there, but made a point not to acknowledge them. Dendrox was made aware that they also knew now about the trouble they had last night, as they were doing the same. "No sign of the men from last night," he whispered to Weena.

"Not so," she informed him, "Ducked into the kitchen when he saw us enter. You must have been looking the other way. I barely caught a glimpse of his face, but I'm sure it was one of them. Probably going to spy on us, see if we slip up. Good thing magic shops and bookstores aren't the usual thing for a thief to be interested in, am I right?"

"Yeah. And you're sure about..." he whispered.

"Yes, I'm pretty sure," she replied, "Better safe than sorry anyway, right?" Weena walked up to the desk saying, "Excuse me, innkeeper?"

"Oh yes, miss? Something I can help you with? Oh, you're one of the ones from last night. I take it the incident wasn't about you and your friends, was it?"

"Oh, of course not," said the wizard calmly and inquired, "I was just wondering if there were a magic shop or perhaps a bookstore or maybe a library of some sort? I'd like to do some research on old legends, mysterious artifacts, and the like. Would you happen to know where I might find something like that or perhaps of who to talk to?"

"Well, Shirkint for sure," he replied right away, "but as I advised before, not wise to travel that way with bandits and The Black... well, you know who. But for Vackiindmire... There's a bookstore at the end of the street just across from this tavern. I think there might be a magic shop around in that area of town as well, but the entrance I believe is over by the market place. It's at the end of the street just before the marketplace. You'll see a bakery and that's the street where you would turn down to find it. I've never been there myself, but I'm pretty sure that's where it is. Oh, you know, if you really get desperate in your search, you might even want to try the marketplace. That'd be on that same side of town, but just all the way south to the far edge. You can't miss it, especially if you are able to get to the magic shop all right. The marketplace is just a jumble of stalls various merchants rent to sell their wares."

"Thank-you, you've been most helpful," she politely said and then turned to Dendrox and asked, "Shall we head out then?" Weena giggled to herself, *"I'm kind of enjoying this take-charge attitude I'm using, although it definitely isn't me and I feel guilty about acting this way."*

The morning sun shone brightly as Weena and Dendrox began to walk side-by-side along the cobblestone street.

"We shouldn't appear to be in too much of a rush. We are supposed to be sight seeing," Weena whispered to him, slowing her pace to a very slow stroll, "Besides, we might as well enjoy ourselves a bit, especially after all we've been through."

They were slowly passing by the town entrance and could see the street opposite the tavern, the one they were supposed to head straight along in order to reach the bookstore as instructed by the innkeeper. The street edged along the northern outer wall of Vackiindmire, passing by several shops until ending at the far eastern wall.

Dendrox walked over to the side of the nearest building and sat down on a little wooden bench that was there. From here they had a clear view of The Twisted Eye Tavern and its stable, the town entrance, and down the dead end street leading to the bookshop. The main street leading south and into the rest of the town was obscured from sight.

"Come and sit with me for awhile," he said to her, motioning her over to him.

When she had seated herself beside him, he explained, "I don't really want to rush off in search of information either. Like you said, we should enjoy ourselves for awhile. We can worry about all that later. Besides, it's amazing how much information is available to you just by listening to the

<Zaylyn ><Quest For The Sword Of Anthrowst ><By Katrina Mandrake-Johnston >   <Ch 56> < 173 >

conversation of others. We might get lucky and hear something about the bounty hunters and if there has been any sort of trouble we should know about."

"Okay," she said, eager to learn.

There weren't many people in this area of town, but the few that did pass by them nodded a friendly 'hello' to the two travelers.

"I need to pick up some more daggers," Dendrox commented, "I lost three fighting the beasts in the tunnels. Those were some of my best daggers, damn it, and half of what I started out with. But, I guess I shouldn't complain as they helped to save our lives. Candra was down to having only three arrows left. She had eight at the beginning of all this. I doubt we'll have much of a chance if we run into any more trouble. No, she only has two left. She broke one getting us the meat back at the camp."

"We should be wary then of the place where she'd find arrows, if we're not to be seen with her," Weena advised, "We shouldn't even be talking about her, should we? Am I right?"

"Yes, it's a good idea," he breathed with a heavy sigh, clearly not enjoying the situation.

A carriage, drawn by two tired but sturdy looking horses, stopped just outside the town gates. Both the horses were dark grey. They were small, but strong, and were no more than four feet high to their backs, as was common in Zaylyn. The carriage was painted deep burgundy-brown and was faded with age. The carriage driver got down from his seat near the top of the carriage and gave both of the horses a loving pat on the nose.

He was an average-sized man and looked as if he could handle himself in a fight well enough. He had greyish-green eyes and a thin narrow nose, under which was a large bushy mustache. He had a cleft chin and on his left side he had a deep scar along his jaw line. His shoulder length hair, tied back in a ponytail, had once been dark brown but now was streaked grey by age. Weena thought he might be just slightly older than Nodwel.

There was a dark blue scarf around his neck and he wore a black long-sleeved shirt, over which was a brown leather jerkin. His billowy, light brown pants were tucked into the tops of his high black leather boots.

There were two small windows on either side of the carriage. Both were open to the air, and on the side closest to the road was the door. They could see a passenger within the carriage, and opening the door wide, he got out.

He was a short man of five feet and was human. He had short black hair and a heart-shaped face ending in a small pointed chin. His large dark blue eyes looked about his destination and he seemed relieved to have arrived. He wore a light blue tunic and loose fitting pants of a dark blue color. A small burlap bag was tucked under his arm.

"Enjoy the ride?" the carriage diver asked with a smile.

"Actually, it was a little frightening traveling through the forest at night as we did," the man admitted.

"Dookarnim, is it?" the driver inquired.

"Yes. Thank-you for giving me a safe passage. I've heard many frightening tales," said Dookarnim.

"Well, if you ever need to travel through the forest again by carriage, be sure to ask for me by name then," he told him with a happy chuckle.

"It was Vexcindor, wasn't it?" he asked.

"That's me," he answered, "So where you headed? Me, I'm going straight to The Twisted Eye to get some much-needed rest. I just have to wait until the other carriage driver arrives to relieve me, and so he can feed and water the horses. It will either be Koosenor or Mantoez. I'm not sure who. You ever travel with either of them? There's only the three of us now."

Dookarnim said to him, "I'm just after a book on rare plants. My wife and I own a shop at the town of Shirkint with all manner of vegetation. It's a fair distance from Leekkar where we live, but Shirkint is definitely where all the business is. Anyway, it's urgent that I get this information and Vackiindmire is supposed to have a great shop with a wide selection of books, old and new alike. I am not very familiar with Vackiindmire. This is the first time being here since I was a small boy and same

<Zaylyn ><Quest For The Sword Of Anthrowst ><By Katrina Mandrake-Johnston >   <Ch 56> < 174 >

for taking the carriage. Is the bookshop very far from here? Oh and may I ask why there are only three drivers now? It seems odd to have so few, with so many passengers back and forth."

Vexcindor shook his head sadly, "I shouldn't have said anything. Let me just say that you had good reason to be frightened during our journey. There are things out there, which your wildest imagination couldn't dream up. The bandits, as of late, are nothing compared to some of the horrors I've seen. Very few are brave enough to travel through the forest anymore. It's not very often that we get many passengers going to and from Vackiindmire. Most of the passengers we pick up are north of the forest, traveling from village to village or to Shirkint. In fact, I believe there are only two people, at least that I know of, who dare to travel back and forth between the towns on a daily basis on their own. I give them each a ride once in awhile, when they want to leave their horses at home. Colex works at the Old Scabbard Inn at Shirkint. Beanvit, I think his name is, works at the animal shop. You know, where they sell exotic animals and steeds and what not. He was telling me about all the wonders they have there, and he said they are always getting new creatures in stock. Anyways, they both live in Vackiindmire and travel to work through that damn forest. If I were one of them, I'd introduce myself to the other real quick and travel together through there, as to not have to go alone. There's a better chance of survival that way."

"Of survival?!" the man asked shocked that he had taken such a risk in coming to Vackiindmire and had not known it.

"Yeah," Vexcindor said simply, "Anyway, the bookstore is just down this street here. It's a dead end street and it's the last shop. You can't miss it."

"Ah, thank-you. I'll try to return during the day then. Thanks for the warning," he said heading down the street and passing by Weena and Dendrox who had been listening in on the conversation from the bench.

A man came out of the inn, and Vexcindor exclaimed with a grin upon seeing him, "Mantoez! It's about time you got here. I'm exhausted and so are the horses."

Mantoez clearly wasn't human. He stood just under four feet tall and had pink eyes. "He must be one of the fairy folk," Weena commented in a whisper to Dendrox, "There are all different sorts, so many that everyone has just categorized them all into one big group."

This small man had short and curly red hair, a round cheerful face, and a small round nose. He had on a pair of plain brown pants and his shirt was dark blue with a yellow vest over it. "Sorry. You have any trouble during the night?" asked Mantoez with a concerned look.

"Nothing unusual, if that's what you mean," he gave him a knowing look.

"Okay, well that's good news," he commented detaching the horses from the carriage and leading them toward the stable.

"I'm heading to the inn. Take care out there," Vexcindor said with a wave and entered The Twisted Eye Tavern.

Weena and Dendrox decided they had better be on their way and continued down the street after Dookarnim.

"I think we had better travel during the day as well, like the carriage driver told that man. Perhaps we can get enough money somehow to buy all of us passage in one of the carriages," said Weena.

Dendrox told her, "It looks to me as if there is only the one carriage with three drivers each taking turns. I agree though. They would know better than us what dangers are out there, and that is besides the Killnarin."

They could see Dookarnim racing ahead to the end of the street where the bookstore was located.

"Hey, a cobbler," Dendrox pointed out as they passed the open door. There was a wooden sign overhead with a picture of a shoe and a tiny hammer painted on it. They could hear the cobbler going about his work within and they caught the faint scent of leather as they passed by. "Candra really needs a new pair of boots. She was complaining about the ones she has on, all the way over the mountains into this valley," Dendrox commented.

"Is that why she has been a little cruel now and then, because her boots have been hurting her feet?" Weena asked trying not to sound too offensive, but she meant what she had said.

<Zaylyn ><Quest For The Sword Of Anthrowst ><By Katrina Mandrake-Johnston >   <Ch 56> < 175 >

"Unfortunately, no," Dendrox chuckled and gave her a smile, "She's pretty much like that all the time."

"Great," she said sarcastically.

As they were passing by the window of a clothing shop, Weena exclaimed, "Oh, would you look at that dress!"

"It's nice," Dendrox said, clearly not very interested.

"It's so beautiful. The amount of work that must have gone into something like that! The intricate patterns, and…" she trailed off seeing that Dendrox didn't really care. Weena decided, "Maybe we should just hurry on to the bookstore. It's probably going to take a long while to find what we're looking for. A lot of people are counting on us."

The two of them approached the end of the street and the shop with a large wooden sign hanging over the door displaying a picture of an open book. They entered the shop and a little bell tinkled to announce their entrance.

<World of Zaylyn ><Quest For The Sword Of Anthrowst ><By Katrina Mandrake-Johnston ><Ch 57>

CHAPTER 57 =   THE BOOKSTORE

They found the place to be dimly lit by lanterns and that the whole shop had a musty smell to it. There were rows and rows of shelves and each long shelf had books packed very tightly along them. Many of the books, for which there was no more room for on the shelves, were neatly stacked in piles on the tables, the back counter, and even the floor.

There were three long tables placed end to end running down the center of the shop, and one rickety looking wooden chair positioned neatly at each. There was only a tiny area at each table that was free of books, and the books were stacked so high that you would feel as if you were in a miniature fort if you were to sit at one of the tables.

On each side of the tables, were three rows of long shelves that ran the length of the shop. Between the shelves there were books stacked neatly in a row down the length of the aisle. The smallest stack of books was piled as high as Weena's waist, while many towered high above her head.

The back counter, which they could barely see, was all the way at the very back of the shop. This also had stacks and stacks of books piled very high on it and also along the side of the counter all the way to the back wall.

"Well it looks as if it's all very organized, I guess, just incredibly crowded," Weena commented.

"What? Is someone there?" they heard an old man call out.

"Yes, we have a few questions," she called out blindly.

"Well come down to the counter, child, where I can see you," the old man's voice said in a quick snappy tone, "Just please, I beg of you, do not knock over any of the books. Everything is precisely organized, and most importantly, perfectly balanced. I will not be meeting my end under a landslide of books, you hear?"

They carefully began to make their way to the end of the shop.

"Didn't that man come in here? The one from the carriage? If he's in here, I don't see him anywhere," said the thief, as he skillfully maneuvered between the books and shelves.

As she inched along, Weena tried to hold her robes as closely to her as possible, being worried they would get caught and bring everything down upon them.

When they reached the counter, she called out again, "Hello?"

"There's no need to shout. Was there something I can help you with?" the voice said.

"Where are you?" she questioned with curiosity.

"I'm here at the counter, you silly girl," said the voice from behind the wall of books on top of the counter.

Weena tired to peer through the stacks of books, which completely obscured and obstructed whomever was behind the counter. Finally, she found a tiny space between the piles and was able to see a tiny white-haired man with a long, neatly combed beard and a little red cap on his bald head. He was dressed in white robes with a dark blue sash tied tightly at his waist.

<Zaylyn ><Quest For The Sword Of Anthrowst ><By Katrina Mandrake-Johnston >   <Ch 57> < 176 >

"Oh, there you are," she exclaimed almost laughing at how ridiculously overstocked this place was.

"I've found the book on tracking I was looking for, Karnez," a man's voice called out from somewhere at the front of the shop, "Thank-you. Maybe I'll be better for detecting ambushes, and animal attacks, and hopefully other things after reading this through."

"Good-day to you, Koosenor, and you're welcome," Karnez called out from behind the wall of books. They heard the tinkle of the bell, which meant that the carriage driver had left the shop. "That Koosenor is one of my best customers. He has such a yearning for knowledge," Karnez commented.

"We're trying to find out some information about a sword. We thought there may be a legend or something about it," Dendrox told the shopkeeper.

"Oh, a legendary sword? That does sound interesting, doesn't it?" he exclaimed a little too overzealous. Dookarnim emerged from out of the rows of books and shelves to approach the counter. "Oh, but it will have to wait just one minute," the shopkeeper told Weena and Dendrox.

"I think I've found it," Dookarnim told Karnez, "How much do I owe you?"

"Well let me see." The little man crawled out through a small space, just large enough for him to fit through, and escaped his tiny enclosure. Dookarnim handed him the book. "Oh, what's this? A book on rare plants, eh? I see you have marked off the pages with Silbreen and Dilkane. Now what would you be wanting to know about those for, eh?" Karnez asked raising an eyebrow as he looked up at the man.

"Would you just tell me how much I owe you? I don't have time for you to be nosey. I assure you, my intentions are noble. I really would like to get home as quickly as I can, for more reasons than one," he said with urgency in his voice.

"Alright, that will be two gold pieces, sir. When you are finished with the book, we will purchase it back from you for one gold piece," Karnez explained.

"Very well," said Dookarnim as he rummaged inside the burlap sack he had with him.

Dendrox heard the jingle of coins within the sack and he got a certain gleam in his eye that only Candra would have noticed if she had been there. Dendrox waited until the exchange was just about to take place and then positioned his boot in the right spot to execute his plan.

Dookarnim stepped forward, money in hand, and with his sack balanced loosely on his arm as he outstretched his hand to accept the book. Dookarnim tripped over Dendrox's boot, practically falling on top of Karnez. His sack fell to the floor spilling some of its contents.

"Oh, my goodness! I'm so sorry, I must have stumbled," he apologized to Karnez who appeared to be quite shaken by the experience.

"Here, let me help you," Dendrox offered, "You must have tripped over my boot. It's so terribly crowded in here, it forces one to stand so close to another. Anyway, let me help," he said bending down and helping Dookarnim to pick up the spilled contents of the sack, "It's the least I can do."

"Here, I'll help too," Weena offered.

"No, it's quite all right, we have it," Dendrox told her. Dendrox palmed one of the gold coins off the floor, but that was all he was able to manage.

"Thank-you," Dookarnim said to Dendrox for the help, "I really must be going now."

Karnez handed him the book and bid him good-bye. Once he had left, the tiny man turned to Weena and Dendrox and said, "Now you were saying something about a sword?"

"Yes," Weena told him, "The Sword of Anthrowst. Do you know if there is a book about it? Or perhaps, if you have heard any bit of information about it?"

Karnez looked at them both suspiciously, "I have heard of it. I'm probably one of the few that have. I have a book here with a bit about the legend. I'll get it for you." The little man disappeared amongst the shelves and books.

"Well this is good news, isn't it? At least we don't have to search for the book ourselves. That's what I was dreading," commented Weena.

"I don't know. I don't like the way he was looking at us," he told her.

"It will be fine. He was suspicious of the other man as well. I suspect he is so overprotective of his books that it pains him to let them out of his possession. I mean look at this, he's practically made himself a little house out of books at this counter," she explained. Weena then lowered her voice, "How are we to pay for this though? Do you think he will let us take a look at the book without buying it?"

"Don't worry about it. I think I've figured a way to get us what we want," he assured her.

"You're not planning to steal the book, are you?" she whispered.

"No, but I managed to swipe a coin," he whispered back to her, "Just let me handle this."

Karnez returned with a small book with a leather cover that had been dyed green. "It will be two gold pieces to purchase, and we will buy the book back from you for one gold piece when you are finished," he explained holding the book out to them.

"What if we just quickly look up the information we need here?" Dendrox suggested, "Wouldn't that be the equivalent of one gold coin for the use of the book?"

"I suppose, but the book may not leave the premises. I will be watching you very carefully," Karnez said eyeing both of them with a stern expression.

Dendrox deposited the coin into the man's tiny hand, and then taking the book from him, passed it to Weena.

Weena took the book over to the nearest table and sat down. She opened the book and began to read within the tiny area of table that was clear. Weena found herself actually enjoying the little enclosure the books made for her. Dendrox watched patiently over her shoulder as she read.

"I hope you two are not thinking of retrieving the sword. Only an utter fool would wish that kind of doom upon the world," Karnez commented.

Weena continued to read by the dim light of the lanterns for quite some time.

She whispered to Dendrox finally, "Well it is an actual sword. I thought that maybe there was a chance it wasn't a sword at all and that it was just a name. You know how they sometimes do that?"

"Yeah, yeah, like the Wings of Aramist or the Gem of Irigite," Dendrox said, getting impatient, "What does it say about the damn sword?"

"I've never heard of those," Weena said hoping to learn more and ease her curiosity.

Dendrox let out a sigh, but indulged her by saying, "The Wings of Aramist is a suit of armour supposedly so light it allows the wearer to move with great speed. The Gem of Irigite isn't a gem at all. It's a large polished seashell that, when the sunlight hits it, shows the location of the cave entrance leading to the massive treasure trove. I used to love that story as a child. I can't believe you never heard it. But, what about this sword?"

"Yes, sorry," said Weena and then she went on to explain, "This sword, if used to kill a wizard, will undo all the magic he or she has ever conjured. No wonder this sword was broken into pieces. Three, to be exact. The extent of the damage this could do, it's incredible. If what this says is true, and for example, if it was used on me, and remember that I have not cast very many spells at all in my life, this is what would happen," she paused thinking back, "Candra's wound would open up and she would become poisoned once more, the wound of the spider I healed would reopen, and the wound in me from the second arrow Candra fired at me would also open up. Well I guess the wound in me wouldn't matter because I'd be dead anyway if I were killed by the sword of Anthrowst. The Shield spell I used twice, once to save Asdella and myself from the blast in the tunnels and the second time to block Candra's arrow, in those it wouldn't have any effect if the spell was to be reversed as that would be turning back time and altering physical events. Same with the Shield spell cast back at the tavern. I hadn't realized just how many spells I've cast. I guess I have had more success than what I give myself credit for. Pure luck is more behind my spells than anything really. I would never be as foolish to think that I could rely on my spell casting abilities. I'd get us all killed for sure. But, anyway, about the sword, what I'm saying is that with the Shield spells, Asdella and I wouldn't suddenly be engulfed in flames and an arrow wouldn't just appear to punch into me. Do you see?"

Dendrox said, "Yes, it only undoes things the magic has caused to happen. Which means all the damage the Killnarin did and all the deaths they've caused will not be reversed, only the spell that summoned them here. They would be drawn back to wherever they came from and we would have

<Zaylyn ><Quest For The Sword Of Anthrowst ><By Katrina Mandrake-Johnston >   <Ch 57> < 178 >
stopped them from doing any further damage."

"Yes, exactly," said Weena. *"Well, I see now that he not only knew about Candra taking my mother's ring, but also about her shooting a couple of arrows at me."*

"And this is only if the sword even exists and only if what this book says has any truth to it," Dendrox reminded her.

"Well, yes. But anyway, you can see what kind of damage this sword could do if it fell into the wrong hands," and then she added, "And here's another thing to consider, how do we know that this wizard, Dranngore, hasn't done some good with his spells throughout his life? If everything reverses, we may be doing more harm than good. And still, what if a spell which was intended for evil actually made it possible for things to be better in the end?"

"Does it say anything of where the pieces of the sword might be?" he asked her.

"No, it doesn't," Weena told him with disappointment.

"So all we've really learnt is that an impossible sword to find has now become even more difficult because the damn thing has been broken into pieces and no doubt scattered all over the damn place. Forget it. It's all completely useless. I'm done with all of this. I'll be at the tavern," Dendrox said despondently and quickly left the shop leaving Weena sitting alone at the table.

"Dendrox, wait!" she called after him, but he was already out the door.

"I take it, you're done with the book then?" Karnez asked the young wizard.

"Yes, and thank-you," she said politely, and then she began to slowly and carefully make her way down the aisle to the exit.

Dendrox was already at the tavern door, when she emerged from the bookstore.

"Wait! Please!" she called out, but he didn't seem to hear her.

Weena finally caught up with him inside the inn. The carriage driver, Vexcindor, was seated at one of the smaller tables eating a hearty meal. Asdella and Vordin were sitting at one of the tables as well, but they purposely avoided eye contact, still being wary of the bounty hunters.

"We still have the rooms until nightfall, right? I'm going to get some sleep," he told her.

"Why did you run off like that?" she asked, feeling hurt by his actions.

"I didn't want to have to listen to some big speech on why we shouldn't give up and bla, bla, bla. It's just hopeless or at least that's how it seems. I'm just tired, that's all," he admitted, "It's been so much already with everything, and now we find out the sword has been broken into three separate pieces. That means we will have to go on three perilous quests instead of one just to get the sword! And then there is the matter of getting the pieces back together again. I just want all this to end and for everyone to be okay. I need to get a bit more sleep, hopefully clear my mind."

"Alright. I'm going to get some rest as well then, in my own room," she told him.

Dendrox retired to his room, but Weena stopped to speak with the innkeeper.

Vordin whispered to Asdella, "Three pieces? That can't be good. At least some of us have so far found out something about the sword."

Asdella suggested, "Maybe we should get some sleep too. This time in a real bed. Candra and Nodwel's rooms are still free, we might as well use them. It doesn't seem right to come all this way and not even get a chance to sleep in a proper bed."

"I agree. I'm still extremely exhausted," Vordin told her.

They too retired to the two remaining rooms the innkeeper had provided for them.

<World of Zaylyn ><Quest For The Sword Of Anthrowst ><By Katrina Mandrake-Johnston ><Ch 58>

CHAPTER 58 = FURTHER EXPLORATION OF VACKIINDMIRE

"Excuse me? I was just wondering where everyone was," Weena said to the innkeeper.

"I don't quite get what you mean, dear," he replied.

"Outside, there weren't many people out on the street. Is there some event that we haven't heard

<Zaylyn ><Quest For The Sword Of Anthrowst ><By Katrina Mandrake-Johnston >   <Ch 58> < 179 >

of?" she inquired.

"Oh, I see. You aren't from within Dee'ellkka Valley, are you? The towns and villages are quite tiny within the valley compared to the towns and villages of other lands," he explained and then he motioned her a little closer as he said, "Plus, it doesn't help the population much to have so many people go missing and with all the unusual deaths and all. It pains me to realize just how accustomed we have become to all of it."

Weena commented, "Oh, that's awful."

"Yeah, I believe the population here in Vackiindmire is anywhere from a hundred and fifty to two hundred at any given time. There's only about forty houses here, most of our number comes from visitors. A lot of merchants come here to our marketplace and end up staying for several months at a time before moving on to another location. The villages north of here have most likely anywhere from seventy-five to a hundred people each."

"Really? I had no idea," said Weena.

"I bet you haven't really had time to explore Vackiindmire as of yet. It's actually quite small compared to something you're probably used to," said the innkeeper. "The marketplace takes up a fair amount of space, but after that, there is just a small cluster of shops on the east side of town. On the west side, there is this inn of course and its stable, then farther south are a few houses, then a blacksmith's, and farther south still, are more houses along the south wall. If you travel all the way west, behind the tavern, you'll find the rest and majority of the houses all along the length of the west wall."

"I hadn't realized Vackiindmire was so small. I guess I wasn't really paying much attention to how big the town was when we traveled here," said Weena.

He told her, "Actually, miss, Vackiindmire is the largest in the valley by size. I believe Shirkint may have a larger population though, could be two hundred and fifty to three hundred people there. I can never tell, as that place is always swarming with adventurers and the like. At times, I'm sure there must be near four hundred or more, especially during the competitions they hold."

"Well Dexcsin was a tiny little place, only a cluster of a few buildings really, but I had no knowledge about the other places in the valley," she explained, "It's good to know. All I had heard was that this was the best place to learn spells, Shirkint in-particular."

"Yes, I've heard Shirkint is the best place also. The magic energy is supposed to be more concentrated there or something like that. I don't really know very much about spells, but I've heard it's far easier to learn them there, and supposedly taking less time. But you've been to Dexcsin, have you? That's the smallest village in the valley. I've been there a couple times. It's a really peaceful place. Hardly anyone bothers to travel there; it being so far out of the way. Not many people there either, fifty maybe sixty is all. They do have some wonderful festivals though. Were you lucky enough to see one of their dances?" he asked.

"Ah, no," she said as the memory of the village gave her a chill. She didn't have the heart to tell him what had happened there, plus he probably wouldn't have believed her.

"Now that's a sight to remember," the innkeeper commented, "During one of these festivals, there is such a variety of food with dancing and music all outside by firelight. Merchants from other villages and towns sometimes set up their tables in the main hall displaying their exotic wares. Some of the younger women dress in colorful flowing costumes and perform a dance involving different colored sashes. The coordinated dance gives the viewers a wonderful and vividly colorful show of beauty and youth, and the feeling that they are beholding something rare and magical. It's as if a rainbow falls in love with a lightening bolt and they have a wild and passionate dance together, which is what the story behind the dance portrays. It's a shame you missed it."

"I should probably get some rest. Thank-you very much, you've been most helpful and very kind," said Weena and retired to her room in the back of the inn.

Candra, who had been wandering the streets of Vackiindmire for most of the morning, ended up at the blacksmith's. She had struck up a conversation with the blacksmith about different types of

<Zaylyn ><Quest For The Sword Of Anthrowst ><By Katrina Mandrake-Johnston >   <Ch 58> < 180 >

weapons and the damage they are capable of, in hope that she might gain some knowledge of how to battle the Killnarin with less difficulty. Her efforts were futile, but she was enjoying herself. She was examining the various weapons and asking the friendly blacksmith many questions about his work.

The blacksmith was a dwarf and had a wide barrel-like chest. His muscular bare arms and his face were marked with soot and he was covered in a gleam of sweat from the heat of the forge. He wore a thick leather apron down the front of his body, and his leather boots came all the way up to his knees. The dwarf was bald except for a thin fringe of light brown hair around the edges with a closely cropped beard and a thick mustache.

Unlike the traditional workshop of a blacksmith, the building was enclosed on all four sides by thick stone walls and only the roof was open to the air. She assumed that there had to have been a good reason for the design, but dared not ask. The door opened and sent a cool breeze into the shop, which Candra welcomed. She had not minded the heat from before, as the blacksmith worked at his craft, and it had not been uncomfortable for her to have stayed there as long as she had already.

An older man, a human, perhaps a little over the age of fifty, entered the shop. He scratched at his squarish jaw saying, "Pretty warm in here, ain't it?" He was a little shorter than Dendrox with a thick upper body and his head was completely bald except for a pair of bushy black eyebrows. A small leather sack was slung over his shoulder. Candra just nodded a polite 'hello' and then continued to inspect a finely made short sword. "Gornam? That blade I ask for ready?" the man asked the blacksmith.

"Garnash, you best be comin' back later today. That multi-bladed dagger has proved to be a bit more troublesome than I had first thought. As you can see, I'm still working on it. Feel free to wait if you'd like, but I know how you mind the heat of the forge so."

"You know me well, friend. So later today then? Late afternoon perhaps?" he asked Gornam.

"Yes, I'm certain that I will have it for you by then. How's the butcher shop of yours up at Torrnell?" the blacksmith asked Garnash as he began to hammer the piece of metal at the anvil again.

"Oh, well enough. We're still having a bit of trouble with the raids from the trolls, but we do our best despite them. There's a dragon now as well. Snatches up a couple of sheep now and then, but it hasn't put too much of a damper on my business," he explained, "If anything, I think the beast may be the reason the trolls have eased up on their attacks."

"Don't know how you can be so calm 'bout all that," and then Gornam questioned, "Your younger brother, Gulair, he's doing all right in his job at The Old Scabbard Inn? Don't know, some of the stories I hear about Shirkint make me pretty nervous if you ask me. I hear The Black Shadow frequents that very inn. Gives me the shivers to think your brother is in the same room as that... that..."

"Whoa, hush now. You know you shouldn't speak of such things," he said in a frantic tone, "I'll be back later this afternoon. Take care Gornam and remember to watch what you say." Garnash left the blacksmith's, closing the door behind him.

Candra now had a curious interest in the multi-bladed dagger that the blacksmith was making. She thought of Dendrox and how he would marvel over such a weapon. She considered an attempt to steal it when it was finally finished, but she knew such a thing would draw unwanted attention and she needed to be careful for both their sakes in case the bounty hunters were still about.

<World of Zaylyn ><Quest For The Sword Of Anthrowst ><By Katrina Mandrake-Johnston ><Ch 59>

CHAPTER 59 = DENDROX'S NIGHTMARE

Dendrox had the dream again...

He found himself alone in the dark of night, the moon and stars shining brightly in a cloudless sky. He could see the tombstones around him and he let out an angry curse, as he knew this dream all too well.

An eerie unnatural mist began to roll along the ground. The fear inside him began to rise, as he knew what would come next and that there wasn't any chance of escape or anywhere to escape to.

He could smell the damp musty smell of the soil, and the cool crisp air chilled his skin. It all seemed so real and every time he had this dream, he could never bring himself to overcome his fear and realize that this was only a dream and nothing more. Except for the sound of his heartbeat quickening and his breathing becoming more rapid with fear, there was only silence.

Then he heard a horrible haunting wail from somewhere nearby. There was the faint but distinct sound of crumbling dirt, as a skeletal hand worked its way up from its grave to the surface.

He could see now that there were more rising out of the soil from all around him, escaping their graves, and shambling out of their tombs toward him. Weapons, in the hands of the slain, were being made ready once again as the corpses pulled themselves into life and action in their battered and broken armour.

Dendrox frantically looked all around in a panic for somewhere to run to, as the moaning and wailing horde of bone and rotting flesh began to close in on him.

It was now too late for they were upon him. Bony fingers pulled him to the ground, tearing at his clothes and clawing into his skin. Rusty weapons were thrust into his gut again and again, as the undead creatures stared with blank, lifeless eyes. Dendrox was screaming in sheer terror and was still screaming when he violently awoke.

He was thankful no one was around, as he was embarrassed and knew that this was just the type of thing Candra would love to ridicule him about. It was one of her ways of dealing with weakness in others where she thought there shouldn't be. This is why he hadn't told her about his frightful reoccurring dream. For him, it was not something that he could just laugh about or simply overcome for fear of being teased about it.

There was a knock at his door and the sound of Weena's voice calling his name. "Dendrox? You all right? Dendrox?"

When he came to the door and opened it, she suggested that they go to the magic shop the innkeeper had spoken of, in hope of discovering more information about the sword. He had fallen asleep fully dressed, so he simply nodded and followed her into the main room of the inn. He still felt as if the odds were stacked impossibly high against them for finding the pieces of the Sword of Anthrowst, but he didn't want to give up all hope just yet.

Weena could see that the innkeeper, who normally was at his desk, was absent and that Narten had taken his place instead. No one else was in the tavern at that moment as far as they could tell.

Narten was wearing the same clothes he had the night before and still had the apron tied about his waist. Weena wondered if he had gotten a break at all from his work since then. His hair had been neatly combed away from his handsome face and his bright blue eyes kept looking expectantly around to the point where Weena got the impression that perhaps he was waiting or hoping for someone to show.

Before Weena or Dendrox could say anything, Narten announced, "Innkeeper is asleep. I watch the place for him so he can get some rest. Otherwise, he runs the whole tavern by himself, night and day. If it's something urgent, I can wake him. It isn't, is it?"

"Oh no," Weena answered, "We just need directions to the magic shop is all."

"Sorry," Narten apologized, "I always get nervous when he puts me in charge of things like this. Just go south down the main street from the town gates, then turn left when you come to the bakery, go all the way to the end of the street, and that's where it will be. It's right across from the marketplace."

"Thanks, it shouldn't be too hard to find then," said Dendrox leaving the inn with Weena.

CHAPTER 60 =   THE THIEVES

It was late afternoon by the time they left the tavern, and Weena and Dendrox walked side-by-side down the well kept main street of Vackiindmire. They passed by the bench on the far end just outside the cobbler's shop where they had been sitting earlier that day, but this time they continued farther into town down along the main road. On this side of the shop, there were two small windows and both of them had their little blue curtains drawn.

<Zaylyn ><Quest For The Sword Of Anthrowst ><By Katrina Mandrake-Johnston >   <Ch 60> < 182 >

A teenaged couple holding hands, their faces beaming with large smiles, walked past Weena and Dendrox. "*Isn't this what we should have? Dendrox won't hold my hand or even hardly look at me,*" Weena said to herself with disappointment, "*I don't know what to think anymore.*"

Farther ahead they could see a white door with pink trim, which was the door to the teashop. As they passed the shop, they could smell a splendid combination of teas coming from within. A pregnant woman, who had been waddling very slowly down the street rubbing and trying to support her enormous belly with her hand, entered the teashop.

Next to the teashop was the butcher shop, and a father and his tiny son exited. The little boy was holding his father's hand and wearing a large happy smile. The father, who was looking affectionately at his child, carried a big package of meat for their dinner. The little boy waved at Dendrox and Weena as they passed by.

Next to the butcher was the bakery and the scent of freshly baked bread filled the air as they approached. A mother and her young daughter were coming out of the bakery. The daughter had a large bag of rolls in her tiny arms. The mother smiled at how independent her daughter was trying to be and looked prepared to rescue their purchase in case it was too much for her. Weena giggled as the bag was almost as big as the girl and her little eyes were trying to peer over the top to see where she was going.

On the other side of the street, opposite the butcher shop was an alley in-between the tavern and a small row of houses. Up ahead they could see two boys running around in the street with wooden swords pretending to be on some grand adventure. Their mother called out from one of the houses telling them that it was time for their dinner.

Dendrox noticed the two rough-looking men whispering back and forth over by the entrance to the alley.

"Bad news, those two," Dendrox whispered to her, "We should stay clear. We can't afford to draw attention to ourselves with all that has been going on."

"Hey you!" the younger of the two called out. He wore a simple long-sleeved white shirt, reddish-brown pants, and a pair of black leather boots. He was a fairly handsome man except that there was something unnerving and definitely unfriendly about his dark brown eyes. "Yeah, you!" he said to Weena and Dendrox, "Come here a minute, we have something to show you!" The younger man, who had short black hair and a thin mustache, now started to casually stroll over to them, while the older man kept eagerly waving them over to him.

"Damn it! Listen, don't do anything stupid," Dendrox whispered to Weena, "Do what they say. I don't want to give those bounty hunters a reason to get involved if they're about. If this gets serious, don't worry; I can handle them. Just don't panic if there is a need for blood."

Weena gave him a frightened nod. She wasn't sure which frightened her more, the two men or the fact that Dendrox was prepared to fight them to the death if trouble started between them.

The older man had a stupid grin on his face, not realizing that Dendrox knew exactly what they were intending. He had blonde hair and a short-cropped beard. Under his light brown eyes was a large crooked nose, obviously having been broken several times in the past.

The man with the thin black mustache came up to them and firmly ushered them over toward the alley and then a little way into it, all the time saying, "You won't believe what we found! You just have to see this! It won't take but a minute."

"*Not very original are you? This actually works for you two? A pair of pathetic amateur fools is what you are, and if either of you try anything, you'll be a couple of dead ones,*" Dendrox thought to himself in anger.

A dagger tip pressed up against the small of Dendrox's back once they were away from the street and far from curious eyes, just as Dendrox had expected.

"Alright girly, hand it over," said the older man. Under his black jacket which fell open at his sides, this man wore a blue tunic over his fair sized belly. Weena wondered if he had a weapon concealed within the folds of his clothing. She suspected maybe a knife at his side, hidden from view under his jacket, as she caught the glint of metal every now and then. She knew Dendrox was being

<Zaylyn ><Quest For The Sword Of Anthrowst ><By Katrina Mandrake-Johnston >   <Ch 60> < 183 >
threatened with a dagger by the other man.

"Hand over what? I don't know what you mean," said Weena.

The man let out an impatient sigh, resting his hand at his side near the edge of his jacket where Weena was sure now that he also had to be carrying a weapon. As he stared into her wide and frightened blue eyes, his gaze was cold and threatening and he said to her, "Don't make us resort to violence, honey. That fat pouch hangin' 'round your pretty little hips there. It's ours now. Hand it over." At first she hesitated, but then remembering that Candra had taken her mother's ring and that it no longer was in the pouch, she handed it over to them. The ring was safe in the elf's possession as far as Weena hoped. She was thankful, as she would have lost her most precious possession to these thieves now if Candra hadn't taken it. "Thank-you kindly," he said with a smirk as he accepted it.

The younger one, still holding the dagger to Dendrox, said, "Now get lost if ya know what's good for ya, and don't try anything neither."

"Alright, we don't want any trouble here. We'll go peacefully," Dendrox said. He wanted to punch the smug look off the older man's ugly face. He had a feeling that it was he who had instigated this little plan of theirs. Dendrox was afraid for Weena and didn't want to aggravate the situation any further.

Weena and Dendrox left the alley, and Dendrox muttered, "We're skipping the damn magic shop. Let's just go back to the inn." He took her by the arm and started leading her quickly back in the direction of the tavern door.

"I definitely agree. That was really frightening. Good thing there wasn't anything of value in there," she commented.

Dendrox looked furious that this had happened and that he couldn't really do anything about it. He wasn't being very gentle leading her back to the inn as he was. It made her feel as though she were a misbehaving child being dragged back to safety and to be scolded.

"Well let's just hope they're not the type that decide we somehow did that on purpose and come after us. Some blame and even attack the victim for not having anything of value when they have gone to all the trouble of robbing them. I've met people who are that insane before," he told her pulling her quickly along and opening the door.

Weena and Dendrox entered the inn, and upon seeing Nodwel, came to seat themselves at the large table next to him closest to the fireplace. They were still wary of the bounty hunters and didn't want to take any chances.

<World of Zaylyn ><Quest For The Sword Of Anthrowst ><By Katrina Mandrake-Johnston ><Ch 61>

CHAPTER 61 = FATE OF THE THIEVES

Lurking in the shadows, hidden from sight, The Black Shadow had watched as the two thieves had taken Weena's pouch. He had watched as Dendrox and Weena headed quickly back to The Twisted Eye Tavern trying to maintain a low profile. He watched until his insatiable hunger could be restrained no longer.

His eager dark form crawled along the side of the building like a spider, his black cloak moving like liquid about him until it was hard to determine if he even still had a humanoid form. His eyes began to glow a deep red as the hunger burned inside him.

He leapt across the street with incredible speed and landed like a great black cat with grace and silence. The two men were below in the alley. He could sense their presence and the hunger intensified.

Instead of rushing in for the kill like the beast inside him desperately wanted, he held himself back. He crept into the shadows near the back of the alley where the rooftop met the high wall of one of the houses. There he sat trying to fight his evil nature and the need to feed. The row of houses, their side walls connecting, ran the length to the north wall of the town. The backs of these houses formed a wall of sorts continuing the alley north along the back of the inn where most of the windows to the rooms were. Dendrox's room had its window facing the alley, but it was situated just before the alley turned to the right and around the corner of the tavern.

"Am I no better than Dranngore? He does not care about who he hurts in his ludicrous plan for power and revenge. I care, don't I? At least a small part of me does and doesn't want to hurt anyone anymore.

"I do care. I think about all the people I hurt when I take a life. I have to admit that the larger evil part of me gets excited at the thought of this, but it's the good part, no matter how small, that has to be the one that matters. I don't want to be a monster anymore. I don't want to be known as the creature in the dark that takes friends and family members away.

"I could simply kill Dranngore and end all of this he's causing, even send the Killnarin back to where they belong. But I don't want to get involved like that. If I kill the wizard, in doing so, I'm giving in to my evil nature no matter if the outcome is for good. I don't want to intentionally kill anyone, no matter what the reason. I may not be able to get control over myself again before I've killed several others after Dranngore is slain.

"Sending the Killnarin back would mean I'd be using more of my powers than I've been allowing myself. The hold over myself and my evil nature is so fragile as it is, sending them back would probably weaken that hold. I'm afraid of what might happen. Being so close to those creatures and knowing their evil, may fuel my own enough to lose control of it. Then I'd be no better than one of those beasts. I'd be much worse and do far more harm than any of them for sure. I can't allow that.

"I have the most power in all of Zaylyn. I can do pretty much anything and everything I wish with ease. I have all the power in this whole damn world, and all I really want is what they all take for granted.

"I can make people do what I want, feel and believe what I want them to, but in doing that, I can't fool myself. Love and friendship can never be real when I know it to be fake. I suffer in this loneliness I am forced to endure. Must it always be so? No matter how hard I fight the evil inside me?

"I could fool people into thinking I am one of them, but that just angers me, knowing that if they knew who I really was, that they would despise me and that any kindness they would have shown me would immediately become lost and meaningless. Although, maybe I should try to interact with people once again. I feel that perhaps I could be around this group without the risk of casualties.

"What, am I trying to fool myself? With me, there is always an incredible risk of death. No one is safe around me.

"But I have to try, don't I? Otherwise, why go to all this trouble to fight and go against my evil nature in the first place? There has to be some sort of reward for me, however small, otherwise I will find myself slipping, relaxing my hold over the evil and find myself starting to think 'What's the use in trying?'. It's so hard to control myself and there has to be something to fight for, as it would otherwise be hopeless.

"When the urges start to take over, my reasons for sparing lives, for holding back even though it will mean the urges will become stronger, my reasoning simply seems to dwindle away until it loses all its importance and until only the need to feed remains. I cannot bring myself to stop before I drain them completely. The hunger is always stronger than the few good intensions I may have had beforehand. And then, the evil is forever pushing at me to do far worse, whether the hunger is still in need of being satisfied or not. Every time I try to fight it, the hunger and my evil urges become more and more intense, and with it, a greater chance of me losing control altogether. If that ever happened, the evil monster within me would slaughter hundreds just for the fun of it, and I wouldn't be able to stop myself, no matter how hard I tried. I'd be no better than one of the Killnarin, only far deadlier and far more cruel and malicious.

"Is that a risk I am willing to take? I am constantly fighting a battle within myself; that massive amount of evil against my few good intensions. Do I want to take the chance that the evil will finally and completely consume me? Is it worth it to endanger the lives of many in the effort to save a few?

"I need something that will scream out to me, to make me stop myself, to make me fight no matter how strong the need to feed is, even if it means the hunger and the urges will become stronger. The chance for friendship is strong enough, isn't it? Enough to maintain a firm hold over the hunger? The chance for love? I don't want to be alone anymore. Perhaps I am being selfish to think I can have

<Zaylyn ><Quest For The Sword Of Anthrowst ><By Katrina Mandrake-Johnston >   <Ch 61> < 185 >
more.

"If I can prove to myself that I can be among others without being afraid of what I might do to them, that is definitely worth it. So many people fear me and I know it's for good reason, but I, in fact, am the one who fears myself the most, for I truly know what I am able to do… and of all the things I find myself wanting to do.

"I was able to stop myself from killing my last victim, the man in the forest. That's a start in the right direction, isn't it? But I fear, in doing so, that it has made it harder for me to hold the evil back. It burns within me, so greatly intensifying the hunger, furious that I have dared refuse its will."

He could hear the two thieves below.

"Nice fat pouch, eh?" the older man said to the other.

The younger man tucked the dagger into a tiny scabbard hidden inside the top of his boot and he said to the other, "Well, whatcha waiting for? Open it up."

The blonde portly man opened the pouch and took out the contents. "What's this?!" he exclaimed, looking at the doll Weena had picked up earlier.

"Eh?" the younger asked with curiosity.

"There's just this doll inside it, and a flame box!" he told him.

"A doll? Are you sure there's nothin' else in there?" he asked, "Gold, maybe a couple gems, a bit of jewelry, anything?"

"I'm telling you, no," the older man replied firmly.

"It must be cursed," the man with the black mustache told him, his dark brown eyes growing wide with fear.

"What are you talking about?" the other laughed.

"She was a sorceress or somethin', right? And look, how this doll looks sort of like her? Yellow hair and blue dress or robes or whatever, just like hers? She's out for revenge now, she is. Waiting for us to turn our backs," he suggested looking all around for any sign of danger.

The blonde man with the short beard tossed the doll, flame box, and empty pouch to the ground as he ridiculed the other saying, "Don't be such a damn fool."

The black haired man got a strange confused look on his face, and then he said starting to panic, "Hey, all of a sudden I can't move!"

"Quit playin' around," the other scolded, "The damn thing's not cursed."

"Well somethin's goin' on that's not right," he snapped back at him, annoyed that he wasn't taking him seriously.

The older man was getting frustrated with him. "Listen," he said to him, clearly irritated, "I'm serious, quit playing around. I'm not puttin' up with one of your idiotic pranks!"

"No, it's the truth!" he said honestly, "I can't move!"

The blonde man just stood there glaring at him for a few seconds, and then the younger man said with fear, "What was that?!"

"What now?" asked the other with a sigh.

"I thought I saw somethin'…" he told him, his eyes straining to see into the darkness at the back of the alley.

"Quit fooling around, I mean it!" the older thief warned.

A worried and terrified look crossed his face as he said hurriedly, "Hey! There it is again! There's somethin' crawling down the wall! Down at the back of the alley!"

"I told you, quit playing around!" he warned again, now becoming extremely angry with his companion's apparent foolishness.

The other man was very frightened now and still could not move from the spot where he stood. "It's somethin' awful, I just know it!" he whined.

"Look, there's nothing there," the older man tried to tell him, staring into the darkness at the back of the alley.

Then he saw two blood red eyes start to glow in the blackness like two orbs of fire come into view. Then The Black Shadow leapt from the shadows at the astonished man, while the other tried desperately

<Zaylyn ><Quest For The Sword Of Anthrowst ><By Katrina Mandrake-Johnston >   <Ch 61> < 186 >

to run but found that he still was unable to move as before and that something magical must be holding him there.

The Black Shadow viciously bit deep into the throat of the older man. The younger man cried out in terror, but found that not only was he unable to move, that now his voice had no sound.

The Black Shadow drank heavily. He was going to kill this man, if he continued. Most of him wanted to, but a little part of him was screaming out at him to stop. This little part of him was so very faint in his mind, but he knew it was there, and he desperately wanted himself to listen to it. But so many times before, it had been drowned out by the excited pounding of his heartbeat, the incredible hunger, and the viciousness inside him. He feared that this would happen once again and that he would end up killing this man despite his efforts. It was so hard to think clearly, his dark and savage instincts taking over in a warm flood into his mind.

"*Don't kill him. Don't kill…*" the little voice called out from his mind.

But he wasn't stopping. He was trying so hard to pull himself away, but found he couldn't, no matter how hard he tried. He was a slave to the hunger and his evil nature, and it was too much for him to fight. He had gone too long without feeding fully. He had held his evil desires back too long for them to be subdued any longer.

"*No!*" he screamed at himself, feeling the man's body becoming limp as he began to pass out from the loss of blood. "*It's not too late, if you stop right now! It will take him a long time to recover, but it's not too late!*" he told himself.

When he finally dropped the man's body to the ground, he was dead. The evil inside him had won yet again, as it always did in the end.

The Black Shadow's entire body burned with the pleasure of the kill, while his evil nature sent a cold chill throughout him as he started to imagine all the terrible things he was wanting to do. He stared at the remaining man from beneath his black hooded cloak. He let out a low and malicious growl, which sent shivers down the frightened man's spine.

He wanted to tear this helpless man to pieces. He wanted to hear him scream in terror, which would also bring him more victims when others came to this man's aid. He wanted him to run, providing him with a chase that would open up all sorts of possibilities for inflicting terror upon the entire town. He had felt this man's fear growing as he had helplessly watched his friend being fed upon. The fear he had caused this man excited The Black Shadow greatly. An evil grin began to spread across his blood-stained lips.

However, the hunger was the strongest need in him at the moment, not the desire to create chaos and terror. The Black Shadow approached the man from behind and firmly grasped his shoulder. With a vicious snarl, he then grabbed the man by his short black hair with his other hand, yanking his head back to expose the flesh of his neck. His fangs eagerly bit in deeply, making the man cry out in fear and pain. He made sure that everyone else in the surrounding area was deaf to the man's cries, as he did not want to be interrupted.

He drank slowly this time and increased the pain the man felt, enjoying his suffering. The man was screaming, and uselessly and desperately trying to struggle free.

The Black Shadow then noticed the doll lying on the ground. It had become soiled lying there in the dirt within the alley, and its black button eyes seemed to be looking right at him, as if sadly watching him destroy all he had fought for.

"*What am I doing?! No, I have to stop! I already killed his friend! I have to stop! I can't let myself become nothing more than an evil monster! The horrible thoughts going through my head, I can't lose myself to the point where I decide to act on them. And of the others? What will I do to them? Weena, Dendrox, Nodwel… they are so close and in danger… as is everyone else in the town. The increased suffering I'm causing this man, prolonging his death, it's just not right. No, I can't simply not prolong his death. I have to stop myself from killing him, not simply make it a quick and painless death. I can't allow myself to kill this man!*"

The Black Shadow released him and pushed him away, sending him backwards to land on the ground. The frightened man instinctively put his hand up to his neck in an effort to try to stop the

<Zaylyn ><Quest For The Sword Of Anthrowst ><By Katrina Mandrake-Johnston >   <Ch 61> < 187 >

bleeding, even though he knew he would surely bleed to death in a very short time. The Black Shadow caused the wound beneath the man's fingers to heal, and the man felt at where the wound had closed in amazement, finally taking his hand away and all the time staring in disbelief at the mysterious black figure in front of him.

The Black Shadow wanted to dive at him again, the blood still warm in his throat. He felt his mind starting to cloud over as he began to lose control again.

"Please," the man sobbed, "I promise. I won't steal ever again. Please, I'll do anything you want!"

Again, a low deep growl rumbled within him, his eyes flashing red. His fangs were eager to pierce warm flesh again. "*No,*" his mind told him, as he tried to control himself. The evil grin that had spread across his lips, faded away, his mind saying, "*I must do what I must, and that is feed, but the evil inside me will not get the satisfaction of another kill!*"

"That guy I knifed a month ago? I didn't really mean it. I'm sorry. I won't do anything like that again. Please, I beg you! ...Wait! You're The Black Shadow, aren't you?!" the man said, his voice trembling and his fear rising even more, "What the hell are you?! Oh no, please no! You can't be him!! I'll do anything! I swear!! Just don't!! Please! Let me go! I won't tell anyone what I saw, I swear!! You don't have to kill me!" he begged.

"*I will not be the monster anymore. I'm no better than a Killnarin then. I don't want to be hated like that,*" he said to himself sadly. There was a horrible pain in his gut forcing him to almost lose control again. "*Damn it! I still need to feed!*" he thought in anger and frustration, wondering if he would be able to stop himself a second time.

"Why won't you say anything?!" the man wailed. He grabbed the man by his shirt and lifted him up from the ground with incredible strength. "No..." he screamed as The Black Shadow bit once more into the man.

This time he took the pain of his bite away. The man had suffered enough.

He was able to stop this time, leaving the man alive, but barely, and unconscious. The Black Shadow collected Weena's belongings and simply walked through the wall of the tavern as if it were air.

Making himself invisible, he walked through the large kitchen where Narten was preparing several dinners, and then he passed through yet another wall to enter Weena's room. Realizing that there was no real reason for her to return here except for her lantern, he entered Dendrox's room and laid the items on the bed, as he knew about the problems they were having with the scissors.

The Black Shadow would have killed again and perhaps others within the town had the doll not been there to help him to get himself back under control. He would not allow himself to become a monster.

He had wondered if his interest in Dranngore and the wizard's actions were motivated because he and the Killnarin were simply threatening his food supply. The Black Shadow had heard Candra suggest the same thing on their way to Vackiindmire. He always made it a point to avoid harming children if he could help it. He had often wondered if the reason could have been that it was simply to ensure that his food supply would not be depleted.

He knew this now; that it was not so. He had returned the doll to Weena as sort of an unspoken thank-you.

"*So many children, so many families, the Killnarin will not be allowed to kill anymore. I will help this group on their quest if I can, although I am unsure of how much longer I can hold myself back. I fear I may be putting them in danger, the more I try to help and the longer I stay around them.*

"*Why is it that I am so fascinated with this group? Could it be that, in each of them, I see a little of myself, some similarity now and then? Some aspect in each of their personalities and the way they think, that reminds me a bit of myself? Perhaps I did have more to do with them coming together than I realize. If I did, I was unaware of it.*

"*Perhaps it goes all the way back to Rasindell. I did feel for him when he lost his love and I protected him from the Killnarin. I even provided him with a daughter of sorts, so he wouldn't have to*

<Zaylyn ><Quest For The Sword Of Anthrowst ><By Katrina Mandrake-Johnston >   <Ch 61> < 188 >

be completely alone, even though he had chosen to be after her death. And then, for Vordin, I do the same. I saved him from a Killnarin and placed him and Lorenta under the care of the two thieves and Weena. I even delayed their travel just so, in order for them all to meet.

"I will continue to watch them as I have been doing and help when I feel I am able to safely do so. I guess it makes me happy to watch them; it makes me feel as if in some way I am one of them somehow. They are the closest thing I have to calling friends, and Lorenta in a bizarre way is my child as I did have a hand in her creation.

"No, you stupid fool! You have no friends or family and that is how it must be! Do not start to create an illusion in your mind that they are in some way, or they will be the first ones you turn on if you lose control! You know that! And from experience, damn it! There is a reason why you gave up on friends… why you gave up on love. There are no families that would take you in as one of their own."

He could hear Nodwel, Dendrox, and Weena in the main room of the tavern, and The Black Shadow decided to leave, but kept part of his mind aware and focused on the group as always.

<World of Zaylyn ><Quest For The Sword Of Anthrowst ><By Katrina Mandrake-Johnston ><Ch 62>

CHAPTER 62 =   REUNITED

After some time, the dwarf got up and went to the desk. "Thank-you so very much for your hospitality. I didn't catch your name though," Nodwel said to the innkeeper.

"Declort," he replied with a smile.

"And your friend's name was…" he added trying to remember.

"Oh yes, it is Yorif. Please send me word, if you find him." He hesitated a moment. "Even if the news is unfavorable," Declort told him.

"I will," the dwarf assured him and then whispered, "I see that not many of my companions arrived back here yet. Any word on any of them?"

Declort replied, "If you're worried about the bounty hunters, I believe they left town sometime around mid day. I don't think you'll have to worry about them. Most hired thugs, as such, don't have much patience unless it's bought with a high price. If the price on your two friends wasn't worth the time and effort, most likely they headed off in search of a less evasive bounty with a higher price on his or her head."

"I hope you are right, but somehow I highly doubt they would have just given up," Nodwel commented.

"You'd be surprised then at how lazy some are. There are definitely many who are precise and meticulous when it comes to bounty hunting, but that bunch did not seem the type," Declort told him.

"I hope you're right. I'll just sit and wait for the others then. Would it be too much trouble to get a mug of ale? I made far more than I had hoped helping out the merchants at the marketplace. I should have enough to pay for a couple of rooms for tonight as well," he told him.

"Well, that's great," the innkeeper said with a cheerful smile, "I'll get you that ale right away."

"You're sure about not seeing my friends though?" Nodwel asked, still dreadfully worried about their welfare.

"I'm the only one running the inn. Narten watches the front when I do manage to catch a bit of sleep. He would have woken me if there had been some sort of problem," Declort explained, "I'm sure they are just fine. The warrior woman and the young man were in here early this morning for breakfast. Sorry I don't remember their names."

"No, I saw them just before that. I'm sure they are all okay, like you said," said the dwarf placing payment for the ale on the desktop. The innkeeper gave him a friendly nod. "Thank-you once again," Nodwel said with a smile and then seated himself once again at the large table by the tavern entrance. A few moments later, Declort presented him with a frothy mug of ale and then went back to his duties.

Nodwel leaned over to the next table and said to Weena and Dendrox, "Looks to be that the hunters left town, as strange as that sounds. There's been no sign of them for quite awhile."

"Well that's a relief," Weena commented moving over to Nodwel's table to join him, as did Dendrox.

<Zaylyn ><Quest For The Sword Of Anthrowst ><By Katrina Mandrake-Johnston >   <Ch 62> < 189 >

"Have you seen any of the others?" Dendrox asked, eager to hear about Candra.

"No, nothing so far," Nodwel answered, "I have seven gold coins left for tonight. So, unless the others come up with anything, it's enough for one room and a bit of food to split between all of us."

The three of them sat chatting about the day's events for some time before Weena suggested, "We should get the item out of the room now, don't you think?"

"Yeah, alright," Dendrox agreed, "We'll be right back, Nodwel. We left a few things back in the rooms." Nodwel gave them a nod as they headed down the hall.

When Weena and Dendrox entered his room, they immediately noticed the stolen items neatly laid out on the bed. Weena asked in confusion, "Dendrox, did you go after the thieves?"

He replied, "No, when did I have the chance? I've been with you the whole time."

"Then who?" Weena asked, still very confused, wondering what could have happened, "Did the thieves return it somehow?"

"Please," he laughed, "not very likely. But I have no clue either. Something odd is going on here. We should check to see if the scissors are still here. I want you to leave the room, very slowly and very carefully. I'll remain and check the room for any traps that may have been laid."

Weena simply nodded and followed his instruction. Dendrox departed the room shortly after and handed Weena her pouch with the flame box and doll within. "There was nothing strange," he told her. He placed his backpack on the floor containing his empty water skin and the two blankets he and Candra had brought with them. He then tied his small leather pouch around his waist, positioning it at the small of his back, and told her, "Everything's back where it belongs." Next he swung the backpack over his shoulder and said to Weena, "Well, I guess we better get back to Nodwel then."

"I left my lantern back in my room. I should get it?" she asked.

"Might as well. We don't know if we're going to have enough money between us all to rent the rooms for the night. Besides, we might get different rooms assigned to us. Hell, depending on how much we have, we may end up all in one room, if the innkeeper will allow such a thing," he told her with a miserable look on his face.

"Okay, I'll just be a moment," she told him and then, after an unnerving thought, added, "You don't suppose someone has been in my room, do you?"

"I could check," said Dendrox, but he didn't look at all pleased with the suggestion. He followed her to her room and took a few moments to gaze about the room standing from the doorway. "Looks all right," he decided, "Get your lantern, but make it quick."

Weena had hoped that he would have taken this opportunity to steal a kiss from her now that they were alone once more. He did no such thing. He just waited impatiently for her to retrieve the lantern and then headed down the hall quickly with Weena following after him.

Weena and Dendrox returned to the main room of the tavern and sat at Nodwel's table once again. It was then that Candra entered through the door followed by Asdella and Vordin.

"They've left," Candra told them all, talking about the bounty hunters, "Doesn't look like we'll have to worry about them. Overheard one of them saying that they'd lined up something far better."

Weena wondered, "*Could it be that they backed off because I said that I was a magic user? I know that most people tend to be nervous, not really knowing what is to be expected, but could it really have deterred the bounty hunters as far as to leave? Being so wary of what I might be able to do, that they deemed the bounty on the thieves not worth the trouble? It's a little hard to believe. Did they really imagine that I could be so powerful? I suppose it could be true.*"

Vordin told them, "Asdella and I, we had a quick look around after getting some sleep, but we didn't come up with much. We ran into Candra on our way back here."

Nodwel told them that he had managed to get some money for the night, and Dendrox and Weena told them what they had learnt about the sword.

Some time later, Lorenta entered the tavern. The man she had entered with had his arm draped over her shoulder. They were talking back and forth, smiling and laughing. Lorenta didn't even seem to notice that the others were sitting at the large table together. If she had noticed, she showed no sign

<Zaylyn ><Quest For The Sword Of Anthrowst ><By Katrina Mandrake-Johnston >   <Ch 62> < 190 >
that she had.

The man she was with sat down at the middle large table, beside the table with Lorenta's companions and next to the fireplace. Lorenta went to the desk to speak with the innkeeper.

The man's black long-sleeved shirt had a tan colored vest over it and he straightened this slightly before smoothing his black greasy hair with his hand. He gave Lorenta a large toothy grin and spread himself out over the bench, his legs spread out beneath the table and his arms resting outstretched on the back of the wooden bench on either side. He wore an incredibly smug look on his round clean-shaven face and there was something deceitful about his expression. His dark brown eyes watched Lorenta a little too closely as she spoke to the innkeeper.

Someone in the inn whispered loudly, "Oh no, not this arrogant bastard again. There goes my whole evening."

"Poor girl," another whispered, "Maybe someone should warn her about that creep, although I doubt it will do any good."

"What is she doing? Who is this guy?" Vordin whispered, as he leaned forward so only his friends could hear him.

The innkeeper gave Lorenta a handful of gold coins. She turned with an excited look on her face as she smiled and nodded to the man.

He clapped loudly and bellowed across the room to her, "Alright! Great news!"

The other patrons were obviously annoyed, as he was acting as if he owned the entire place and everyone in it, intruding on their privacy with his uncouth behavior. He kept looking at everyone with just a hint of a smile on his thin lips, as if he were challenging everyone around him. Most of the people just ignored him, while a few returned him cross looks.

Declort, the innkeeper, set up a chair on the small stage and announced, "I didn't have anything planned for tonight, but this young lady here has agreed to tell a couple of stories for your enjoyment. Now, this is her first try at storytelling, so go easy on her."

This man, who had come in with Lorenta, had obviously been here before. Everyone appeared to be hoping this man would be quiet and keep to himself for the duration of the storytelling.

Lorenta sat down upon the chair, her face clearly blushing, and she looked nervously around at all the people staring expectantly back at her. The man clapped a little too loudly again in the quiet tavern, making sure everyone was painfully aware of his presence.

<World of Zaylyn ><Quest For The Sword Of Anthrowst ><By Katrina Mandrake-Johnston ><Ch 63>

CHAPTER 63 =   LORENTA THE STORYTELLER: THE FARM

"Once long ago, there was a man," Lorenta began keeping her voice strong despite her nervousness, "He was a good man with a kind heart and had a kind and loving wife.

"This man was a farmer, but luck had not smiled on this unfortunate couple for their tiny piece of land only contained dry and barely useable soil. Still, he worked very hard at that piece of land. Each time, he would plant the seeds that contained all their hopes of survival into that hostile ground, water them as best he could, and beg them to grow.

"This went on year after year. But they struggled on together in the face of their misfortune, always hoping for better days in the future. Come market day, they would take what few shriveled vegetables they had managed to produce in hopes that someone would buy them, providing them with the money they desperately needed to be able to keep their land. As it was, the poor farmer and his wife had to go hungry several days at a time just to be able to have something to bring to the market.

"All day, they would wait patiently, trying not to lose hope as the potential customers passed them by, sometimes letting out a surprised laugh at how miserable their produce looked, but most of the time they gave a disgusted look at the shriveled vegetables neatly laid out and moved on. The farmer and his wife tried not to look at the plump delicious vegetables and the healthy well-fed people that had brought them, as it was too much for the couple to bear.

"Thankfully, at the end of each market day, out of pity, a few people would offer them a few coins for their produce merely to give to their horses as a treat for the ride home. It wasn't much, but at least it

<Zaylyn ><Quest For The Sword Of Anthrowst ><By Katrina Mandrake-Johnston >   <Ch 63> < 191 >
was enough for them to keep their farm.

"One night after coming home from a most depressing and disheartening market day, the farmer came out to the field after his wife had gone to bed. The farmer looked bitterly at his miserable excuse for a farm and then collapsed to the ground weeping heavily. It was the first time in a long time that he had let their misfortune get to him and he wept, lying distraught for several hours on the hard dry dirt in the dark.

"Then he saw something very odd and something he had never noticed before. There in the hard-packed soil was what looked to be a long blue and wispy tuft of grass. He reached out and gave the plant a tug, but it held fast.

" *'Could it be that this odd plant is what has been causing all of our problems?'* he wondered, and he also hoped this was so, as then everything could be solved so easily just by removing it.

"He got up, and kneeling on either side of the little blue plant, gave it another tug.

" *'I've never heard of a plant like this,'* he told himself, *'It must be magical and here to forever curse my land. All I have to do is pull it out.'*

"This time he yanked with all of his remaining strength and he fell backwards as it came free of the dirt. When the farmer looked at his hand, he was amazed and shocked to see that it was not a plant at all that he had pulled from the ground. It was a tiny man that he held by the long wispy locks of blue hair that were on top of his small head.

"The tiny man let out a deep bellowing laugh, which surprised the farmer even more, and he dropped the tiny figure.

" 'Why do you weep?' the tiny blue-haired creature asked.

" 'Just look all around,' answered the farmer, 'Nothing fit to eat or sell grows here. My wife is nothing but skin and bones. Why she stays with me is beyond me. I am so weak myself, that I can barely even work this field anymore and I'm failing to see the use in it. I'd have better luck trying to grow crops in a field made up entirely of dust and salt.'

" 'Is that what you wish?' bellowed the little man.

" 'What?! No, of course not," exclaimed the farmer.

" 'Would you rather have a field of rich dark soil perfect for growing grand vegetables of exquisite flavor?' the tiny man asked.

" 'Well of course. I'd be happy with less, just as long as my wife and I don't slowly starve to death,' the farmer grumbled getting even more upset and annoyed by this being's questioning.

" 'Would you give your first born son to gain this?' the strange little man asked.

" 'What are you talking about?! I doubt we will even live much longer, and to bring a child into this kind of life would be murder, especially where we can't even feed ourselves,' the farmer explained with tears in his eyes, as he and his wife would have liked to have children but clearly wouldn't be able to provide for them.

" 'Is your answer yes?' the tiny man asked, looking up at him with black beady little eyes.

"The farmer now despised this little man for all he was doing was bringing more tears to his eyes and heartbreak at his situation, making him feel worse and worse for failing to provide a better life for himself and his wife.

" 'I don't know, sure. Will you leave me be now?' he said hastily with annoyance, 'All you are doing is making me feel worse!'

" 'I will leave, but I shall one day return,' bellowed the man, and he vanished.

"The farmer, too tired to return to the house, fell asleep right there in the middle of the field thinking to himself that he surely had finally gone mad with hunger and that he had started to hallucinate.

"He awoke the next morning and was so astonished to feel dark moist and loose soil at his fingertips that he believed he was still dreaming. His wife, upon seeing this, ran out to him rejoicing. Neither of them dared question what had happened, as they feared doing so would somehow end their miracle.

"Years past. Each market day, they would bring such grand vegetables that everyone would come to them first and everything would be sold in a manner of minutes. Their farm grew such an abundance that half the time they didn't really know what to do with so much extra food.

<Zaylyn ><Quest For The Sword Of Anthrowst ><By Katrina Mandrake-Johnston >   <Ch 63> < 192 >

"The farmer and his wife ate well, and eventually after several years of good fortune, gave birth to a son. The farmer was wary that perhaps the little blue-haired man had not been a dream, but they had many years of harmony and his wife gave birth to two more sons.

"When his children were old enough to help him work the land, he showed them what to do in great detail. His eldest son was incredibly lazy and did not pay attention to his father's instructions and had no intention of doing any of the work at all. The father told them that he and their mother were going to town and that when they returned he would inspect their work. He divided the land into three parts assigning one part to each son and then left for town.

"The two younger sons started on their chores right away, while the oldest son sat relaxing under an apple tree. When his brothers spoke to him about this, he told them that he would give them part of his allowance if they would do his part of the work. They agreed and finished their lazy brother's work first before continuing with their own.

"When the father and mother returned, he was disappointed to see that his two younger sons had not yet completed their work. He praised his eldest for doing such a fine job, not knowing what had occurred.

"Come nightfall the farmer was admiring the work of his sons when he heard a bellowing laugh. There was the tiny little man with the wispy blue hair. 'I have returned. Give me your eldest son.'

"The farmer didn't know what to do. He begged, 'Can't we make some sort of deal? I can't lose one of my sons!'

" 'Alright, I am feeling generous,' said the little man.

" 'If your sons can work the land to my satisfaction in a specific amount of time, you shall keep all of your children. Should one of them fail, they will be mine.'

"The farmer agreed, as it was his best chance at saving his oldest son, but he feared for his two younger children as he thought they worked so slowly. The next day the little man called forth the farmer, who in turn called forth his three sons. He explained to them the story of their farm and the deal he had made with the strange little man. The two younger brothers looked nervously at their older sibling for they knew he would fail. The sons were sent out to do their task.

" 'Brothers, help me. I do not know what to do,' the eldest said.

" 'To help you would mean our own doom. We cannot help you. Watch what we do and try to follow, for you are dear to us and we do not wish you a horrible fate.'

"The allotted time passed and the little man inspected the land. 'Fine work. Fine work. Wait! What do you call this?!' he exclaimed with a wicked grin.

" 'Son!' the father said in disbelief, 'Just yesterday you were finished first and with beautiful work. What happened?'

" 'I am sorry father. I did nothing that day, while I paid my brothers to do my work,' explained the son with great shame.

"The little man chuckled, 'And now you will forever make up for your laziness.'

"The eldest son was transformed into a tiny bee, and the mysterious little man vanished. Every day, the brothers would see a bee which looked slightly different than the others, working harder than ever pollinating the flowers of the farm and forever knowing the punishment for his laziness."

Lorenta looked sheepishly around hoping for approval and was pleased to hear everyone give their applause. The man she had entered with, of course, was making a point to clap the loudest and watching to see if Lorenta had noticed this.

"Tell us another one!" he called out, "That was great! See, I told you that you could do it! Come on! Lorenta, tell us another!"

A spider crawled across the stage in front of Lorenta.

"*This used to be me,*" she thought to herself looking at the spider crawling innocently across the smooth wooden boards of the stage, "*Funny, it's so hard for me to believe. This is not me anymore. I am no longer the same as this spider here. This is not what I am anymore. I can't even remember what it was like to be this. I don't even know who I am. One thing I do know is that it feels right to be*

<Zaylyn ><Quest For The Sword Of Anthrowst ><By Katrina Mandrake-Johnston >   <Ch 63> < 193 >

accepted as a human. This is what I want, but that would mean I would have to hide my true self, which is something I wouldn't be able to stand. This man I met last night seems to accept me, seeing more in me than the others. The others, even Vordin, they don't really see me as part of their group. I bet they've already discussed any information they've collected and have made their plans of what to do next in our quest without me as usual. I shall have to discover things for myself second hand, as it seems I always shall have to."

Declort told her, "Go ahead. Tell another, if you have one. You're doing very well. You're a natural at this."

"I shall tell another, if you wish," Lorenta said blushing.

<World of Zaylyn ><Quest For The Sword Of Anthrowst ><By Katrina Mandrake-Johnston ><Ch 64>

CHAPTER 64 = LORENTA THE STORYTELLER: THE CLOSET

"The old woman reluctantly put up a notice advertising her house for sale," Lorenta began, this time having more confidence in herself, "When a young man showed interest in the home, the woman seemed very pleased, as she wished to live with her son and his family in her old age. The man was amazed at the low price the old woman was asking for the large and beautiful house.

"The man told the woman that he would purchase the house from her, and this is when the old woman pulled him close and whispered, 'Then I must tell you the secret of this house.'

" 'What is this you speak of? What secret could there possibly be?' the man asked with curiosity.

" 'You must swear that you will be very careful if you decide to use its power. I have been so wary of selling this place because of it. Follow me,' the old woman said leading him up several flights of stairs.

"So the man followed the old woman to the attic. There was a closet door here, and this is where the old woman stopped.

" 'What is it that you're talking about?' the man exclaimed, 'I see nothing here.'

"The old woman put a bony finger to her lips. 'Watch,' she said as she knocked once, twice, three times upon the closet door.

"Then she slowly turned the rusty doorknob and opened the door. To his amazement, he saw a wondrous and amazing world through the doorway. He could do nothing but stare in astonishment.

" 'You may go through, and the passageway will lie open to you until you return here to this house. None of the beings within can come into our world, and although you will be able to interact with the wondrous beings within, none can do you harm. You must remember to knock only three times to activate the magic of the doorway. Promise me, that you will knock only three times and never four. Please, I must have your most sincere promise.'

" 'Alright,' he agreed.

"So the man bought the house and the old woman went to live with her son and his family. The man could hardly wait to explore the magical world.

"He however was wary of doing so alone. He told his best friend about the closet door within the attic, and he of course didn't believe him until he came and saw for himself.

" 'Shall we go in?' he asked his friend.

" 'I don't know, are you sure we'll be safe?' his friend asked, extremely nervous.

"The man answered, 'The old woman who sold me the place said we would be, and she seemed to know what she was talking about.'

"His friend was still not convinced and he said, 'But are you sure it will be safe for both of us? Maybe it only works for the one who knocked.'

" 'Well, we'll never know unless we try,' the man told him, 'Besides, we can stay close to the doorway in case there is any trouble.'

"So the two men entered through the doorway and found themselves in a wondrous and amazing world. Here everything shimmered in a strange light. Large colorful crystals had sprouted from the ground like trees. The ground itself was as smooth and white as an eggshell. A small stream was nearby, but it was not water that flowed in it. It was filled with a white cream-like substance.

"Overhead in a light purple sky, an immense serpent-like dragon beat its wings. They edged toward the doorway, but the dragon seemed to ignore them. Landing beside the white milky stream, it dipped its snake-like neck beneath the surface and a few seconds later rose with an odd creature between its teeth. This creature had a round scaly body with eight spider-like legs and three eyestalks on the top of its body. The creature screamed a shrill cry as the dragon devoured it. The dragon then continued its flight into the sky.

"The two men looked at each other in astonishment and quickly decided to leave.

"The next day, they went through the portal again. This time the scenery was a little bit different. They realized that they were in a different location within this strange world. Here there were blue fuzzy plants surrounding a pool of black water. Many strange colorful bugs chirped and buzzed around the plants.

" 'Wow, would you take a look at that!' his friend exclaimed.

"There, sitting around the pool was a huge green insect which half resembled a large grasshopper. It had no wings and instead of two large legs used for jumping, all six of its legs were large. What was most odd about this creature, was that its size was that of a full-grown cat.

" 'There are more of them, look!' the man said to his friend.

" 'We haven't seen you two before. Where is the old woman?' the insect asked the two men.

" 'It just talked!' both the men exclaimed together.

"The man finally told the bug, 'She sold me the house and went to live with her son.'

" 'Oh, I see,' said the large green insect, 'I do hope that she reminded you to only knock three times and never four. You wouldn't want to be responsible for unleashing that kind of evil into your world.'

" 'What do you mean?' he asked, 'What will happen if I knock four times?'

"The insect told him, 'Return tomorrow and I shall tell you more. You must always keep your visits short.'

" 'But we just arrived!' he told the bug, wanting to find out as much information as possible about what would happen if he knocked four times and what evil it was speaking of.

" 'There are two of you,' the bug explained, 'so it's more draining on the magic of the portal. You should leave now and return tomorrow.'

" 'Alright,' agreed the man, and he and his friend left, returning to the house.

"The next day, the man met his friend and asked him if he wanted to enter the world again.

"His friend replied, 'Maybe you should go by yourself and find out all the information you can. It sounds more dangerous than what it's worth.'

"So the man went home and went up to the attic.

"Knock. 'One,' he counted. Knock. 'Two,' he said.

"Then a voice called out to him from outside. It was his friend. 'Maybe I should come with you after all,' said his friend.

" 'Alright,' the man shouted back, 'Thanks. Let me just activate the portal so I don't lose count. Come on up. The door's open.'

"The man returned to the closet door. Knock. 'Two,' said the man. Knock. 'Three,' he said.

"He opened the door and was astonished to see himself looking into a mirror. No, it wasn't a mirror, because a wicked grin spread across the lips of his reflection.

"Before he could do anything at all, his double had stepped across the threshold and pushed the man into the closet and closed the door after him.

"The man found himself in a black void where the only thing visible was the transparent doorway back into his house. From this side, the door was invisible. He could see that his duplicate had a vicious looking dagger behind his back. His friend entered the attic.

"The man pounded furiously upon the door trying to warn his friend, but he remained unheard no matter what he did.

" 'So are we going in then,' his friend asked.

" 'No,' the imposter replied, 'You were right. It's just too dangerous, especially when we don't know very much information about the other world. We wouldn't want to accidentally unleash a terrible evil, now would we?'

" 'Well no. What are you going to do?' asked the man's friend, totally unaware of the danger.

" 'I don't know, board it up perhaps?' the evil thing suggested, eagerly fidgeting with the dagger behind his back.

" 'Well, I have wood and nails at my place. Let's do this right away then,' said his friend turning around to head downstairs.

" 'Yes, let's,' the evil being said, as he grinned a viciously wicked smile at the trapped man within the closet. Then he followed his friend out of the room with the dagger in his hand, ready to strike.

" 'No!' the man screamed pounding on the door.

"A few minutes later, the evil being returned, its hands and the dagger drenched in blood. He opened the closet door without knocking upon the door at all. He tossed the dagger into the closet. The man tried to escape but found he couldn't. The evil creature then dragged his dead friend into the closet.

" 'What have I done!' the man wailed, 'It's all my fault! I must have knocked four times by accident.'

"The evil being, laughing, set the house on fire.

"The creature said to the man, 'There will be no one to let you out now, and I shall be free to terrorize this world. Thank-you for letting me take over your life. No one will know the difference, until it is too late that is, like your foolish friend here.'

"The house burned to the ground with the man watching the doorway slowly vanish before his eyes until he was in complete darkness within the void."

Once again, Lorenta received applause. She stood up and took a slight bow to announce that she had finished her storytelling, and then came to sit with the man, not her companions.

"Oh, that was excellent," the man said to her, putting his arm around her.

"Thank-you," replied Lorenta looking up at him.

"Both of your stories didn't have very happy endings like I had expected. Why was that?" he asked, lustfully eyeing her body.

"Life rarely has happy endings, at least as far as I've seen. Why should it be any different in the stories I tell? Besides, it's not as if they are real. There is no one to protest," she said to him.

"You obviously haven't been looking in the right places then. There are plenty of happy endings as well as beginnings and middles. It's just that most people tend to dwell on the bad parts instead of the good, sometimes so much that they themselves become unaware and unable to see the good in their lives," the man told her.

"Yes, that is true," Lorenta agreed, "I shouldn't have said that."

"Isn't it a good turn of events that we happened to meet? Don't be shy. Why don't you sit a little closer?" he coaxed caressing her shoulder.

"Perhaps," Lorenta said, unsure of herself.

Asdella had a foul grimace on her face, as she watched the man and Lorenta speaking to each other.

CHAPTER 65 = ASDELLA'S RAGE

Asdella got up from the table, her sword in hand, and came to stand before the table Lorenta and the man were at.

"Asdella, what are you doing?" Weena whispered to her.

"Best to not get involved, whatever she's up to," Nodwel explained to the group, "She's been known to start fights. Nothing to worry about, usually just a few heated words. I have no idea why she is so upset. He is annoying, yes, but Lorenta can make her own decisions. I'm sure Lorenta will be joining us before it's time to leave this place."

"If you're looking for a whore to brutalize, you're looking in the wrong place. Preying on innocents now I see?" she said with a vicious sneer and looking at the man in disgust.

"You call that normal?" Candra whispered.

"No. What's the matter with her?!" Nodwel exclaimed, "You know, it's probably best just to

<Zaylyn ><Quest For The Sword Of Anthrowst ><By Katrina Mandrake-Johnston >   <Ch 65> < 196 >
leave it be."

"How dare you insult and embarrass my lady friend here by making such accusations about me. I'm sure she would not associate with me, if such terrible things were true," he said to Asdella.

"You just met her. Shut up you filthy cur," she snarled back at him between clenched teeth.

"You don't know that for sure," he said glaring at her in a degrading manner from beneath his brow, "It just so happens that this is true. I did only meet her last night, and she asked that I join her again tonight for her attempt at storytelling. Which, I might add, is very good for a beginner. We spoke throughout that entire night, and she is a very interesting and talented girl. Now leave us be, you monster of a woman."

Asdella did not falter in her stance and said in a firm voice, "There is only one talent you are interested in."

The man removed his arm from around Lorenta, trying his best to sound completely shocked by her accusation, saying, "You are implying... You must have me confused with someone else." Asdella just stood there with a bitter look on her face. He shook a finger at her and said viciously, "How dare you! You horrible person!" Then he let out a cruel laugh as he added, "The way you are dressed would suggest that this is your line of work. Being a whore? You accused me of looking for one, didn't you? What the sword is for, I can only imagine. I obviously can see that you don't even know how to care for one. Look how it's all banged up. You don't even have a scabbard for it, do you? Anyway, as I was saying, if you think that this fine woman here beside me is that type of person and interfering with your section of town, you are so wrong. Now leave and take your uncouth behavior with you. How dare you suggest such a thing about her or myself?! I've never been so insulted in all my life!"

Asdella remained standing where she was, unwavering, her lips pressed firmly together as she continued to stare the man directly in the eyes. She seemed to remain strong in this man's onslaught of hurtful words, but her sword arm had begun to tremble with emotion.

Seeing that his act of innocence wasn't going to deter her and that he would probably have to give up on Lorenta to deal with her, he said with contempt and changing his tone to have a malicious edge to it, "Get lost. Can't you see I'm busy?" He knew well who she was. He had recognized her when he had entered and wondered if she had recognized him. He had hoped that she had, as he knew it would pain her to remember. "Hey, you look real familiar," he said with a wicked grin, "I know where I've seen you before." He smiled at the tension and the frightened look building beneath her angry face, "Didn't you used to belong to old-what's-his-face?"

He loved how his words cut her like a knife. She could do nothing about it either, which pleased him even more. The hurt he had caused her when he was pretending to be an innocent was wonderful; suggesting that she was a whore when he knew well she had been forced to behave as one and that he in fact had abused her physically and mentally several times. To everyone in the tavern, he was the one being harassed by this hateful woman. He felt like laughing out loud at her, but instead just expressed it in a mocking grin. He wondered, "Hey, whatever happened to him?"

"I got revenge," she snarled, as she suddenly thrust her sword deep into the man's belly and then yanked her sword upward until it caught on his ribcage. With an insane look in her eye, she grinned a large insane and satisfied smile at his horrified expression. She pulled her bloodied sword out of his gut and then thrust it into his throat.

Everyone in the tavern stared in horror and shock at what had just happened. Lorenta had been splattered with the man's blood. His body slumped slightly forward but remained on the bench as his blood spilled down onto the floor beneath the table.

No one dared approach Asdella, as she stood there with a wild look in her brown eyes, holding her sword up as it dripped with blood, as if she were daring for someone to challenge her actions of revenge.

"What are you doing?!" Lorenta exclaimed, "He liked me. He was nice to me. Why did you kill him?"

"He deserved it," Asdella answered plainly.

"How? He didn't do anything," she questioned, but lacked the emotion one would normally have

<Zaylyn ><Quest For The Sword Of Anthrowst ><By Katrina Mandrake-Johnston >   <Ch 65> < 197 >
in the severity of such a situation. She appeared merely curious.

"Yes he did. You have no idea. He would have hurt you," Asdella tried to explain.

Many of the people were trying to cautiously edge their way toward the exit. Others tried to get to the back rooms in an attempt to hide, while a few remained seated but drew their weapons in case they were forced to use them. None of them had the gall to say a single word, not even Nodwel, Dendrox, Candra, Weena, or Vordin, who all felt that they somewhat knew Asdella and had a rough idea of what to expect from her.

Lorenta continued, "He wasn't being violent, and if he started to act as such, I could have protected myself. Remember the man with the medallion? You heard about what happened with him on the way to this town."

Asdella said through gritted teeth, "You can't protect yourself from that kind of hurt."

Vordin finally got the nerve to say something, wanting to know what had driven her to murder this man, "He knew you before? What did he mean when he said you used to belong to someone?"

Asdella shot him an icy glare saying, "He hurt a lot of women I used to know, and I was one of them."

"Maybe he had changed, you don't know that," Lorenta added, "He appeared to be a different man than what you remember, didn't he? He didn't make any unwanted advances toward me or any sign of being a violent man."

"I don't really care, now do I?" Asdella said in a bitter voice, but it showed signs of cracking. She was extremely upset and was desperately trying to hide it.

Lorenta began to cry, and Asdella headed out the door into the night.

<World of Zaylyn ><Quest For The Sword Of Anthrowst ><By Katrina Mandrake-Johnston ><Ch 66>

CHAPTER 66 =   DRANNGORE'S PLAN

The innkeeper said to the group in a stern voice, "I suggest you leave, before the fate of your friend affects you as well. Murder is not something to be taken lightly. I doubt she'll make it very far without having to face the consequences. That woman is clearly insane. I want you to know that I am not judging you as a result of her actions. I wish you well and hope you will find some trace of what happened to my friend Yorif and can get word to me about it. There should be a carriage leaving soon. You should depart before the authority arrives and I pray you escape before any of his companions find out what has happened here. I shall try to keep as much information as I can from them and I'm sure I can sway the other witnesses to do the same with promises of ale and what not, at least until the authorities can handle the matter properly."

"Thank-you," said the dwarf, feeling that he should have been able to stop her, especially where he was the one who had known her the longest.

"Just go, and quickly," Declort said.

The carriage was situated just outside the town gates. The two dark grey horses were hitched and looked well rested. Vexcindor, the carriage driver, was standing nonchalant beside the carriage. He was leaning up against its side calmly twirling his fingertips around the side of his dark brown full and bushy mustache. Vexcindor had a relaxed expression upon his face as his greyish-green eyes searched the blackened sky above, but Candra thought she detected a hint of nervousness in his eyes. He then adjusted the snug fit of his dark blue scarf about his neck, never taking his gaze from the sky and the dark clouds drifting high above.

Nodwel asked, "Excuse me sir, how much is it to buy passage to Shirkint?"

Vexcindor gave the dwarf and his companions a large friendly grin as he said, "You nearly startled me there for a moment. Welcome, welcome. I was beginning to think that the flow of customers had finally slowed to a full stop, at least coming out of Vackiindmire that is." He clapped his large hands together continuing, "Well, let me start with names. I always like to do introductions before a journey. No need to feel defensive either. Whether you give me real names or fake ones, it makes no difference to me. It just makes the journey a bit more pleasant knowing what to call each other is all. I don't take

<Zaylyn ><Quest For The Sword Of Anthrowst ><By Katrina Mandrake-Johnston >   <Ch 66> < 198 >

to anyone questioning me about my passengers either, past or present so no need to worry there. By the expressions on your faces, I would assume you're in a bit or trouble. No business of mine though. The name's Vexcindor. And yours?"

Nodwel told him quickly, "I'm Nodwel, this here is Vordin, Weena, Lorenta, Dendrox, and Candra. We're expecting a friend of ours shortly, a woman named Asdella."

Candra shot Dendrox a glance to mean that perhaps Nodwel shouldn't have been so hasty to give up their proper names as he did. Dendrox waved it away, and Candra tried to dismiss her worries.

"Well, I'm pleased to meet you all," said the carriage driver, "So there will be seven of you traveling tonight then? Might be a tight squeeze. There are two benches within the carriage, rather nice too, with soft cushions and the whole bit. Each bench will seat maybe three on each side in quite a snug fit. If you squeeze the smaller passengers together, you might be able to fit four. Well, I'll let you figure things out for yourselves."

"We may not have enough to buy passage, as we are a little short on money," Nodwel explained and then asked again, "How much will this cost us?"

"Oh yes, sorry, I guess we should take care of the business side right away then. It is ten gold coins for the voyage. It matters not the number of passengers, it is just a little more difficult for the horses to pull a heavier weight. As such is the case, especially with seven of you, I ask that you give me time to slip the horses a bit of a treat before they make the journey. It's not much, but I'm sure they'll appreciate it."

"Oh yes, of course," Nodwel told him, "We have to wait for our friend as it is. As for payment, I have seven coins left from all the odd jobs I did at the marketplace, but that is all."

"I made three with the storytelling, so we have enough," Lorenta spoke up, "I don't think we should wait around for her though, after all she's done."

"I'm sorry, but I can't just leave her here," the dwarf told them all, "For one, doing so might result in more violence directed on innocent people because of her anger. Besides, I can't just abandon her, no matter what has happened. I know she would not do so, if the situation was reversed for any one of us."

"It would never be the reverse!" Weena exclaimed.

"That doesn't matter," he snapped, clearly upset about the entire situation.

Vexcindor entered the stable to retrieve a special treat to pamper the horses with.

When the carriage driver was out of sight, Weena said, her words filled with emotion, "She can't just go around killing people!"

"I know!" Nodwel told her, "But we can't do anything about it, at least not right now. You know what she would say, if you said that to her? She would say something like, 'Oh yeah, I just did'. It wouldn't do a bit of good. Would it make things right, if she were killed in return for her actions?"

"Well no," Weena admitted, but then added, "Unless it's the only way to stop her from doing something like that again."

"I think we should just be on our way," Nodwel said, "Besides, if we are to continue in our quest for this sword, we will need her, and you all know this. We can't afford to make this an issue, all of Zaylyn…"

Lorenta winced in pain, holding her head.

"What's wrong?" Vordin asked with great concern.

"I think… the spider leader… is trying to… contact…" she managed to get out before she went into some sort of trance.

"Lorenta?" Vordin questioned, "Are you all right?"

She simply stood motionless, her body rigid, and her eyes blank and staring.

In her mind, Lorenta could see things clearly through the giant spider leader's eyes. She was experiencing his memory of recent events, as if they were taking place right before her eyes.

Lorenta could see a young girl in her early teens standing within a forest clearing. She estimated that she might be thirteen maybe fourteen years of age. The girl was dressed in a tattered grey dress tied with a piece of cord at the waist. Her feet were bare and blistered, obviously from a long trek over the countryside. Her hair was a lovely deep reddish color and her skin was a pale creamy white. Her blue eyes were vacant and staring.

The giant spider had recognized this at once as a Possession spell being used, similar to their own abilities. Lorenta was amazed that she was aware of the thoughts the spider had had within this memory as well.

It had to be Dranngore; Lorenta was sure of it. The girl, in a strong commanding voice which didn't seem her own, addressed the Killnarin that had crowded around her upon her arrival.

"Do not go above ground from now on. Stay below in the tunnels and practice your spells. I want to have the wizard's guild worried. Any spies within the two villages and any along the way would have been killed. They won't have a clue as to what's going on. I will have my revenge, but first all of you need to prepare and practice those spells. They won't be as easy to defeat as weakling villagers. All of you are here now to hear my instruction? Let me see," Dranngore said, using the girl's body as his own. He appeared to be counting the number of his evil creatures. "Some of you are missing," he announced in an angry tone, "Where are they?!"

Deep guttural noises were made by one of the Killnarin.

"They were killed?" Dranngore asked in a surprised voice, "How is this possible? I see that two of you are wounded, but no matter as they should be able to regenerate in time. Tell me what has happened here."

The same Killnarin replied with more guttural noises.

"Resistance in the tunnels? Giant spiders, eh? Clearly they were no match for you with your magical resistance and your poison resistance, which would include their venom. The most they could do, would be to weaken you slightly, not enough to kill one of you," he said.

The beast made more noises.

Dranngore laughed, "A few measly adventurers trying to survive my unstoppable army? They are of no consequence. No one would believe what they say. But if you come across them again, finish them off. "

The girl stood silent for a few moments. The spider had thought that Dranngore must have been considering his plan, from the satisfied look on the girl's face.

"Only I would be so bold as to attempt such a glorious revenge," Dranngore announced, "They will regret the day they denied me my seat within the guild. Now get below and practice, damn it! I will not have my plan fail! You'll have plenty of time to go off on your own now and then later, when we make our next move. But that won't be for several days, perhaps as long as a week. I want them all to worry themselves sick wondering what is happening. 'Who could possibly be so powerful to do all this?' they will say to themselves. And then, won't they be surprised when they see that I, Dranngore, have commanded an army of Killnarin! They said it was impossible, that the risks were too great. But I have done it, and they will perish miserably for laughing at me. Anyway, go, go! You had plenty of fun at the two villages and apparently in the tunnels as well, so now it's practice, practice. Good-bye."

The vacant look in her eyes faded. Dranngore had left the girl's body.

"What? Where am I? How did I get here?" she said very disorientated and confused. "What… what are these strange creatures?" the girl said frantically in fear.

The Killnarin, that had been speaking to Dranngore, bit the girl in half with a sudden twist of its powerful jaws.

The giant spider leader ended the connection, having shown her his memory. Before he left her mind, he warned her to be careful and that he would contact her again if they came to learn anything new.

Lorenta relayed all she had seen and heard to the others.

Dendrox, a little relieved, commented, "Well at least we know for certain now that none of the other villages have been attacked in any of the other areas."

Candra said to him, "Yes, Cranok is safe at least for the moment and so are your parents. It seems

<Zaylyn ><Quest For The Sword Of Anthrowst ><By Katrina Mandrake-Johnston >   <Ch 66> < 200 >

that their goal is here in Dee'ellkka Valley now."

Lorenta, rubbing at her temples, advised Vordin not to attempt the mind link they had established unless in a dire emergency.

Vexcindor returned with a wooden bucket filled with a wide variety of treats. Vordin wondered where he had found such an assortment, as he hadn't noticed such things the night before during his watch within the stable.

"Oh please, feel free to sit within the carriage. There's no need to wait outside. Might as well be comfortable while you wait for that friend of yours," the carriage driver added as he presented the bucket to the two horses and let them each grab a large mouthful.

They all agreed and entered the carriage after Nodwel and Lorenta had paid him the fare. It was in fact quite comfortable and elegant inside, not what they had expected at all. Vordin hung his magical lantern on a small hook improving visibility within the seating compartment. The women and Vordin managed to all seat themselves on the back bench while Dendrox and Nodwel sat on the other, leaving enough room for Asdella if she ever decided to show herself again.

"I wouldn't be surprised if the Killnarin started to use their fire magic, when and if we next meet them," Vordin said to them all, "They used fire magic at the attack of Nilnont, don't forget that. We should be prepared for such an attack, just in case. We're becoming more resistant to their spells and starting to recognize their mind games. They are likely to resort to more damaging methods."

"Well said," Nodwel commented, "At least we know now, that there is some sort of insane plan and motive behind this horrible man. He cares for nothing other than himself. He doesn't even realize that the other wizards probably made that comment about the Killnarin because they were aware that the creatures kill and destroy everything in their path. Simply letting them do this, is not controlling them. They do seem to show some sort of loyalty to him, probably for summoning them into this world from wherever they came from, but I doubt that he could stop them if he wanted to. A stream can be directed along a certain path easily enough, but when you try to stop it however, it merely decides to simply flow around whatever is trying to block it, forming an ever growing pool and spreading outward over everything."

"Okay, we get the picture," Dendrox told him, "We are all doomed unless we kill Dranngore with the sword and reverse all his spells including the damn Killnarin."

Weena added, "Well, if we are to find out anything more about the sword, it will definitely be at Shirkint. I'm actually a little excited about going there."

Asdella knocked at the side of the carriage saying, "You didn't think I'd let you all leave without me, did you?"

Asdella climbed inside to sit farthest from the door on the bench beside Nodwel. Everyone sat in silence as Vexcindor gave the command and the carriage began its journey. Asdella stared out of the window with her arms crossed defensively in front of her chest with her murder weapon, which she had cleaned, beside her.

****

NEXT = <u>WORLD OF ZAYLYN</u> = BOOK # 2

(Quest For The Sword of Anthrowst = Part 2)

Quest For The Sword Fragments And The Hunt For Dranngore

****

Quest For The Sword Fragments And The Hunt For Dranngore
By *Katrina Mandrake-Johnston*
World of Zaylyn

Quest For The Sword Of Anthrowst - Part 2:

Enter the World of Zaylyn. This is a world filled with strange creatures, magic, and mystery. This is the continued story, in the quest for the Sword of Anthrowst.

Evil, malicious creatures called Killnarin have entered this world to do the bidding of an insane wizard named Dranngore. Can this horrible man control these beasts as he believes?

Vordin has been told that the evil wizard had to be slain by the Sword of Anthrowst in order to send the creatures back to where they came from.

Lorenta, the mysterious being who is spider by day and human at night, has taken on this quest with him. The two thieves, an elf named Candra and Dendrox her human companion, have also joined Vordin in this quest, as has the amateur wizard Weena, Nodwel the axe-weilding dwarf, and the berserk warrior woman Asdella.

Discovering that the sword had been broken into three pieces and hidden away in three separate locations, the group continues on what seems like a hopeless quest. Through the help of the giant spiders, a message was relayed to Lorenta that Dranngore is seeking revenge on the wizard's guild for denying him membership and that it would be several days before the Killnarin made their next move.

After Asdella brutally takes revenge on a man from her past, the group must flee Vackiindmire and have decided to make their way to the town of Shirkint. They desperately hope that they will be able to discover more information about the sword there.

Vexcindor, the carriage driver, is to take them through the forest to Shirkint, but will they run into trouble? They were warned about the increasing raids by the bandits within the forest.

Are the rumors true about a thieves guild being located at Shirkint?

It seems that The Black Shadow has been guiding them along from the beginning. Does he have some sinister plan for the group?

He eventually asks them to perform a task for him, but what are his true motives for helping them as he has?

Will he eventually turn on them as Asdella fears? Does Asdella know more about The Black Shadow than she is letting on?

His hold over the hunger is quickly diminishing the more he resists. Will he be able to keep himself from killing? Will The Black Shadow be able to stop himself from attacking and feeding from one of the group?

Zaylyn Code: Z3K8S6E4S0M9

About the author ::

    I have been writing stories all my life starting as young as seven years old, with this book being my first book published at the age of twenty-seven. I've always been a big fan of fantasy, sci-fi, adventure, and horror, enjoying movies, comics, books, and video games with good story backgrounds. Writing has always been my passion. Being a big fan of 'choose your own adventure' books and 'fighting fantasy' game books at a young age, most of my early writing followed this similar style, creating stories with endless possibilities to be explored in whatever mystical world I had imagined.

    One of my first attempts in writing a straightforward story, stemming away from the multi-choice and dice rolling adventurers I usually wrote, was at the age of eleven. This story is actually what inspired the idea for the first book in the World of Zaylyn series. The first three chapters are taken from this story, being modified to fit the rest of the book. Not much was changed actually, just elaborated on. So I encourage all the young writers out there to write if the ideas are there, because years later those dreams and adventurers can be relived and re-imagined and perhaps one day shared with others.

    As a young writer, I found that I was bursting with ideas, always writing beginnings of stories, scenes and situations, or even just character personalities and backgrounds. But my problem was that I had a hard time finishing a story as another better and more exciting one would come into my mind and I would begin on this instead, always planning to get back to the others. So I found that I had an enormous collection of story bits and ideas. I was looking through them and found that most had to do with the world I had created in my mind over the years to explore as I try to fall asleep each night.

    Originally, in my mid to late teens, I had attempted to create a game based on my dream world. Over a course of three years, I complied a large number of characters and backgrounds, quests, places, mystical and magical objects, spells, riddles, puzzles, houses and families, and much more, even daily routines and work schedules of the minor characters the others would be interacting with. Basically, it became so complicated and elaborate, and more and more life like, that, in my late teens, I decided to write a series of books about the world I had created instead. I began, but found that I was still having the problem of starting, getting stuck, and wanting to move on to other later events that were fresh and exciting in my mind.

    So, at twenty-two, after the birth of my first child, I was looking over my growing collection of story bits, both from when I was younger and from my teens and those meant for the game I had designed, and saw that I could incorporate many of them into several stories about the same world. I began to write, not start to finish, but in many, many pieces, jumping around from scene to scene and piecing the bits together like a giant puzzle into their proper order and chapters. Many times, I found myself writing twenty to forty chapters all at once. So, my advise is, if you discover that you have writer's block and still have ideas, move on to later sections and come back when you have a better idea of how things are to flow together.

    After five long years, the first book in the series was ready for others to enjoy, with the second book following close behind.

****

Special Thanks ::

**   Thanks to those who modeled for my cover.

**   Extra thanks to my two main editors, my husband and mother, for their extensive time and effort.

**   Thanks to my father for the support and encouragement in my writing.

**   Special thanks to my mother for the encouragement, support, and readings at all stages.

**   Extra special thanks to my children for their patience, enthusiasm, and encouragement with my writing.

**   Special thanks to my grandmother, who inspired me to write as a child with her own storytelling and for the encouragement, enthusiasm, and support in my writing.

***   Thank-you to all that have shown an interest in my writing over the years and to those that have inspired me to continue with my ideas and writing.

****

Printed in the United States
By Bookmasters